# SONGS
# UNFINISHED

Visit us at www.boldstrokesbooks.com

# SONGS UNFINISHED

*by*

Holly Stratimore

2015

ISBN 13: 978-1-62639-231-1

This Trade Paperback Original Is Published By
Bold Strokes Books, Inc.
P.O. Box 249
Valley Falls, NY 12185

First Edition: January 2015

**Credits**
Editors: Victoria Oldham and Ruth Sternglantz
Production Design: Stacia Seaman
Cover Design by Gabrielle Pendergrast

# Acknowledgments

First, I must thank Radclyffe for seeing my potential, encouraging me to keep at it, and taking a chance on me. The talent you have assembled at Bold Strokes Books is second to none. I am continually inspired by the works of my fellow authors, and I love being part of this incredible family.

A gazillion thanks to my amazing editors, Victoria Oldham and Ruth Sternglantz. The appreciation I have for each of you is immeasurable. I will always be grateful for your insight, contributions, guidance, hard work, encouragement, and humor. Collaborating on this project was a remarkable experience that I will never forget. Thank you for bringing out the best in me.

Many thanks to everyone on the Bold Strokes team for their tireless efforts in pulling everything together. Special thanks to Stacia, Cindy, and Sandy. You ladies rock!

Gabrielle, your cover took my breath away! I love how beautifully you brought my vision of these characters to life. Thank you so much for sharing your incredible talent.

Behind every written work are unsung heroes that deserve our appreciation and recognition: our teachers. I salute you all.

Thanks to my friends, past and present, old and new, who have supported me, shaped me, and been there for me through all the ups and downs in my life.

Thanks to my parents for providing the foundation that makes everything good in my life possible. Not a day goes by that I do not acknowledge how fortunate I am to have such a wonderful family. I love you all so very much.

Penny, I don't know what I'd do without you. Thank you so much for your unconditional love and support, for putting up with my funky moods when I'm "in character" or writing scenes in my head, for giving me the time and space I need to write (despite how neglected you must feel in the process!), and for always believing in me. I love sharing my life with you. You are my rock, sweetheart. I love you to the moon and back!

And of course, thanks to the readers.

For you, Mom.

You are forever in my heart.
I miss you every day.
You are my hero.

# PROLOGUE

*Los Angeles*

Shawn Davies checked the pulse of the unconscious man sprawled on the bed. Still alive. *Thank God, I didn't kill him.* She quickly checked the wound on his head. Through his thick black hair, a lump and a small amount of blood were visible. She wiped the lamp clean with her shirtsleeve and put it back in its place on the nightstand. She left his nearly empty glass next to it, poured hers and the rest of the wine bottle into the bathroom drain, rinsed out the sink thoroughly, and set the bottle next to his glass. *Whoever finds him will just think he passed out drunk. He won't call the police...What would he tell them anyway?*

She threw on her jacket, dropped her own glass into the pocket, and silently slipped out the door of the second-floor motel room, making sure it was locked before she latched it shut.

She blew out a deep breath of relief and sucked in another, thinking it was the first time since she had arrived in Los Angeles that the smog-infected air actually smelled refreshing. She charged down the stairs as quickly and quietly as she could.

She clutched her keys in a white-knuckle grip to ensure they wouldn't jangle, slipped a key into the lock of her beat-up compact car, and fell inside. She did her usual swift inspection of the backseat, lifting up the blanket strewn across it. Guitar case and amplifier were still present, along with the backpack containing her life's work. She turned the key in the ignition and sped out of the motel parking lot, made her way to Interstate 405, and headed south toward Long Beach.

Twenty-five minutes later, she pulled into a convenience store and dropped open her glove compartment. She knew the way back by heart, but considering the night she was having, she wanted to refresh her memory by making sure she had the sequence of routes correct. She clicked on her dome light, unfolded the map, and confirmed that yes, she did know her way. She checked her gas gauge, and then her wallet. Was there enough? She sifted through the bills, counting and recounting, trying to figure out how much she would need later.

*Doesn't matter,* she thought. *I can't stay here. Especially now.* She went inside and picked up a few munchies, bottled water, and an extra-large steaming cup of coffee, and then drove a block and filled up with gas.

It wasn't until she had been on the freeway for almost an hour that she finally allowed herself to cry.

# CHAPTER ONE

*New Hampshire*

Jaymi Del Harmon locked the door behind her and dropped her keys on the bar. She stared at the disheveled apartment, with its secondhand furniture and piles of cardboard boxes, and thought that maybe now she would find the ambition to unpack and make this place a home. Up to now it just hadn't been important. She removed her long coat, made her way down the hall to her bedroom, and sat heavily on the bed. Reaching into the pocket of her gray blazer, she pulled out the small card with the scripted print. There it was in black and white: her mother's full name, followed by two dates, marking the beginning and the end of a life. Below the dates was a short poem intended for comfort, little consolation for the insurmountable loss she was feeling. It wasn't enough, but it was all that was left.

The discomfort of her dress clothes finally prompted her to get up and undress. After stripping down to a gray thermal tank and underwear, she commenced throwing each article of the discarded clothing one by one against the closet door, as if she were a Red Sox pitching ace throwing blazing fastballs past Yankees batters.

"Why, God, why?" Jaymi screamed into the empty room. "Why would you take Mom away from me? She was so young!" She pushed her anger into each thread of material as she flung her clothes across the room, the only way to get out the impotent rage swallowing her whole. "There are assholes out there molesting kids and killing people, and you take my mom instead of them?"

Sobbing uncontrollably, she lowered herself onto the bed and curled into a fetal position, drawing her pillow into her arms and soaking it until her tears ran dry.

She felt no passage of time, only the sensation that all the energy that remained within her was quickly draining away. She forced herself into the shower and, feeling slightly better, slipped into jeans and a sweatshirt and convinced herself to eat a bowl of soup. The sun had set. A single table lamp lit up the one possession in the living room that had been unpacked and stayed that way since she had moved in—an acoustic guitar. She lifted it off the couch and strummed it absentmindedly.

She had moved out of her parents' house and into her own place three months ago, at the urging of her mother, who was determined to help her daughter regain some sense of normalcy in her life. It had been an excruciating year. She'd given up her music career in Los Angeles just when it was about to take off in order to care for her mother, who'd been diagnosed with breast cancer. She'd left everything, including her girlfriend, Peach. Well, ex-girlfriend. They'd had problems, and Peach had just finished entertaining someone else in their bed when Jaymi had gone home to try and work things out. The betrayal had hurt, but it was soon eclipsed by the need to take care of her family. She hadn't actually seen the other woman, who had slipped out the back door as Jaymi had moved toward the bedroom, but it didn't really matter who it was. What mattered was she was moving on with her life.

Jaymi had returned to the apartment with her best friend Nikki and collected her belongings while Peach was in class. After three weeks of giving notice at their day jobs and tying up loose ends, the band set out on their long return trip to New England. Rather than give up entirely, the band followed Jaymi to New Hampshire so they could keep working together, a fact she would be forever grateful for. It wasn't LA, but at least they were still playing.

Once in New Hampshire, Nikki and their bassist, Kay, worked frantically to keep the band going by calling old contacts and setting up auditions at clubs at which they had played before they had headed west to pursue their dream. Drawing on her desperate need to escape her heartbreak over Peach's infidelity and the agonizing turmoil of watching a wretched disease eat away at her mother's life, Jaymi's presence onstage stole the show every night. Audiences connected with the honest and vulnerable sincerity in her delivery. Her sweet voice carried beautiful melodies with evocative lyrics that were a welcome contrast to Nikki's wilder hard-rocking style. And Jaymi could kick ass playing electric guitar just as well as she could acoustic. She let go at every show, putting her raw emotions on display and letting them carry her away. It was catharsis, and if she hadn't had that opening, she would never have made it through the pain.

She wrote more songs in that year than she had in all the previous years combined. Every one of them was about Peach. When she finally reached the point where she felt she would puke if her creative mind came up with just one more angry, brokenhearted song, she wondered if she would ever be over her. One day she tried to imagine how it would feel. She *pretended* she was over her. She took out a pen. She filled a page. She cried. She didn't bother to wipe the teardrops off the paper. She closed the notebook. She dropped it in a desk drawer and forgot about it. It was the last time she cried over Peach.

One day she was washing dishes when a melody came into her head. She rushed to her recorder and quickly hummed the tune over and over. She played it back a few times and dug out her guitar and worked out the notes and a chord progression. Within a day, she had recorded keys, drums, bass, and acoustic rhythm guitar. No lyrics came to her, so she played the melody in a beautiful electric guitar solo. Satisfied with the results, she decided it needed no lyrics. It was the first song she had written in months that actually gave her feelings of hope, and she entitled it "On My Way"—acknowledging that she wasn't quite 100 percent yet, but it was a sure sign that she was getting there.

Now, months later, reflecting on her mother's funeral, she knew life would never be the same without her mother in it. She could never again pick up the phone and talk to her mom about her day. Or ask her, again, for the ratio of vinegar to water to get the stains out of a coffeepot, or what seasoning she used on her roasted chicken, or to tell her one of the many amusing anecdotes about her grandfather so that she could keep the facts straight.

The questions she wished she had asked formed themselves from ink to page, and thus another song was born. Guitar wasn't right for this one, though, and she found herself sitting at the piano and pecking out the chords and working out the melody in a quiet hum. After a few run-throughs, she attempted to sing the words. And that was when she lost it. The waterworks were on again in full force and she had to walk away.

❖

Jaymi's low beams barely lit the salt-worn paint that defined the lanes. It had been a long, harsh winter in New England, though not atypical. She didn't care. At least the frigid February morning air told her she was alive. The relentless sunny days of Southern California, along with the heartache of a cruel city and an unfaithful lover, were behind her now.

There were times that she questioned whether or not she would survive her broken heart. There had been too many nights of uncontrollable sobs, pleading prayers, and a desperate desire to escape her own skin. There were times, over the last six months, she'd thought losing her mother to cancer would be the final push over the edge. She'd felt completely and utterly out of control. Her career had been up in the air, and her heart had been torn to shreds.

But her band, Passion Play, was back on track now. They had sent home recordings of four of their songs to an independent radio station in Boston. The station now featured the group regularly on a weekly show that played local unsigned artists. Increasing requests for these songs were giving them more airplay every day. With a strong lesbian following and a growing fan base, it was only a matter of time before they hit it big.

Jaymi smiled as she parked her truck and headed inside Blayne's Courier Service. It wasn't a bad job and it paid the bills for now. And being alone on the road all day allowed her to work on songs in her head. Sometimes new songs would come to her, and when she got home she'd hum the melody into her trusty 4-track recorder.

Giving up on California didn't mean she was giving up on her music career, and she refused to let the choice diminish her determination. Boston also had its fair share of bragging rights when it came to launching the careers of many successful musicians: Tracy Chapman, The Cars, John Mayer, its namesake band Boston, and New Hampshire's own Aerosmith, just to name a few. Even Jaymi's hero Melissa Etheridge spent a year at Berklee College of Music and started playing clubs in Boston before she went to LA.

As her workday dragged on, her good mood faded. To cheer herself up, she decided to have lunch at New Horizons Bookstore and

Café, which was within walking distance from where she worked. Her friend Devin still worked there part-time, while she continued to write for *Happenings,* the magazine she'd done an article for on Jaymi's band. Like Jaymi, she was paying her dues with jobs that paid the bills until she found a way to become a full-time working novelist.

Devin welcomed her with a hug.

"Do you greet all your customers like that or am I special?" Jaymi asked, unzipping her coat and shaking off the cold.

Devin smiled widely. "I think you know the answer to that question."

"It would boost sales, you know."

"Or prompt harassment charges."

"Anyone who'd complain about a hug from you would be crazy. You had lunch yet?"

"I'm just going now. Your timing couldn't be better, but that's normal for you musicians, isn't it?"

"True, all true!" Jaymi smiled and thought about how much Devin had come out of her shell since coming out of the closet. A dark-haired, brown-eyed woman with an athletic five-foot-six build and a warmth and sweet innocence to melt anyone's heart, Devin Carita was always a welcome sight. Sara had been good for her. *They're good for each other,* she thought. *I used to think that way about me and Peach, before...* She forced herself to discontinue the thought and instead focused on making a selection from the café's menu board.

They made themselves comfortable in a booth and began to eat.

"What's on your mind, Jaymi? You okay?"

"Is it that obvious?"

"It is to me," Devin said.

"Just missing my mom, I guess." Jaymi sighed. "God, I can't wait for winter to be over."

Devin gave Jaymi's hand a squeeze. "I hear you, Jaymi."

"And to make matters worse, I've had the worst writer's block this winter. I haven't been able to write a damn thing."

"I know how frustrating that is. Would you like to come over for dinner tomorrow tonight? Maybe getting your mind off things for a little while will help."

"I'd love to. I've got a gig, so I'd have to leave by seven thirty. You sure Sara won't mind?"

"You kidding? She'd love it. And you're safe, since it's my turn to cook." They both chuckled at Sara's reputation for not quite mastering the cooking thing.

"Well, in that case, what time?"

"How's five?"

"Perfect."

Devin stood up and cleared the table. "I have to get back to work. Would you like a coffee to go?"

"Sure. I'll take it here, though. I got out of work early today, so I thought I'd hang out for a while."

"You got it."

She thanked Devin and took out the notebook she always carried with her to jot down ideas for lyrics. She opened it and stared at a blank page. She was still working on the tribute song for her mother. She sipped her coffee and gazed across the café. She was surrounded by people and felt completely alone. Life was going on without her. Something had to give.

She looked at the page again. A year ago, it would have poured out of her effortlessly. *This used to be my best outlet and I can't write a friggin' thing!* She slammed the notebook shut and drained her cup. *That's it. Screw writing. I need to focus on something else for a while.*

She sought out Devin on the sales floor and had her recommend a few new lesbian romances. It had been far too long since she had indulged in a quiet night of reading. She bid her friend good-bye, pleased with the purchase of four new books, and then headed to the craft store down the street. She needed a new scrapbook. She had a stack of photos and clippings of the group that had been collecting dust for months. Perhaps delving into the old hobby was another tool she could use to return to some sense of normalcy. She made one last stop at the video rental for two romantic comedies and eagerly made her way home.

Dinner at Devin and Sara's the next night was a welcome reprieve as well. She avoided the subject of her mother, knowing the inevitable waterworks that would follow. Not that she didn't feel safe enough with them to let her guard down. Quite the opposite, actually. It wouldn't have been the first time she lost it in their company. Still, her survival instincts reminded her that she needed to conserve her emotional energy for Passion Play's gig.

There was one aspect of the visit that was tough to take, and that was being in the company of two people so in love that there were times it seemed they had forgotten Jaymi was even there. *What's it feel like to be so at home with someone you love, that you can always be yourself? I've never had that with anyone.* Jaymi watched in envy and wondered if she'd ever have that kind of love with someone. *Shit. Don't start longing for a lover, you idiot. You've got too many other things you need to focus on right now—namely, your career.*

She left feeling grateful that she would be spending the rest of the evening onstage, losing herself in the music.

# CHAPTER TWO

"Aunt Betty! Hello? Aunt Betty, it's me, Shawn!" Shawn pressed the doorbell again. *Strange. Her car's in the garage. Where could she be?* She leaned over the porch railing and peered through the picture window, shielding her eyes from the bright afternoon sun. It was impossible to see inside with the reflections of the snowy front yard and nearly cloudless winter sky bouncing off the glass. She stepped off the porch and was just tall enough on tiptoe to cup her hands around her eyes and press her face to the window. Aunt Betty always had at least one plant hanging in that window, and plenty scattered about the living room. She said it added life to her modest surroundings. But Shawn couldn't see a single plant anywhere.

*I should have called first.* What would she have told her? That her life was in the toilet? That she hadn't called or written for nearly six months because she was too ashamed of the immoral methods of survival she had resorted to? That she had been homeless and having one-night stands with strangers just so she could sleep in a real bed? That she had hit rock bottom and agreed to have sex with a record executive in exchange for a promised record deal?

"Hey!" The shout of the neighbor prompted Shawn to jump back from the house. The lanky senior stepped closer to the wooden fence dividing the small lots and jabbed his cane in the air in Shawn's direction. "What're you doin' pokin' around over there? I'll call the police—"

"No! Please don't. I know the person who lives here—she's my aunt."

The old man frowned and narrowed his eyes. "That so? A relative, you say? Obviously ain't a very close one."

"Do you know when she might be home?" Shawn asked, ignoring the comment.

The man shook his head and his look turned sympathetic. "Listen, kid. I don't know what you're up to, but the lady that lived in that house died last month." The look on Shawn's face must have convinced him she was telling the truth, for his eyes immediately softened. "Too bad, too. Nice lady. Always smiled an' waved hello to me. Never had to call about noise like I do with those damn college kids across the street over there." He gestured with his cane, muttering something about Massachusetts going down the drain.

The man's weathered tan parka became a blur, and his voice faded into insignificant ramble. Shawn mechanically walked to the car and collapsed into the driver's seat.

❖

Shawn pulled into the long driveway and stopped as soon as the car was off the road. Only pure desperation would have brought her to this place. *This is a mistake.* She shut off her headlights and was grateful for the tiny sliver of a moon. The car wouldn't be seen from the house at this distance. There weren't any lights on, and she knew he'd probably be in bed at this hour.

Her anger had been difficult to subdue as she sped away from Aunt Betty's house. It was easier to feed off the anger than to let herself feel the grief and despair that had tempted her to park her car on the tracks in front of the oncoming southbound Downeaster half an hour ago. She knew it was her own fault she hadn't been notified of Aunt Betty's death, because there had been no way to contact her since she ran away to California. She had kept in touch with no one except Aunt Betty. Shawn hadn't had a permanent address for nearly a year, so even if someone had found evidence of their correspondence and tried to track her down, they would have reached a dead end.

Now she ignored the pounding of her heart, rehearsing what she would say when, or if, he opened the door. She switched on her parking lights and pressed the accelerator. The car started to creep closer to the house, and the closer she got, the harder her pulse pounded. She cut the engine as soon as she could and took a deep breath. She got out and gave the door a gentle nudge with her hip to close it without a slam.

An automatic porch light came on as she approached, momentarily stopping her in her tracks, but she bravely forged on. She climbed three agonizing stairs to the front door, pried open the storm door, and knocked. She inhaled a frigid breath of New Hampshire's February night air. She nervously shifted her weight back and forth from one foot to the other. She knocked again, slightly louder this time. The door flung open, revealing her father. She hadn't seen him since that awful scene at her mother's funeral, and she was shocked at the sight of the man standing before her now. He looked heavier and older than she remembered. His matted hair had grayed and his tattered white T-shirt stretched over his gut. The hems of his pajama pants were dirty and worn from dragging on the floor. His sagging jowls were unshaven and his bushy eyebrows hung heavy over his blazing dark eyes. Gone was the solid physique of the proud, accomplished auto mechanic who longed for his only child to succeed in a more prestigious career than his own.

"What the hell do you want?"

Shawn swallowed hard and stared at her feet. "I need a place to stay. Just for a few days, I promise—"

"I told you never to come back here."

Shawn choked down threatening tears. "Please, Dad. I have no place else to go." She raised her head and looked him in the eye. "How long are you gonna go on blaming me for Mom's death? Huh?"

He winced and averted his eyes, clenching his jaw in an apparent effort to squelch his words.

"You think this is what Mom would want? It's been seven years, Dad. Seven years! For God's sake, I'm your only child." Her vision blurred as tears surfaced. "Please...I need you."

He met her gaze, his expression unchanged. In one swift motion, he stepped back and slammed the door.

The porch light shut off and she made her way back to the car, enveloped by the blackness of the night.

Shawn wiped away the tears as she drove back out into the night. Her father's reception hadn't surprised her but she was stubborn about giving up that last shred of hope for acceptance by a parent. She was haunted by that little voice inside that says parents are supposed to love their children unconditionally. Eternally. Without fail.

It was a love she had experienced from her mother, until that summer day when Shawn told her she was a lesbian. Shawn had been prepared for the typical reactions—guilt, disappointment, and so on. She had expected the usual comments: *You just haven't met the right guy! Don't give up so easily!* or *But you're such a pretty girl!* or *What did I do wrong?* or *Don't go telling this to everybody...it's just a phase. You'll outgrow it.*

Shawn knew her mother loved her, and the last thing she expected was rejection. But her mother had been furious. Insulted. Shocked. Humiliated. Her mother had focused on possible repercussions on her own life and disregarded the magnitude of feelings Shawn was dealing with. She'd been more concerned about what people would think and the state of Shawn's soul than the actuality of her well-being.

Shawn had been devastated. And though her mother didn't ban her from her life, Shawn was forbidden from ever again mentioning the subject in her mother's house or presence. "I will pray for you," she had said, "and I suggest you pray for yourself, too." Instead, Shawn prayed for her mother's understanding and acceptance and agonized over how the hell she was ever going to change her mother's mind. She figured that maybe it was one of those things in life that just took time. She clung to the hope that it wasn't possible for a mother to shut off the love for her kid completely. Months passed and nothing changed. Eventually, Shawn learned to harden her heart on the subject. She buried herself deeper in her music and grew more isolated by the day. *And here I am, years later, still alone, still struggling to find my way. Without my parents to guide me.*

Shawn checked her gas gauge. Almost empty again. She hadn't been in this town for years, but she still knew it like the back of her hand. She drove to a station downtown that was open twenty-four hours and filled up. She pulled away from the pumps and onto the far side of the lot. *Where the hell do I go now?* She was low on funds and hated to waste any more money on motel rooms. And it was way too cold to sleep in the car.

It had taken almost a month to get across the country. She had made it to Flagstaff before she had run out of money. She had scoped out the town until she found a street with heavy foot traffic.

After charming a coffee-shop manager into letting her play music for nothing, she collected enough donations to afford a tank of gas and a cheap meal. That night she parked next to the trees along the perimeter of a strip-mall parking lot and slept.

After a week at the coffee shop, she headed east again until she was too low on money to go any farther. She repeated the routine along the entire route, staying longer if the money was good, and hitting the road if it wasn't. Her only scare occurred when a grumpy storeowner threatened to call the police and have her picked up for vagrancy.

She cringed at the memory. If she hadn't been so afraid, she might have let him do it—just so she could sleep inside for a night. She propped her head in her hands and fought off another wave of tears. She jumped when the hard rap of knuckles sounded on her window. *Oh shit! A cop! Okay, stay calm. Act composed.* She slowly rolled down her window.

"Evenin', young lady. Everything all right?"

"Yes, sir."

"Where you headed?" he asked.

"Uh, home, sir."

"California plates. Kinda late to be starting such a long trip, isn't it?"

"Oh, I mean home here. I'm originally from New Hampshire. Visiting family."

"I see. May I see your license and registration, please?"

"Sure, uh, right here, I've got them right here." Shawn retrieved them both and tried desperately to hide the shaking of her hands, as well as the nervousness in her voice. The officer retreated to his cruiser.

She watched the officer in her rearview. *What's taking so long? Please, God, please. No complications.*

The officer finally returned with her documentation. He pulled out his ticket pad and began writing. "Are you aware that your passenger-side taillight is out?"

"No, sir. No," she answered, shaking her head.

"This is just a warning," he said, tearing off a page and handing it to her. "You'll need to have that replaced within ten days, okay?"

"Okay." Shawn tried to conceal her relief. "I will. First thing tomorrow."

"You take care now. Enjoy your visit."

"Thank you, sir."

The cruiser pulled away and Shawn headed back out on the road, unsure of where to go. She cracked her window, welcoming the fresh, cold New Hampshire air, hoping it would keep her awake. She hadn't realized how homesick she had been. She found herself cruising through old familiar neighborhoods, noticing the crops of new businesses, new sets of traffic lights, new houses. It still felt like home, regardless of the bad memories mixed with the good ones.

She tuned in her old favorite radio station, paying little attention to it until a familiar voice began to sing. *My God, that's Jaymi's voice! They're on the radio!* She pumped her fist and turned up the volume. "Passion Play's on the fucking radio!" she yelled. "Shit, they come back here and start making it while I go nowhere in friggin' LA? Are you kidding me?"

She pulled off the road into a shopping plaza, realizing that maybe there was someone in the area she could turn to after all. She had first met Jaymi Del Harmon and her band, Passion Play, at an open mike in Long Beach. They'd continued to run into each other after that, since they often played the same venues.

Jaymi had approached after Shawn had performed one night, greeting her with praise. As they got to know one another and learned they were from the same area in New Hampshire, a friendship began to develop. Jaymi sweetly and tactfully offered bits of constructive criticism, and Shawn's usual defensive response was stifled by respect and admiration she hadn't known before. Jaymi unknowingly became a mentor to her.

Jaymi had advised Shawn to adjust her guitar strap so her right hand would fall naturally in a better position on the strings. And when Shawn had admitted that she struggled at times to coordinate her vocals and accompaniment, Jaymi suggested that she rehearse the two separately and repeatedly so when she put the two together, each would flow more effortlessly and expertly, and she could focus on her emotional delivery of the song rather than its technical accuracy. As all these improvements culminated, people began showing up specifically for her, and she, in turn, fed off the audience's energy.

They'd run into each other less frequently when Passion Play began moving up the musical world's food chain. Shawn's increasingly nomadic existence hadn't helped. Then Passion Play suddenly disappeared. Shawn had learned through the grapevine that Jaymi's mother had fallen ill and the band had moved back East.

Shawn looked at her watch. It was after eleven. She had no place to go. She was almost broke. She was cold and hungry. But she recognized the name of the club the radio DJ said Jaymi's band was playing. Finally, something might be going her way.

# CHAPTER THREE

After they finished loading up their gear and said their good nights, Passion Play's members dispersed to their vehicles and left the lot one by one. Jaymi climbed into her pickup and turned the key. A sluggish *whirr, whirr, whirr* ground itself out of the engine.

"Damn it! Not again." She waited thirty seconds and tried again. Same result. She looked around. There was one car left in the lot, a tired-looking compact with faded blue paint and California plates. It slowly approached. She tensed up, hoping she wasn't in danger. It pulled up next to her and she cautiously peered into the vehicle. A young woman poked her head out the driver's side window.

"Jaymi?"

Jaymi looked closer. "Do I know you?"

The girl brushed her hair off her eyes and away from her face. "Shawn Davies. We met in Long Beach, remember? Open mikes?"

Jaymi nodded. "Oh my God! Shawn! Of course I remember you. But what are you doing here?"

"It's a long story. You need some help?"

"Yeah. It won't start. I think my battery's dying. Can you give me a jump?"

"Sure, no problem." Shawn climbed out as Jaymi popped her hood and retrieved jumper cables from behind the seat. Shawn took the cables from her and had everything hooked up and the truck running in a matter of minutes.

"Thanks. You're a lifesaver. Did you catch our show tonight?"

"Uh, no. I, uh…didn't have money for cover. I was hoping I'd catch you before you left."

"You must be freezing. How long have you been out here waiting?"

"I don't know. Maybe an hour. What time is it?"

"Almost one. You poor thing." Jaymi glanced at Shawn's backseat, which was packed to the gills.

"Listen, Jaymi, I have a huge favor to ask."

"Well, you just did me a huge favor, so name it."

"I need a place to stay, just for a few days. I just need time to find a job and then I'll get my own place and be out of your hair."

"Yeah, of course you can stay with me." Jaymi felt like she knew Shawn well enough from their time together in LA to be comfortable having her in the apartment, and some company might actually be nice for a while.

Tension visibly drained from Shawn's features, replaced by a smile. "Really? Thanks so much. Peach won't mind?"

"Peach and I aren't together anymore." Jaymi hated the sudden feeling of insecurity that hit her at the mention of Peach's name. She thought she was beyond that now.

"Oh shit, I'm sorry. I feel like a jerk now."

"That's all right, you didn't know. We split up almost a year ago. But whatever. Follow me back to my place—it's cold out here and I'm wiped."

Jaymi's headlights stretched down the long driveway when they got there twenty minutes later. Passing the old farmhouse on the left, she made a slight right to park in front of the barn. Part of the barn's loft had been converted into a two-bedroom apartment by the couple that owned the property, and her living quarters occupied a good portion of the upper floor.

Jaymi told Shawn to make herself comfortable in the living room while she brought Shawn's bag and guitar into the spare bedroom. But Shawn was pacing the room when she returned, her arms wrapped around herself as though she was cold. Jaymi could understand why that would be. Shawn was unseasonably dressed in a denim jacket over a gray hooded sweatshirt. There was a frayed hole in one knee of her faded Levi's 550s and the cuffs at the bottom were tattered. The pants had probably fit her perfectly at some point, but now they barely clung to her small hips and nearly mimicked the oversized style of popular hip-hop artists. The rubber soles of her Converse tennis shoes were cracked and blackened with age, their red canvas faded and soiled.

When Shawn nervously swiped back her bangs, her eyes beneath were dark with exhaustion.

"Sorry. I needed to stretch my legs. Been on the road for ages. Listen, I don't want to impose—"

"You're not imposing, really. And I know you well enough to know you're not some psycho," Jaymi said, turning up her thermostat.

"You have no idea how much I appreciate this." She shivered and rubbed her hands on her arms. "I didn't know who else to turn to. You're the only person I could think of. I heard your song on the radio and remembered you'd moved back here."

"Look, it's late, and I can see you're exhausted. Other than rehearsal in the afternoon, I'm free all day tomorrow. So you can fill me in then, okay? Right now, you need to rest. I don't know what's going on with you, but I can tell you've had a rough night. Are you hungry? I could fix you some soup."

Shawn's smile was shy, but her eyes lit up. "Starving, but I don't want to be any trouble. I think I still have some munchies out in my car."

"It's no trouble, Shawn, really. Go get into some pajamas. The bathroom's down this hall on your right. If you'd like a shower or you just want to freshen up, please, go right ahead. Either way, I'm fixing you something to eat."

The genuine gratitude in Shawn's eyes reminded Jaymi of a rescued puppy. She studied the worn face. It was obvious she hadn't had a professional haircut in months—her hair was unkempt and much longer than Jaymi remembered, a mop of light brown hair with a hint of rust, parted on the side in a style similar to the young Paul McCartney's. It fell loosely layered, with overgrown bangs reaching well below her dark eyebrows. They practically hid her soft hazel eyes, which in certain lighting, Jaymi remembered, appeared a faded brown that matched her hair. Jaymi thought her eyes beautiful, the sad and insecure face cute, and the mysterious, quiet manner intriguing.

Jaymi showed Shawn to her room, set up the bathroom with clean towels and a brand-new spare toothbrush, and told her to help herself to anything else she needed. Content that Shawn was all set, she put on a can of soup and made a tuna sandwich.

As she prepared everything, she wondered what had happened to her friend. Shawn had seemed insecure when they'd first met, but everyone starting out was insecure, and she certainly hadn't been the frail and timid refugee who showed up at her show tonight. Had she gotten into the drug scene out there? *God, I hope not. I already dealt with one addict in my life. That was enough.* She didn't recall Shawn ever doing drugs before. She'd seen her have an occasional beer or two, but that was it.

Why was it that she had no one else to turn to? She'd grown up here. Didn't she have any family to take her in?

Jaymi finished making the sandwich and cursed when she noticed the soup bubbling. She turned down the heat and gave it a stir. Come to think of it, Shawn had never spoken of her family. If she had, Jaymi didn't remember it. Even if her parents weren't an option, she must still have friends or relatives in the area.

There was also the question of how long she might need to stay. If she truly had nowhere else to go, that might throw a monkey wrench in Jaymi's plans. She was finally in the clear to focus on nothing but her own needs and career. *I don't need any complications in my life. Not now. I need this time for myself.* She almost immediately felt guilty for having such thoughts, but it was true. She had worked hard to overcome the impulse to put everyone else's needs ahead of her own.

On the other hand, the condition of her friend broke her heart. The look in Shawn's eyes when she offered to feed her was a good indication that it had been a very, very long time since anyone had treated her with kindness. What had happened to her? Jaymi was curious to find out, and that alone was enough temptation to let her stay awhile—at least until she could get back on her feet. *A few weeks can't hurt, right? Besides, I always liked Shawn.*

She heard the bathroom door open as she placed a glass of milk next to the soup and sandwich. She turned and caught her breath. The transformation was remarkable. Shawn's damp hair was combed back, so Jaymi could see her face better. Jaymi smiled, and Shawn's eyes twinkled when she returned the smile, and she shyly clasped her hands together and shrugged. She wore navy-blue cotton sleep pants with white music notes on them and a heather-gray pocket T-shirt. She looked absolutely adorable. *I might be in trouble here.*

"Feel better?"

"You have no idea."

"Good. Sit and relax, okay? You're not intruding. I wouldn't have said yes if I didn't really mean it was okay. My God, you look scared to death. You're safe here, honestly."

Shawn nodded, concentrating on her soup. The way she devoured it made Jaymi wonder when she'd last had any real food.

"Mmm. That hits the spot." She gobbled down several crackers, added a handful to the soup, and finished it off. She then bit into the sandwich. By the look on her face, Jaymi would have thought she was tasting filet mignon for the first time.

"Again, I can't thank you enough. Do you...would you mind... shit, I've got some nerve showing up here..."

"We'll talk about it tomorrow. Tonight, relax and know that you're welcome here. Okay?"

She gave Jaymi another warm smile that made her face light up. "Thank you, Jaymi. Really."

Jaymi retrieved the pot of soup from the stove and emptied its remaining contents into Shawn's bowl. There would be time to talk later. Tonight was about rest and food. Tomorrow would take care of the rest.

# CHAPTER FOUR

Shawn sank her head into the plush pillow and let her weary body melt into the cushions. *This is heaven.* She relished the feel of clean sheets and inhaled their crisp scent. She cuddled into the cocoon of warm blankets, without shivering once. No sharing a room with cockroaches and traffic noise tonight.

She awoke to the welcome aromas of bacon and coffee. She stretched and yawned, blinking lazily as she recalled where she was. She smiled contently. She had slept through the night—no small thing after what she'd been through.

Bright sunlight filtered in through the curtain and Shawn wondered how late she had slept. She figured she could probably sleep for several more hours, but already felt more rested than she had in months. Her stomach grumbled and the need for nourishment prompted her to get up.

"You sleep okay on that futon?" Jaymi asked when Shawn shuffled into the kitchen after a brief stop in the bathroom.

"Better than I have in weeks, thank you." *First night this week without nightmares.*

"Sorry that room's kind of a mess. I've used it more for storage. There are some hangers in the closet if you'd like to hang any clothes."

"It's fine, Jaymi. You weren't exactly expecting company." *Beats sleeping in the car.*

As Shawn stood in the hall at the edge of the kitchen, she absorbed the surroundings that exhaustion and anxiety had hindered her from noticing the night before. Starting at her immediate left began the U-shaped wraparound of appliances and countertops that ended in a small bar. On the left wall was a window above the sink, complete with country-style red, beige, and blue plaid curtains that pleasantly complemented the textured beige paper on the wall. In front of her against the right wall was a round natural-finish pine table with four matching chairs. Though the rest of the apartment was carpeted, the kitchen retained its stained maple hardwood floor, its prominent knots adding character to the charm of the place.

The breakfast bar separated the kitchen from the entrance to the apartment on the left. Looking beyond the kitchen was the living room, and there seemed to be another room off to the right. There was a bay window on the left wall and a glass patio door led to a spacious balcony. Shawn marveled at how much she felt at home already, yet at the same time, it felt very strange. She hadn't had a real home in so long. Until this moment, she hadn't known how badly she wanted one. Suddenly, she ached for the stability of having the same place to go to every night. A place that was actually hers. A place where she could be herself. A place where she would feel safe and comfortable.

A place like this. *I could get used to this.* She quickly reprimanded herself for having the nerve to think such a thing. *Don't think like that. You're only setting yourself up for a big fat fall.* "That smells so good. You didn't have to do all that for me."

"Who says it's for you?" Jaymi teased. "I always treat myself to a big brunch on Sundays. When I'm really ambitious I make omelets or pancakes. Gotta admit, it's nice to have someone to share it with. Want some coffee?"

"Yes, please. Black." Jaymi poured her a cup and placed it in on the table. Shawn pulled up a seat and thanked her. *Yeah, I could definitely get used to this.* Of course, the odds of that happening were probably zilch once Jaymi learned what a screwup she'd become. She stirred in a spoon of sugar and sat quietly sipping her coffee. Jaymi returned to the stove and started flipping the bacon.

Shawn had a perfect view from behind and took full advantage of the fact that Jaymi's attention was on the food. Jaymi held an imaginary guitar pick in her right hand and absentmindedly played air guitar on her thigh and nodded rhythmically to the song playing in her head. She was wearing dark blue New England Patriots boxers and a long-sleeved hunter green T-shirt. On her feet were fuzzy red slippers with *Peanuts* characters all over them. *Damn, she's cute.*

Jaymi turned her way to open the fridge, and Shawn quickly looked away and faked a cough. *I'll bet my face is as red as those slippers right now.*

"You okay?"

"Yeah. Just a tickle." Shawn faked another small cough just to be on the safe side.

"Here, this'll help," Jaymi said, pouring a glass of orange juice and handing it to her.

A plateful of scrambled eggs, two strips of bacon, hash browns, and a slice of wheat toast followed. Jaymi joined her and they sat in silence as they each dug into their meals.

"LA's a tough town, huh?" Jaymi finally said.

Shawn closed her eyes for a moment and nodded. "The worst. Well, for me, anyway. Some people like it. I just couldn't stay. It got too hard." She could feel tears beginning to well up and turned her head, hoping Jaymi wouldn't notice. "Anyway, I need a job. I'll find one this week, I promise. I don't expect you to put me up here for nothing. My first check, I'll give you some money, and I'll work on finding my own place. Then I'll be out of your hair."

Jaymi looked at her for a moment, but her face was unreadable.

"Okay. I know a few temp agencies in town. You might find work through them until you find something more permanent. If that's what you want, anyway."

Shawn nodded, her mouth too full to answer, and avoided Jaymi's gaze, afraid she'd see Shawn's shame in them. Yet she wanted to look into those eyes, crystal blue and wise.

Contemplating the woman in her company, with song lyrics practically writing themselves in her head describing the beauty before her, Shawn wondered how in the world Peach could have ever let this amazing woman get away. Or was it Jaymi who ended it? There was an air of aloofness to Jaymi—not distant or detached, but in the sense that her focus was elsewhere, and that focus was so strong and so intense, it seemed unbreakable. When that focus was on you, it held you, penetrated you, leaving you frozen and motionless. You couldn't escape; you didn't *want* to escape. It was as if Jaymi could see inside your soul, and she loved you for what she saw in it. You wanted to surrender to her sweet embrace forever.

It was no wonder Jaymi had named her band Passion Play, for the passion she exuded when she sang, or strummed her guitar, or gently played her piano, was just as intense as her eyes. Her voice was sweet, sensual, provocative, rebellious, tender, and sometimes full of angst, all rolled into one. Each emotion released in its most appropriate time, flowing effortlessly and believably with each note, each phrase. As she lost herself in her song, you too were lost, as if the two of you were one, and through her voice, she was expressing your feelings, in a way so eloquent and revealing you would never dare expose such confessions on your own. Certainly, Shawn had been captivated every time Jaymi took the stage.

Jaymi didn't have the stereotypical features sought after by modeling agencies or tabloid magazines. But there was something about her, something unique that made her stand out. She had a soft-edged oval face, unpronounced cheekbones, a petite sharp, straight nose, and thin lips. She looked serious, contemplative, and damn sexy. Shawn felt drawn to the somber ache in Jaymi's expression that suggested she understood things most twentysomethings didn't. Like she was an old soul or something.

As Shawn finished off her breakfast, she realized she had been staring at Jaymi. She took a long swallow of coffee and decided she would try to talk. "So, last I heard, you guys left LA because your mother was ill. How's she doing?"

Jaymi looked down at the table and her long, elegant musician's fingers wrapped around her coffee cup. One hand remained still, while the fingers of the other absentmindedly stroked its handle. Shawn watched the nervous gesture and knew immediately she had hit a nerve. And she tried to dismiss the awareness that she suddenly wished she were Jaymi's coffee cup. Jaymi's voice forced her attention back to her face.

"My mother was diagnosed with cancer. When I got the news, I had to come home," Jaymi said softly, her eyes still glued to the cup. She took a deep breath. "We lost her, not long after."

Shawn bit her lower lip, pinched her eyes shut for a few seconds, and sighed. "Oh, Jaymi. You must think I'm the biggest jerk. I didn't know. That's twice I've stuck my foot in my mouth. First with Peach, now this. I am so sorry."

"It's okay, how could you have known? We didn't exactly stick around to say good-byes to everyone before we headed back here."

"I noticed. I really missed you, you know? You were one of the only real friends I had out there." She stole a brief look at Jaymi, and with a shrug and another sigh, picked up her spoon and needlessly stirred her coffee. Without looking up, she quietly said, "It's been seven years since I lost my mother. Stroke."

Jaymi looked up. "Looks like we've got something in common—besides music, that is." They sat in silence once again. It was obvious neither of them felt like discussing the topic any further. Jaymi stood up and began to clear the table and Shawn followed suit, and insisted on washing the dishes, despite Jaymi's objections.

After cleaning up, Jaymi poured Shawn another cup of coffee and suggested she hang out in the living room while she showered. *Cozy place,* Shawn thought. *Even though it's big.* Natural pine walls were tastefully decorated with photos. A navy, tan, and forest-green tweed sofa had a matching recliner, and both faced a television positioned in the left corner. There was an elliptical coffee table and what looked like an antique wooden rocking chair, fully restored and refinished, with quilted cushions.

Through the open door to the right was Jaymi's music studio. Her upright piano and multi-guitar stand flanked a desk with a digital multitrack recorder on top. There were notebooks and musical lead sheets galore. To anyone else, it might have looked like a scattered mess, but to a fellow musician like Shawn, the disorder was the sign of a creative genius at work. She listened and, satisfied that the shower was still running, gave in to the temptation to peek through the papers on the recording desk. Page after page of lyrics, purposely written with space between lines to write in chord names, were scribbled in frantic handwriting, as if the ideas might escape quicker than they could be written down. She knew that feeling. She kept a tiny handheld tape recorder with her at all times, one she could readily pull out of her pocket to record an idea, lyrical or musical, before it was lost. It had become indispensable. It was amazing how quickly an idea could come into your head—a phrase, a sequence of words that perfectly expressed that thought, that feeling, that emotion. And if you didn't get it down that instant, it could be lost forever.

Jaymi had many good songs. Maybe even great songs. *Better than mine,* thought Shawn, as she jealously skimmed over page after page. "It's about time someone shook the dust off that pile."

Shawn jumped at the sound of Jaymi's voice and nearly dropped the papers. She quickly set them down and spun around to face her, hoping to God she wasn't red with embarrassment.

"Oh shit, I'm sorry, Jaymi. I wasn't snooping." Again, she tried desperately to avoid Jaymi's eyes, but it was hard not to look at her. Dressed in blue jeans and a forest-green ribbed Henley, she had walked silently into the room in her stocking feet. The men's clothing gave her slender physique a slightly masculine figure, though it couldn't hide her fine feminine curves. Her ash blond hair was towel-dried and still damp, and her eyes captured the sunlight, making them sparkle. Jaymi stepped up beside her and picked up the top sheet.

"I've been stuck on this one for months. Terrible writer's block this winter," Jaymi said, studying the page. Shawn noticed her clean scent and tried to inhale it without being obvious.

"I should get showered and dressed, too," Shawn said, thinking a cold shower was definitely in order.

❖

Shawn let the hot water ease the tension from her shoulders. Her thoughts raced with the explanation she owed Jaymi. She wanted to explain why she was here. But how much should she tell her? How much could she tell her, without risking rejection? Jaymi seemed like an unconditional friend, but that didn't mean she didn't have her standards.

She would tell her only what she had to—for today, anyway. She'd let time dictate whether she would need to tell her any more. She'd get to know Jaymi better before she told her the dark truth about herself. Jaymi was way out of her league, so it wasn't like she was misleading a potential lover.

She fumbled through her knapsack for something decent to wear. After several years of living in Southern California, her selection of cold-weather clothing was limited. She settled for a heavyweight navy New England Patriots sweatshirt that was still in decent condition and a pair of carpenter's jeans. She wiped the steam from the mirror and checked herself. *Damn, I need a haircut. First thing I'll do when I get a job—after I give Jaymi some rent money.*

She gave herself a pep talk to gather up her courage and made her way into the living room. Jaymi was sitting on the edge of the sofa, quietly strumming her guitar. And despite her desire to simply stand in the shadows, unnoticed, and watch Jaymi play, Shawn caught her breath and focused on what she needed to say.

Jaymi sensed her presence and the music stopped.

"Don't stop on my account," Shawn said, but it was too late. Jaymi set down the guitar, resting its neck on the arm of the sofa.

"I'm just noodling," Jaymi said. "I like your sweatshirt. I see you haven't lost your loyalty to our hometown team." She smiled that sweet smile and Shawn took a seat in the recliner.

"Never. New England's in my blood. It's home. I'm even more fanatic about the Red Sox."

Jaymi laughed. "Yeah, I remember. It sucked not being able to watch them play when I was in California. Unless they had a series in Anaheim or were on a nationally televised game against the Yankees or something."

"It was so sweet when they won it all last year."

Shawn could have easily talked baseball for hours, but she needed to get the talk over with. She took a deep breath and sat at the other end of the couch, braced her forearms on her thighs, and slowly began wringing her hands. *Here goes.* "I guess you're wondering why I showed up looking for you last night."

Jaymi nodded. "I am curious, I admit."

"My plan was to stay with my aunt Betty down in Lowell. Other than my father, she's the only family I have left here. Anyway, when I got to her house…" She swallowed hard, unsure if she could continue without bursting into tears. She glanced over at Jaymi, whose gaze was sympathetic.

"What is it?"

"Her neighbor told me she died a month ago." She straightened up and hardened as Jaymi gave her condolences. "So I went to my father's house, but…" She shuddered with the memory of the encounter. "I thought by now he would have forgiven me. I just was hoping he might…well, anyway, that's another story. The bastard still hates my guts. I didn't know where else to go. Then I heard your song on the radio, and the DJ said you were playing at Sparky's, so—"

"Shawn"—Jaymi leaned forward, her expression serious—"what happened in California? I thought you were doing pretty well, getting gigs."

Shawn covered her face with her hands and slowly shook her head. She prayed again for courage. She slowly brought her head up. "I screwed up, Jaymi. Bad. My gigs started dropping off 'cause the clubs were constantly trying to bring in new talent, to keep it fresh. I couldn't afford an agent, so every night I was just driving to any place I could audition, or if they had open mikes. I'd drive a hundred miles if I had to. And that was getting me nowhere, and I couldn't afford the gas. Wannabes like me are a dime a dozen in LA, and most of the places either dealt only through agents, or they said I could leave a demo and they'd get back to me. Well, the only recordings I have of my stuff are pretty low quality, so I was out of luck. Then to make matters worse, I lost my day job."

"Oh no. That sucks."

"Tell me about it. I'd been waiting tables at this dive, and the guy that ran the place, I swear he had it out for me. Anyway, I had this tendency to show up a little late sometimes. Not all the time, just once in a while, and it was only by five minutes or so, never more than that. Usually because he was a bastard and kept putting me on the breakfast shifts, even though I kept telling him I was a musician and worked late playing clubs. I told him I'd do better with the lunch shifts, but he did it just to spite me, I think."

Shawn watched Jaymi's face for signs of disgust, but all she saw was compassion. She struggled on, her stomach in knots and her palms damp with sweat. She rubbed them on her jeans.

"Anyway, I guess he finally got fed up and one day he fired me. I had a hell of a time finding another job. I think he was giving me bad references. Money ran out and I lost my apartment. I haven't had a steady job in more than two years. I guess I'm just not good at much. Every job I got, somehow I'd screw up."

Jaymi sat silently, waiting for her to continue. She knew she had to get it all out now.

"I can't catch a break. I've either been staying in motels when I did have a few bucks, or sleeping in my car, or..." She faltered. She couldn't say the rest out loud. Not yet, and maybe not ever.

"My God, Shawn, that's awful. You didn't have any friends you could stay with?"

Shawn chewed on a knuckle before answering with only a shrug and averted eyes. Hearing it from Jaymi made it sound even worse, like she really was totally alone.

"It's okay if you don't want to talk about it."

Shawn swallowed hard. "It's not that I don't want to. I'm just not sure I'm ready to—"

"It's not like it's any of my business. I'm sorry, I shouldn't have pried."

"No, Jaymi, I'm sorry. It's not that I don't trust you, I'm just... let's just say I was desperate and broke and I did some things I'm not too proud of."

"Listen"—Jaymi leaned forward and looked into Shawn's eyes, her voice soft and calm—"we all make mistakes, and we've all done things we're not proud of. I know I have. So stop being so hard on yourself and try to look at this as a new start, okay?"

Shawn managed a weak smile and nodded. Jaymi stood up and for a fleeting, hopeful moment, Shawn thought Jaymi was going to hug her. Instead she walked by her and retrieved a guitar case from the studio.

"The band's rehearsing today, so I need to get ready to go," Jaymi said, placing the guitar gingerly in its case. "You want to come along? Or you can hang out here if you want. You can watch TV, play your guitar, whatever you like to do to relax. I know you've had a long trip, so maybe you don't feel like going anywhere. I have time to help you unpack your car if you want. Make yourself at home in that spare bedroom. I know there isn't much in there, but maybe we can go to the Goodwill store or something and pick up a dresser for your clothes. I hate to see you living out of a suitcase."

"Wow. I appreciate it, but really, I feel like I'm intruding here. I'm not moving in or anything, I wouldn't expect you to put me up for any extended period of time—"

"Hey," Jaymi said, "I've been meaning to set up that guest room for months, and now I have an excuse to stop procrastinating." She picked up her guitar and set it by the kitchen door. "Besides, I like having a guest. And by the way? I've missed you."

"Thanks, Jaymi. I can't tell you how much I appreciate it. I won't let you down. And, yeah, I'd love to come to rehearsal, of course." She felt safe in Jaymi's presence, something she hadn't felt in a long time, and she was desperate to keep the feeling. She'd been alone long enough. Now she just wanted to be near people who didn't want anything from her.

Jaymi nodded and opened the door. "Then let's get to it. We've got music to make."

# CHAPTER FIVE

Rehearsal turned out to be at Jaymi's aunt and uncle's house. They were kind enough to let them use their finished basement, since their son, Brian, was the band's drummer. He greeted Shawn with a big hug and didn't pry into the circumstances surrounding her return. They'd spent many nights talking sports together and had gotten pretty close in LA, and he said he was glad to have his baseball buddy back.

It was a no-brainer for Shawn to come to rehearsal. Being in the presence of other musicians was always where she felt most at home. Jaymi had insisted that she bring her guitar, in case she felt like jamming with them. She was hesitant, feeling much too inadequate to play with such an accomplished band, but inside she couldn't have been more excited and hoped she would get the chance to join in for at least one song.

Jaymi was almost finished setting up when the band's bassist, Kay Burnes, arrived with Nikki Razer, the lead singer. Shawn was surprised to get a hug from Kay. She hadn't gotten to know her very well in LA, but now Kay treated her like an old friend.

"Well, what have we here?" said Nikki, peeling off her leather biker jacket as she sized up Shawn. "Long time no see, cute stuff." Her skin-tight black sweater revealed the inviting swell of her obviously cold breasts. She accessorized with silver and turquoise jewelry around her neck and on several fingers. A wide studded leather wristband adorned her left wrist. "Where you been? Ethiopia? You need to put some meat on your bones, girl."

Shawn shrank away from her. The last thing she needed was

someone like Nikki bringing attention to how pathetic she felt right now. Shawn had always thought that if it were possible to mate two women, Nikki could be the offspring of the sleek, sexy, beautiful Pat Benatar and the tough, punk, rebellious Joan Jett. Her indigo hair and ebony eyes could lure any woman she wanted from across any size room into the uninhibited confines of a bedroom. And she let people know it. Shawn had never felt comfortable around Nikki. She was jealous of Nikki's confidence, for one. But she also wondered how Jaymi kept Nikki's ego in check to keep peace within the group.

Thinking back to the Passion Play performances she'd seen in California, she was reminded of the flirtatious interactions between Nikki and Jaymi onstage. They were just part of the show and the audience ate it up, but they were always initiated by Nikki. Shawn got the impression they were Nikki's way of sending a message to the audience that Jaymi was hers—even though she wasn't. Shawn had to admit they *were* magic onstage, a kind of musical chemistry maintained between Jaymi's reflective sweet melodies and Nikki's fiery edge.

"Down, girl," Jaymi said. "Shawn just got back from California. She's staying with me for a while and I invited her to hang out while we practice."

Nikki nodded, her eyes still fixed on Shawn, a sly smile upon her lips.

*She thinks she can have me if she wants,* thought Shawn. *She is so wrong.*

"Sure. Why not?" Nikki grinned. "You might learn something."

Shawn glared at her, and she knew her contempt was probably apparent, but she was having a hard time caring. *Fuck you, Nikki.* She stayed silent and crossed her arms over her chest to keep from lashing out. She wasn't about to let someone like Nikki fuck up the one good thing that had happened to her in years.

Once the band started to play, Shawn relaxed. Jaymi had made sure she was comfortable on a couch with snacks and a soda, as if she were sitting back to watch a movie. But once the music started, she quickly forgot about the spread in front of her. At last she could keep her eyes glued to Jaymi without it seeming weird.

The band ran through a few covers to warm up, and then through a few of their own well-established songs. They stopped periodically to fine-tune certain parts, solos, or instrumental arrangements, more often than not under Jaymi's direction. It was obvious that she was the creative force behind it all.

After listening to them work through the creative parts of their music, Shawn felt inspired to get back to work on her own material. The need for survival had forced music to take a backseat lately, but surrounded by it now, she thought maybe she could return to it. An hour and a half later, they took a break, and Jaymi joined Shawn on the couch while the others went upstairs.

"So, how do we sound?" Jaymi asked.

"You guys are awesome. I always thought you were. I like the new songs, especially that last one you did."

"Thanks. I just wish I could contribute more."

"What do you mean?"

"I've been battling writer's block for months. All those new songs are Nikki's and Kay's. Brian writes with them a little, too. I feel like I'm not contributing at all."

Shawn heard the frustration in Jaymi's voice. *That explains why Jaymi wasn't singing lead on any of those songs.* She gave Jaymi a light pat on the back. "You just lost your mom. Cripes, give yourself a break. It'll come back." The sorrow that filled Jaymi's eyes at the mention of her mother broke Shawn's heart. "Besides, even if you're not writing, you're helping with the arrangements and drum fills and stuff like that."

Jaymi smiled. "It doesn't help that I'm my own worst critic. I'm scrapping every idea I come up with lately."

"I know what you mean," Shawn said. "I toss half the shit I write."

Jaymi smiled. "But we keep at it, don't we?"

Before she could answer, the others had reentered and assumed their positions. Nikki had a beer in each hand, one of which she had already begun consuming. Shawn glanced at the clock. It wasn't even three o'clock yet.

"Nikki, why do you always have to drink?" Jaymi said, clearly annoyed, and snatched the unopened bottle from Nikki's hand.

"Hey!" Nikki tried to grab the bottle.

"I need you sharp. We're working on new stuff and I need you sober."

"Ah, fuck, I need more than two to de-sober me." She laughed at her made-up word. "De-sober! That's a good one."

Shawn clenched her teeth. She hated the disrespect Nikki was showing Jaymi. She knew Jaymi could hold her own, but it didn't matter. She had to say something. She got up and with Nikki's attention on Jaymi, she easily slipped the open beer from Nikki's other hand.

"I think you ought to show Jaymi a little respect. Drinks can wait till *after* rehearsal."

When Nikki looked at her, Shawn expected her to look pissed off. Instead, she saw what looked like a bit of respect.

"Wow," Nikki said, "so you do have a backbone after all." She smiled widely. "I like that, cute stuff." She then linked Shawn's arm in hers and walked her away from everybody. "In fact," she whispered so no one else could hear, "I find it sexy. I like a woman who can put me in my place."

Shawn wasn't flattered but did begrudgingly enjoy the confidence boost. She managed to slide her arm out of Nikki's grip, and Jaymi quickly broke up the rendezvous and managed to get her singer refocused on the task at hand.

They struggled through the next two songs, talking through changes and experimenting, until they had all grown hungry and tired and were getting cranky. Shawn was champing at the bit to play but figured it would have to wait until next time. *I hope there is a next time.*

When it seemed they were ready to wrap things up, Jaymi stopped everyone and looked in Shawn's direction with a smile. "Well? Wanna sit in for a few Beatles tunes or something?"

Shawn lit up. "Really?"

"Well, yeah, we always try to end on a high note. No pun intended." Jaymi laughed. "Go on, get out your baby and get in tune. You can plug in here."

A mixture of excitement and anxiety swelled through Shawn's entire body. She couldn't wait to play, but she had never played with a full band before. The closest had been jamming at home with the stereo. What if she messed up? What if she sang off-key, or forgot the lyrics, or screwed up her timing?

The band was waiting. There was no time to dwell on what-ifs.

Shawn quickly set up and dove right into a lively version of "Can't Buy Me Love," the band joining in after the first line had escaped her mouth. It was amazing. Once Shawn made it through the first verse, she felt herself slide into her zone. Line by line, the butterflies dissipated and the rest of the world slipped away.

Jaymi switched to electric guitar and they followed with "Get Back." Shawn was impressed with her skills on lead guitar. Jaymi's impeccable timing, expressive phrasing, and energetic strums accompanied the entire group singing together through every chorus. Shawn's high was rising, note by note, verse by verse. This was what she lived for. The oneness with the band, with the song, with the music. It was better than sex.

Well, almost better.

❖

"I can see you haven't lost your touch," Jaymi said on the drive home.

"Well, thanks. Thank God I didn't sell my guitar. I thought about it. I was that desperate. But what's it say about me that I was willing to live in my car before I'd give up my guitar?"

"Sounds like a good line for a song," said Jaymi, who immediately began singing Shawn's words and tapping out a rhythm on the steering wheel.

"I would live in my car
Before I'd give up my guitar."

Shawn joined in. The second time through, she instinctively harmonized in her raspy alto. They broke into laughter, and then Jaymi, who seemed genuinely impressed, looked at Shawn with a huge smile. "Wow, that was cool. You should play with us on a couple songs on our next gig. You wanna?"

Shawn's eyes rounded and her jaw dropped. "Are you serious? Me?"

"Uh, yes, you." Jaymi playfully looked around to either side of her passenger, as if looking for someone. "Who else would I be talking to?"

"But…will the band be okay with that? I mean you guys are tight, man, the band's really tight. I'm not as polished as you guys. I mean, you're on the radio now and everything. What if I screwed up? I'd hate to think I'd set you back."

"You're not going to screw up. Geez, Shawn, you don't give yourself much credit. You're good, you know. *Really* good. As far as the polishing goes, I can help you with that. I always thought you were the best one at all those open mikes we used to do."

Shawn couldn't believe what she was hearing. Jaymi Del Harmon thought she was the best? *Maybe she's just saying that to be polite.*

"I'm starved," Jaymi said. "You like Chinese?"

"That sounds good, but I can't. I've only got a few bucks left."

"Hey, don't worry about it. It's on me. You've got to eat."

"Yeah, but…"

"But what? Listen, if it makes you feel better, after you get a job, you can treat."

Shawn shrugged, embarrassed, but also too hungry to argue. And, if she was completely honest with herself, it felt really nice to have someone care whether or not she ate. There was a time she would've been too proud to accept Jaymi's offer, but months of going to bed hungry and doing whatever she had to in order to survive had taught her that a person couldn't live off their pride. She just hoped this, too, wouldn't slip away from her.

## CHAPTER SIX

Shawn woke the next morning to silence and the wonderful aroma of perked coffee. She shivered as she crawled out from under the covers, slipped on her Patriots sweatshirt, and went into the kitchen. The only light came from the low-wattage bulb over the stove. She flicked on the overhead light. On the kitchen table was the local phone book opened up to the Employment Agencies section of the yellow pages, and next to it, a twenty-dollar bill and a note from Jaymi that read:

> Shawn,
>     Hope you slept well. Maybe one of these places can help you find work. I circled the one I used—they were very helpful. Give them my name if you need a reference. And you can also use my address and phone number as your contact information. Here's my spare key to the apartment and some money in case you need gas. Good luck and I'll see you when I get home tonight.
>     Jaymi
> PS: By the way, you played awesome yesterday!

Shawn grew warm inside with Jaymi's words. She felt undeserving of such praise, let alone the kindness and generosity Jaymi had shown her so unconditionally. She wondered if that would change if she knew the truth about why she had left LA.

*She does know the truth. I lost my job and my apartment. I was broke.* Shawn argued with herself, as she often did. *She doesn't need to know about all of my despicable bad decisions. Or that I had a huge crush on her when we were friends back in LA.*

Inspired by Jaymi's generosity, she quickly downed a cup of coffee, showered and dressed, and headed out, the phone book tucked under her arm. She signed up for work at five agencies, each of them promising to call her should anything come up that fit her skills and qualifications. Since she didn't need gas, she stopped at a supermarket—she'd thank Jaymi by having dinner ready for her when she got home.

She put away the groceries, prepared chicken breasts in a marinade, and made a sandwich with the bread and tuna she had bought. She was cleaning up when there was a knock on the door. She jumped. *Fuck. They couldn't have found me. No way.* She took a steadying breath and cautiously peeked out the kitchen window toward the landing outside the door. Nikki.

*It's only one thirty. Doesn't she know Jaymi wouldn't be home from work yet?* If she did, it meant she wasn't there to see Jaymi, which instantly made Shawn even more nervous. *Shit.*

Nikki knocked again, this time with a little more force. Shawn conceded and opened the door.

"Hey, cute stuff, how's it going?" Nikki said as she removed her sunglasses and stepped in without an invitation.

"Okay. Jaymi's not home yet—"

"Oh, I know. She doesn't get out till five. I wanted to stop by and see if you needed anything." She walked into the living room and made herself at home in the easy chair.

"No, I'm fine. And my name's Shawn." She followed Nikki into the room but remained standing, hoping it would indicate she didn't expect her company to stay long.

Nikki grinned, sat back, and crossed an ankle over her knee. "But you *are* cute. You do know that, don't you, *Shawn?*"

Shawn folded her arms across her chest. "Is there something I can do for you, Nikki?"

The grin grew wider for a second before she answered. "You can tell me what you're doing here, for starters."

"I think Jaymi already explained that to you yesterday."

"Right, right. You just came back from LA, needed a place to stay, and my dear friend didn't have the heart to turn you away—"

"Look, I don't know what your problem is with me, but if you're worried about me taking advantage of Jaymi, I'm not—"

"That's it exactly, *Shawn*." Nikki's eyes were cold and the grin vanished. She dropped her foot to the floor and leaned forward in the chair. "You see, Jaymi and I have been friends a long time—since we were sophomores in college—and I've seen her screwed over way too many times because she's too nice for her own good. I look out for her because I don't like seeing her get hurt."

"Well, you must not be doing a very good job of it if she keeps getting screwed over," Shawn blurted. It was easier for her to feel courageous with someone she didn't like.

Nikki stood and moved close to Shawn. "You know what," she said, the grin returning, "I like you. You've got spunk. But I do have to warn you, Jaymi's not interested in getting involved with anyone right now, not for a long time—in case you had any thoughts of making a move on her. She's made it quite clear that her career is all she cares about right now. And I'm going to make sure nothing interferes with that, understand?"

Shawn took a step back and reclaimed her personal space. "Well then, you've got nothing to worry about, because a relationship is the last thing on my mind right now." She knew it was the truth, yet something sank in her heart just the same. "And I have no intention of doing anything that would hurt Jaymi. I know what a good person she is, and I wouldn't dream of taking advantage of that."

"Good. Glad to hear it," Nikki said, though Shawn didn't miss the sarcasm in her tone. Nikki's breast brushed the side of Shawn's arm as she swept past her, and it took all of Shawn's willpower not to wipe at the spot on her arm, as though to wipe Nikki away. She left without another word, as though she'd already dismissed Shawn from her thoughts.

Shawn made herself a cup of coffee and spread the newspaper out on the kitchen table. She circled several *Help Wanted* ads and began making phone calls, crossing out dead ends as she went. Not much out there for a struggling musician looking for a day job.

At five, she began preparing dinner, anxiously peeking out the window every two minutes. When Jaymi arrived, Shawn was glad to see she looked surprised rather than upset at the activity in the kitchen.

"You're cooking supper?"

"My car didn't need gas, so I used the money you left to buy some food. I hope you don't mind." Shawn smiled and tried not to check her out, but she couldn't help noticing that she looked damn cute decked out in her khakis and a collared black uniform shirt trimmed in violet and yellow.

"Mind? Are you kidding? This is sweet, coming home to someone cooking me dinner. I can't even remember the last time…" Jaymi's smile faded suddenly. "Yes, I can, but let's not talk about that. That's really sweet of you. You didn't have to, you know."

"Oh, I know. I just thought I should earn my keep around here. And it's only fair—you've been feeding me since I got here, so I figured it was the least I could do."

"I appreciate it," Jaymi said, then went down the hall to her room. She returned a few minutes later in blue jeans and a flannel shirt. "So how did your day go? Any luck finding a job?"

Shawn proceeded to tell her about the temp agencies she visited and the ads she answered. She debated telling her about Nikki's visit and decided it was probably best not to keep it from her in case Nikki mentioned it. Part of her was worried that Jaymi would take what Nikki said seriously, and would think taking Shawn in was a mistake. But it would probably be worse if Jaymi thought she'd lied to her. They finished dinner and cleaned up, but she still hadn't worked up the nerve to bring it up.

Jaymi pushed away from the table and said, "That was delicious. Where'd you learn to cook like that?"

"My mother taught me. Well, she made me learn, is more like it," Shawn replied. "I'm grateful for it now, but at the time it just felt like another part of her denial that I was gay. She tried everything she could to make me more feminine, and she thought cooking was a woman's duty. She was probably hoping that if I tried it, I might find I like doing girly things. And that would somehow translate into me liking men. Never worked, obviously." There was a moment of awkward silence, and Shawn wondered if she'd overshared. They cleared the dishes in silence, and then headed into the other room.

"I had a visitor today," Shawn said, sensing it was a good time to change the subject.

"Let me guess. Nikki."

Shawn's eyebrows shot up. "You talked to her?"

Jaymi shook her head and curled her legs beneath her on the sofa. "I don't have to. I'm sorry, I should have warned you. She gave you the *Jaymi's been hurt and I'm looking out for her* speech, didn't she?"

Shawn nodded, let out a deep breath, and bit her bottom lip. "You know her well."

"Don't take it personally, Shawn. She pulls this protective act every time I make a new friend. Not that you're a *completely* new friend, but, you know. I keep telling her to give me a little credit. Remember what I said about us all making mistakes? Well, I haven't always made the smartest moves when it comes to women, but I can at least say I've learned from my mistakes. And seeing a therapist helped, too."

"You've been in therapy?"

"Oh yeah. Sanest decision I ever made in my life, ironically. I learned a lot about myself, and I'm much stronger and more confident because of it. It helped me with losing my mom, as well as other things. And I've learned to watch for red flags so I don't fall into old behavior patterns and neglect myself."

Shawn shifted in her chair. "Red flags, huh? Like what kind of red flags?"

"Well, let's see. I dated a girl for a couple months who always criticized how much people drank at the clubs, yet she got smashed every time we went to one. I suspected she had a problem, so I subtly tried to fix her. She'd had a tough childhood, and I felt bad for her. I thought if I loved her enough, that I could single-handedly cure her of her addiction. I would take her places that didn't serve alcohol, like the mall, or a movie, or the beach. But every time, without fail, we'd end up at a bar or a club because she insisted we had to properly end every date with a nightcap. When I finally told her that I thought she had a drinking problem, she flipped out and dumped me. Another girl I went out with talked about her ex a lot, and I didn't think much of it. Everybody does that to an extent when you first start dating. A month into the relationship, though, she was still obsessing over this girl. And then one night she called me her ex-girlfriend's name when I was making love to her."

"No shit! Now that's bad." She couldn't believe all those women didn't know what a good thing they had in Jaymi.

"Yeah, no kidding. She kept apologizing, saying it was just old habit, and it didn't mean anything. Well, I finally smartened up and accepted that she was still in love with her ex. I should've picked up on it earlier, but I ignored the signs because I was so attracted to her. I ended up breaking it off, and then I found out that less than a week later, they were back together."

"Guess that's why they say love is blind." Shawn had begun to fidget when Jaymi said *making love*. It was stirring up fantasies and hormones she needed to keep under control.

"I'm ashamed to say I could give you more sordid stories of my failed relationships, but I don't want to bore you. I've been fortunate that I've never been physically abused, but I've certainly been psychologically abused." Jaymi shrugged, and it almost seemed like she was shrugging away the memories.

Shawn noticed the omission of any mention of Peach. Why was that? Was that breakup still too painful to talk about?

"So now that I've worked on my confidence issues, I know what to look for, and I can spot those red flags a mile away. But Nikki's still afraid I'll fall head over heels for every woman I meet and go right back to my old naive ways and get screwed again."

Shawn wasn't sure what to say. A part of her was intrigued and questioning her own possible need for therapy, while another part was flattered. *Does Jaymi think of me as someone she could fall for? Is she already on her guard? Am I her type?* She forced the thoughts from her mind. She was subtly aware of the reawakening of her old crush on Jaymi but knew it would have to remain just that. *No way in hell Jaymi would be interested in a screwup like me.* She had to find her own place soon. There were definitely complications she didn't need.

"Shawn? You okay? You got quiet on me."

"Oh yeah. I'm fine. Tired, I guess. It's been a long day."

Jaymi got up and picked up her guitar. She returned to the sofa and began to strum. "This always helps me relax after a long day. Why don't you get yours out?"

Shawn couldn't get down the hall fast enough to retrieve her guitar. *I'm going to jam with Jaymi! In her living room! Stay calm now, you fool, you're acting like a crazed fan, for God's sake.*

They tuned up and Jaymi began to play the intro to one of her songs. Shawn studied her fingers and picked up the chord sequence. Jaymi began to sing softly, and that sweet voice carried over their strumming perfectly. Shawn couldn't bring herself to sing along on the chorus; she wanted only to hear Jaymi's voice.

"Now one of yours," said Jaymi when the song was over.

Shawn froze. Her mind went blank.

"Come on, don't be shy. I've heard you play at open mikes, remember? You've got lots of great songs. And a great voice. How about 'No Foolin' or 'Crazy For Your Love'?"

They dove into both suggestions, Jaymi picking up the chords just as easily as Shawn had. But Jaymi wasn't shy about singing along, adding beautiful harmonies and countermelodies above Shawn's lower, raspy voice.

When they finished, both were smiling from ear to ear. "That was so much fun," said Shawn, her skin alive from the music they'd shared.

"We sound pretty damn good together. You're not used to playing with anyone, are you?"

Shawn felt a little ashamed. "No, it's always been just me, solo. I never really had anybody to jam with. I've never been in a band. My parents thought music was a waste of time. As a career, anyway. Especially my father. So I just played by myself, rather than have to explain to other people why my parents weren't cool with it."

Jaymi set down her guitar and placed her hand on Shawn's knee. Shawn's skin tingled at the warm touch. "Trust me, you're not wasting your time. You're very talented, Shawn. I love your music. I loved watching you perform in California. You've got a lot of heart and it comes through every time you play. People love that."

"You really mean that? You think I've got talent? I mean, I know I've got some, but enough to make it?"

"Well, yeah, of course I do. I wouldn't say that if I didn't mean it." Jaymi stood and pulled Shawn up by the hand. "Now come on, let's go to bed—I mean—" She blushed and laughed nervously. "I'm sorry, that didn't come out the way I meant. Okay, now I'm embarrassed. What I meant was that we both need to get some sleep."

Shawn laughed, too. "I knew what you meant, Jaymi."

"Well, good night. Thanks again for dinner." Jaymi started down the hall toward her bedroom.

"Jaymi," Shawn called. Jaymi stopped and turned around. "When it comes to us being friends…I hope there aren't any red flags."

Jaymi smiled. "So do I." She closed the bedroom door behind her.

It wasn't exactly the response Shawn had been hoping for, but it was a start.

## CHAPTER SEVEN

Jaymi was actually enjoying her workday, the memories of the last few days replaying in the background. Not that she ever hated her job—it would do until she could support herself with her music. She felt a new spring in her step. She found herself cracking jokes and unable to keep from smiling. And when Jaymi noticed that the supervisor was wearing two different shoes, she couldn't resist teasing her. It was funny, and her mood seemed to be contagious because her normally humorless boss laughed despite herself.

She knew she had to keep her feelings in check. Enough time had passed since her breakup with Peach that she wasn't in rebound mode anymore, but she still wanted to be careful not to repeat past mistakes. Had she been single when they'd first met, she might have gotten to know Shawn better. But she'd always felt like Shawn had a good heart.

Shawn seemed hesitant to open up about her life in the time they'd lost touch. The few details she had shared since her arrival three days ago didn't place her in a favorable light, but she had still been honest enough to share them. Her inability to keep a job was a concern, and although the stories were funny, it also meant Shawn might not be very reliable. Shawn said she'd find her own place once she found steady employment, if, of course, she could find and keep a job.

To her surprise, she had mixed feelings about that part of the plan. The shared living arrangement might actually be mutually beneficial. Musically speaking, of course. She was already feeling more inspired to write. And it would take some of the financial pressure off both of them. After all the years Passion Play had been playing together, maybe she needed something to shake things up a bit.

Jaymi had plans to meet her sister Laura at New Horizons for lunch, and she spotted her from the sidewalk just as she was pulling into the parking lot next to the store. She scooped up some fresh-fallen snow, waited until Laura came around the corner, and nailed the tall, slim blonde in the shoulder with the snowball. "Gotcha!"

Laura pretended to be angry and glared at her younger sister. "You brat. Just for that, you're buying lunch."

"No sweat, sis." Jaymi brushed the snow off Laura's coat and continued to unnecessarily brush at snow that wasn't there, knowing the exaggeration would get her goat. "Wouldn't want you to look unpresentable in public."

"Don't worry. I don't embarrass easily."

"No, but I do."

Laura rolled her eyes. "Shut up. Let's go in. It's freezing out here."

They ordered and dug into their meals. Jaymi exchanged a wave across the room with Devin, who was helping a customer.

"Have you seen Dad lately?" Jaymi asked, after swallowing a bite of her BLT. "I haven't been over there for a couple weeks."

"I saw him last weekend. He's doing okay. You know, hanging in there like the rest of us." She took a drink. "Teddy stopped by, too."

"When's our next dinner?" Since her mother's death, she and her siblings made a point of getting together with their father at least once a month, to share a meal and some quality time together. They had always been close, but after going through such a painful loss together, they were acutely aware of an unspoken bond they knew would last forever.

"That depends on you. You're the budding rock star with the busy weekend schedule." Laura smiled proudly and nibbled off a bite of her veggie wrap.

"I'll look over our schedule and let you know."

They ate in silence for a few minutes, and then talked a little about how their jobs were going.

"We have a new designer on the team," said Laura, who had a successful interior design career. She smiled mischievously, and then drawled out in a sing-song voice, "And she's gay."

"No."

"No what?"

"No fixing me up. You know I'm not into that."

"You're not seeing anyone, are you?"

Jaymi immediately thought of Shawn. *Where'd that come from?* "No, but—"

Laura playfully slapped Jaymi's hand. "I won't fix you up, just introduce you. Who knows? She might be just your type."

"I don't have a type."

"Oh, come on, everyone has a type."

At that moment, Devin walked up to the table. Jaymi sighed in relief. *Devin, you've got perfect timing.*

"Hey, Jaymi. Hi, Laura."

"Hi, Devin."

"How's it going, Jaymi?"

"Good. I'm good. Can you join us?"

"Not today. But I saw you come in and I wanted to say hi."

Laura grinned at her sister and then looked at Devin appraisingly. "Well, perhaps you can help Jaymi look for that book she's been wanting."

Jaymi glared at Laura and then spoke to Devin. "Actually, I can't today. I only have fifteen minutes left before I have to get back to work."

"No problem. Me, too. I'll catch you guys later."

They watched Devin walk away and Jaymi readied herself for what she knew was coming.

"She's sweet. And I'm straight, but she'd turn my head."

"She's also very taken."

"Now that's a shame. I could see you with her. What if she wasn't? Would you be interested?"

Jaymi wasn't sure how to answer that one. There was no doubt she found Devin attractive, but Devin had been in love with Sara since Jaymi met her, so she hadn't thought of her in that way before. "Well, she's definitely got some of the qualities I'd want in a woman. She's got a heart of gold. She's easy to talk to. She makes me laugh."

"She's a writer, isn't she?"

"Yes."

"So you're both creative."

"Yes."

"Something else you'd have in common with our new designer."

"Will you let it go, already? I don't want to be fixed up."

"Okay, okay. I'll drop it." She finished off her iced tea with a slurp. She then looked at Jaymi seriously. "Just promise me one thing, will you?"

"What?"

"Next time you get involved with someone, make sure it's with someone who appreciates you, all right? Peach abandoned you when you needed her most. I don't want to see you get hurt like that again."

"That makes two of us, Laura."

"I'm just saying this because I love you."

"I know you do." She smiled weakly at her sister and glanced at her watch. "I have to go or I'll be late."

They exchanged a hug before parting, and Jaymi realized she hadn't mentioned Shawn at all. *That's interesting, since I couldn't stop thinking about her the whole time.*

❖

Shawn shuffled into the kitchen. She started a pot of coffee and popped two slices of bread into the toaster. She rubbed her eyes and yawned, pondering the best course of action for the day. Breakfast, even though technically it was closer to lunch. Shower. Use Jaymi's laptop to go online and look for jobs. Maybe pick up the guitar for a little while and work on some songs. Cook dinner for Jaymi again.

It all seemed so surreal—her life was so far removed from what it had been only a week ago. She wanted it to stay this way. She was getting her life back on track and that was all there was to it. Her mind strayed to last night's conversation about making bad choices and not listening to her instincts.

She jumped when her toast sprang from the slots and nearly toppled onto the counter. She finished preparing her meal and sat down to eat. Her thoughts then wandered from the last few days with Jaymi to Aunt Betty. With all that had occurred since her arrival, she realized she hadn't given herself time to deal with the loss.

How had she let her life get so out of control that she didn't know Aunt Betty had died? When was the last time they'd spoken? She'd spent the last seven years estranged from everyone—her father, her cousins, her few friends—everyone except Aunt Betty. Shawn had never been very close to any other relatives. She'd chosen to distance herself from them rather than come out to them and risk rejection.

She cleared her dishes and within an hour was on the road. She knew the drive would eat up a good chunk of gas, but she didn't care. The need to pay her respects was stronger than anything else right now.

She only wished she had enough money to buy a bouquet to place by the grave. She only wished she was able to shed tears when she found the plot and saw Betty's name engraved beneath her uncle's on the stone. But the tears wouldn't come. And it made her angry that they wouldn't come. Was she so far gone that her heart had hardened? *What's wrong with me, for Chrissake?*

❖

Once again, Jaymi came home from work to the aroma of a home-cooked meal. Broiled steak tips, seasoned steak fries, steamed corn, and crescent rolls were the menu tonight. She could get used to having someone home to cook for her.

"Shawn, you're going to spoil me rotten if this keeps up," she said as she shed the burden of her gloves and jacket.

Shawn took the garments from her and put them away in the hall closet. "It's the least I can do since I'm not working yet. Go get changed, it'll be ready in a few minutes."

When Jaymi returned, there were two goblets of wine on the table and Shawn was plating their meals. After a few bites, she praised Shawn's cooking talents, thanked her, and asked her about her day.

"Well…it didn't exactly go as planned." Shawn stared at her plate, moving the fork a millimeter one direction, and then back again. She filled Jaymi in on her impulsive drive to the cemetery in Lowell to see her aunt's grave. "I just needed to say good-bye, you know? I just needed to see it." Shawn paused, as if contemplating a fry. "I know I should've spent the day job hunting."

"It's okay, I understand, believe me. You needed closure. Better you take care of those needs sooner rather than later."

"So you're not mad?"

Jaymi chuckled. "Of course not. Look, it's not like you're under some deadline to move out of here or anything. Give yourself a break— you've only been here a few days. I'm sure you'll find something soon."

Shawn took a long swallow of wine and sat back in her chair. She swiped a napkin across her lips and shook her head.

"What?" Jaymi asked, puzzled by Shawn's look of confusion.

"Why are you being so nice to me?"

"What do you mean?"

"I mean, I show up here after we haven't seen each other in ages, and you give me a place to stay. You're not worried about how or when I'm going to be able to help you pay for anything. You know about a few of the dumb-ass things I've done. You're not using me for sex—"

"Whoa, wait a minute. Who says I'm not gonna use you for sex?" Jaymi did her best to keep a straight face, until Shawn's face turned as red as the wine and her eyes grew as wide as the rim of her glass. Jaymi burst into laughter. A minute later, Shawn joined in. They managed to compose themselves long enough to finish eating.

Jaymi insisted on clearing the table and washing the dishes. She joined Shawn in the living room afterward and settled into the recliner.

"So you never answered my question about why you've been so good to me."

"I could ask you the same thing."

"Huh?"

"Let me put it to you this way. Did you make dinner the last two nights because you think you owe me something?"

"Well, I guess that might have been part of it. But mostly, I wanted to do something to thank you for everything you've done for me."

"Would you have done it if you had found a job and were already helping me pay the bills?"

"Well, yeah, of course I would."

"Okay, then. Friends do that, Shawn—they take care of each other. Friendship is meant to be unconditional. And as far as the dumb-ass stuff? That was out of desperation and for survival. I know that's not who you are. It's done, it's over with, and you're focusing on the future, right?"

Shawn stretched back out on the couch and grinned at Jaymi. "You really are the sweetest person I've ever met."

"We'll see if you still feel that way tomorrow night. I'm cooking. I may kill us both."

❖

Jaymi climbed into bed and proceeded to toss and turn. She couldn't believe she had made that comment to Shawn. *Who says I'm not gonna use you for sex?* What was she thinking? It wasn't like her to so blatantly flirt like that. But the look on Shawn's face had been priceless. *God, she's cute when she blushes.*

But for one instant, she had seen fear in Shawn's eyes. Was that what she was used to? People using her? Or was she the one using people? There were still pieces missing to the puzzle. She'd been homeless in California. Where had she lived? In a motel? In her car? Had she been so desperate for money that she'd prostituted herself?

She hated thinking that Shawn might indeed be taking advantage of her hospitality. Yet something in her gut didn't believe that. Shawn had already taken positive steps to change her life. What was past was past.

# Chapter Eight

Two weeks went by. Shawn managed to fill her days while Jaymi was at work. She continued her job search. She wrote songs. She practiced her guitar and brushed up her skills on keyboards. She did housework. She cooked dinner. She accompanied Jaymi to some rehearsals and gigs. She wandered the lonely acres of the ranch and made friends with the horses.

And she attempted to fight off the growing crush on her roommate. It wasn't going well. If anything, they seemed to be getting closer each time they spent time together. Talking about losing their mothers, talking about their families, talking about how Shawn's closeness to Aunt Betty had compensated for the declined relationship with her mother, and talking about Jaymi's surrogate mother in her landlady, Alice.

And of course, there was always the music. They shared their dreams, their ambitions, their childhood stories, their obsessions. When they weren't talking, they were playing music.

Then finally, she found work—a three-month assignment at a gourmet coffee distribution center, picking orders and packing them for shipment. Not the most thrilling work, but it was income. The shift started at six a.m. Each morning, Shawn struggled to make it out of bed and on the road, setting her alarm extra early to give herself more than ample time to arrive punctually. But even after she managed to drag herself up and into the shower, her body was sluggish, and each day she made it with barely a minute to spare.

The supervisor, Karla, wasn't impressed with her last-minute arrivals, shooting Shawn stern, annoyed looks and exaggerated sighs as Shawn frantically rushed to the time clock and punched in with only seconds to spare. In spite of this, Shawn kept to herself and worked quietly, determined to do well.

The warehouse wasn't large. There were four aisles, each approximately forty feet long, and the coffee was stored on shelves on the left, with a rolling rack along the right, which traveled into U-turns at each end and continued its path into the next aisle. Each order picker began the sequence by assembling the necessary number of boxes at the beginning of the aisle, pushing them along the rollers, collecting the products listed on their order forms, until they reached the end of the line where a quality inspector verified the accuracy of the orders, and another worker prepared them for final shipment. The sequence was then repeated for each order.

Since each picker had their own orders to fill, they worked independently, far enough apart to discourage much interaction. This was fine with Shawn; she wasn't in any hurry to participate in friendly banter about who she was or why she was temping. By Friday, she felt pretty comfortable with the routine and relaxed enough to free her mind to work on music while she labored. She hadn't realized it was slowing her pace until one of the other five pickers was suddenly rear-ending her.

"Hey, wanna speed it up a little? You're clogging up the works here."

"Oh, sorry. I'll get out of your way," Shawn said, hastily grabbing the next few items on her list and cramming them in her box. She pushed her orders along, nearly jogging to reestablish a workable space between them. But when she came to the end of the aisle, she failed to negotiate the U-turn. Three of the five cases tipped, spilling their contents onto the floor. Feeling the heat of her coworker's glare, she gathered them up and began repacking them. She hustled into the next aisle and tried to refocus on the next items on her list. Then she remembered she hadn't checked off what she had just packed and reached for her pen in her shirt pocket, only to discover it was missing. *Shit! Nothing I can do about it now—I can't fall behind.* She continued on and, upon arriving at the quality station, borrowed a pen from the inspector to make her check marks.

Just as her lunch break began, she heard herself paged to Karla's office.

"Close the door, please," Karla said without looking away from the screen she was reviewing.

Shawn studied Karla's round, pockmarked face as she waited. Karla's appearance was masculine, emphasized even more so by tiny tight black curls cropped above the ears and collar. Shawn remained standing and braced herself for the impending reprimand.

"Your performance today has been well below standard," Karla began.

"I know, I'm sorry—"

The woman's dark eyes flared behind her black-rimmed glasses. "Don't interrupt me, young lady. Although I must say I'm using the term *lady* loosely here." The insult shocked and confused Shawn—a homophobic slur was the last thing she expected. "I just want to make one thing clear—even though you're here through a temp agency, you are still required to uphold the same quality standards as our company employees do."

Shawn remained quiet.

"That last order you filled was completely unacceptable. There were three items missed, none of the items were packed in the order of the packing list, seven bags were damaged and had to be re-picked, *and* your checklist was incomplete." Karla leaned forward and raised her eyebrows, which Shawn interpreted as a request for a response.

"I'm sorry. It won't happen again, I promise."

"You better hope not. One more slip-up like that and I'll be making a phone call to the agency. And another thing. You'd best be to work on time, or I'll have to add that to my list of complaints." Karla leaned back and folded her arms across her chest. "Now get back to work."

Shawn clenched her jaw to keep from saying anything. She needed this job, and she wasn't about to let some control freak boss get her down. If she could keep her head in the game, she'd be okay. The last thing she wanted to do was fail. Again.

❖

Jaymi could hear the driving barre chords thundering from her apartment before she had even pulled into her parking spot. She entered quietly, careful not to startle her new roommate. She knew what it was like to be completely immersed in a high-volume world of her own, unbridled emotions bursting their way from within, expressed in a flurry of fingers on the fret board, while the other hand engaged in seemingly random and wild swings on the strings, sounding in perfect rhythm and time.

There was a voice wailing along with the tune, and Jaymi merely stood and admired the sight before her, trying to capture the barely audible lyrics, since Shawn wasn't using a microphone and her voice was nearly drowned out by the guitar. The song was in rough form and she could tell Shawn was working through it. The chord progressions and lyrics seemed to be intact, and the melody was definitely taking shape each time Shawn repeated a verse.

But the bridge was giving Shawn trouble. After four run-throughs, she grunted in frustration and stopped altogether. She noticed Jaymi leaning against the door frame watching her and jumped.

"How about this?" Jaymi said, and then proceeded to sing her own version of the bridge lines, using nonsense sounds since she didn't yet know the lyrics.

"Yeah! I love that." Shawn pulled out her pocket recorder and held it up to Jaymi's face. "Quick, sing it again." She pressed *record* and Jaymi sang it again. Shawn moved the guitar slung over her shoulder and only then seemed to realize it was Jaymi's Fender Stratocaster. "Thanks for letting me play your Strat. I don't have an electric anymore, and this song...it really needed an electric."

"Not everyone cares for their instruments like you do. So I know you're not going to abuse mine if you want to play them." Jaymi's stomach turned a bit and she sighed. "When inspiration hits, you've got to go with it. I know how it is—well, at least I used to. It's been a long time since I've felt inspired to write much of anything new."

Shawn powered off the amp and placed the guitar in its stand as if it were a priceless relic. "I'm sorry to hear that. I go through spells like that, too. It sucks." She began to wipe down the guitar and its strings with the soft cotton cloth Jaymi kept handy.

Jaymi slumped into her La-Z-Boy. "Thanks. That song...you just write that today?"

"Yeah. I had a bitch of a day and I had to let out my frustration somehow." Shawn sat and ran her hands through her hair. "How do you do it?"

Jaymi cocked her head to one side, trying to ignore how sexy she found the gesture. "Do what?"

"How do you deal with working at these meaningless jobs when all you want to do is make music, twenty-four hours a day?"

"It's not easy. It's a mind-set. We're paying our dues, Shawn. You have to. I mean, you have to eat and you have to have a roof over your head, so there has to be a paycheck coming from somewhere until you're earning one from your music. On a *regular* basis, that is. You think I enjoy driving all over the county delivering legal documents and medical records all day long? Besides, the way I look at it is, as long as these jobs stay meaningless for us, they'll keep us motivated to keep working toward our ultimate goal."

"You are very wise, Madame Del Harmon, you know that?"

"Wise-*ass* maybe, I don't know about wise!" She laughed and headed to the kitchen. "Anyway, let's be thankful we both survived the week. And I've got a gig tonight, so I'm going to make a light supper."

Shawn sprang from the sofa. "You have a gig tonight? Can I come?"

"Of course you can. It *is* open to the public, knucklehead! See, *that* would be the wise-ass I was talking about."

"Oh, and I got paid today, so I'll be able to pay my own cover," Shawn said, pulling a modest wad of cash from her jeans pocket. "And here's some money. It's not much, since I only worked three days this week, but I can give you more next week." She flipped through the bills and gave Jaymi half.

Jaymi took it, reluctantly. "You could have waited a couple weeks—"

"No." Shawn backed away like Jaymi was going to try and give it back. "I told you I wasn't going to take advantage of your hospitality, so please, take it. I did that kind of shit in LA—used people, I mean—and I'm not proud of it. But…that was another life and it wasn't *me*. I don't want to get off on the wrong foot with you, especially since you've been so good to me." Shawn looked at the floor, clearly thinking she'd said too much. Jaymi stood quietly, studying her, absentmindedly tapping the edge of the bills on the counter.

"You don't have to be this way with me, you know," Jaymi said, finally.

Shawn looked up at her. "What way?"

"Afraid. My God, what are you so afraid of?"

"I don't even know where to begin to answer that question. There are so many things…things you don't know about me."

"Things you can't tell me?"

Shawn exhaled deeply. "I don't know. You might think differently of me if you knew about some of the stuff I did."

Jaymi pursed her lips in quiet consideration. "Are you trying to say that *I* should be afraid? Because I'm not buying it. Look, maybe we don't really know each other all that well, but I don't feel like you're taking advantage of me. I trust you enough to open my home to you and let you stay here." She pretended to be stern. "I don't let just anyone play my Strat, missy."

Shawn smiled, blushing slightly before seriousness took over again. "You don't know what that means to me. I showed up here uninvited, out of nowhere, and you had every right to turn me away. I had no place to go. I couldn't go home. I tried, but my father wants nothing to do with me." Shawn's eyes began to water but she forced herself to continue. "All I want is a chance to start over, to do things right this time and prove I'm not such a bad person." The tears began to flow harder. "I don't want to be that person anymore. I need this job, Jaymi. I'm sick of being broke. I don't want to end up on the streets again. I'll clean fucking toilets if I have to." She buried her face in her hands.

After a moment's hesitation, Jaymi took Shawn in her arms. Gradually, she drew Shawn deeper into the embrace. Shawn slowly withdrew her hands from her face and let them find their way around Jaymi's waist. When the desire to pull back just enough to kiss away the tears pulled at her, Jaymi let go and mumbled something about getting Shawn a tissue. *No. Don't do that. Don't go there. Not now, when things are easy.*

When she returned, she handed Shawn the entire box of tissues and began rummaging in the refrigerator. Although Shawn would probably open up and tell her just about anything right now, Jaymi needed a little bit of time to process her feelings. If, in fact, it was even her place to try and help Shawn at all.

"I don't think you're a bad person, Shawn, if that makes you feel any better," she said, taking a frying pan out of a cupboard and setting it on the stove. "Here—you're in charge of the bacon. We're having BLTs, how's that sound?"

Shawn could smile again. "Sounds delicious. Sorry I kind of lost it there."

"Don't be. For what it's worth, I believe you—that you're trying to make a new start. My gut tells me I don't have to worry about you, really it does." She began slicing a tomato. "Thanks for the money, by the way. I'll put it toward the electric bill, which is bound to go up if you keep cranking up my Strat the way you were today."

Shawn filled her in on the disaster at work and the supervisor who'd inspired the angry song.

Jaymi could relate to the frustration of having to hold a job just for the sake of paying the bills, but that was life, and Shawn had to accept that. She tried to explain to Shawn that she wasn't alone—they were all making that sacrifice for the time being.

"Use it as a motivator, Shawn. That's what I do. If I loved my day job, I might not work so hard on my dream. Don't forget—these jobs are just a means to an end."

Shawn looked at her thoughtfully. "You know, I never looked at it that way. I guess I'm just too impatient. I want to make it in music so bad that I get pissed about other stuff taking time away from that."

"Welcome to the club, my friend. If you read about anyone who's made it, they'll tell you the same thing. They held all sorts of jobs to get by before they got their big breaks."

Shawn chewed on a knuckle and seemed to be absorbing the advice. "I'll do better this time, you watch."

She grinned and Jaymi's heart leaped joyfully in her chest. *She's so beautiful when she smiles.*

"I'll be the best damn coffee picker Karla's ever seen!"

"That will perk up your boss."

Shawn groaned and said, "She'll think I'm the cream of the crop."

They both laughed, and Jaymi added, "Just put your nose to the grind—"

"And there won't be any more trouble brewing on my shift."

Jaymi cocked an eyebrow. "I do believe I've met my match."

"You ain't seen nothing yet."

Shawn smiled seductively and Jaymi's pulse quickened. She

forced her gaze away from Shawn's inviting lips and tore into the head of lettuce. *I'm in serious trouble here. Serious trouble.*

❖

Jaymi made sure Shawn was comfortable before joining the band to get ready for the show. As comfortable as she could be at a sports bar and grill occupied by a bunch of straight people. Fortunately, she was seated with some of Jaymi's gay friends, and Jaymi assured her they were great people. Devin and Sara were a couple, and Sara's friend LaKeisha was also with them.

Sara was cute: dirty blond and blue eyed, just below average height, and with the boyish build of a jock—the kind of girl you wanted to give a huge bear hug because she was just too damn irresistible.

Devin was much more reserved; a novelist, Jaymi'd said. A beautiful brown-eyed brunette, about five-six and with the body of a model, with just enough butch in her air to tip off a fellow lesbian. She had an undeniable strength that added to her attractiveness.

LaKeisha was a long and lanky black beauty. Glorious high cheekbones, an infectious smile, and colorful loosely fitted clothing matched her charming outgoing manner. She was a former basketball star at their university and a working psychologist, with a flirtatious sense of humor.

Although Devin and Sara's presence relaxed Shawn and made her want to hang out with them again and get to know them better, sitting next to a psychologist gave her nowhere to hide. She wished Jaymi hadn't revealed her profession to her, and though Jaymi insisted LaKeisha wouldn't be scrutinizing and analyzing her every move and word, Shawn remained guarded, just the same.

Ironically, Nikki helped break the ice. She approached their table before the band took the stage, beer in hand, clad in her ever-present trademark leather jacket.

"Mmm-mmm-mmm," Nikki said, as if she had just sampled a taste of the world's finest chocolate. "I don't know if I can handle seeing this much beauty at one table and not act on it." She made eye contact with each woman before turning her gaze on Shawn. She winked and took a long swig of her beer.

"I thought you weren't supposed to drink before gigs," said

Shawn, refusing to return the smile and feeling grateful that she had ordered a soda instead of beer.

"Hey, what're you, my mother? You been talking to Devin? She pulled this same act with me the first time we met."

"I thought Jaymi said—" Shawn said.

Devin piped in, "Nikki, come on, why do you insist on pushing Jaymi's buttons all the time?"

As if on cue, Jaymi showed up just then. "Consider my buttons pushed. Why are you drinking? We have to go on in ten minutes."

"It helps me relax, you know that."

"Helps you burp, is more like it," Sara said, which lightened the mood and got a laugh out of everyone.

Except Jaymi. "I wish you'd find a better way to relax. Let's go," she said, taking hold of Nikki's arm. "And you can leave the beer here, thank you."

Nikki promptly raised it as if in a toast, finished it off, and left the empty bottle on the table. "Showtime!" she crowed, with a wink, and followed Jaymi backstage.

Shawn could once again feel her blood begin to boil. She hated the way Nikki treated Jaymi. She thought it odd that Jaymi was so aware of keeping herself safe and guarded against people mistreating her, yet she seemed oblivious to Nikki's constant disrespect. *There must be more to their relationship,* she thought. *Maybe there's a side of Nikki I just haven't seen.*

She excused herself to the ladies' room and was slightly unnerved when Sara said she would do the same.

When they were out of earshot of the others, Sara pulled Shawn aside. "Are you okay?"

Shawn shrugged. "Yeah, sure."

"Listen, I know you just met us and maybe you're a little overwhelmed with all these new people, especially since one's a shrink and one's a journalist—"

"Devin's a journalist? I thought she wrote books."

"She does. But she works part-time at the local newspaper—for the entertainment magazine, actually. That's how she met Jaymi. She interviewed her for her first assignment. But anyway, I'm getting off track. I wanted to say I hope you're not intimidated by them. Trust me, they're really sweet people."

"No, I'm fine, really." *Damn, is it that obvious that I'm uncomfortable?*

"Anyway, Jaymi said you were going through a rough time—she didn't go into specifics, don't worry—but FYI, LaKeisha and I work at a center in town that has great support services on a sliding pay scale. It's strictly confidential."

"You think I need a shrink or something?" Shawn felt herself getting defensive and a cold sweat broke out on the back of her neck. She knew that was her shame talking and softened her tone. "What did Jaymi tell you, anyway?"

"Nothing, other than what I just said. I didn't mean to upset you. She's concerned about you, that's all."

"I'm sorry. I'm not upset. I've been on edge lately." She chewed her bottom lip for a moment, disgusted with herself for being such a jerk to this sweet person, who was only trying to help her. "Thanks. I'll think about it, okay?"

"Okay." Sara smiled, slipped a business card into Shawn's hand, and added, "Besides, I'm the craziest one of the bunch, and I've survived—or they've survived me, I should say. So there's definitely hope for you."

Sara headed back to rejoin their party. Shawn liked Sara, it was hard not to. But she felt raw, open. She hated that someone she didn't even know was suggesting she needed help. Jaymi might not have said anything specific, but it was enough to convince a stranger she needed therapy. *Great.*

Passion Play's performance was spectacular, as Shawn expected. She was blown away by how much they had improved in the few years since she'd heard them in California. Which said a lot, considering how good they already were back then. Despite her buzz, Nikki was electrifying, singing lead on just over half the band's songs. She played a solid rhythm guitar as well. Jaymi sang lead on the other tunes, except for two songs sung by Kay and one by Brian. On several songs, Jaymi switched to piano and proved she was equally amazing on the keys. During one blues-rock jam, Nikki killed with her skills on harmonica. Kay proved she was no slouch on bass either, as she was featured in one song with a funky slap-bass interlude that simultaneously showcased Brian's brilliance on percussion.

"Wait'll you see them play at the gay club," Devin told Shawn during the first intermission. "They're even hotter there, since they have an entire gay audience that *really* gets them."

"Yeah, and Nikki eats up the way the women flirt with her when she's onstage," said LaKeisha. "Of course, she eggs them on."

"And then she sleeps with half of 'em, too." Sara shook her head, beaming that mischievous grin. "Nah...she's not that bad."

"Yeah, it's more like a third, not half," said Devin soberly. "Speaking of which, here comes the *better* half of the band's lead singers."

"So, you guys enjoying the show?" Jaymi asked.

"You kidding? You guys are awesome." Shawn was dying to hug her but held back. Jaymi's hair was mussed and sweat glistened on her chest. She looked gorgeous. "Here, have a seat." She grabbed a chair from a neighboring table. "You want a drink of water or something? Tea to soothe your throat?" She motioned to their waitress, who responded with a nod and a just-a-moment gesture.

"Yeah, tea with lemon sounds good. Oh, shoot, my money's in my other pants backstage."

"That's okay, I got it." Shawn grinned. "I owe you at least one cup of tea."

"And let's not forget about dinner. Chinese takeout, to be exact," Jaymi said, smiling.

Shawn ordered Jaymi's drink and couldn't keep from pouring out a review of each song they had done so far.

"Wow, I guess if I need a thorough critique, I know who to go to." Jaymi squeezed Shawn's hand when she finished her analysis.

Shawn felt herself flush slightly and realized she was dominating the conversation. "I'm sorry."

"No, it's okay. I love how passionate you are," Jaymi said. "I'm glad you're enjoying it so much."

"Yeah, and so much attention to detail, too," said Nikki. "*I* didn't even know some of that shit was in our songs. Those are some really profound observations there, cute stuff."

"You could learn a thing or two from her, Nikki," said Jaymi. Nikki's response was once again the opposite of what Shawn expected.

"You may be right, Jaymi. What do you think, Shawn? You want to teach me something? Show me something new?" She leaned over the table, and Shawn looked away from the cleavage exposed by her low-cut top.

"All right, that's enough." Jaymi got up and grabbed Nikki by the sleeve. "We've got our second set to do."

At the next intermission, Shawn was washing her hands when Devin exited a stall and joined her at the sink. After being in the dimness of the club, Shawn finally got a better look at the gorgeous woman.

"Great show, huh?" Devin said with enthusiasm.

"Yeah." Shawn extracted towels from the dispenser and began drying her hands, stepping aside so Devin could do the same before holding the door for her so they could exit together. Shawn took a step toward the bar and asked, "You want something? I need another drink. I'll get one for Sara, too, if you want."

"Yeah, I suppose I should get her something so she won't be jealous of me joining you for a drink at the bar without her." Devin smiled as they stepped up to the bar. Shawn realized she must have looked as panicked as she felt, because Devin quickly said, "I'm just kidding. Sara knows I only have eyes for her."

Shawn relaxed and smiled. There was a warmth about Devin that immediately put Shawn at ease. Shawn glanced over to their table and saw Sara smiling at Devin as she joked with her friends. "That's obvious. Bet she feels the same way."

Devin simply grinned back at her girlfriend and nodded. They ordered drinks and Devin resumed the conversation. "Jaymi's pretty awesome up there, huh?"

"She's the best."

Their drinks arrived and Shawn insisted on paying for all three. Devin leaned close so she could speak softly. "Don't tell anybody, but I had a little crush on Jaymi when we first met." She giggled. "Uh-oh, maybe I shouldn't have ordered another drink…loosens up my tongue way too much." She smiled widely and blushed.

Shawn would have been jealous had she not felt so comfortable with Devin's refreshing honesty. "I can't blame you for that. I've practically idolized her since I met her." She looked away, hoping her real feelings, whatever those were, didn't show on her face. "But not in a sick way, I'm not a stalker or anything. I admire her and what she's doing. I look up to her—there's nothing wrong with that, is there?

I'm a musician, I love her music, and now I'm getting to know her as a person, and…" Shawn stopped talking, realizing she was digging a hole.

"And you're learning that the person behind all those wonderful, soul-moving songs is just as amazing. And not only that, she also happens to be one of the sweetest, most genuine people you'll ever meet."

"Ain't that the truth."

"I was a bit starstruck around her at first, too. I think it actually makes her uncomfortable when people act nervous around her. She couldn't care less about being famous. She's fine with just hanging back playing guitar while Nikki gets all the attention."

"Yeah, I got that, too," Shawn replied, feeling a bit stupid about the times she'd acted like a crazed fan herself.

"She is damn good, though. She's crazy if she thinks no one's paying attention to her."

"Yeah, no shit." *I can't take my eyes off her.*

Devin patted her on the arm and picked up their drinks. "And from what she's told me, you're not so bad yourself. Maybe next time we'll get to hear you sing."

Shawn followed her back to the table. Jaymi had talked about her. And not just her problems, as Sara had mentioned, but about her voice, too. What did that mean? *Nothing. Don't be stupid. They're her friends, and you tell friends things. That's all.* At the end of the third and final set, the women were still at their table raving about the performance when a large shadow drifted across the table from behind Shawn. She swiveled around to see who had drawn the attention of her new friends.

"Karla! What're you doing here?" Shawn managed to say. Karla was dressed in a similar fashion to that day's work clothes: khaki pants and a dark-colored sweater vest over a plain white collared shirt. Clearly it was her standard uniform.

"Same as you, I assume. I'm here to see Passion Play, have a few drinks, and relax with friends. They're my favorite band."

Shawn was still too shocked to respond. *The bitch has friends?* She despised the woman and wished she would go away. Why had she even come over? She certainly seemed to dislike Shawn as much as Shawn disliked her.

"They're awesome, aren't they?" said Sara. "Karla? How do you know Shawn?"

"We work together."

"Oh. Well, hey, I'm Sara, and this is my girlfriend Devin, and my most bestest friend LaKeisha." They took turns shaking hands.

"Well, anyway," Karla said, showing no signs of discomfort at Sara's openness. "I just wanted to say hi, Shawn."

Shawn watched Karla as she exited with the rest of the crowd. She let out a sigh of relief, accompanied by a roll of the eyes and a swig of her soda.

"What was that all about?" asked Sara.

"I have no idea. She's the supervisor at the warehouse where I'm working. She treated me like shit today. Now she's suddenly sweet as pie to me? Oh, and she's straight. Can you believe that?"

"I can," said Devin. "I haven't been out that long, myself."

"Well, it's possible she needs to be a totally different person at work," LaKeisha said. "It's tough being the boss with all that responsibility on your shoulders. I'm not condoning verbal mistreatment of your employees, mind you, but sometimes that's a person's way of keeping themselves detached. So they don't let personal feelings interfere with decisions and so forth. I wouldn't take it personally, Shawn."

"Yeah, but I got the feeling it *was* personal," Shawn said.

The conversation moved on, but Shawn continued to think about the strange encounter. Was LaKeisha right? Was it just some kind of façade? Maybe underneath she was a big softie who just wanted to be understood. Shawn barely kept herself from snorting. Right.

She shrugged it off. Monday would be interesting. She wouldn't let it distract her from a great night.

❖

Jaymi stretched and curled into the passenger seat of her pickup. She had surrendered to Shawn's insistence on driving so she could unwind after the show.

"You're really lucky, Jaymi. You've got some great friends," Shawn said on the ride home. "They really care about you."

"Yeah, I know." Jaymi yawned. Her eyes furrowed in suspicion. "Hey, wait a minute, what exactly did they say to you?"

"Well, let's see. Sara informed me that you had told her I was going through a rough time and graciously offered me the anonymous assistance of her youth center. LaKeisha gave me some helpful advice on how to handle my asshole boss, who incidentally was there tonight—"

"That mean ol' boss of yours had the nerve to harass you outside of work?"

Shawn squirmed at the thought of Karla and her Jekyll and Hyde behavior. "Actually, she was nice to me. Just came over to say hi and said she was a fan of the band. It creeped me out, but I can't really tell you why. What do you make of it?"

Jaymi just shrugged, and yawned again.

"Sorry, am I boring you?" Shawn gave her a playful shake and thought that maybe for the first time since her arrival she was beginning to loosen up. Her conversation with Devin had helped wash away some of her insecurities. Jaymi was just human, after all.

"No, not at all. I'm sorry. Nothing personal, I'm just really exhausted. Mind if I snooze? You know the way, right?"

"Yeah, Jaymi. Go ahead. You won't even have to wake up when we get there. I'm stronger than I look. I'll just carry you upstairs and put you to bed when we get home." She instantly regretted the words and gripped the steering wheel tightly. *Shit, what did I just say? I'll put you to bed? Home?*

"If you say so, Muscles," Jaymi whispered, nearly asleep already. She dozed off for several minutes, then, without opening her eyes, asked, "What about Devin? What'd she have to say?"

"Devin, yeah, sweet girl. Nice things about you, all nice things."

Jaymi's eyes opened and she looked at Shawn. "Don't want to tell me? That's okay, I can pretty much guess. She's protective of me, too, like Nikki is, only in a much more tactful way. Whatever she said, it's true, every word. That much I can tell you about Devin." She closed her eyes again and drifted back to sleep.

*Yeah, just what I needed—someone else to confirm what I've known all along—that you're a catch and I'm in big trouble here if I can't get a handle on this crush. Shut up, Shawn, and focus on the road, will you?* She glanced in the rearview mirror and frowned. *Is that the same car that's been behind us the whole way home? Is it following us?* She pressed on the accelerator and kept an eye on the car. Two more turns, and it was still behind her. Just when she was about to wake

Jaymi, it turned left and disappeared from sight. She let out a shaky breath. *Nothing to worry about, right?*

❖

Jaymi collapsed into her bed and switched off the lamp. The show had been a huge success. Each gig was drawing larger crowds, and people were coming to the clubs not just for a night out of drinking and dining, but specifically to see Passion Play. The increased airplay of their single was helping, of course, but their fan base seemed to be multiplying at a dramatic pace. What had begun as a smattering of familiar faces in a sparse audience was turning into a sea of new fans crowding themselves into every venue at which they were booked. She couldn't have asked for a more positive sign that her career was progressing in the right direction, and with even more success than they had achieved in Los Angeles.

It was the eve of another month's anniversary of her mother's passing, which made her even more grateful to have some positive energy surging through her as she crawled into bed. Her mother, no doubt, was enjoying her daughter's success from Heaven. She hadn't mentioned the anniversary to her friends because she didn't want any pity or anyone feeling down tonight. But it also made her feel just the slightest bit alone, even in the crowd.

Without warning, her thoughts turned to Peach. She hadn't thought of her in months, which was a good thing. A few years ago, she would have been sharing all this with her. That was the original plan. She wondered how she was doing, and if she was on the way to achieving her dream with as much progress, or if their breakup had set her back and devastated her to the same degree it had Jaymi.

She went over it in her mind repeatedly, trying desperately to make sense of it all. Why her lover had suddenly turned so cold. Why she had suddenly seemed to have fallen out of love with her. Why she had begun to lose interest in all things but her studies. And why she had spent time anywhere but home. And why, when Jaymi needed her most, her suspicions were confirmed that Peach had more than a study buddy.

Now Jaymi's career was taking off. She had another album's worth of songs added to her already prolific catalog, despite the current bout with writer's block. She had the camaraderie and support of friends and family. She had a decent day job. She had this terrific apartment with all the space and privacy she could want. She had accomplished all this as a single woman. And it felt great.

Except there was still something missing. Someone missing: a lover to share it all with. *Yeah, right. You remember how that worked out with Peach. The more the band takes off, the more I'll be on the road. How fair is it to ask someone to stay behind for weeks on end while I'm gone? For all you know, Peach only cheated on you that one time. Do you really want to go through that again? Lovers have needs. Any lover of mine is bound to get lonely. How can I trust that she won't seek comfort in another woman's arms while I'm away?*

She rolled over again and faced the door, still wide-awake and thinking about the guest in the neighboring room. Did Shawn have an ex she thought about? The thought made her stomach turn, a fact she decided to ignore. She wondered if Shawn also suffered through each anniversary of her own mother's passing. Did she just want to hide from the world, too?

Tomorrow was going to be hard. *Don't dwell on it, you fool, that's not what Mom would want. It won't bring her back.*

She tossed and turned for another hour before exhaustion finally swept her into a dreamless sleep.

## CHAPTER NINE

Jaymi rolled over onto her side and stifled a groan when she remembered what day it was. Yawning widely, she pushed off the covers with her feet as she scrubbed her face with her palms. She was tempted to curl up into a fetal position and spend the day with her face buried in her pillow, bawling her eyes out. *If there are times you are sad after I'm gone, promise me you won't focus on my death. I want you to think about my life and the good times we had together. Remember how much I love you.* Her mother's words were enough motivation to drag herself out of bed. The awkwardness of having to explain such behavior to her new roommate didn't hurt, either. She pulled on a sweatshirt and stepped out of her room. The spare bedroom door was ajar. She leaned her head against it and spoke Shawn's name quietly. No answer. She gently pushed on the door and saw the futon unoccupied and its blankets thrown carelessly over it.

"Shawn?" she said again as she entered the kitchen. There was coffee made, but the auto shut-off had already done its job. "Huh." She shrugged. "Must've had someplace to go."

After showering, she heated a cup of coffee and went out onto the balcony. It was shaping up to be a gorgeous day. She squinted from the sun's blinding reflection off the snow-covered pasture. She gazed at the pretty scene and spotted two horses playfully running and loping in the field. They seemed to be enjoying the feel of snow flying up from their hooves as they kicked and rolled in it. Jaymi smiled, fantasizing that the show was for her benefit.

She looked toward the fence, where a human held the attention of the other three horses. Jaymi watched in amazement as they took turns receiving strokes and pets from Shawn, who seemed completely at ease with them. Though she couldn't hear her voice from this distance, she could tell Shawn was talking to them. Their ears perked and twitched as if she spoke their language.

Intrigued, Jaymi slipped on her ski jacket and boots and went outside to join her. She was right, Shawn was talking to them. Her voice sounded sweet and soothing; it was no wonder the horses didn't feel threatened. Jaymi walked up behind her. "Good morning."

Shawn jumped so abruptly that her elbow struck the coffee cup Jaymi was holding and splattered it onto the front of Jaymi's coat. Shawn gasped for oxygen, her back pressed against the fence, one hand still clutching her chest, the other fisted and firmly held up in front of her as if she were ready to block a strike.

"Oh God, Shawn, I'm sorry. I didn't mean to startle you."

Shawn held her pose, breathing heavily, her eyes wide and serious. She looked terrified.

"Are you okay?" She reached out to touch her, but Shawn shrank away, and she pulled her hand back.

Shawn's hands moved up to her face and then pushed their way through her messy hair as she released a huge breath. "Yeah," Shawn finally said, shaking her head. "Yeah, I'm okay. You just surprised me. Don't…please, don't do that. Don't sneak up on me like that."

"I didn't think I was sneaking up on you. I'm sorry, I'll make more noise next time."

Shawn nodded slightly. Her eyes softened and she looked away, obviously embarrassed.

"Well, I better go in and clean this off."

"Shit, your jacket. I might have a tissue…" Shawn fumbled through her pockets, spilling out half a roll of mints and some loose change, which she quickly snatched up off the ground.

"It's okay. It's nylon, it'll wash."

"I'm sorry." Shawn shoved her hands in her pockets and looked at the ground.

"Don't worry about it, really. You're good with the horses." Jaymi motioned toward the pasture where the horses, alarmed by Shawn's jump, had scampered off.

"I used to work at a stable when I was a teenager." She smiled slightly and sighed. "Geez, come to think of it, it's the only job I was any good at. We lived down the street from a place a lot like this one. People had a couple of their own horses, and they boarded a few others."

"That's cool. I don't know much about them myself." Jaymi settled her cup securely into the snow and leaned over the fence. Shawn settled next to her in the same position.

"If I don't make it in music, I'll do something with horses."

Jaymi turned to face Shawn. "What do you mean, if you don't make it?"

"I don't know, Jaymi. I don't know if I've got what it takes. I don't know what the hell I was thinking, going to California," she scoffed. "I made such a mess of things. I can't believe how bad I...Shit, maybe my father's right. I see you up there with your band, and you're all so confident and polished, so *professional*. And I'm so, I don't know...I'm not—"

"Hey." Jaymi placed her hand on Shawn's shoulder and turned her so they faced each other. "What kind of talk is that? Don't compare yourself to us...to anybody. You think we always sounded this polished? It's taken a long time and hard work to get as good as we are. It doesn't happen overnight. Unless you're in some pop boy band that was put together by some marketing guru who's trying to make a fast buck with a flash-in-the-pan teen idol album."

"Yeah, but—"

"But nothing. Shawn, I don't know why you doubt yourself the way you do. You're *good*, damn it, and I'm not just saying that to make you feel better. Your songwriting alone is good enough. No, your songs are *better* than good enough. They're great songs. You just have to work on your confidence. Listen, you may not believe this, but before I met Nikki, I had the worst stage fright—"

"You? No way!" Shawn playfully slapped Jaymi's arm with the back of her hand.

"I did. It was awful. I was a nervous wreck during my college recitals. That's where I met Nikki, at UMass in Lowell. Anyway, I'd get so nervous I thought I was going to throw up. My hands would shake wicked bad, and I could barely fret the strings, and I'd mess up or sound sloppy. I was so preoccupied with thinking about everything I was doing that my performances must have really sucked. There was no emotion in them, no passion. Oh, I was in tune and on key and all that, but it wasn't until I started hanging out with Nikki that I learned to let go and just *feel* it, you know?"

"Really? I would have thought it was the other way around—you teaching Nikki, I mean."

"Well, I helped her with her guitar lessons. That was the deal that started our friendship. She helped me learn to trust my instincts—to remind myself that I knew the piece by heart, so quit practicing and just *play,* and to trust that I wasn't going to screw up. After all, how could I? I practiced everything to death! Forget about the audience, just play, and have fun. Like I did when I was a kid, alone in my room, just wailing away, jamming with my records." Shawn's face lit up. "You did it too, right? Pretended you were in the band? Shawn, you just need more time onstage. It gets easier, really it does."

They looked out over the pasture for a few minutes and watched the horses in silence.

"What about you, Jaymi? Do you have a backup plan?"

"Sure do. Teaching."

"What, like be a professor or something?"

"No, I'd like to do private guitar lessons. I wouldn't mind doing some workshops, too. Maybe teach some basic music theory, or have ensembles for kids who want to practice playing music with other kids."

Shawn picked at a loose splinter in the fence. "I could see you doing that." Shawn turned shyly to Jaymi. "You're a good mentor, you know. I learned a lot from you, back in LA."

"I'm glad. It means a lot to me that you feel that way."

"Maybe you could help me find some open mikes around here?"

"Now you're talking! I've got a whole list upstairs, come on."

As they turned to head back up, a woman approached them from the main house.

"Hey, that's Alice, my landlady," said Jaymi. "I'll introduce you."

A rugged farm girl in her late fifties, Alice was dressed in jeans, a red plaid flannel shirt, Timberland work boots, and a tan heavyweight canvas parka.

"Beautiful morning, isn't it, Jaymi?" she said. Her leathery face beamed with energy and kindness and was framed with thick gray curls and rimless glasses.

"Yes, it is. Alice, this is my friend, Shawn."

Alice accepted Shawn's handshake with a grin. "Glad to meet you, Shawn. That your car over there I've seen the past few weeks?"

"Yeah. Is it okay parked where it is?"

"Oh, sure. Not like Peter and I ever have much company. Peter's my husband."

"Sorry I haven't taken the time to introduce you two sooner, Alice," Jaymi said. "It's not a problem if Shawn stays with me for a while, is it? She's just come back from California."

"Oh no, no, no, of course not, honey." Alice winked at Jaymi, then turned to Shawn. "You stay as long as you want. If you're a friend of Jaymi's, that tells me right off you'll be no trouble."

"I really appreciate it. I'll be looking for my own place as soon as I have the money. I could even help you out with the horses if you need it, you know, to help pay my way."

A wide smile spread across Alice's face. She looked Shawn up and down then turned to Jaymi. "Girl wants to earn her keep. I like that." She studied Shawn's face for a moment. "I was watching you this morning. You know your way around horses, don't you?"

"Yes, ma'am. I do."

Alice burst into laughter. "Ma'am? Cripes, that makes me feel like a hoity-toity ol' lady! Ma'am! You know, your timing couldn't be better. My stable boy up and quit on me a few weeks back. Got himself a job down in New York City. My knee's bothering me something fierce today. Tore up my ACL a few years back, and if I start favoring my knee, then my damn hip'll start in, and don't even get me started on when it rains 'cause, well…Oh, you don't want to listen to my bellyaching. Are you free to help me out today?"

"Anything you need."

"And I don't expect you to work for nothing, so I'll pay you, same as I was paying him, but on one condition."

"What's that?"

"You put a kibosh on this ma'am stuff. You call me Alice. You call me ma'am again, and I'll put you in charge of the fertilizer shed, and that'll be all I'll have you do. Understand?"

"It's a deal, *Alice*."

Jaymi watched them walk away together, already laughing and joking like old friends, and she felt a moment of envy. She wished

Shawn was that free with her. It wasn't surprising that Shawn would take so easily to Alice. Alice and Jaymi's mother had been longtime friends, and Alice's down-to-earth ways were as comforting as a bowl of soup and a warm blanket on a cold winter's night. The fact that Alice warmed up to Shawn so quickly was encouraging. Jaymi trusted Alice's instincts.

She thought of the way Shawn had jumped and settled into a defensive position when Jaymi had startled her, and she wondered just what the hell was so frightening in Shawn's past to elicit that kind of reaction. The terror is Shawn's eyes had been very real, and it had taken more than a few seconds for her to realize she wasn't in danger. Jaymi's heart ached for her. She couldn't imagine being that scared of anything.

Alice and Shawn disappeared into the barn, and Jaymi turned to go back inside. With time, maybe Shawn would open up. And by then, maybe Jaymi would know how to respond.

After three hours cleaning out stalls, replenishing oats, hay, and water, Shawn walked up the porch steps to the house to show Alice the results. Peter, who was just as friendly and full of country charm, dressed similarly in jeans and flannel and puffing on a pipe, greeted her. He called to his spouse, who walked to the stable with Shawn. Satisfied with what she saw inside, she suggested that Shawn assist her with bringing in the horses so that she could introduce them. One by one, Shawn learned their names, was briefed on their personality quirks and any special needs, and was given information about their owners. Of the five, only two of the horses belonged to Alice and Peter.

"I can see you have a love for animals," Alice remarked, after they settled in the last horse. "Thanks for keeping a lookout for Charley, too," she added, referring to her golden retriever. "He tends to get underfoot when I'm bringing in the horses."

"I've always loved animals." She watched a tiger kitten playing in some hay on the floor, sliding into it as if it were third base, then flinging a strand of it into the air with its paw and batting it around. "I thought about a career with them, once."

"Well, why not? You'd be terrific. What is it you do?"

"I'm a musician. Well, an aspiring one anyway. That's my number one love."

"Ah, like my Jaymi. She's something else, isn't she?"

"Yeah, she sure is."

Alice smiled warmly. "I've known Jaymi since she was a little girl. Her folks and us have been close friends for years. Such a shame when Yvonne died." Alice bit her bottom lip, closed her eyes for a moment, and pressed a palm to her heart. "Nearly broke my heart, losing a friend like that. Oh, dear, I've got to go up and give poor Jaymi a good ol'-fashioned bear hug. They were very close, you know. Only person I ever met that was as sweet as that dear lady was her own daughter. I missed Jaymi terrible when she moved out there to California. Only wish she could have come back for better reasons than to…Well anyway, what's done is done. We built that apartment for our daughter, but she got married and moved out, so it worked out good for Jaymi and us both when she needed a place."

Shawn couldn't help but smile, but her heart was heavy as she thought of Jaymi's pain. She had heard muffled sounds of the guitar coming down through the floorboards while she worked in the barn. She had wished she could hear it more clearly, and she had to force herself to not be distracted by it.

"Well, I wish you luck with your music. It's important to have dreams. But you have a gift with animals, too, remember that. Here"—Alice said, extending some folded-up cash—"you did a great job today, and I appreciate it."

Shawn looked at her with surprise. "No, really, you don't have to. It was only a few hours."

Alice took her hand and folded her fingers around the money. "You earned it. I told you I'd pay you, now take it."

"Okay. Thank you. I enjoyed it. I'd forgotten how much I miss this. I'd be glad to help tomorrow, too, if you need me. During the week, I have a temp job for now, but on the weekends…"

"I'll take you up on tomorrow, but you've got to have a day off, so only if you're up to it."

"I'm up to it. What time?"

"Meet me here at eight o'clock. Sharp."

❖

After she had finished her work in the barn, Shawn found Jaymi absorbed in her music studio and sensed it was best not to disturb her. After showering, she gave Jaymi the rest of the day to herself and used some of her earnings to purchase some much-needed winter clothes and to get her hair cut. When she got back, Jaymi seemed in better spirits.

"Giving up the sheepdog look, are you? You look…" Jaymi stopped and stared at her for a moment. "I mean, I love your haircut. I can see your face now!"

"Thanks. It was driving me crazy. I haven't had the money to get it cut in a long time. Feels like she must've taken twenty pounds of hair off my head."

"Twenty pounds? Wow, are you feeling light-headed?"

Shawn rolled her eyes and laughed. "Terribly! I think I'm going to faint! You better come over here and catch me!" She tipped her head back slightly and daintily put the back of her hand on her forehead.

"Oh, brother. You're a terrible actress. No wonder they kicked you out of Hollywood."

"Hey, I left voluntarily, remember? And I never claimed to be an actress."

"And you definitely can't pull off the helpless female role."

"Thank God for that."

She picked up her packages and carried them into her room. She dumped their contents onto her bed and one by one removed the tags and added them to her other clothes in the small closet. A deep sense of satisfaction stole over her. It had been ages since she had been able to buy new clothes, and now she had clothes and a haircut. Small things that felt huge. How long had she been living out of a suitcase now? Maybe she could buy a secondhand dresser with her next paycheck. But then again, it probably wasn't a good idea to get too settled here. Her thoughts on the subject were aborted when she noticed the apartment was silent.

She tentatively made her way down the hall and stopped at the threshold of the studio to find Jaymi hunched over the piano with her face in her hands. A wineglass in front of her was empty. She hadn't known Jaymi to drink alone. Ever. Shawn froze, not sure if she should leave her alone and go back to her room. She watched as Jaymi's right hand returned to the keyboard and pecked out a few notes, her head still resting in the other hand.

"That's pretty," Shawn said softly. Jaymi barely moved but lifted her head and stared at the wall, keeping her back to Shawn.

"Too bad I can't finish it," she murmured. Shawn walked over and stood behind her. She leaned over, peering at the papers propped up on the piano in front of them. Absorbing the lyrics, she didn't realize her hands had begun massaging Jaymi's tense shoulders.

"Mmm. That feels good," Jaymi whispered.

"It's about your mother, isn't it?" Jaymi nodded. "Man, you're really tight. I dated a massage therapist once, so don't worry, I know what I'm doing." Shawn swallowed the lump in her throat, enjoying the feel of Jaymi's body under her hands far too much.

"That's what I'm afraid of."

"Very funny. Though it is a good way to pick up women. I can give you some pointers if you want."

Jaymi swung her body around to straddle the bench, breaking Shawn's touch. "Are you implying that I need pointers to pick up women?"

Shawn could feel her face flush, but with the encouraging day she'd had, her confidence was riding higher than usual. She dropped onto the bench in front of Jaymi. "Definitely not. Trust me, you don't need any help in that department."

"And how would you know that?"

"Er…"

Jaymi slid closer to her, so close their knees touched and Shawn could smell the wine on her breath. "Something tells me you don't need any help either."

Shawn sat motionless. *Is she going to kiss me?* Nikki's warnings ran through her head as Jaymi's hands slid up her thighs. *Shit. Shit, shit, shit.*

Every instinct within her was battling her willpower. *I made a promise to myself when I left LA that I was going to change. The old me would be taking her to bed right now, not giving a damn about the consequences. I don't want to do that with Jaymi. She's too special. She's too vulnerable. I won't do that to her.* Shawn cleared her throat and backed away, moving off the bench. "Jaymi, how many glasses of wine have you had?"

"Three…no, three. Four? Shit, I lost count." She giggled. "Count it off! A one, a two—"

"And have you eaten?"

"Nope."

"That's what I thought." Shawn took Jaymi by the hands, led her to the sofa, and gently sat her down. "I owe you a dinner. I'll run out for Chinese."

She turned toward the kitchen, but Jaymi grabbed her hand and stopped her.

"No…don't go. I don't want you to go back out. I'm sorry, I'm having a rough day."

"It's the song, isn't it? You miss your mother."

Jaymi nodded. Her eyes welled up and she tried to speak through sobs. "I can't…every time I try to finish it, to sing it, I can't get the words out."

Shawn sat beside her and, after a long, awkward silence, tentatively put her arm around her shoulders. Jaymi burrowed her face into Shawn's neck and cried. "It's okay," Shawn whispered. "I understand how you feel. I'm here for you. I'm here for you." *Dear God, if you're testing me, this is a really cruel way to do it.* She held her until the tears ran dry. When Jaymi pulled away, her eyes swollen from crying, it tore at Shawn's heart. She wiped a few tears from Jaymi's cheeks and gave her a gentle smile. "Time for food, I think."

What she wanted far more than food was to hold Jaymi close, to draw her in and not let go, to take away the pain. But it wasn't like she was the right person to do that. She had enough baggage of her own, and although Jaymi was hurting today, every other day she had her crap together in a way Shawn couldn't even fathom.

She tried to pull away, and when Jaymi hiccupped they both started laughing, and the moment was broken.

"I don't want you to go. Please stay. We'll put on a movie or something. Order pizza." The pleading look was all it took. Shawn grabbed the phone and ordered while Jaymi fumbled with the DVD player. When she sat back down on the couch beside Jaymi, her insides shook slightly when Jaymi curled up against her and promptly fell asleep, her arm thrown over Shawn's stomach.

Shawn tried to pay attention to the movie, but all she could think about was the way Jaymi's body pressed against her own, the way her breasts felt against her biceps, the way her hair fell over her face. Shawn let her head fall against the back of the couch. *God give me strength.* She rested her hand on Jaymi's back and gave in to the feeling of peace. It wouldn't last, so she might as well take it while she could.

❖

Jaymi woke later than usual on Sunday morning. Her head was pounding from the wine, but worse than that was the restless night she had suffered. She couldn't escape the image of Shawn sitting in front of her on the piano bench. She tried to tell herself it was the wine that had given her such a strong urge to kiss her. Where did that come from? Was she finally ready to start dating again?

She quickly dismissed the possibility. *No, probably just loneliness. And maybe I was a bit horny, too. I am human, after all.* The timing couldn't be worse. *I'm finally focused on my career and it's taking off. I can't let anything disrupt that.*

But she also remembered how good Shawn's hands felt on her shoulders, her touch soothing and caring. Jaymi knew it had been a spontaneous gesture, a simple absentminded massage that she didn't even realize she was doing. But later, when Shawn had woken her so she could answer the door to the pizza man, it had felt so good to have Shawn's hand resting lightly on her back, their bodies pressed together. She hadn't meant to fall asleep at all, but waking in Shawn's arms made her feel something she couldn't define, but something intense nonetheless. They'd eaten in silence, both of them pretending to watch the movie. And when they'd finished eating, Shawn had insisted on walking her to her room and tucking her into bed. In that moment, in that single instant, she had very nearly asked her to stay. Not for sex, although that might have been nice, too. But she wanted Shawn's body next to her, she wanted to be wrapped in those strong arms. Instead, she'd closed her eyes and listened as Shawn left the room, closing the door softly behind her.

She forced herself up and into the shower. A cool shower. As she washed, she worked her mind back into focus. She wouldn't allow herself to become vulnerable. No, she definitely wasn't ready to date again. She would be a friend to Shawn and help her through this rough patch, and before long, she'd be on her way, back on her feet. Besides, she hated to screw up the budding friendship that was forming between them. She was sure Shawn felt the same, for she was just as determined to pursue her dreams as Jaymi was. They could help each other, and anything more than friendship would just mess everything up.

So why did that make her sad?

# CHAPTER TEN

Shit!" Shawn threw off the covers and in the early morning blackness tripped over them rushing across the room. She turned on a light and frantically grabbed her clothes and headed for the bathroom.

After a three-minute shower, she went into the kitchen and found Jaymi seated at the table, half-asleep and sipping coffee. She was in a hurry but didn't fail to notice how cute Jaymi looked with her tousled bed head, in an oversized T-shirt and flannel sleep pants. She entertained a fleeting wish that they could both play hooky but knew she would only get herself into trouble if they did.

"You want some coffee?"

"No, thanks. I'm already late," said Shawn, putting on her coat. "She's gonna kill me!" she added as she ran out the door.

She spent her commute praying for God to take away her crush, praying she wouldn't be late, and replaying images of yesterday's rehearsal with Passion Play. She knew her feelings for Jaymi would only lead to heartache, and she mentally prepared herself to face her crazy-ass boss.

Yesterday, once again, she had gone with Jaymi to rehearsal. She assumed that Jaymi had spoken to Nikki about the way she had been treating her, because Nikki didn't make a single rude or wise-ass remark. In fact, she'd pretty much ignored her entirely, which suited Shawn fine. And this time, when she joined the band for their wrap-up jam, Jaymi insisted that Shawn play some of her own songs. With Jaymi, Nikki, and Kay grouped together to follow Shawn's lead sheets, the band did two run-throughs of each song.

It was the first time Shawn had heard her songs performed with a full band. Reliving the exhilaration of their praise and interest triggered goose bumps. She could feel her determination awaken, and she recommitted herself to pursuing her career. *Open mikes. This week! I'll do at least one. Gotta check that newspaper again. Maybe Jaymi will go with me.* She reluctantly told herself that next Sunday she wouldn't go to Jaymi's rehearsal, but instead would spend the day alone to write and practice.

Waiting impatiently at a red light, Shawn checked the time. No use rushing now, since there was no way she could get there in time. Not without speeding and risking a ticket.

She crept into the building and discreetly punched in seven minutes late. No sign of the dragon lady. Good. She went right to work. But five minutes later, Karla paged her to her office. The dread lodged itself in her throat and she resigned herself for the inevitable.

"Please, close the door and have a seat." Karla motioned to the chair but the condescending tone she had used on Friday was missing, and there was a slight smile on her thin lips.

Shawn sat and clasped her hands between her knees.

"So," said Karla, her smile widening, "did you have a good weekend?"

*What is this? Her twisted way of sneaking in for the kill?* "Uh… yes."

"Good show Friday, wasn't it?"

"Yeah. Listen, you don't have to waste your time with the small talk. I'm sorry I was late today. Please don't fire me, I—"

"Fire you?"

"I'm so sorry. I really need this job and I'll stay late to make it up, or I'll work through lunch. I know I can do better this week. I'm really starting to get the hang of things. Anything, I'll do anything, just please give me another chance."

Karla rose from her seat and came around to the front of the desk. She sat on it's edge and crossed her legs at the ankles. "Look, I know I was a little hard on you last week. The big bosses have been riding my ass lately, so I was under a lot of stress. I didn't bring you in here to fire you. But, since you offered, there is something you could do for me."

Shawn released a deep breath, but not without skepticism. "Thanks. Yeah, anything. Whatever."

Karla lowered her voice, as if she was afraid of being heard from outside the office. "How well do you know Jaymi Del Harmon? I saw you talking to her at Sparky's."

*Ah. Right.* "We're friends. Why?"

"You live with her, don't you?"

Shawn turned her head slightly and narrowed her eyes. "How did you know that?"

"It's on your application. You put her as a reference, and you both have the same phone number."

"Oh, that. Sure." Shawn cleared her throat and sat back in her chair. She didn't appreciate the invasion of her personal space. "You want an autograph? I'm sure she'd sign a photo for you or something."

Karla leaned forward. Her breath suggested that she drank as much coffee as they shipped. "I want to meet her."

"Oh. Well, I think they have another gig next weekend and sometimes they do meet-and-greets after their shows. I could introduce you to the whole band if you want."

"No. I don't want to be treated like just any other fan. I mean just me and Jaymi, somewhere private." Karla's smile seemed forced but her tone lost some of its edge. "Maybe I could buy her dinner or something. I don't care about meeting the rest of the band."

"I don't know…I'd have to ask her." Shawn squirmed. Her face was beginning to burn with the rising explosion she was struggling to squelch.

"Look, I don't see why it should be such a big deal. She seems nice enough and she must appreciate her fans, right?"

"Oh, she does, believe me, she's grateful. It's just, she's a very private person, and I don't want to disrespect that, you know?"

"Well, I do have her number from your application. I suppose I could call her myself."

"No! No, please don't do that."

"Then ask her. Ask her tonight and maybe I can tear up that written warning I filled out for your constant tardiness rather than turn it in to the temp agency. I'm sure they would think twice about giving you any more assignments."

"What?"

"You heard me."

Shawn clenched her teeth. "I'll see what I can do."

"Good. I'll be waiting."

❖

"She actually threatened you if I didn't agree to meet with her?" Jaymi looked at Shawn incredulously.

"Yes. I'm so sorry, Jaymi, I couldn't see any way out of it. You know I can't afford to lose this job. I feel terrible."

"Hmm." Jaymi took a bite of her dinner and a long swig of milk. Shawn had known the news wouldn't go over well with her. Not that Jaymi didn't enjoy meeting her fans or appreciate their admiration and support. But to be coerced into a private meeting hardly seemed appropriate. And to threaten Shawn in the process was unacceptable.

Shawn shook her head. "You know what, forget it. I'll just deal with it. You don't have to do this. This is bullshit. It's like blackmail or something, isn't it? It can't be legal."

"Are you sure?" Jaymi asked, obviously relieved.

"Yes. I'll just get to work early every day so she won't have any reason to write me up. Shit, it's just one warning, so what. I've dealt with worse. I'll start looking for another job if I have to. And besides, she told me to ask you, and I did. I held up my side, right? She can go to hell."

"I'm sorry, Shawn, I'm just really not comfortable with someone demanding to meet me, and to threaten you like she did? I don't trust it. It sounds like she's got a screw loose or something."

"You know, this is only a three-month assignment. Maybe I can just stall her until I get my own place or find another job. I'll tell her your schedule's booked solid and it'll have to wait."

"I'd appreciate that."

Shawn changed the topic, asking about Jaymi's day. Even though it might mean she could lose her job or, worse, have the dragon lady on her case more often, she was relieved Jaymi wouldn't be meeting her stalker-fan boss.

And for the moment, she was grateful for the reprieve.

❖

Jaymi woke, startled, at an angry, unintelligible voice coming from Shawn's room, and once she had her wits about her, realized the voice was Shawn's. She slowly opened Shawn's door and through the darkness could see her body flailing beneath the covers.

Shawn continued screaming. "Get off me! Get off me! No! *Get off me!*"

Jaymi carefully sat on the side of the bed and placed a hand on Shawn's shoulder.

"Shawn? Shawn, wake up. It's just a nightmare." She shook her gently. Without warning, Jaymi was suddenly pushed backward onto the carpet and Shawn was on top of her, pinning her arms down. Jaymi shouted Shawn's name at the top of her lungs. Shawn finally came to, shaking her head and gasping for air. She jumped to her feet and stumbled backward.

"Shit! What am I doing? Jaymi, are you okay?" She stood wide-eyed, her breathing still labored.

Jaymi sat up and caught her own breath. "Yeah, I'm okay. Are you?" She could see Shawn's shoulders lurch as the sobs began.

"I don't…no." She shook her head and wrapped her arms around herself as she cried. Jaymi approached her cautiously.

"Do you want a hug, or will I get tackled again?" Shawn held up her arms and Jaymi pulled her close. *God, she feels good in my arms,* thought Jaymi, surprising herself. *Shit, don't be thinking that! It's just been a long time since you've been with anyone, that's all.* She pulled away. "I'll go get you a tissue." She returned to find the bedside lamp on and Shawn sitting cross-legged on the futon, wiping the tears from her face. "You want to talk about it?" Jaymi asked, as she handed her the tissue and sat beside her.

"I do, but I'm afraid to."

"It's just me. Nothing to be afraid of."

"I know it's just you. That's what scares me."

Jaymi frowned. "I don't understand. Are you afraid of me for some reason?"

"Oh no, not at all. Shit, I'm sorry, that's not what I meant." Shawn slid off the bed and began to pace. "I'm afraid of what you'll think of me if I tell you."

Jaymi caught her by the arm and stopped her midstride. "Just tell me. Let it out."

Shawn returned to her position on the bed and inhaled deeply.

"Before I came back here, things were really bad for me. I did some really stupid things."

"And that's okay, Shawn. You told me you were trying to make a new start."

"But I haven't told you everything. Remember I had lost my job and my apartment? That actually happened to me more than once. I'd get fired from some two-bit shit job, and then I'd get kicked out of wherever I was living 'cause I couldn't pay for it. Twice I lost my own place, and two other times I rented rooms where my roommates kicked me out. So the times I was homeless, I would hang out at the clubs and I'd pick up girls just so I'd have a place to sleep. I didn't even know their names half the time." She paused, clearly expecting judgment. When she didn't get any, she kept going.

"I felt awful. I mean it's not like me to use people like that. Shit, Jaymi, I was desperate. I was living in my car." She wiped her tears away with the back of her hands. Jaymi shifted closer to her and, after a slight hesitation, placed a hand on her back and began to lightly move it in a soothing circular pattern.

"Shawn, were you homeless when I was living out there?" Shawn stiffened and stared at her clenched hands, but she didn't say anything. "You were, weren't you? My God, Shawn, why didn't you say something? We would've given you a place to stay!"

"You guys were so successful, and I was such a loser and I knew there was no way you'd want someone like me staying with you. I didn't even consider it an option."

"Why would you think such a thing? I've never thought of you as a loser! My God, I feel awful. I didn't know, Shawn. I would have offered had I known."

"I realize that now." Shawn finally lifted her head and met Jaymi's eyes, despite feeling even more ashamed now. She was on a roll, so she might as well tell her the rest. "Jaymi, it gets worse. After I lost that last job at the restaurant, I met this guy from a record company. Warren Brinkman. He saw me play, promised me he could get me a recording deal. He showed me his credentials and everything. He set up an appointment for me to meet him at this restaurant so we could go over the paperwork and sign contracts and so forth. I thought it was odd that we didn't meet at his office, you know, with a lawyer or an agent or something, but hey, what did I know? By then, I didn't care what it took. I was broke, homeless, and I was starving. I hadn't eaten a decent meal in a month. I told him I'd sign wherever he wanted me to sign. But there was one catch." Shawn coughed, clearing her throat as she choked out her next words. "He said I had to give him something first."

"Come here," Jaymi said in a near whisper, giving her a gentle tug. Shawn moved next to her and couldn't believe she was letting herself cry on Jaymi's shoulder. With Jaymi's arm wrapped around her, she actually felt safe again. Almost completely safe. *Almost.* She had yet to tell her everything. But still, it was safer than she had felt in a long time.

Shawn wiped her sleeve across her nose. "He said I had to sleep with him. And, oh God, I can't believe I'm going to tell you this, but I was gonna do it, Jaymi. We left the restaurant and I followed him to this motel. He was lying on the bed waiting for me. I started to unbutton my shirt, and I thought I was going to throw up. I've only slept with a guy once, and I hated it. But at least I *liked* that guy and I was in high school when that happened. But this creep…I told him I wanted to freshen up first, 'cause I needed to buy some time to work up my nerve. Well, I took one look at myself in the mirror and I hated myself. I *really* hated myself. I stood there asking myself, What have I become? I know that sounds corny, but that's really what I thought. In the few minutes I was in there, I changed my mind. I knew I had at least one ounce of self-respect left and I knew I had to get out of there. When I came out, he had poured us each a glass of wine. I took one sip, to calm my nerves a little, and I told him forget it and grabbed my coat and started to leave. He was pissed. He grabbed me by the wrist, so hard I thought he'd break it and I'd never play again, and then he threw me on the bed and climbed on top of me and held me down. When I struggled, he punched me in the face—"

"Oh my God, Shawn. He hit you?"

Once again the tears flowed, and she felt her body shaking as the memory swept through her. "He tried to rape me, Jaymi. He tried to rape me." Jaymi squeezed her tighter. "I kept telling him to get off me, and he laughed and said that I asked for it, and he was gonna give me what I asked for. I got an arm free and I grabbed the lamp on the table next to the bed. I swung it as hard as I could and hit him in the head, and then I got the hell outta there."

"You killed him?" Jaymi's eyes were wide.

"No, I made sure he was alive. At least, he was alive when I left, I'm sure of it. I could see him breathing. I left that night, and I headed back here and never looked back."

They sat in silence for a few minutes, and then Jaymi asked, "You didn't go to the police?"

"The police? And tell them what? That I agreed to sleep with this guy to further my career but I suddenly changed my mind?"

"No, I mean, what he did to you, it's a crime. What if he comes after you? What if *he* calls the police and says you assaulted him?"

Shawn shook her head violently. "No way. What's he going to say? That he promises music contracts in exchange for sex? No way. I'm just glad to be here. Away from that asshole and away from that place. The whole godforsaken town."

She got up and went to the bathroom. She splashed cold water on her face and tried to quell the need to vomit. In a way it was good to have it all out in the open. She thought about that weird feeling of being followed and wondered if she should mention it, but like she'd told Jaymi, there was no way the guy would come after her, let alone be able to find her when she'd gone clear across the country. She steeled herself to face Jaymi and returned to the bedroom.

"So see? You sure you want such a loser staying with you?" Shawn shrugged, her guard back up, ready for the rejection she was about to face.

"Loser? Brinkman is the loser."

Shawn couldn't hold back her smile, but it quickly faded. "But I said I would sleep with him. I was willing to—"

"So what? It doesn't make it right, what he did to you."

"But what about the women I slept with? I used them."

Jaymi placed her hand on Shawn's shoulder. "You were alone, and desperate, and scared," she whispered. "I know that's not who you are, Shawn. Sometimes we do crazy things when we're in desperate situations. It doesn't mean someone's a bad person."

"How do you know that's not who I am? You're probably seeing red flags swarming all over me now."

Jaymi laughed and shook her head. "No, I don't. You wouldn't have told me all this if that were the case, you'd still be living that way." She wiped a tear from Shawn's cheek and then playfully tousled her hair.

"But how do you know I'm not using you, too?" asked Shawn, a chill running up her spine from Jaymi's touch. Or was it from the fear of rejection she was still fighting off?

"I've heard your music."

"Huh?"

"You heard me. It's in your songs. There's a purity in your lyrics, and honesty when you sing. I know you better than you think I do."

Shawn shook her head. "How can you be so willing to just accept someone like me into your home, Jaymi? I mean, you didn't know me all that well to begin with, and now that you do, you're still okay with me. I don't get it."

Jaymi squeezed Shawn's hand. "My parents taught me to be kind, Shawn. You fell on hard times and didn't have anyone to help you. Do you think those women you slept with didn't use you, too? Didn't they get something out of it as well?"

"I guess I never thought of it that way. I was just so aware of why I was in bed with them, you know?" Shawn thought back to the various women and considered what Jaymi said. She'd picked them up at bars, not book readings. They were out for a hook-up, and that was what Shawn had given them. The fact that it meant she hadn't needed to sleep in her car and that she got an occasional hot shower out of it in the bargain didn't mean they didn't get what they wanted in the process. Suddenly the knot in her stomach loosened a bit.

Jaymi gave Shawn's face a light caress, wiping away the last of the tears. "Sometimes life really sucks, Shawn. And it sucks worse for some people than others. We all do what we need to in order to keep going. But beating yourself up, blaming yourself for other people's actions, that's just self-torture. Let it go, and be the person you want to be." She got up and went to the door. "Shout if you need me. We'd better get some sleep."

Shawn watched her, perplexed and relieved. She'd told Jaymi the worst of it, and she still had a place to live and, maybe, a true friend. She'd been so convinced she'd be out on her ass again, she wasn't sure how to process the fact that nothing had changed.

She flopped back onto the bed, exhausted and feeling strangely empty.

# CHAPTER ELEVEN

With her secrets out in the open, Shawn became more relaxed than she had been in ages. But she noticed that now that her guard was down, Jaymi's seemed to be up. Not that there was any tension between them—they talked the way they always had, maybe even a bit more. It was in Jaymi's body language. There were no more signs of the affection she had demonstrated that night. Once, Shawn had brought up girlfriends she had had and asked Jaymi about her exes. Jaymi instantly changed the subject.

Remembering the conversations with Nikki about Jaymi's lack of interest in a relationship, as well as her history about getting hurt, Shawn told herself not to take it personally, although she had to admit it hurt her a little that she had shared her darkest demons with Jaymi, and in turn, Jaymi had seemed to shut down. They focused on preparing her for an open mike, and she decided not to push—after all, Jaymi hadn't pushed her. She'd give Jaymi the same consideration and just hope that over time things would get better. The insecure, injured part of her wondered if Jaymi wasn't as okay with everything Shawn had told her as she had seemed. A kernel of doubt stayed lodged in her heart. But the days slipped by and for the most part they were easy ones.

Fortunately, Karla was buying Shawn's excuse that a meeting with Jaymi would have to wait at least a month, since the band was booked solid with rehearsals and gigs, and they were working on material for another album. An autographed eight-by-ten photo and the promise of a signed CD had mollified her for the time being. She still questioned Shawn on a daily basis, and Shawn had managed to arrive at least ten minutes early for work every day. Karla seemed to have resigned herself to being cordial in order to maintain her connection to Jaymi.

Thursday night's open mike night finally came, with support from all the usual suspects: Devin, Sara, LaKeisha, and Kay. Much to Shawn's relief, Nikki bartended at the club and was on duty that night. The last thing Shawn needed was Nikki's strange brand of flirtation and put-downs.

The room filled to about half its capacity. The small platform stage was at one corner of a dance floor. A DJ booth occupied a nearby corner, and a bar and billiards area were at the other end of the room.

After spending some time with Jaymi's friends at the Sparky's gig, Shawn was a little more at ease with them tonight. Still, by the time her turn to perform came around, her nerves were shot.

"Come on, Shawn, you're up next." Jaymi motioned to the stage.

"I don't know if I can go through with it. I haven't performed in months."

"You'll be fine."

"Yeah, and you know we're all here for you," Sara said. The others added their encouragement.

"Hey," said Jaymi, resting her hands on Shawn's shoulders, "just sing to me. Pretend there's no one else in the room, okay? Just like you did all week at home. You're gonna be great."

She stared into Jaymi's eyes and her stomach flipped. At home. The sound of that, combined with Jaymi's touch, settled her. The warmth of Jaymi's hands stayed with her as she made her way to the stage. Shawn was introduced and greeted with a polite spattering of applause, making the overzealous eruption from her tiny group of fans more obvious. She locked eyes with Jaymi, stepped up to the mike, and began to play. The chords were a bit choppy at first, and there was a slight tremor in her voice, but when Jaymi nodded and began lip-syncing the words with her, calm washed over her and she allowed the song to take over. Before she had finished the first verse, she noticed that the hum of a distracted crowd had diminished and faces began turning in her direction.

After a solid round of applause, Shawn dove into her second song, an upbeat rocker that prompted the audience to clap along. Shawn felt her confidence growing and she swore she saw pride in Jaymi's face.

By the time she finished her third and final tune, she knew she had completely captivated the audience. She thanked them shyly, bowing and making her way back to the table with a huge grin as they cheered with hoots and hollers, whistles, and applause. She gladly received a round of hugs from everyone waiting. She then looked to Jaymi, who was standing aside watching, arms crossed, and a huge smile across her face, her blue eyes sparkling with pride.

"So how'd I do?" Shawn asked.

"Are you kidding me? Did you hear this crowd? You were unbelievable!" Jaymi reached for Shawn's hand to pull her into a hug.

"Not bad, cute stuff." Nikki pushed between them, forcing Jaymi to drop Shawn's hand. "Not bad."

A woman stepped up next to Nikki. "Are you nuts, Nikki? That was shitloads better than not bad. That was fucking awesome!" The woman extended her hand to Shawn. "Hi. I'm Randi. I'm a friend of Nikki's." She grinned and Shawn noticed how tightly her clothes hugged her body. "But don't let that scare you off, honey."

Shawn managed a smile and looked inquisitively in Jaymi's direction. Jaymi shrugged.

Randi continued to hold her hand. "What're you drinking, honey? You must be parched after all that singing."

"Uh…"

"Aw, don't be shy. You must be used to fans buying you drinks." Randi's dark eyes cruised Shawn up and down.

"Not really." Shawn's pleading look strayed back to Jaymi, who finally came to the rescue.

"She'd like a hot cup of tea with lemon, right, Shawn?"

"That so?" asked Randi. Shawn nodded. "You got it." Randi took a step toward the bar, stopped, and turned. "Anyone ever tell you how sexy you are when you sing?" Without waiting for a response, she smiled and sauntered away. Shawn felt herself blush.

Jaymi glared at Nikki. "You want to tell your friend to ease up a little?"

"Lighten up, Jaymi. You know Randi's a flirt. She doesn't mean anything by it. Besides, I think they'd be cute together."

"What? Shawn's trying to get her career back on track. She doesn't need a player like Randi distracting her."

Nikki moved in closer to Jaymi and said slyly, "You're being awfully protective of her. I think maybe you're jealous."

Shawn realized there was subtext here she wasn't catching, history between Jaymi and Nikki. She wondered what the hell had just happened but figured it wasn't the time or place to ask. Maybe Jaymi would tell her at home later. She accepted the cup of tea Randi brought over and followed her to a quiet table in the corner. It wasn't what she wanted to do, but she felt like she needed to stay away from Jaymi for a second, after the weirdness with Nikki. *It's all so fucking complicated.*

"So, Shawn—I love that name for a woman, by the way," said Randi, "why I haven't seen you in here before?"

Shawn winced at the cheesy pickup line. "I've been living in California for the last seven years, you know, trying to make it in the music business. I just came back recently." She shifted in her chair and tried to focus on her present company, though she found it hard. She wanted to be with Jaymi.

"Well, I can't believe you're not already a big star. You really were fabulous up there." Randi smiled, and both the smile and the compliment seemed genuine. "I'm sorry if I came on a little strong earlier. Just my nature, I guess. I have trouble containing myself when I meet an attractive woman. I see beauty, and I flirt. I can't help it."

"I think I've suffered from that condition myself on occasion." Shawn took a long look at the brunette sitting across from her. High cheekbones, chiseled jawline, a wide bright smile with perfect teeth, and deep brown eyes surrounded by thick eyelashes. She was attractive, no question.

Randi responded with that beautiful smile and raised her beer in a toast. "Welcome back, honey. Eat your heart out, Hollywood."

"To new friends," added Shawn, noticing that Jaymi was at the bar with Devin ordering a glass of wine. As they walked back to the table, Shawn noticed that Jaymi made no effort to make eye contact with her. Her heart sank as she quickly reminded herself to keep her feelings in check. *Maybe she doesn't want to intrude. Or maybe she needs a break from me. I've been depending on her for everything, including my social life. I do need to start making my own friends.*

"Hello?" Randi leaned forward on her elbows, her penetrating dark eyes seeking Shawn's attention. "Where'd you go?"

"Sorry. I'm just really tired, I guess. No, that's no excuse. I'm sorry, I'm being rude."

"No, you're not. Look, I don't want to keep you from your friends, so it's okay if you'd like to go back to your own table."

"Well, you can join us if you'd like."

Just then Jaymi walked up to their table. "Shawn, you about ready to go? I'm beat. Kay's headed out already, and you and I both have to work in the morning."

"Yeah, sure. What about the others?"

"They're going to hang out a little longer."

Shawn stood up and thanked Randi for the drink.

"Don't mention it. Hope to see you around again."

After another round of hugs and congratulations from the gang, Jaymi and Shawn left.

❖

"Third time's usually the charm," Jaymi said.

Shawn turned the key, once again attempting to get Jaymi's truck started. It rumbled to life.

"Guess my battery's going. Thanks for driving, Shawn." Jaymi yawned as she spoke. "I shouldn't have had that last glass of wine."

"I don't mind, you drove on the way down." She let out a sigh of relief, grateful for the success of her first open mike since returning from California. She let the truck warm up for a few minutes and then reached to shift into gear, but as she did so, she took notice of something across the club's parking lot.

"What's wrong?" asked Jaymi.

"That big black pickup over there looks familiar. Does it belong to one of your friends?"

Jaymi didn't bother to open her eyes. "No one I know drives a black truck."

Shawn shrugged it off and pulled onto the street. A few minutes later, they were on the highway and Jaymi was struggling to stay awake.

Shawn decided to tease her. "You falling asleep on me *again*?"

Jaymi chuckled. "It's becoming a habit, huh?"

"So, I pour my heart out onstage, I'm a big hit, I get hit on, and I'm driving home with a woman who can't even keep her eyes open to celebrate with me."

Jaymi grinned and mimicked playing a violin. "Aw, you poor thing."

"Damn right! You know I could've gone home with any number of women there tonight."

"Yeah, I know." Jaymi mimicked a raspy, sensual drawl, "Since you're *so sexy* when you sing."

Shawn began to sing in an exaggerated sultry style, complete with gestures and facial expressions, and the two laughed even harder.

"So why didn't you?" asked Jaymi when the giggles subsided.

"Why didn't I what?"

"Go home with Randi. Or anyone else, for that matter?"

"Not interested," Shawn said, uneasy with where the line of questioning might lead.

"Why not?"

"I'm just not. I'm not into one-night stands anymore. Besides, I have enough on my plate right now." She could hear her voice speeding up with nervousness. "You know, like you said to Nikki, I'm really trying to focus on my career and get my life in order—same as you. Get a steady job, get my own place, get my own paying gigs." *I can't very well say it's because I don't want anyone but you, can I?*

"Yeah. Gotcha." Jaymi slunk down into her seat and closed her eyes.

Shawn silently took a deep breath, glad Jaymi was willing to drop it. She glanced in the rearview mirror. "Shit, there's that truck again."

"What truck?" asked Jaymi, looking at her side view mirror. "The one you saw outside the club?"

"Yeah."

"How can you tell? It's so dark."

"It's got that row of lights across the roof, see?"

"Oh yeah, it does."

Shawn pressed on the accelerator and checked the mirror again. The truck picked up speed.

"I'm just curious," Shawn said, speeding up a little more, and then moving into the right lane. The truck did the same. Shawn took the next exit. "Shit, Jaymi, it's following us."

"Are you serious? Where are you going?"

"I don't know, but I'll betcha they go where we go." She found a gas station, turned around, and got back on the interstate. Within a few minutes, they spotted the truck again, several vehicles back.

"Holy shit, Shawn, you're right. But why would someone be… You don't think it's that Brinkman guy, do you?"

Shawn's stomach soured at the thought. "No. He wouldn't waste his time coming way out here," she said, thinking it sounded more like she was trying to convince herself. *Would he? Or does he have some other loser doing his dirty work for him?* "Besides, it has Maine plates. I don't want to freak you out or anything, but the night you played at Sparky's, I could have sworn someone followed us home from there."

"Now you're just being paranoid."

"Jaymi, listen to me"—Shawn grabbed Jaymi by the sleeve— "what if you have some crazed fan out there?"

"Oh, come on, Shawn! That's crazy."

"No, it isn't. You don't realize how famous you're getting. You and the rest of the band. You don't see their faces like I do when you guys are onstage. Not up close, anyway."

"Great, now you're making *me* paranoid."

"We're at our exit. What if they follow us to the house?"

"Geez, now I wish you *had* brought Randi home with you."

"What? Why?"

"She's a cop."

"Are you shitting me?" They were approaching their driveway. The truck was still behind them.

"Tell you what, pull in and go halfway up, and if they turn in, too, or even stop at the end, just start honking like crazy. Alice and Peter will be out in a heartbeat to see what's going on."

"No. Not yet. I don't want whoever that is to know where we live." Shawn drove past the house to the next intersection and turned. This time, to her relief, the truck didn't follow. As an added precaution, she turned again and headed back toward town. When she was sure the truck was gone, she brought them home.

"You know, maybe whoever it is lives up this way," said Jaymi, sounding as relieved as Shawn felt.

Shawn was still skeptical. "Well, maybe so, but something just doesn't sit right. Why would they exit the highway and speed up to keep up with us?"

"I don't know. You think we should call the police?"

Shawn hesitated, still fearing the possibility of the authorities connecting her to Brinkman. *What if he's dead and someone saw me with him?* "I'm not sure. I mean, they didn't really commit a crime or anything."

"I'm at least going to go see Alice and Pete in the morning and give them a description of the truck. Then they can keep an eye out for it."

"Yeah. I guess that's a start."

They gathered up Shawn's things and climbed the stairs to the loft. Jaymi drew the blinds in the kitchen and living room as Shawn brought her guitar to her room. She peeked through her bedroom window, and for a moment thought she saw movement in the driveway. She shook her head and figured her mind was playing tricks on her. She walked out of her room, only to bump into Jaymi, who had just come out of the bathroom.

"Oh, sorry," said Shawn, and then made a move toward the bathroom. When she was finished, she emerged to find Jaymi waiting in the hall. "I'm sorry, were you not finished with the bathroom?" Jaymi was leaning back against the wall, eyes sleepy, a smile on her lips.

"You really think Passion Play's getting famous?"

"Yeah, I do."

Shawn made a U-turn into her room and tossed her dirty clothes onto a pile of laundry in the corner on the floor. Jaymi followed her and plopped down at the foot of the futon.

Shawn climbed under the covers and propped herself up onto her pillow with her hands behind her head.

"Peach used to joke around and say she didn't want me to become famous because she thought I'd have a bunch of women after me all the time," Jaymi said, staring blankly across the room. "Ironic, isn't it? She acted like I wouldn't be able to resist all that temptation, and then *she* turns around and cheats on *me*."

Shawn was taken aback; she had been living here for a month and this was the first time Jaymi had shown any inclination to talk about her ex-girlfriend.

Shawn sat up. "I'm so sorry."

Jaymi hugged her knees into her chest. It obviously was a painful memory, but Shawn's instincts told her it was key to understanding Jaymi. It would also explain why her friends were so protective of her when it came to dating. Shawn decided to test the waters.

"Was it just a one-time thing or did she fool around on you all the time?"

"I only know of one time, but that was enough." Jaymi sighed deeply. "And the worst part was that it happened on the night I told her I was coming back here to be with my mom. It was right after she'd been diagnosed."

Shawn nearly bolted out of the bed. She wanted to throw something. She wanted to hunt down Peach and tell her she was scum. "Are you fucking kidding me?"

"I wish. We had this huge argument. I was a mess, trying to figure out what to do. I didn't want to derail my career, or our relationship, but I *had* to come home."

"Of course you did. I mean, duh, that's a no-brainer."

"Peach didn't think so. She assumed I wanted her to quit law school and come back with me."

Shawn shook her head in disbelief. "She didn't come with you? How could she do that to you?"

"The thing is, I didn't ask her to come with me. I told her I'd be back, but as far as she was concerned, my leaving to be with my mom meant I was leaving her."

Jaymi fell silent and Shawn wasn't sure what to say. She didn't want to push. She figured she'd let Jaymi decide if and when she wanted to open up more on the subject. Jaymi made no move to leave, and finally, she continued.

"I needed her that night. Probably more than I ever needed anybody in my whole life up to that point. But instead of staying to work things out with me, she accused me of having an affair with Nikki and took off to go study with her friend Suri. Friend, my ass."

Shawn had never heard Jaymi speak with such contempt. *An affair with Nikki? No way. Not possible.* Shawn wanted to choke the living shit out of Peach and her so-called friend. She wanted even more to hold Jaymi and take away her pain. For now, she settled for taking her hand and gently caressing it. Jaymi still showed no inclination to get up.

"I can't believe she thought she couldn't trust you," Shawn said, sensing Jaymi might have more to say. "Seems like she would have known you better than that."

"I thought so."

"So she got jealous easy?"

"Actually, no. The only person she was ever jealous of was Nikki, for some ungodly reason. Nikki and I have been close for a long time, but there's never been anything romantic between us. Peach never lacked confidence when it came to women, especially me. She knew she could trust me. I think she just liked to throw Nikki in my face to keep me on my toes. If she had seriously been jealous, she wouldn't have stopped coming to our gigs. I understood. I mean, I didn't expect her to go to every one. And she was, after all, studying law, which monopolized most of her time."

"No wonder I never met her. You'd still think she could've made time to go to a show once in a while, though."

"Yeah." Jaymi pulled her feet underneath her. "I've had a lot of time to reflect on things since we broke up, and I've decided it was ultimately for the best. We were so different in many ways. I'm surprised we didn't have more fights."

"You don't seem the type to fight."

"No, not at all. But Peach, she thrived on debates and arguments."

"The fine makings of a good lawyer."

Jaymi released a long breath, and then laughed halfheartedly. "I don't know how we lasted as long as we did. Stupidity, I guess. I was young and stupid and thought I was in love. You don't think straight when you're in love—"

"We're gay, Jaymi—we're not supposed to think straight when it comes to love," Shawn teased, sitting up and giving Jaymi a playful push.

"Very funny." Jaymi returned the gesture, as Shawn jokingly exaggerated a fall back onto the bed, then sat up again.

"Don't feel so bad, Jaymi. Everybody does stupid things when it comes to love. And if it's any consolation, I think Peach wasn't as secure as you thought she was."

"You think she sabotaged our relationship on purpose?"

Shawn shrugged. "She probably convinced herself that someday you were going to cheat on her anyway, or you'd leave her when the band got more successful and had to travel. So why not beat you to it? Save herself the humiliation. I mean, it's the way I would've thought, when I was younger."

"Yeah, well, she humiliated herself anyway, because now everyone knows she's a damn cheater."

"She's a damn fool is what she is," Shawn said softly. She leaned forward and without thinking, moved her hand to Jaymi's shoulder. "I mean, shit, didn't she know what she had?"

They sat frozen, close enough that one of them just needed to make the next move, close the gap. After a moment she felt Jaymi's hand squeeze hers, and then remove it. She saw tears well up in Jaymi's eyes and her heart sank.

"Good night."

She heard the sound of Jaymi's bedroom door closing firmly behind her, followed by muffled sobs Shawn was sure she didn't want her to hear.

*Smooth. She's in pain, and all you can think about is kissing her.* Shawn pulled a pillow over her face and muffled a frustrated groan. She lay back down, shut off her light, and looked at the clock: 1:57. She had to be at work in four hours. It wasn't like Jaymi to keep her up talking until the wee hours knowing she needed to work the next morning. Which told Shawn she must have really needed someone to talk to. Jaymi'd needed a friend, and once again, Shawn's crush had blurred that line and she'd almost crossed it. And it was her comment about fame that had triggered the conversation in the first place.

But Shawn also sensed these crazy feelings were becoming mutual. Peach had obviously hurt Jaymi badly, which was making her push Shawn away whenever they got close. There was also the focus on her career that she was determined to keep on course.

*Maybe I shouldn't have come here. I'm disrupting her life. I'll never be able to live with myself if I screw things up for her. If she starts to have feelings for me, I don't want to put her in that position— thinking she has to choose between her lover and her career. I'd just hold her back.*

She made up her mind that she would start looking for her own apartment after work tomorrow. *Today, actually.* With that decision made, she tried to fall asleep. The sobs in the neighboring room had finally subsided, but Shawn's heart was aching with the pain she knew Jaymi was feeling, and with the sense of loss that came with her decision to move out.

She hated Peach for causing Jaymi such heartbreak.

*It's no use. I can't sleep.* She turned on the light, opened her notebook and began to write. The pen scribbled out word after word, line after line, and as the words began to flow into a rhythm, the melody began to emerge simultaneously.

❖

Jaymi refrained from slamming the door after she left Shawn's room. After all, that wouldn't be fair. She wasn't angry at Shawn. *No, it's me. What the hell is wrong with me?*

She fell onto her bed and began to sob. *Why can't I just admit I'm attracted to her? Shawn. Who was down and out and came to me for help. After her own father turned her away. She's probably as vulnerable right now as I am. And what if I'm falling into that same pattern of being the rescuer? No, I can't let anything happen between us. We're not ready. Maybe I should give her a deadline to move. I'll feel like a jerk, but it's probably for the best. Remove the temptation, right?*

*Except I like having her here. Sara's right, she is cute. What if it doesn't work out? We're getting to be such good friends. And she said herself that she's not interested in dating, that she's trying to focus on her career, too.*

She tried to sleep. But she continued to ponder the feelings that were growing between herself and her new roommate. At two thirty a.m. she gave up trying to sleep and turned on the light. She reached for the notebook she religiously kept in her nightstand and let her feelings escape through her pen. And when she turned the ink-filled page, she acknowledged the miracle which had just occurred: the dissolution of the writer's block that had plagued her for almost a year.

Excitement consumed her as she reread what she had written. She let out a huge breath of satisfaction and smiled. She didn't want to sleep now; she wanted to play it. To share it. With Shawn. Now.

She approached Shawn's room and stopped in her tracks. There was light filtering out beneath the door. She inched it open and peeked in to find Shawn sitting on her bed with her guitar on her lap and a notepad in front of her. She was so immersed in lightly tapping the strings and penciling notations onto the paper, that she didn't notice Jaymi until she was beside her. She finally looked up and let out a slight gasp of surprise.

For the first time since Shawn had moved in, Jaymi acknowledged that living together wasn't hindering their careers. It was helping. She handed Shawn the page she'd written and watched as Shawn scanned it before looking up at her.

"Can I hear it?"

Jaymi experimented with a few chord progressions, humming along, making adjustments here and there as she worked through it. She then cleared her throat, smiled, and sang through a rough cut. She handed the guitar back to Shawn, after she had applauded vigorously, and Shawn played her song to Jaymi, who then gave her a standing ovation. A quiet shyness loomed in the air for a few minutes.

"I never did get to give you a hug after you sang tonight," Jaymi finally said.

"Does that mean I get one now? Or do I get two after my next gig?"

Jaymi took Shawn's hand. "Oh no, I can't wait that long." She pulled Shawn into her arms and lowered her head, their cheeks briefly brushing before she rested her chin on Shawn's shoulder.

A faint whinny rose through the floor from one of the horses in the barn below. They both chuckled and Shawn said softly, "See, our songs are so good even the horses are applauding. And you can tell everybody you heard it straight from the horse's mouth." Her breath caught when Jaymi brought her right hand to Shawn's cheek, resting it there so lightly it sent a quiver through her body. She gently brushed back Shawn's bangs and then combed her fingers through her hair, her forearm coming to rest across her shoulders.

Jaymi whispered, "You are *so* cute."

"And I am *so* calling in sick this morning."

"And why is that? You look fine to me."

"Because if you're thinking of kissing me, I'm not going to stop you."

Jaymi inched her face even closer and when she gently pressed her lips to Shawn's, it was even more amazing than Shawn had imagined it would be. After several sweet, teasing presses, Jaymi's lips claimed

Shawn's, pulling a moan from Shawn's throat. She could sense Jaymi's reluctance slowly diminishing, and ultimately surrendering, to the moment. Aware of Jaymi's fears, she allowed Jaymi to take control. She made no move toward the bed, but simply followed Jaymi's lead, responding with passion, but without aggression. Shawn tenderly ran her fingers through Jaymi's hair and then caressed her back. Jaymi kept her arms wrapped gently around Shawn's torso as the kiss continued.

After several minutes, Shawn felt Jaymi's hand slide under her shirt and onto her bare back. A shiver ran up her spine from a touch so light and soothing that she thought if Jaymi simply ran her hands over her entire body and nothing more, she could die a happy woman. No one had ever touched her that way before. She contemplated slipping her own hand under Jaymi's shirt but decided it best to be patient and let Jaymi continue to dictate where this all was going. She wanted her to feel safe, despite the aching desire throbbing between her legs.

As if she had sensed her holding back, Jaymi ended the kiss and looked into her eyes. "Are you all right?"

"Yeah. I just don't want us to rush things."

"You're right." She sighed and rested her head on Shawn's shoulder. "Do you want me to go back to my room?"

"Yes."

Jaymi let go and backed up a step, her face scrunched up with hurt, when Shawn smiled and took her hand.

"Jaymi, you don't understand. I want to go with you."

"But I thought you didn't want to rush things?"

"Just to sleep. You have the queen-sized bed. It would be a hell of a lot more comfortable than this tiny futon. I would love nothing more than to just hold you in my arms while you sleep."

The look of surprise on Jaymi's face was enough to melt Shawn's heart. "I think that's the sweetest thing anyone's ever said to me."

They nestled under the covers and curled up in Jaymi's bed. "Mmm, your bed is so comfy," murmured Shawn.

"I'm sorry you've had to sleep on that old futon for a month."

"No, don't be sorry, the futon's fine. Believe me, after living in my car, I feel like I've been staying at a five-star hotel."

"I hope this doesn't sound insensitive, but I'm glad your father turned you away."

"Me, too." Shawn yawned and gave Jaymi a squeeze. She then

propped her head up on one elbow and caressed Jaymi's sleepy face. "Hey, you falling asleep on me without a good-night kiss?"

"Too dangerous," she whispered, her eyes already closed.

"Don't you trust me?"

Jaymi opened her eyes. "Not as much as I don't trust me. I haven't had sex in far too long. So believe me, even though we've been up for almost twenty-four hours and we're both completely exhausted, I'm horny enough and have just enough wine in me to throw all my willpower out the window and attack you anyway. And wipe that shit-eating grin off your face, or I'll have to send you back to your room." She rolled back onto her side and closed her eyes.

Shawn kissed her head, spooned her, and slid an arm around her waist. "Good night, Jaymi."

"G'night, Shawn."

## CHAPTER TWELVE

K arla, it's Shawn. Listen, I won't be in today. I'm not feeling well."
"You won't be in? On a Friday? You know Friday's one of our busiest days," Karla snapped. "And you haven't been here long enough to have earned any sick time."

"I know, I'll have to take it without pay." Shawn knew she could make up the difference if she offered to help Alice today. Although with Jaymi also having the day off, she knew it was going to be hard to drag herself out of the house. She didn't care. The barn work would only take a couple hours, and Jaymi would be nearby the whole time, right upstairs, merely yards away for the whole day. Unquestionably less torturous than spending nine hours away from her in a room full of coffee beans and indifferent coworkers.

"You seemed fine yesterday."

It was 5:23 a.m. and Shawn had slept only two hours. She knew Karla had a right to be pissed. She also knew she was less likely to lose her job if she called out, than if she showed up sleep deprived and screwed up all day. "Karla, I'm sorry, but I won't be able to come in today. I'll see you on Monday," Shawn said and hung up quickly.

Shaking off the frustration, she stood in the doorway of Jaymi's room and marveled at the thought that she was about to crawl back into bed with her. The sun was just coming up, and a thin line of daylight was peeking through the window between the blinds. She hoped that the look on Jaymi's face reflected an inner peace as she slept. For it was obvious that, while awake, there was a lot going on in that head of hers. Shawn wanted to know her inside and out, and she hoped that

Jaymi would, over time, continue to let her in and share more, as she had begun to last night.

She slipped under the covers, pulled herself close, and savored the feeling of their bodies pressed together. As she tried to fall back asleep, it occurred to her that despite sharing kisses last night, they had yet to discuss their feelings for each other. Not that she knew what the hell she was feeling anyway. *I have to be careful. I don't want to scare her off and screw things up. I'm shocked that she came on to me. Shit, I hope it wasn't just because of the wine, or I'll feel like I took advantage of her.*

Her thoughts lulled her back to sleep until she felt Jaymi stir and place a kiss on her cheek. Jaymi's fingers were lightly caressing her face and hair. Shawn opened her eyes.

"Good morning, cutie," whispered Jaymi.

"Morning. Cutie? I like that," Shawn said, grinning. "What time is it?"

"About noon. You want some breakfast?"

"Are you on the menu?"

Jaymi's face flushed. She was obviously not expecting such a flirtatious answer to her question.

"Look at you blushing," teased Shawn. "Has it really been so long?"

"Yes. Since Peach and I broke up."

"Wow. That's a long time."

"And it'll be even longer if you keep rubbing it in."

"I'm sorry. I'm not pressuring you or anything. And I hope you don't think I'm only interested in sex. I mean, don't get me wrong, not that I wouldn't *want* to, 'cause believe me, I…Ah, shit." Shawn buried her face in the pillow.

Jaymi pulled the pillow away and laughed. "You have quite a talent for embarrassing yourself, don't you?"

"I have talents in many areas." She winked and flashed what she hoped was a devilish grin. Sex was one area in which she wasn't lacking self-confidence. "Last night was only a preview."

"Oh, Shawn." Jaymi bit her bottom lip and looked up at the ceiling. "About last night…"

*Oh shit, here it comes. I blew it…*

Jaymi cupped Shawn's chin in her hand and lifted her face to look her in the eye. "Last night was amazing," she said softly.

Shawn looked at her in awe. "It really was, wasn't it?"

Jaymi's lips slowly turned up as she nodded. "I have never shared a night like that with anyone."

"Yeah, I know what you mean. The songs, the talking, the making out. Then sleeping all cuddled up—hey, what's wrong?" Shawn reached up and wiped a tear from Jaymi's cheek.

"I don't know if I can do this. I didn't expect this, and with everything going on in my career right now...I've had too many setbacks already and I can't afford to get distracted."

"I have no intention of interfering with your career plans." Shawn could see the protective wall going back up. They both sat up in bed. Perhaps regret was settling in after all.

"No? Then what exactly *are* your intentions?"

"I don't know. I want my music career, just like you." Jaymi remained quiet, and Shawn felt the panic churning in her stomach. Just as she'd thought, she'd gone and fucked up a good thing.

"Jaymi," Shawn finally said, "do you still love her?"

Jaymi's eyes turned a darker shade of blue as she looked at Shawn in alarm. "No. Maybe. I mean, I don't feel anything for her. I don't want her back."

"Then why are you still letting her hurt you?"

"She's not."

"But you're still letting what she did to you control you, so yes, she's still hurting you." Jaymi's eyes softened and then began to water. Shawn cautiously raised a hand to her face and swiped away a tear. "You're scared. I understand. If you're not ready for anything more than what we shared last night, that's okay. This took me by surprise, too, you know."

Before Jaymi could respond, they were interrupted by a knock on the apartment door. Jaymi shrugged, indicating she wasn't expecting anyone, and left to answer it. Shawn followed.

The words *good morning* were barely out of Jaymi's mouth when Nikki strolled past them and sat down at the piano. "Hey, listen to this, will you?" she said, as she began banging out chords on the keyboard. "I've been working on it all morning and I can't seem to get this one part right. You have to help me."

Jaymi rubbed her face with her hands as she let out a big sigh. "We're rehearsing tonight, can't it wait till then?"

Nikki spun around on the bench. "You sick or something? It's after noon and you're not even dressed."

"I'll put on some coffee. Would you like some, Nikki?" asked Shawn.

Nikki scrutinized her boxers and sweatshirt, and then turned back to Jaymi with a glare, which Jaymi returned in full.

Shawn maintained an innocent front, while she inwardly gloated over Nikki's assumptions.

Nikki swiped her song sheet off the piano and stood up. "No, thanks. You're right, Jaymi, we can work on this tonight." She let herself out.

"What's with her?" asked Shawn, as Jaymi collapsed into a kitchen chair.

"Same shit, different day," Jaymi muttered.

Shawn placed a steaming mug in front of her and then went about cooking eggs and toast. "She has a problem with you dating, doesn't she?"

"It's none of her damn business."

"Yeah, well every chance she gets, Nikki makes it quite clear that you're determined to stay single and focus on your career."

Jaymi got up to pour juice and keep an eye on the toast. "Determined to focus on my career, yes, but as far as the single thing goes, to be honest, I haven't stayed single on purpose. The timing just hasn't been right. I needed time to get over Peach. At the same time I was dealing with that, my mother was ill. Then I had to deal with her passing away." Her voice grew tight. "I've really needed this time for myself."

She buttered the toast as Shawn served the eggs. They sat and ate quietly, without much eye contact. They finished, and when Shawn got up to do the dishes, the silence was thick in the room, like a third person just waiting for an opening.

"Shawn, to be honest, it's very tempting to jump headfirst into a relationship. But I'd like for us to get to know each other better before we let this go any further. And I know that must sound hypocritical right now, because I know that I'm the one who initiated things last night—"

"Alcohol can do that." Shawn's pain was evident in her hurt tone.

Jaymi walked over to her, and when Shawn's gaze remained

down, staring into the sink, Jaymi touched her hand to Shawn's cheek and gently turned her face.

"Alcohol had nothing to do with it. Last night would have happened either way. I'm sorry. I need more time. And I'm afraid if I don't take it, I'll just repeat past mistakes and you'll end up getting hurt."

Shawn pulled the drain plug and dried her hands. "*I'll* get hurt? Jaymi, I'm the one worried about hurting you."

"What makes you say that?"

"Because I've never been in a serious relationship before. The longest I've ever lasted with someone was three months, and that was with my first girlfriend in high school. I've never even *tried* being in a relationship. I can be wicked impulsive when it comes to women. I just act and don't think. And not that it's bad to just go with your heart, but I think I've finally smartened up and realized you need to use your head, too. See, that's where we're different, and I think maybe it's a good thing. Because we can learn from each other.

"I've changed so much lately. You know, living on the streets really opened my eyes and made me realize that I had to start making better choices, or I wasn't going to survive. I thought the only person I had left in this world was my aunt Betty, and she's gone. I wanted to die, Jaymi. Seriously. Wanted. To. *Die*. You might think I'm bullshitting you, but I believe it saved my life when I heard you on the radio that night. Because something in my gut told me if I could find you, you wouldn't turn me away. And maybe, just maybe, I could find something to live for again. And I have.

"Since I've been here I've done nothing *but* think—about everything. My life, my health, my music, my career. You. I thought about how grateful I am that my father is such a bastard and wouldn't let me stay with him when I got back here. I've thought about how lucky I am that you live over a barn and I can indulge in my other love and take care of those beautiful horses. I've thought about how grateful I am for all you've done for me. You helped me find a job and you've supported me musically, and you've let me jam with Passion Play, and last night…last night that open mike fired me up so much! And to come home with you and spend the night together the way we did. I've thought about you and how badly I didn't want to make mistakes with you either. You say you don't want to repeat mistakes? Well, neither do I." She ran out of words, feeling emptied and raw.

"Shawn," Jaymi finally said, "do you think last night was a mistake?"

The sink gurgled as it swallowed the remaining dishwater.

When she finally spoke, it was quiet and genuine. "Only if it's ruined our friendship, because that's the one thing I don't think I can live without right now. And even if that's all we ever are, it's still a hell of a lot, and I'd be okay with that."

"I don't regret what happened." Jaymi spoke quietly. "But I do need you to be patient with me. It would be irresponsible of me to commit to a relationship right now. With you or anyone else. But I'm not a one-night stand kind of gal, you know what I mean? Don't get me wrong—last night was really special and I do care about you, Shawn, but—"

"But we can't get involved. I understand. You have nothing to be sorry about. Last night was as much my doing as yours. I'm sorry, too."

"So we're okay?"

"Yeah, we're okay. No pressure, I promise."

"I appreciate that."

Shawn smiled. "So, I guess that means no sex tonight, either."

"You're not going to make this easy for me, are you?"

"Oh, all right. Patience it is, then."

When Jaymi left the kitchen to shower and dress, Shawn meandered into the living room. She sipped her coffee and took in her surroundings. Afraid of getting ahead of herself, she fought the inclination to consider this place her new home. She had no idea whether she had a future with Jaymi or not. Being in a relationship would be taking everything to a new level of unexplored territory. Gone would be the days of casual sex and being on her own. It meant nothing less than a mature and serious commitment. All or nothing.

Fear crept up her spine in a way she had never felt before. How was she going to live up to those expectations? The only thing she knew about being in a relationship dated back to her high school days with Mel when she had first come out of the closet. That was no comparison to the magnitude of what she would be entering into with Jaymi.

For the first time since she'd arrived, Shawn took a good look at the contents of the large bookcase that took up most of the wall that separated the living room and kitchen. Aunt Betty once told her you could tell a lot about a person by their book collection. Shawn thought shamefully of her single photo album, one book on songwriting, and twenty or so paperback songbooks stuffed into the threadbare duffel bag on her bedroom floor. Not surprisingly, Jaymi's books were as organized as her CD and record collections, grouped by genre and, in the case of fiction, alphabetized by author.

Paperbacks filled the top two shelves. At least half were lesbian fiction, but there was a wonderful mixture of mysteries, young adult, and series collections. There were also old childhood favorites that she had saved—many of which were collections of comic strips, such as *Peanuts, Garfield,* and *The Family Circus.*

The next two shelves were all hardcovers. There were a few coffee-table books about the Red Sox. Martin Luther King Jr., Eleanor Roosevelt, Abraham Lincoln, John Lennon, and Melissa Etheridge were among the biographies. She had also kept many of her college textbooks. Most were from her music studies, but there were other subjects mixed in, including psychology, philosophy, Greek mythology, world history, and geography. Suddenly Shawn felt utterly ignorant. She had barely managed to graduate from high school. Jaymi had a BA and interests in a wide variety of subjects to boot.

On one side of the bottom shelf were two neat stacks of music magazines and four large scrapbooks on top of a pile of newspapers. On the other side stood high school and college yearbooks and a row of seven or eight photo albums, all arranged chronologically.

Curious, Shawn withdrew the oldest photo album and opened it to the first page. She beamed when she saw, in black and white, the beautiful, pudgy-faced baby grinning back at her. She slid the top entry from its sleeve and flipped it over. On the back, in what she assumed was Jaymi's mother's handwriting: *Jaymi Lynn, one month old.*

Shawn jumped slightly when Jaymi appeared in the doorway. "Haven't changed much, have I?"

Shawn grinned, feeling like a kid caught with her hand in the cookie jar. "You've only grown more beautiful."

Jaymi ran a hand through Shawn's hair and she could smell Jaymi's clean scent, making her pulse race. Jaymi leaned in and gave her a quick kiss on the lips. "You are not making this easy, you know."

"I thought we agreed to take things slowly?" Shawn said, stepping back and sliding the album back into its slot.

"Yeah, well, tell my hormones that."

Shawn let out a frustrated groan. "Just get outta here and go to rehearsal before—"

"All right, all right. I'm going." Jaymi disappeared around the corner to the music room to get her guitars. A moment later, she came back through and said, "If you see anything in there you'd like to look at or read, feel free." She then added with a grin, "But if you tease me about my hair in my high school pictures, you're in big trouble, missy."

Shawn laughed. "Sorry—can't promise that."

"Fine. I guess that is asking a lot." Jaymi hesitated, and Shawn wondered if she was fighting the temptation to kiss her good-bye.

"You're going to be late."

"Yeah. Right. I'll see you later."

"Okay."

Shawn waited for the sound of her exit and resumed perusing. She pulled out the scrapbooks, which Jaymi must have started filling as a child. There were crayon doodles of singers and guitars and rock bands. There were album cover designs. There were spiral-bound notebook pages with song lyrics written in pencil in the whimsical handwriting of a child. There were newspaper clippings and magazine photos of her musical idols. There were picture advertisements for guitars that Shawn was sure Jaymi'd coveted and had most likely begged her parents for as birthday or Christmas presents. Shawn had done the same thing. *I bet Jaymi had better luck with that than I did.*

The most recent scrapbook chronicled Jaymi's college years and her career with Passion Play. Everything from college recitals, to a byline mention in a list of entertainers performing at a local craft festival, to local club dates, to participation in benefit shows, to promotional photos, to the interview in *Happenings* that Devin wrote. There were also numerous photos of the band, both onstage and random candid shots. Shawn recognized Sara and LaKeisha in some shots taken at a party.

Shawn smiled deeply and fought a sting of jealousy. If only her career had gone as well. She gently reminded herself that it didn't matter now—she was on the right track, and she wasn't going to let the past deter her any longer.

She laid the scrapbook back in its place and checked the time. Maybe she'd peek at a few more photo albums for the hell of it, though she did not want to linger too long with them. She needed to get to work in the barn. Her heart warmed as she imagined looking through them together with Jaymi, Jaymi reminiscing and filling in the blanks of the when, where, and who for every picture. The prospect of learning everything she could about Jaymi engulfed her with an excitement about the future she had never felt before.

She skimmed quickly through the photo albums, randomly opening to three or four pages in each. When she got to the high school years, she squelched a chuckle. *Nice do.* She bet every gay girl in school had had an enormous crush on Jaymi.

She spent more time with the last album—Jaymi's college years and beyond. Filled with a mix of curiosity and dread, she went through page by page, scanning the faces, recognizing Nikki and Kay. About midway through, there were gaps. Random empty sleeves. Not one photo of Jaymi with another woman other than her bandmates or friends. Apparently, Jaymi's sentimental side reached its limit when it came to ex-lovers.

Shawn replaced the album on the shelf and wondered: *Will there ever be a picture of me in there?*

❖

Jaymi arrived uncharacteristically late for rehearsal, though only by ten minutes, which by her own standards was unacceptable. Normally she looked forward to practice, but today she walked in feeling indignant and defensive. During the drive she'd wished she were lying in Shawn's arms rather than driving to practice, and that thought alone made her cranky.

Today's rehearsal was of particular importance, though. They had the first of four booked gigs at a popular club in Boston tomorrow night. They'd played there twice last year, and those performances had drawn the attention of a local independent station known for showcasing unsigned New England artists. The station had been playing their songs ever since.

Brian, in addition to his skills on drums, was also the mastermind creator and manager of the band's website. He'd set up a live chat session with the band on the site for the day after the show, and based on RSVPs, they were anticipating a large crowd. Though her bandmates were looking forward to it, Jaymi was dreading it. She had always been fiercely protective of her privacy, despite knowing that the group needed the publicity. She had terrible nightmares about the invasive treatment celebrities received from tabloid magazines.

She shook off the cold as she made her way downstairs, bracing herself for the attitude and teasing she was sure to get from Nikki after their awkward encounter earlier. She apologized for keeping everyone waiting.

"No need to be sorry." Kay shrugged. "For God's sake, you're the one that's always here first."

"Well, looks like we can get started now, since Her Highness has decided to grace us with her presence," Nikki said as she descended the stairs.

"Stuff it, Nikki." Jaymi knelt on the floor and opened her guitar case and Nikki cornered her.

"Ooh, a little testy, are we? I would think you'd be on cloud nine. After all, it's not every day the princess of pure gets laid."

Jaymi sensed the withheld gasps of surprise from Kay and Brian and shot up in front of Nikki. "What did you just say?"

Nikki smiled widely, then feigned a look of apology. "Oh, I'm sorry. Was I not supposed to say anything? Or maybe she sucked in bed and that's why you're so tense. Sexual frustration is an awful thing, isn't it?"

For the first time in her life, Jaymi felt an uncontrollable surge of anger overcome her. The others watched in amazement when Jaymi grabbed Nikki by the shirt and got within inches of her face.

"What goes on between me and Shawn is none of your fucking business. I've had it with you and your bullshit! I'm sick of your disrespect, and your drinking. You strut around like you're God's gift to women and fuck anything that feeds your overgrown ego. You think just because you can sing and prance around onstage that makes it okay to treat people like shit? What fucking right do you have to call me out on who I sleep with?"

Kay and Brian managed to pull Jaymi away and direct her to the couch on the other side of the room. Nikki brushed herself off, shaking her shirt back into place and trying to finger-comb her gelled hair. She was obviously trying to appear calm, but her flushed face and shaking hand betrayed her. Jaymi sat sandwiched on the couch between Kay and Brian, each with an arm around her, and she finally began to calm down.

Nikki glared at the threesome, pursed her lips, and nodded. "I can see how I rank around here. Jaymi assaults *me,* but let's not comfort Nikki. It's poor Jaymi. It's okay. I'm fine. Not that any of you gives a shit."

Jaymi freed herself and walked over to Nikki. "I'm sorry. I lost it, I know. But what do you expect, huh? How many times do you think you can taunt me and treat me that way and think it's okay? It hurts me, Nikki. I thought we were friends. And I don't understand it. I don't understand why you're so bothered by my friendship with Shawn— which, by the way, that's all it is. What you assumed happened last night never did, and even if it had, what difference does it make? What's it to you? You should know by now that the band is my number one priority. Nothing, not even a girlfriend, if I had one, is going to change that. Can't you have a little faith in me? Can't you have just a little confidence in the person I've grown into over the past few years?"

Nikki's expression softened and she dropped her gaze to the floor. For the first time in years, Jaymi saw the warmhearted friend she had come to know in college.

"I'm sorry, Jaymi."

"Nikki," Jaymi said, "you've changed. I mean, yes, you've always been a little cocky, and that confidence is a big reason why you've helped us become so successful. But a slice of humble pie would do you a world of good."

"Hey, you can't deny I'm just as much a driving force behind our success as you—"

"I'm not saying you aren't. And"—she motioned to the other members of Passion Play—"so are you two. But lately, when we're not onstage, it just hasn't been fun, and it's because of you. You've become unbearable. Because, honestly, Nik, if your head has swollen this much with the little success we've seen so far, I don't think I can bear seeing it get any worse if the band really starts to take off. It'll destroy us, and it'll make for a very bittersweet career. And that's not the career I want."

Nikki stared intensely into Jaymi's eyes. "What are you saying?"

Jaymi shook her head and felt tears form. "If you can't get your ego in check, I'm not sure I want to stay with the band."

"Are you crazy?" Brian shouted. He and Kay were both on their feet.

"No way," said Kay. "Jaymi, without you, Passion Play doesn't exist." She looked at the other two. "Without any one of us, it doesn't exist. This has been a four-person effort from day one. We've all contributed, we've all made it what it is, and we can all take credit for our success." She turned to Nikki. "Jaymi's right, Nikki. You need to shape up. We've all held our tongues for far too long because we know how good you are and how much we need you. But enough already. Enough showing up late, and drinking during gigs, and your goddamn ego. You're going to ruin it for all of us if you don't get your act together."

Nikki stood alone, facing her three partners lined up like a firing squad, waiting anxiously for her reaction to their implied ultimatum.

She slowly regained her haughty composure, took three steps backward, and pulled her leather jacket from the back of a metal folding chair by the stairwell. "Fine. I'll get my *fucking act* together." She sneered. "My fucking *solo* act, that is. I don't need you. I don't need any of you. If you're so fucking tired of me, I'll go." She flung the jacket over her shoulder and sprinted up the stairs, slamming the door behind her. They heard her Mustang speed away from the house.

The remaining members of Passion Play stood motionless and silent. Jaymi's heart hammered in her chest. *My God, what just happened here? How the hell can we replace Nikki? She's the lead singer, the front man, the main attraction.*

"Now what?" asked Brian, looking to his cousin for guidance.

"We rehearse. We've got a show to do tomorrow and I don't want to disappoint our fans." Jaymi tried to disguise the fear rising into her throat. She retrieved her guitar from its case and slung it over her shoulder.

Kay took a step toward her own instrument and stopped. "Don't you think they're going to be disappointed when they show up and our lead singer isn't there?"

"I guess we'll find out, won't we?" Jaymi said, plugging into an amp and beginning to tune. "Which means we better put on one hell of a show."

"What're we going to tell them?" asked Brian.

Jaymi let out a long breath. "We'll just say she was ill and couldn't make it." She strummed a few chords with a bit more force than she intended and adjusted the volume on her Fender Stratocaster. "Don't worry. Once she cools off, she'll be back."

Kay sighed and shook her head. "I hope so. I wasn't trying to tell her she had to shape up or ship out, I was just trying to wake her ass up. Besides, I was getting sick of the way she's been treating you, Jaymi. You don't deserve it. You've been the glue holding us together, and honestly, girl, I'm surprised it took you this long to blow."

"Yeah, me, too," said Brian. "I've never seen you lose your temper like that. It was like…" He proceeded to tap into a drumroll, which started quietly then gradually grew louder until it finally exploded into a series of booms and crashes. "Whooooo! Look out!" he shouted above his dramatics. "She's gonna blow!" He punctuated his demonstration with an ear-shattering cymbal crash.

"All right, all right," Jaymi bellowed. "Come on, let's get to work. We've lost enough time already."

## CHAPTER THIRTEEN

After sweeping out the entire barn and making sure they fed and watered everyone—including the cats—Shawn and Alice brought in the horses. Shawn welcomed the cool air and physical labor. Not only did she need the exercise, but Alice's charm and easy manner were good company and a distraction she needed until she could sort things out. Alice then bid her good afternoon as Shawn went to work cleaning saddles.

Shawn inhaled and felt herself relax. The dry, dusty scent of the hay, the faint smell of hot wood, the sensual musk of leather, and the natural odor of the horses were as pleasurable as a bouquet of flowers. As she scrubbed and buffed, she enjoyed the fragrance of the polish and the feel of the tacky cloth in her hand. Two fluorescent shop lights occupied her work area, and a series of dimmer bulbs dotted the ceiling along the hall of stalls, creating a soothing atmosphere. She easily worked up a sweat. Alice kept the barn well heated, and that explained the cozy warmth in Jaymi's living space above. Alice had explained how she and Peter had designed the apartment so its occupant would receive plenty of sunshine through the kitchen window each morning, and in the afternoon, the rays would pass through the balcony doors into the living room.

She mentally reviewed the events of the last twenty-four hours. Things were going well, she thought. But she was scared to death. She hoped desperately that her lack of experience in relationships wouldn't screw things up. She also hoped that she would be able to keep her libido in check. Jaymi was right—they did have a lot to learn about each other, and it would be best to take things slowly. It wasn't going to be easy.

Shawn had shared a bed with many women over the years, but after sleeping with Jaymi curled up in her arms last night, her body was screaming for relief. She needed to dismiss it from her mind quickly or she would go crazy. She forced herself to think about other things, and after several attempts, her thoughts landed on the one person who was Jaymi's polar opposite: her father. In a matter of minutes, her mood was completely altered. She was inundated with slideshows of chaos and instability.

When she was little, Shawn wondered if her father wished she'd been a boy. Her parents tried for years to have another baby, hoping for a boy, but her mother had been unable to conceive. As fate would have it, from an early age Shawn was a tomboy. Though it confused her mother, it seemed to be some compensation for her father, considering the pleasure he took in playing catch with her, watching football together, teaching her how to change the oil in the car, raving over the skills she demonstrated with any tool placed in her hand. Some days she caught him looking at her strangely, but he never said anything out loud. Having a tomboy daughter was the next best thing to a son, which to Shawn was the closest thing she felt to acceptance.

Until the day she told him she was a lesbian.

Then, her mother told her she couldn't accept something against God's will.

That night, with only two months left of her senior year of high school, Shawn secretly began making plans to leave for California. She purposely made no waves with her parents, going through the motions of focusing on her schoolwork and saving the earnings from her part-time job at the stables next door.

The day after graduation, she set her alarm for five a.m. and loaded up her car. She left a note on the kitchen table, then drove away without looking back, her vision blurred with tears of relief, of pain, of anticipation.

She planned one stop along the way, to visit her aunt Betty, the only relative she'd ever felt truly close to. She'd been the only person in her life to support her plans for a career in music and had always encouraged her to not give up when her guitar or piano lessons became increasingly difficult. She'd even insisted on sending her the money for lessons, because her parents couldn't see the purpose in giving their child unrealistic ambitions. Not that they disapproved of her playing, as long as it remained only a hobby—something Shawn's heart wouldn't allow her to do.

Aunt Betty had accepted her as a lesbian. She'd known Shawn was gay before Shawn had figured it out and told her she had lots of gay friends. But when Shawn arrived at her aunt's house that day on the first leg of her journey west, Betty greeted her in shock, with the terrible news that her mother had died of a stroke.

Shawn had lost everyone that had mattered in her life. Her mother was gone. Her father had disowned her. Aunt Betty had died without her even knowing. *I can't lose Jaymi, too. She's all I have.*

❖

Jaymi had expected to come home to the hopeful, flirtatious woman she had left earlier in the day. Instead, she walked in on a crying mess on the couch, surrounded by tissues. Her guitar was facedown next to her, and the coffee table was covered with scattered pages of scribbled lyrics. Several flickering candles around the room provided the only light.

Jaymi immediately set down her things and stripped off her coat and gloves. Resisting the strong urge to gather Shawn up in her arms, she gingerly sat next to her instead and asked her what was wrong.

"I never got to say good-bye," Shawn sobbed. "She died thinking I hated her…"

"Who? Your mother?"

"Yes. And you want to know the worst thing? I *did* hate her the last time I saw her. At least, I thought I did."

"I'm sure she never thought that."

Shawn extracted a tissue from the box and blew her nose. "I took off the day after graduation and all I did was leave a note. Two hours later, I'm sitting in my aunt's house and she's telling me my mother's dead. She never even knew I was leaving. I didn't tell them—I just left."

"You were just a kid. You were mad at them, that's all. What teenager doesn't get mad at their parents? If you *really* hated her, you wouldn't have left a note. Unless…what did the note say?"

"I don't remember. Something about them not accepting me for who I am and that I was going to California to go after my music career."

"That doesn't sound hateful to me, it sounds like what a lot of kids say to their parents. Especially gay kids."

Shawn wiped her face and shook her hands through her hair. "Yeah, I guess it does. And I did sign it *Love, Shawn*."

"See? She knew you loved her, even though maybe you weren't getting along at the time. And give yourself a break—you couldn't have known she would have a stroke that day."

"My father blamed me. He said she was so upset about the way I left that I caused her stroke."

Jaymi handed her another tissue to wipe her tears. "That's awful. But you know that's not true, don't you? There are underlying conditions that build up for years that can cause a stroke. It wasn't your fault. I think everyone goes through some feelings of guilt when they lose someone close. Even me, and we *knew* my mom was dying. I had a very close relationship with her, but to this day, I still think of things I wish I had said or done. Time passes, and you figure out you're going to have regrets no matter what. You just have to accept that you're only human and no matter how hard you try, you're never going to be perfect." She placed a firm hand on Shawn's shoulder and told her again, "It's not your fault."

"That's not all." Shawn had stopped crying but looked like she could start again any second. "My father freaked out at the funeral and went off on me—yelling and swearing at me, blaming me in front of everybody—until I was so humiliated I had to leave before the end of the service."

"Ah, geez, I'm so sorry."

"That's the last time I saw him until the night I showed up here." Shawn got up, went to the kitchen, and brought them each a tall glass of water. "You guys played a long time tonight."

"Actually, we got a late start, thanks to me."

"You were only running a few minutes late—"

"No, not because of that. Nikki and I had it out. It got really ugly."

Shawn returned to her seat next to Jaymi and watched as she gulped down half her drink and set the glass on the coffee table.

"She quit the band."

"What? Are you shitting me?"

Jaymi closed her eyes, nodded, and told her the story. When she had finished, she began to cry, as the aftermath of the altercation hit her. Keeping up a strong front for the band had been a survival reflex. Now she faced the uncertainty of how receptive her audience was going to be without the band's popular and extremely talented lead singer, and how it could impact the future of her life's work.

Shawn put an arm around her. "Why do you think Nikki's so threatened by me?"

"My history with Nikki is a long story."

"I've got all night." Shawn leaned back into the other end of the sofa, casually crossing her arms over her stomach and stretching her legs out and crossing her ankles, ready to absorb Jaymi's long story.

Jaymi smiled and settled back into the sofa, imitating Shawn. "When we met in college, I needed someone like Nikki. I was shy and lacked confidence. Keep in mind, too, that I'd only been out of the closet a little over a year, so I was still finding myself in that respect. She took me under her wing. I was fascinated by how confident she was, how blatantly bold and strong. I wanted to feel that way, too. She didn't give a shit about what anyone thought of her. She didn't let anyone tell her she couldn't make it as a singer. She was so determined and had the most stubborn belief in her talent…I'd never seen anything like it.

"When we started to become friends, I latched on to her and found that just by being around her, my own confidence began to grow. She saw how insecure I was, but she also believed in my talents. It helped me believe in myself. We made this deal: she would work with me to improve my stage presence and overcome my stage fright, and I would work with her on improving her guitar playing. It worked wonders for both of us." Jaymi smiled at memories of simpler and happier times.

"So you guys must have a lot of mutual respect," said Shawn. "What happened?"

"Well, for years we focused so hard on our music, and putting the band together, and so on, that I never really had many friends outside the band. I mean, Kay and I get along great, but it's always been more of a working relationship with her. Nikki was my one and only close friend, until Peach and I started dating. But she was my *girlfriend*—that's different. I'm talking strictly friends. I couldn't quite define what it was at the time, but now that Peach is out of my life and I've had time to process things, I can see that there was definitely a power struggle between those two when it came to me. Nikki was used to being the one I depended on for everything, and it was an adjustment for her. She never came right out and said it, but she let me know in subtle ways that she didn't want Peach tipping the balance and interfering with what was becoming a well-oiled machine, so to speak—"

"Like Yoko breaking up the Beatles."

"Something like that. We were all pretty serious about maintaining certain boundaries when it came to the band. No visitors at rehearsal, for example. The band was everything to Nikki. Anything—or anyone— that threatened what we were setting out to accomplish was bad news in her eyes."

"Well, that explains why she wasn't thrilled when you brought me along to watch you guys a few weeks ago."

"Yeah, you could say that. Anyway, when we moved back here, I took a hiatus from the band. I wanted to spend every possible moment with my mom. I watched the most important person in my life fight for her life every day. And when she died…well, you know how much something like that changes you. My priorities changed. It's not that my music means any less to me, I just realized that I had been so isolated from everyone—including my family—that there was a part of me that was cheating myself out of things that make your life whole. Like friends. I began to make friends outside the band and the music scene. *And* I began to limit how much time I spent with the band so I could have a life apart from it. I started to socialize more, like with Devin and Sara, my family, and a few other people."

"And you don't need Nikki the way you used to, and she can't handle it."

"Yeah. I think she liked the idea that she had that hold on me— that control. And I know deep down, beneath that giant ego, there's an insecure little kid who's afraid of losing her best friend. That I won't need her anymore, and she'll get discarded by me just like she was discarded by her family. Her father kicked her out of the house when she was fifteen when he found out she was gay. The only reason she was able to go back home and then eventually go to college was because a week later she lied and told him that she wasn't gay after all, that it was just a phase." Jaymi finished off her water and traded it for a glass of wine, handing one to Shawn. "She used to brag about how she outsmarted him, tell me how stupid he was to pay for his lesbian daughter's tuition so that someday when she was famous she could come out publicly and humiliate him by telling the world how her clean-cut father was really a bastard who had rejected his multitalented daughter. I don't need to explain that to you."

They sipped on their wine in silence for a few moments, and then Jaymi got up and walked over to her CD cabinet. She looked them over thoughtfully, fingering several cases before making her selections and firing up the stereo. She sat back down with Shawn, this time right next to her, their knees touching, as the sounds of Shawn Colvin emitted from the speakers.

Shawn took the bait and leaned toward her. "You know something, Jaymi, whether Nikki comes to her senses and rejoins the band or not, I believe the band will still be a huge success. And you guys are going to kick ass tomorrow night, with or without her. *You,* not Nikki, are the reason Passion Play is so good, don't you know that? You write the best songs, you do the arranging, the producing, you keep the focus. Jaymi, you run the show, and whether you realize it or not, it's you the audience goes crazy for. I've seen it. Yeah, Nikki's a showman, she's attractive and sexy, blah-blah-blah. And maybe to some, she's the center of attention. *She* thinks so. But when you sing, Jaymi, holy shit—it's like the whole world stops to listen. And watch. And you can't see it, obviously. But to me and a ton of other people, you are the sexiest thing on that stage. And that, angel, is another reason why Nikki is so threatened by you."

Jaymi shyly tried to deflect the compliments, pondering whether what Shawn was saying was really true, or if her perceptions were skewed by attraction. "How do you always know the perfect thing to say?"

Shawn merely shrugged and raised her eyebrows.

Jaymi finished her last swallow of wine and not so innocently leaned her body over Shawn's to set her goblet on the end table behind Shawn, rather than on the more convenient coffee table in front of them.

It wasn't the apprehensive kiss of the night before, but a firm, passionate one that spoke of confidence and no fear of rejection. After a slight hesitation, Shawn surrendered and within minutes was easing Jaymi onto her back and letting her own body relax into her arms, their lips never parting, their tongues caressing, their hands exploring.

It wasn't until Shawn felt Jaymi's hand slide into her bra that she heard the argument begin in her head. *Oh God, I don't want to stop this, but I have to. She obviously wants it, too. No, it's the wine, it's weakening her—our—willpower, but subconsciously it's because we both want it. I'm confused—she wants to slow things down, yet she keeps coming on to me. Oh, just sleep with her, but what if she backs off again in the morning, when she's sober and regrets this...and then what?*

Shawn drew her lips away, and pulled away slightly. "Jaymi, I can't do this. I thought—"

"Stop thinking." Jaymi cupped Shawn's face between her hands. "I don't want to think. All I've ever done is think. For once, I just want to go with my feelings."

Shawn gently took Jaymi's hands, pulled them away from her face, and stood up. "But what about my feelings, Jaymi? I've done nothing *but* act on my feelings without thinking, and where has it gotten me? One-night stands. Homeless. Disowned by my father. And almost raped. Don't you understand? I need to think now. I've screwed up my whole life because I didn't think things through. It's like we've reversed roles."

"Oh God..." Jaymi covered her face. "You're right. I'm so sorry." Jaymi reached for a tissue and continued. "I don't know what's gotten into me. Normally my willpower is so strong, but I don't know what it is about you, Shawn. This is the first time since Peach and I split up that I've had feelings for someone and I've actually felt safe to do something about it. But I got so caught up in how I was feeling that I didn't think about your feelings."

"So, it's not just the wine and my compliments making you horny?" Shawn couldn't resist teasing. Suddenly what Jaymi was saying sank in when she didn't laugh, but focused those intense blue eyes seriously on her. "Jaymi—are you saying you have feelings for me? Like, real feelings?"

"I didn't want to. I didn't expect to. None of this would have happened if I didn't. I don't just make passes at women. I haven't met anyone I've wanted to date." She slowly stood up and took Shawn by the hands and gave them a squeeze. "That is, until now. I made up my mind that the next time I got involved with someone I would take my time, I'd evaluate and analyze and examine every aspect of who that person was, and I'd make absolutely sure that we were right for each other. And that I could trust her, completely. I've been telling myself for so long that I didn't want to be with anyone. That I was better off single. That I wasn't going to put my heart on the line again unless I had no doubts that it was absolutely right."

Shawn held Jaymi's eyes. She could feel her heart pounding like a jackhammer. Her head spun as Jaymi's words began to sink in. *She's falling for me.* "Have you been doing that with me this whole time? Studying me to see if we're compatible?"

"No. At least not consciously. I think it's just happened naturally, without me trying. With you, everything is so easy. And it seems to be that way for you, too. We just get along so great, and we just keep getting closer every day. If it keeps heading in this direction, it'll only get better, don't you think? Do you feel it, too?"

Shawn's eyes closed as she nodded slowly. "I'm scared, Jaymi."

"Scared of what?"

"Of me, of me screwing this up—"

"How do you know it won't be different this time? What makes you think you'll screw it up?"

"I told you. I've never really had a real relationship. I've only been here a month. There's a lot you still don't know about me."

"Shawn, you're forgetting that we were friends for a year back in California."

"Yeah, I know. But with you, I..." She bowed her head and shook it.

Jaymi lifted Shawn's chin and leaned closer. "Tell me," she whispered.

"You don't understand. You're different. With you it's different, and if I screw it up this time, I'll regret it for the rest of my life."

"Why is it different with me?"

"Because..." *Just say it, damn it! No, once I say it, I can't take it back. It changes everything.*

Jaymi wrapped her arms around Shawn and softly began to sing one of her songs into her ear:

"You don't have to tell me what you're feeling
I can see it in your eyes
You don't have to say the words, my darling
Because your touch holds no disguise..."

Jaymi kissed her gently on the cheek and whispered into her ear. "There's no hurry." She caressed Shawn's face and looked her in the eye. "I thought I wasn't ready but I was wrong. When I told Nikki today that you and I were just friends, it hit me. I don't want to be just friends. It's more than that, and you know it. I have more than enough patience for the both of us. When you're ready, I'll be here. Because something tells me you're worth waiting for." She kissed her again, this time on the lips, and left her standing in the flickering light of the candles. Shawn noticed that when Jaymi closed her bedroom door, she didn't latch it.

## CHAPTER FOURTEEN

Despite her exhaustion, Shawn rose early and went to work in the barn. She was avoiding Jaymi, dreading the awkwardness that awaited them. After reeling in the living room for several long minutes, she had blown out the candles and taken the nerve-racking walk down the hall. She had carefully rested her head against Jaymi's door while *Should I or shouldn't I?* hammered away inside her head for what seemed like an eternity. She finally willed herself into the confines of her own room. As she tossed and turned all night, she wondered if Jaymi was doing the same.

She was so deep in her thoughts she didn't hear Alice enter the barn.

"Whoa, girl," said Alice. "It's a good thing the horses are already out, or you jumping up like that would've scared the bejesus outta them! Sorry, honey, I didn't mean to startle you."

"No, it's okay, Alice. I'm off in my own world today." She stabbed her pitchfork into a bale of hay and wiped her forehead with her arm.

"I can see that. Anything I can help you with, honey? I'm a good listener. Course, Pete always teases me and says I'm an even better talker."

Shawn smiled, touched by Alice's perceptiveness and concern. She reminded her of Aunt Betty. "Thanks, but I think I've got to work this out myself."

Alice studied Shawn's face a moment. "Let me give you some advice. Love doesn't come around that often. When you find it, you have to grab it by the horns and not let go. It's the strongest bond there is, but it doesn't take much to break it either."

"How'd you know?"

"That your troubles have to do with love? There's heartbreak written all over your face. I've seen it on Jaymi's face, too. Give her time, honey. If there's really something there, it'll happen. Can't force it, though. You'll know when the time is right."

"What's Jaymi said to you?"

"Nothing. She's had a rough time of it the past few years, and it's been an awful long time since I've seen her as happy as she's been since you got here. It's obvious you have something to do with it."

Shawn let her smile escape and, for once, didn't care that there was someone there to see it. After they spent a few minutes exchanging stories about the horses, she worked up the nerve to ask Alice a question she'd been dying to ask. "Alice, there's one other thing. I was thinking…"

"What, honey?"

"Well, I used to ride—it's been years—but I thought maybe sometime you'd let me ride Scout? She's such a sweet horse and she seems to trust me—"

"I think Scout would enjoy that. You can take her out today if you'd like. Which means I better start cracking the whip—you missed a spot over in that corner!" She pointed and gave Shawn a playful pat on the arm before disappearing out the door.

❖

Jaymi was on the phone when Shawn came in. "Well, if you see her or hear from her, will you please tell her to call me? We all really want her there tonight." Shawn returned Jaymi's hesitant smile as she rushed by and retreated into the shower.

After dressing, she steadied herself and made her way back to the kitchen. Jaymi was sitting at the table with her head in her hands, the phone's handset in front of her. Shawn prepared two cups of coffee and sat down with her.

"I can't find Nikki anywhere. What are we going to do? This is a really important gig, and I know I'm pissed at her, but I don't want her to quit. I just want her to grow up, you know?"

"Can't you just do songs she doesn't sing lead on?"

"But she sings more than half of them, so we don't have enough material. This is a three-hour gig."

Shawn sipped her coffee. "Covers?"

Jaymi shook her head. "No, not at this place. A couple covers is okay, but they want mostly original material." Suddenly her eyes brightened. "I have a better idea." She grinned devilishly and Shawn knew what she was thinking.

"Oh no. No—" Shawn leaned back and held up her hands.

"What do you mean no? You know most of our songs already. It'll be great. You can play the guitar parts Nikki usually plays, and we'll fill the gaps with your songs."

"Do you really think your fans are going to accept some unknown open-mike singer as Nikki Razer's replacement? Come on."

"No, not her replacement. We'll tell them Nikki's ill, just like we originally planned, and just say you're filling in temporarily. Think about it, it'll be a great opportunity for you to showcase your stuff and get your own gigs going. Before you know it, you'll have your own following, your own fans. We can help you while you're helping us."

Shawn's heart began racing with the idea, though she knew it would add fuel to the fire where Nikki was concerned. She made the mistake of looking into Jaymi's eyes, their expression pleading and hopeful.

Six hours later, after a grueling, crash-course cram and jam rehearsal, she was on the road with Passion Play, headed to Boston.

❖

A crowd of about two hundred made itself comfortable in the intimate forum. Rumors scurried from ear to ear as the band nervously warmed up their vocal cords and tuned up their instruments backstage. They were greeted with an enthusiastic roar when they took the stage. Jaymi, who normally would have been set up to Nikki's right, took center stage and dove in with one of her more upbeat tunes, followed by another song she'd cowritten with Brian. Shawn was in Jaymi's old spot, with a black music stand discreetly placed at the side of the stage to her right. She was afraid she'd need the lead sheets in front of her as a crutch, though once the band got rolling, she ignored them completely.

Seven songs into the set, Jaymi finally addressed the crowd. "As many of you may have heard, Nikki Razer was unable to perform with us tonight." The fans responded in collective disappointment. "But I want to take this opportunity to introduce you to an up-and-coming talent. She was kind enough to fill in at the last minute since, after all, the show must go on. Ladies and gentlemen, please give a warm welcome to Shawn Davies!" She waved her arm in Shawn's direction and Shawn stepped forward with a slight bow. Her heart leaped as most of the crowd applauded politely, but she turned to Jaymi in dismay when she heard some boos and a few chants of *We want Nikki, we want Nikki.*

Jaymi nodded encouragingly and shouted, "Show 'em, Shawn, let's show 'em!" Shawn burst into one of her best rockers and drowned out the skeptics. Without hesitation, she went right into a second song, and before it was over, she owned the crowd. Jaymi smiled at her as the jeers transformed into cheers.

They mixed up the next six songs of the set, each member taking turns singing lead before Jaymi turned the stage back over to Shawn for three songs. Jaymi ended the show with two of her own. They bounced off the stage higher than a kite, with the crowd chanting for an encore.

"What'll we do? We've already played everything." Kay looked elated, but panicked.

"We haven't played everything," Jaymi answered, grinning at Shawn.

Shawn smiled. "No, we haven't."

Kay and Brian gave them puzzled looks.

"You guys just come back out and sit with us onstage, okay?" Jaymi said. "You'll see." They shrugged and followed them out to a deafening noise. Jaymi and Shawn picked up their acoustic guitars and settled themselves next to each other on stools, flanked by Kay and Brian.

"Shawn and I wrote these songs simultaneously, without either of us knowing it," Jaymi explained to the audience. "Now, we'd like to share them with you as a duet."

❖

Despite the long drive home that awaited them, the band was too pumped to head their separate ways. They gathered at a restaurant not far from the club to celebrate and ward off their hunger. Raised glasses, mutual praise, gratitude to Shawn, and regret over Nikki's departure dominated their meal. As the waiter cleared the table and then brought desserts, Jaymi finally brought up the inevitable question.

"So do you guys think we should still try to talk Nikki into coming back?"

The group fell silent.

"Yes, I do," said Shawn. "Face it. Even though this crowd enjoyed this one show, they still want Nikki back. She's way too popular. And talented. Filling in tonight was awesome, guys. It was really an honor, but I can't fill her shoes."

"In my opinion," Kay said, "whether she comes back or not, I think Shawn's doing a great job filling in. The three of us would have to discuss it, Shawn, but I think we should at least consider asking you to join the band temporarily until we know for sure what's going on with Nikki. We have too many gigs lined up and we can't afford to cancel. With or without her, I think you make us even better. I really like what I heard tonight."

Shawn couldn't believe her ears.

"But we don't know if she's coming back," said Brian. "She sure didn't sound like it when she left yesterday. And you all know how proud she can be. It's not like she can't make it without us if that's what she wants. She's got a big enough fan base of her own."

Shawn turned to Jaymi. "I don't know if it's a good idea," she said, knowing Jaymi would be thinking similarly about whether a relationship would cause problems if they were in the same band. Flashes of intergroup turmoil caused by romances between members in pop groups throughout the years bombarded her.

Jaymi smiled at her, apparently taking the hint. "I think it's something we need to discuss. I don't think we should make any rash decisions. Shawn has her own career goals and I don't want to sidetrack her." She hesitated for a moment. "And Shawn and I have some personal issues to work through, too. I don't want the band's interests to sidetrack us from that."

Their companions' eyes narrowed with questions.

"Okay, I'll bite," said Kay. "So, is there something going on between you two?"

Shawn stared at her plate, not daring to answer.

"Well," Jaymi said, "we're not quite sure where it's heading yet, but—"

"Aha!" Brian tipped back in his chair and pointed at his cousin. "I knew it. I knew you guys had a thing for each other." He smiled smugly, crossing his arms and nodding in approval.

"Okay, okay—you're right, okay? But please, keep it to yourselves for now, all right?" said Jaymi. "If word gets out to Nikki, or our fans, she'll really blow, and she'll think I devised some evil plan to get her out of the band so I could conveniently replace her with a love interest." They all had a good laugh and agreed to keep quiet. "And that's another reason why I think Shawn's stint with the band needs to be temporary," she added.

"Yeah, you're right," Kay agreed. "Let's not forget about The Rule."

Shawn cocked her head to one side and looked at Kay, confused. "What's The Rule?"

"Our no-office-romances rule. We made a pact when we started the group that we weren't allowed to date each other. Because we knew if we were seriously in this thing for the long haul, we needed to keep that boundary, or else it would cause problems within the band. It works, and fortunately, we all see each other only as friends anyway."

Jaymi looked at Shawn apologetically. "I'm sorry, Shawn."

"No, Jaymi, it's okay, really. I agree completely. I appreciate you guys giving me the opportunity to play with you, and I'll give it my all if you need me to keep filling in. But Jaymi's right. I have my own plans to make it as a solo artist."

They paid the check and headed out for the hour-long drive.

Brian and Kay waved from the van and took the lead as Shawn climbed into the driver's side of Jaymi's truck. Jaymi assured her she would try to stay awake for the ride this time—she was too wound up from the show to sleep. Shawn squinted against a car's brights in the rearview mirror, irritated that they were so close. She flipped the rearview to deflect the reflection and sped up. The car fell away, but she was uneasy until it finally turned a corner. The feeling stayed with her long after the drive ended.

# CHAPTER FIFTEEN

Welcome to Live Chat with Passion Play! Chat live with members of the local band Passion Play! Here's your chance to get to know Jaymi, Nikki, Kay, and Brian!

**Chatline:** I would like to know who founded the group and where you guys got your start.

**Jaymi:** Nikki and I formed the group when we were in college together. We were both music majors and Nikki knew Kay through a friend and we asked her to join. Brian is my cousin. We asked him if he wanted to play with us after we had auditioned several drummers who didn't quite fit our style.

**Brian:** Yeah, I joined by default! Good thing I like my cousin. It's been fun and a great opportunity.

**Chatline:** Liz here. I caught your show at Sparky's a few weeks ago and loved it! My question is for Brian. What's it like to be the only non-gay member of the band? And, by the way…are you single?

**Brian:** Aw, see, Jaymi? I do have my own fans! Happy to meet you Liz! It doesn't bother me I'm the odd one in the group (those who know me would say I'm the odd one anyway, LOL!). It does benefit me in that I can date the straight women that come to the shows. So, yes, I am single. Wanna send me a pic?

**Kay:** Hey, we're not running a dating service here!

**Jaymi:** Next question, please!

**Chatline:** I love all you guys! I want to thank you for being out—it's really inspiring to other gay women like me to have you as role models and helping our cause. You rock!—LR

**Jaymi:** Thank you, LR, that's nice to hear. We didn't set out to be role models or activists or anything. We've just always believed it would be easier to be open and honest about it.

**Kay:** The more of us who live openly, the more we can open people's minds and hearts to see we're all human and that it's really no big deal. We didn't see any point in being something we're not. We're proud of who we are.

**Chatline:** Jaymi, it sounds like you're the leader of the group. Are there ever any conflicts between you guys?—Jo

**Jaymi:** Hi, Jo. Just like any job, yes, there are times we can drive each other crazy. But we're pretty tight. You have to be when you spend so much time together. It's like having a second family, so yes, sometimes there's some tension and some compromises. Luckily, we always manage to work through them and ultimately put the band first.

**Chatline:** I heard a rumor that there was a big fight and you kicked Nikki out of the group. Is that true? Is that why she wasn't at the show last night?

Jaymi looked sharply at her bandmates. "Who knows about that?" Brian held up his hands. "Got me. I haven't said anything." "Neither have I," said Kay. "Maybe Nikki's been talking."

**Chatline:** I noticed Nikki hasn't participated in the chat, either, which makes me think maybe the rumor is true.

**Kay:** Don't believe everything you hear. Nikki was unavailable today, unfortunately, and we apologize for that. But there is no truth to rumors that she was kicked out of the band.

**Chatline:** Jaymi I saw u smile at me when u sing

**Jaymi:** I do have a tendency to smile onstage—I love what I do!

**Chatline:** No I mean u looked right at ME and smiled last night like u were singing that song to ME.

Jaymi shot a nervous glance at her cousin and shrugged. "I have no idea what this person's talking about."

**Brian:** Jaymi sings to everyone in the audience—she does have that gift of connecting with them.

**Jaymi:** Thank you, Brian. Anyone want to know who our biggest influences are? There're too many to list all of them, but a few of my favorites are Melissa Etheridge, Pat Benatar, Indigo Girls, Shawn Colvin, and Mary Chapin Carpenter. I also listen to some classical sometimes to relax.

**Chatline:** Jaymi I'm your biggest fan and I would love 2 meet u do u ever do any meet and greets and I know it was ME u were looking at

"Just ignore it, Jaymi." Kay grimaced. "She sounds a little obsessed and you don't want to encourage her."

**Jaymi:** Our website lists the dates of all our shows and meet-and-greets. We also run ads in the *Happenings Magazine* insert in the newspaper.

**Chatline:** I go to all ur shows would u play at my birthday party next Saturday

**Kay:** Sorry. Anyone else out there with a question?

**Chatline:** Kay, I play bass and I think you're one of the best female bass players there is! Any advice for me as a woman trying to make it in this male-dominated music world?

**Chatline:** How about Friday nite Jaymi? I could change my party to Friday I don't live far from U

Kay answered her bass player's question while Jaymi and Brian gawked at the screen. "What is with this person?" Jaymi said. "And how does she…she? Or he? How does this person know where I live?"

"Yeah, and can't she get the hint already and quit bugging you?" said Brian.

Kay peered at the laptop again. "Jaymi, that weirdo is still bugging you about her damn party. How do we get rid of her?"

**Jaymi:** I'm sorry, but the band doesn't do private parties.

**Chatline:** Listen, whoever you are, quit hogging the chat! How old were all of you when you started learning to play?—Billie

**Kay:** We do need to limit everybody to one or two questions so it's fair. So, please, sign off so others can participate in the chat. Getting to Billie's question, I was nine when I started piano lessons and twelve when I picked up guitar and bass. I also took flute lessons in grade school. I grew up in a musical family. My mom sang and played piano. My father played guitar and banjo, and my brothers and sisters all played something. So I was lucky. It was like I grew up in a band.

**Jaymi:** I think I was four when I started messing around on my parents' upright piano. I started guitar lessons when I was eight. As far as Nikki goes, she's always saying she started singing in the womb! And besides guitar and piano lessons as a kid, most people don't know she dabbled with the saxophone when she was younger, too. I think Brian was ten when he started drum lessons, right?

**Brian:** Eleven, actually.

**Chatline:** Nadine here. I'd like to know when your next album is coming out?

**Chatline:** Ur going to be sorry for blowing me off Jaymi I love u I'm ur biggest fan

There were three more threatening messages before the exasperated panel managed to end the hour-long session and sign off.

"Well, that went well," said Brian sarcastically, as he began attempts to trace the source of the obsessive fan so he could set up a block.

"It was a friggin' disaster." Jaymi sighed. "What is with that lunatic? Saying she loves me? Being rude to the other people writing in? And it wasn't exactly fun dodging the questions about Nikki, either."

"Yeah, but at least we anticipated some questions about Nikki's absence," said Brian.

A blast of frigid air blew in as Shawn entered after her morning's work in the stables. "Is it over? How'd it go?" she asked as she stamped snow off her boots and then removed them.

"Oh, just lovely," Kay replied, rolling her eyes. "Seems our friend Jaymi here has made quite an impression on one particularly devoted fan."

"What're you talking about?"

They bombarded Shawn with accounts of the crazed fan with the upcoming birthday.

"And the worst thing is," added Jaymi, who began fixing Shawn a cup of hot chocolate, "this person says she doesn't live far from me."

Shawn said, "Oh my God—you think it has anything to do with that truck that followed us that night?"

"What truck?" asked Brian.

Jaymi and Shawn filled them in.

"You might want to talk to Alice and ask her to keep an eye out for any strange vehicles coming into her driveway," Brian said.

"Yeah, and maybe add a few more locks to your doors," added Kay.

"Oh, come on, are you serious?" Jaymi wanted to seem calm but had to admit she was getting nervous.

Shawn blew on her cocoa and said, "This lunatic could be stalking you, Jaymi. And I wouldn't be much of a bodyguard." She smiled slyly and added, "Although I wouldn't mind guarding your body." Her flirtation wasn't missed by Kay and Brian, who grinned, though they clearly resisted the temptation to tease them.

"All right, all right." Jaymi curled up in her chair. "I'll go talk to Alice and Pete right now."

Later that evening, Jaymi found herself looking out the windows repeatedly before Shawn finally wedged a chair beneath the entrance door's knob and slipped a broom through the handles of the french doors to help her feel safer. She even went so far as to tuck her into bed.

"Shawn?" she asked, grabbing Shawn's arm before she could get up from the side of the bed.

"Yeah?"

"Stay with me tonight…please?"

"Are you sure?"

She smiled and playfully squeezed Shawn's biceps. "Ooh, feel those muscles. See? You *could* be my bodyguard. Working in the barn has really done wonders for me."

"For you? You mean for me—"

"Oh no. I mean it's done wonders for me…I get to check out those arms, all cut and muscular. And to think how scrawny and undernourished you were when you got here."

Shawn began flexing her arms and striking various bodybuilder poses. "Ooh, yeah, me strong! I protect you, Ms. Jaymi the Rock Star. Mmm, I be your personal bodyguard, yes?"

"Come here, you nut." Jaymi pulled her onto the bed as they had a good laugh.

Shawn began to tickle her and she shrieked. They wrestled for several minutes before Jaymi managed to flip Shawn over and straddle her.

"Now whatcha gonna do, Muscles?" Jaymi teased, bending over to within inches of Shawn's face. Shawn stretched up and gave her a peck on the lips. Jaymi whispered, "Is that all you got?"

Shawn grinned and pulled Jaymi down onto her. She locked her into a long, sensuous kiss that lasted well into the night, until they fell asleep in each other's arms.

# Chapter Sixteen

Shawn scurried into work with two minutes to spare and went right to work. A month into the job, she was settling in and getting to know a few coworkers well enough to make friendly conversation. Stacy, who usually worked nearby, made a point to approach Shawn as they began their routine that day.

"Look out for the dragon lady today," Stacy warned, keeping her voice to a near whisper. "She's in rare form. She chewed my head off just because I forgot to punch out Friday, and then she went off on Andy about something, too."

"Really? She's so weird. Was she pissed I called in sick Friday?"

"Pissed is not the word. I don't know why, we had a pretty slow day. You feeling better, by the way?"

"Yeah, I'm fine."

"Ms. Davies," Karla bellowed from the end of the hall. "In my office. *Now.*"

She flashed a look of dread at Stacy, who returned it with a look of sympathy and mouthed, "Good luck."

Shawn didn't have to be told to close the door and did so automatically. Karla paced behind her desk for a moment before bracing herself on the back of her chair.

"What have I told you about coming in at the last minute?" she growled through clenched teeth.

"I wasn't late," Shawn said confidently. "I know I punched in on time—five fifty-eight, you can check it—"

"Yes, I can see that, but tell me, did you go to your locker *before* or *after* you clocked in?"

"Right after, but I was still on the floor on time—"

"You think this company's paying you to put your shit in your locker?"

"All I did was hang up my coat. Everybody does it, I didn't think—" *My God, Stacy wasn't kidding.*

"Ah," Karla said, straightening up and squeezing her chin between her thumb and forefinger, "you didn't think. Why doesn't that surprise me? And how are you feeling today?"

Flashbacks of confrontations with her father began pummeling her. She fought them off but was having a difficult time fighting off her temper, which was going to blow soon if this got any worse.

"Fine."

"Of course you're fine," Karla sneered, leaning forward and squinting at her. "You were fine enough to go to Boston Saturday night, weren't you?"

"What gives you the right…?" Shawn yelped, then calmed herself down enough to lower her voice. "Do you do this to everybody? You spy on them outside work? You have no right—"

"You have no right to lie to me. You have one more chance, Davies. I've written you up for this." She handed Shawn a paper from her desk and plucked a pen from her shirt pocket.

"For what? I'm not allowed to be sick? And you know damn well I wasn't late today."

"Don't give me any grief. You weren't sick Friday and you know it. Now sign here, before I write you up for your piss-poor attitude, too."

Shawn pressed her lips together tightly, knowing that the next thing out of her mouth would easily get her fired. She signed her name, resisting the urge to write *Fuck you, I quit* in giant letters across it. Karla snatched the paper from her hand, swiveled to her right to make a photocopy, which she then handed to Shawn—so that she would remember their conversation, she explained—and dismissed her.

Shawn fumed the rest of the day and gave the horses an earful out of Jaymi's Stratocaster when she got home, while chugging down a few beers in the process. It took Jaymi four attempts to get her attention when she arrived home from work. The sun had gone down while Shawn had been wailing away on the guitar and the room was growing dark. Shawn stumbled to the amp and snapped off its power.

She wrangled off the guitar, catching the strap once across her face as she lifted it over her head, and had difficulty setting the guitar into its stand properly, which only made her angrier. She finally managed to secure the instrument, cursing at it the whole time.

"Shawn?" Jaymi looked around at the empty bottles and tried to take her by the hand and calm her down, but Shawn yanked out of her grasp.

"Leave me alone."

"What's going on?"

"She just keeps pushing and pushing, just like...my fucking *father!*" she yelled. "She's gotta be an asshole—"

"Who?"

"Goddamn boss. What do I have to be, perfect? I can't be perfect, don't they know that?" She paced several steps, fists at her sides, teeth clenched.

Jaymi made her way to her Stratocaster. She removed it from the stand and returned it to its case, then leaned it upright in its place among her others against the wall.

Upon seeing the fear in Jaymi's eyes and her protective response to care for the guitar, Shawn began to panic. "Oh no, Jaymi, I'm sorry. I didn't mean to take it out on your Strat...I'm sorry—"

Jaymi stood firmly, hands on her hips. "You know what, Shawn? If you're going to drink, I'd prefer you not play my instruments and that you stay away from my equipment. Not to mention that I could hear you playing from halfway down the driveway—Alice isn't going to put up with you playing that loud." There was little sympathy in her tone, and for the first time, Shawn realized that despite Jaymi's easygoing personality, she was still human and capable of getting angry.

Shawn dropped her head in shame and left the room. She emerged from her bedroom in her coat and headed for the door.

"Where are you going?"

Shawn shook her head and put her hand on the doorknob. "I can tell you don't want to be around me right now."

Jaymi hustled to the door and stopped her from opening it. "I didn't say that. And you're in no condition to drive—"

"Maybe I need a walk to cool off. You want my keys or don't you trust me?" She didn't wait for an answer as she moved around Jaymi to leave. The door clicked softly closed behind her.

❖

An hour later, Shawn came back to the apartment, looking worn out and as though she'd been crying her heart out. Jaymi went to her instantly.

"Shawn, are you all right? Why don't you just tell me what happened? Come on, take your coat off and sit down." Jaymi coaxed her to the couch, fixed them each a cup of tea, and Shawn recounted her encounter with Karla.

"I don't understand why she has such a problem with me. Why's she gotta be so mean?"

Jaymi chose to redirect the conversation. "Shawn, do you always use alcohol to deal with your anger?"

Shawn crossed her arms over her chest. "Are you trying to say I have a drinking problem? Because I don't—"

"No, Shawn, that's not what I'm saying at all. I'm just saying… you have a lot of anger toward Karla, and your father. And drinking isn't the best way to deal with anger, it only makes it worse."

Shawn stared at her tea on the coffee table and stirred it hypnotically. The tea bag's string wound itself around the spoon, and she reversed the spoon's direction to unwind it. She continued this pattern as she began to speak, her voice distant. "When I was a kid, if he pissed me off, I'd lock myself in my room and play my guitar as loud as I could stand it. Used to piss him off even more, and I'd just ignore him and turn it up louder. He threatened to take it away, so I rigged up a lock on my closet so no one could get into it but me, and I kept my guitars and amp in there." She gazed across the room as sadness fell across her face. "If I couldn't play, I thought I'd die. Sometimes I wanted to die. I used to think he wished I would."

"Oh God, Shawn, that's awful." Jaymi put an arm around her, anticipating tears, but there weren't any. Her face was hard and her eyes were cold. After a few minutes of silence, Jaymi touched a hand to Shawn's cheek and turned her face toward her.

Jaymi locked eyes with her and spoke deliberately. "I am so glad you're here with me, and I'm glad you locked up your guitars and kept on playing."

And with those sweet, gentle words, the tears began to flow. "Why can't he be proud of me?" she sobbed. "Why can't he forgive me? I didn't want Mom to die. It wasn't my fault..."

"Of course it wasn't your fault."

Shawn folded herself into Jaymi's arms. "I miss her...I even miss my dad, but he hates me. I don't even exist to him anymore. How can he do that? I'm his only child."

"I don't know, sweetie, I don't know. But you know what? You need to start being proud of yourself. Despite the way your father's treated you, you need to know that you are something special. You're an amazing person, Shawn, you just don't know it yet."

Jaymi's eyes moistened as she thought of her own mother. They lay back on the couch as she continued to comfort Shawn, combing her fingers through her hair and softly expressing her empathy. Shawn squirmed until she had worked her cheek up against Jaymi's neck. She rubbed her face into Jaymi's shoulder, drying her eyes on her sweater.

"I think you're amazing, too, Jaymi," she whispered. She gently pressed her lips to Jaymi's neck and placed featherlight kisses along the length of it. Jaymi gasped and her body quivered as Shawn's lips traveled over her neck and up to her ear and then found their way to her mouth.

Shawn climbed on top of her, kissing her firmly as she pressed herself against Jaymi's body. Their hips rocked up and down, their lips still passionately tasting each other. Shawn yanked out Jaymi's shirttail and then her hand made its way underneath to her breast. Jaymi felt her nipple harden under Shawn's hand. Then Shawn reached down with her other hand and pressed her palm between Jaymi's legs before she began to work the button on her pants.

The phone rang.

They ignored it. Jaymi peeled off Shawn's pocket T-shirt and they rejoined lips. The phone was still ringing. Shawn unzipped Jaymi's pants. The ringing stopped. Jaymi yanked off her sweater and Shawn began to unbutton her shirt.

The phone rang again.

Jaymi separated her lips from Shawn's and breathlessly said, "I should answer that."

"No, don't. They can leave a message." Shawn leaned in to kiss her again, but Jaymi braced her hand to Shawn's shoulder and stopped her.

"It might be important," she said. "It could be my dad. Or Nikki."

"Oh, all right. I'll get it." Shawn stumbled reluctantly across the room. "Hello…hello?" Shawn shrugged. "They hung up. Some asshole with the wrong number has lousy timing." She gazed lovingly at Jaymi and took two steps toward her when the phone rang again.

"God damn it!" She grabbed the receiver. "Hello? I know somebody's there—I can hear you breathing. Who is this?"

"They hung up again?"

"Yes. That's it—I'm not answering it again." She ran back to the couch and hopped on top of Jaymi. "Now, where were we?" She leaned down to kiss her, but Jaymi scooted herself up into a seated position. "Hey, what're you doing?"

"You're drunk, Shawn."

"Nah. Well, maybe just a little." She giggled.

"You're drunk, you're upset, you're vulnerable. I am so turned on right now, but I'm not going to take advantage of that. I care about you too much."

"I don't feel like you're taking advantage of me. Really. It's fine."

"But I do." Jaymi knew it was the right thing to do, even though every nerve ending in her body was screaming in protest. Her clit was throbbing. She felt the fabric of her bra straining from the pressure of her swollen nipples. She wanted Shawn's lips and tongue on her everywhere. She wanted to taste and feel every inch of Shawn's body. *God, give me strength.* "I don't want the first time we make love to be under these circumstances."

Shawn fell back into the corner of the couch. She found her T-shirt and stretched it over her body, as though to protect herself from Jaymi's rejection. The hurt in Shawn's eyes tugged at her heart and threatened Jaymi's resolve. But she also knew it was a clear indication of Shawn's vulnerable state. "So if the phone hadn't interrupted us you wouldn't have stopped me?"

"Maybe. Maybe not. But then I might have regretted letting things go further." The phone rang. "Ah shit. I'll get it this time." Jaymi zipped up her pants before she grabbed for the phone. "Hello?"

"Jaymi. It *is* you, isn't it?" The woman's hesitant deep voice was barely audible.

"Who's this?" No answer. Jaymi flicked on the wall switch to the kitchen light and looked at Shawn, puzzled. "Hello? Who is this?"

"Why won't you meet with me, Jaymi? For my birthday? I told you, I'm your biggest fan."

Jaymi was gripped with horror and she hung up.

"What's wrong?"

"It's that nut from the chat. But how did she get my number?" Jaymi turned around to return the handset to its cradle. She picked up a sheet of paper from the bar. "Oh my God...what's this?" she asked, holding it up and studying it.

"That's the damn write-up Karla gave me today."

"Oh my God."

Shawn walked over. "Yeah, I know, it's bullshit."

"No, it's your boss. That's who's harassing me."

"What? How can you tell?"

"I just put the pieces together—your boss bugging you to meet me, coming up to you in the bar, knowing you were in Boston Saturday night. It all fits. She's been stalking me and you just got caught in the crossfire."

# CHAPTER SEVENTEEN

The lights were still dim on energy-saver mode when Shawn entered the warehouse the next morning at 5:15. She knew that, without fail, Karla arrived at 5:00 sharp every day. She bypassed the lockers, knowing she wouldn't be removing her coat. She wouldn't be punching in today at all.

She turned down a short hall and saw that Karla's office light was on and the door was ajar. She took a deep breath and hoped she hadn't made a mistake in choosing to confront her alone. She hadn't told Jaymi about her plan. But when Jaymi refused to call the police to report the harassment, Shawn knew what she had to do. There was no way she was about to let Karla off the hook.

Shawn wasn't afraid of her, even though Karla had four inches on her and outweighed her by at least fifty pounds. *Hell, if I can fight off that Brinkman asshole, I can handle this bitch.* She pushed the door open farther and stepped in, leaving it wide open. Karla's chair bounced up and back as she jerked upright at the sight of her unexpected visitor.

"Shawn—what the hell? What are you doing here?"

"The jig's up, Karla. The phone calls last night. The threats online—"

Karla's face hardened slightly. "I don't know what you're talking about."

Shawn leaned forward and slammed her palms onto the metal desk. The bang echoed throughout the building. "The hell you don't. Are you also going to tell me that's not your black truck outside that we've seen following us after gigs?"

"How do you know that's mine?"

"It's the only car in the fucking parking lot, Karla. We're the only ones here."

Shawn straightened up and braced for retaliation, but Karla just sat there. Her cheeks began to redden, and then to Shawn's surprise, she pulled off her glasses, covered her face with both hands, and began to cry.

Shawn hadn't anticipated this reaction and she had no clue what to do. She glanced around for tissues, found none, then quickly trotted to the ladies room across the hall and returned with a wad of toilet paper.

Karla collected herself and thanked her as she violently blew her nose.

"I don't know what to do," she finally said through sniffles. She looked up at Shawn, her black eyes bewildered and pleading. "I've been lying to my husband. Every time I go see her play, he thinks I'm out with my friends, playing cards or at the movies or something. We got married right out of high school, but there's always been something missing. I've questioned myself before, but I was scared to admit it. I love my husband and I don't want to hurt him, so I managed to bury my feelings. But I haven't been able to do that with Jaymi. I think about her all the time."

"Karla, what're you saying? You think you're gay?"

"Shh!" Suddenly Karla sprang from her seat, causing Shawn to jump back, but she wasn't headed for Shawn. She rushed past her and slammed her office door shut. She grabbed Shawn's coat sleeve and yanked her down into a chair and sat beside her. "I think so, but how do I know for sure? I'm so confused. How did you know?" Her voice was panicked now, and Shawn actually pitied the frantic woman next to her.

"You really want to get into that now? Here?"

Karla gazed across the room and said dreamily, "I think she's beautiful, don't you? See? Why would I think that? I know it's no big deal for a woman to think another woman is attractive, but it's different with her. I want to look at her. I want to be near her. I even think about what it would be like to kiss her, and then I get all, well, you know." Karla blushed and took a moment to collect herself. "If that's what it's like to be gay, then I must be gay, right?"

"If I say yes, are you going to be pissed and look for an excuse to write me up again?"

"I'll tear that up, okay? You're right, I shouldn't have done that."

Karla stood and checked the clock. She cracked her door open and looked down the hall. After securing the door again, she returned to the seat by Shawn. "Just help me, please. Tell me the truth. I have no one else to talk to about this. Do you think I'm gay?"

Shawn sighed and rubbed her tired eyes. "It sounds like it to me. And I think you're jealous of me and Jaymi, and since you have a crush on her, that's why you don't like me." She again braced herself for the backlash.

Karla remained silent, her body rising and falling with each deep, shuddering breath. She slowly shook her head and spoke softly. "My gosh, you're right. That's what it is. A crush." Karla's voice faltered and her eyes grew dark as she stood up and began to pace. "Wait a minute—I thought you and Jaymi were just roommates. Are you more than that?"

*Oh shit...what are we? What do I tell her? It's really none of her business. But if I tell her we're together, maybe she'll stop harassing Jaymi. But what if it pisses her off even more and it gets worse?*

"Well?"

"Uh, yeah. We're more than just friends," Shawn finally blurted. *There, at least that isn't a complete lie.*

"Hmm." Karla lumbered behind her desk and slumped into her chair. "I should've known. It's not like I had a chance with her anyway." In the distance, Shawn heard her coworkers shuffling into the building. Karla leaned forward and whispered, "Do you still think I could meet her someday? I really am a fan, you know."

Shawn cocked her head and studied her. "I don't know, Karla. You really freaked her out."

"I won't bother you guys anymore. I promise. And I won't give you a hard time at work anymore, either. Really, I just want to meet her. You never know, maybe we could all be friends." Her eyebrows shot up like a child hopeful of acceptance by peers at a new school.

"Okay, okay. I won't make any promises, but I'll ask her, okay?"

"Yeah, right. Okay." The sound of footsteps outside the office prompted Karla to force her shoulders back and straighten her posture. Raising her voice slightly into her supervisory tone, she said, "Now you better go get punched in, Ms. Davies." She smiled a crooked smile and winked as Shawn nodded and let herself out.

Shawn went to work feeling completely baffled. On the one hand, she was relieved to know that it was Karla who had been following them, rather than someone tied to Brinkman. On the other hand, she wasn't about to fully trust Karla, either. If she was gay, would she become more obsessed with Jaymi? Would she continue to take out her frustration and jealousy on Shawn, especially now that she knew they were more than friends?

Her instincts were to quit and find another job. She needed to protect Jaymi. *That would be just like you, wouldn't it? Give up at the first sign of trouble. Or the next time she pisses you off, you'll lose your temper and get yourself fired again.*

Would she be letting Jaymi down if she didn't at least finish out the assignment? The employment agency might not give her another chance. She'd lose another reference, and who knew how long she'd be out of work. Then what? *Jaymi will think all that talk of changing my ways was bullshit. Then she'll really think I'm using her.*

*Wait. I need to stick this out for me, not for Jaymi. Whoa. Where did that come from?*

Shawn made up her mind. *Be a grown-up for once and deal with it. If Karla bothers Jaymi again, I'll just report it to the agency. It'll be her job on the line, not mine. I'm taking control of my life if it kills me.*

❖

Jaymi cringed as she approached her apartment and noticed that once again, Shawn was home but all the lights were off inside. *Great,* she thought, *she probably had it out with Karla and she's in there drunk and jamming on my guitar again.* She made her way up the stairs, grateful that at least if she was playing, the volume was at a more reasonable level. She slipped her key into the lock and pushed her way inside.

Her jaw dropped as she looked around the room in wonder. Scattered around the apartment were tons of lit candles. The mellow acoustic guitar sounds of Ed Gerhard were playing from the stereo. The table was set, complete with two glasses of wine and a bouquet of flowers in the center. An enticing aroma wafted from the oven, and its heat warmed the space.

Just as Jaymi's senses had completed absorbing her surroundings, Shawn appeared from the hallway, dressed in black khakis and a tan suede vest over a crisp white collared shirt. It was an outfit Jaymi had seen her wear for performances. And she looked damn good in it.

"What's all this?" she asked.

"Well…" Shawn made her way around the bar and helped Jaymi off with her coat. "I got to thinking that we've never had a real date. And today I was asked if we were more than just roommates, and I didn't really know how to answer." She hung up the coat, slipped on oven mitts, and pulled a casserole dish out of the oven. "Hope you like chicken pot pie. Homemade, of course. My mother's recipe."

Jaymi, who hadn't been able to wipe the smile from her face since entering, made herself comfortable at the table. "Who's asking about us?"

"Karla. Who, by the way, confirmed everything—the chat, the phone calls, *and* she's the one who's been following us. Don't worry, though. She promised she'll leave you alone—"

"You confronted her? Shawn, I asked you not to do that."

"It's okay, really. I wasn't going to let her get away with harassing you like that. Besides, turns out she's got this huge crush on you, and now she's questioning if she's gay. It was a wicked bizarre morning. But I think she'll stop bugging both of us now. She even tore up that warning she gave me."

"I had a feeling it might be something like that. Well, good. I hope that's the end of that nonsense."

Jaymi was initially a bit upset that Shawn went against her wishes, but it felt good to know Shawn cared enough to go to bat for her. She wouldn't have had the guts—she hated confrontation. *Look how well that's worked out for you. Hold in your anger until it boils over, like you did with Nikki.* Jaymi felt a new sense of pride in Shawn.

"Mmm, that smells so good."

"Wait'll you taste it," Shawn said as she dished out two servings. "She still wants to meet you, though. I told her I wasn't sure if you'd be comfortable with that, but that I'd ask."

Jaymi shrugged. "I don't know. I have to think about it. If so, it would have to be in a public place. Like maybe at New Horizons, in the café. Actually, scratch that. It would have to be a place I never go regularly and don't care if I ever go back. You know how I am about my privacy. It's bad enough she found out where I live. Although now I understand how she got our phone number, obviously. I still don't fully trust her after the stunts she's pulled. And I want you to come with me."

"Oh yeah, definitely. I wasn't thinking you'd meet her alone." Shawn placed the food on the table, sat down, and unfolded a napkin onto her lap.

Jaymi dug into her pie. "This is delicious. You really made this from scratch?"

"All except the crust. I cheated this time and bought the dough. But if I have the time, I can make that from scratch, too. Glad you like it."

"I could get used to coming home to this."

Shawn blushed slightly and stabbed at her meal. They ate in relative silence, pausing between bites to share other tidbits about their day. After they finished, Shawn's face suddenly released a beaming smile.

"What?"

Shawn wiped her lips with her napkin. "I've got good news and bad news."

"Okay…Which do I get to hear first?"

"Actually, the bad news, as far as I'm concerned—and I hope you agree—isn't really bad news at all."

"Shawn, what are you talking about?"

"You've got your lead singer back."

"Nikki's coming back? But how?"

"I talked her into it. Well, I may have told just one little lie, but I had to do it. It was the only way I could convince her."

"All right, spill it. What happened? How'd you find her?"

"Hey, I didn't survive the streets of LA on my looks alone."

Jaymi smiled and raised her eyebrows. "You could've fooled me. Now come on, tell me what happened."

"Actually, it was all luck. After work, I ran into Randi at the supermarket. Nikki's hiding out at her house. Randi invited me over for a drink, and I figured I'd check out the situation."

Stung by jealousy, Jaymi felt her ears grow warm. Randi's attraction to Shawn had been obvious, and Randi's reputation for seduction made Jaymi feel terribly insecure. She tried to shake the old feelings aside and listen to Shawn's story.

"Nikki was pissed when she saw me come in. I didn't stay long enough to have a drink, by the way. I went right up to Nikki and told her the band was talking about breaking up if she didn't come back."

"But that's not true."

"No, but she doesn't know that. So I exaggerated a little. You should've seen her—she went ballistic that you were giving up. She said you're the heart and soul of the band, and she wasn't about to let you throw away your future because she had been so selfish and stupid. She went on and on about how wrong she was to think she could make it alone, and how much she missed all you guys already. She was close to tears."

Jaymi sat quietly for a few moments. "Wow. Maybe she's finally beginning to grow up. So she's definitely coming back?"

"She'll be at your next rehearsal."

Jaymi shook her head in wonder, grinning at Shawn in appreciation. "You really know how to put that charm to work when you want to, don't you? I mean, nobody gets to Nikki like that. Not even me, and I've known her longer than anybody."

"What can I say? Gotta make the most of what skills I have."

"You're amazing." She remained seated and began to gather their dishes, but then stopped. "Wait a minute, you said there was bad news—but *good* bad news…"

"Yeah, well, if Nikki's coming back, that means you won't need me to fill in anymore."

Jaymi frowned. "Is that really what it took to get Nikki to come back? She said you have to quit?"

Shawn shook her head. "Uh-uh. No. It's your no-office-romance rule, remember?"

"So…?"

"So if I'm out of the band, there can't be any objections to you and me dating, right?" Shawn gathered their plates and took them to the sink, as though she needed to put physical distance between herself and the answer.

Jaymi was taken aback. This should be a good thing, the right thing. But she enjoyed being onstage with Shawn. They performed well together. She got along great with Kay and Brian. There were no big egos to deal with. Sure, it meant they could spend more time together. But with Shawn out of the group, their lives would go on separate paths.

What if Shawn joined Passion Play permanently? It was a smart career move for both of them. Would their romance survive?

Jaymi's heart and dreams were both at stake here. *And what about Shawn's heart and dreams? My career is already starting to take off. What if hers goes nowhere? Will she be content to stay behind while I'm out on tour? Is she even thinking that far ahead? How fair is it to expect that of her? What if she gives up on us like Peach did and winds up in bed with someone else?* Her inner voice was mocking her. *The rule was your idea in the first place, you bonehead.* It made sense at the time. It was even kind of a joke, since they all knew their relationships with each other would never be more than platonic.

Great. She finally felt safe enough to take things to the next level with Shawn, and now she was questioning her judgment. There were huge risks whether Shawn was in the band or not. She knew she had to consider the possible consequences not only for herself and Shawn, but for Nikki, Kay, and Brian, as well.

She looked mournfully at Shawn, who was washing the dishes, and completely oblivious to the dilemma spinning through Jaymi's mind. She dried her hands and turned around with a playful glint in her eye. Jaymi promptly smiled, hoping Shawn hadn't caught any sign of her turmoil.

"I just want to make one thing clear. I didn't do all this tonight to seduce you," Shawn said.

Jaymi quirked an eyebrow. "I'm not sure if I should be flattered or insulted by that. It's the work uniform, isn't it? I know it's not my best look—"

"I think you look damn sexy in it," Shawn blurted, and her slight blush didn't prevent her from continuing. "It drives me crazy every time you come home from work."

"Are you serious? This?"

Shawn snaked her arms around Jaymi's waist and pulled her close. "If I had a dime for every time I couldn't keep my eyes off you, I would've been a millionaire a long time ago."

*Oh, Shawn. Don't do this. Don't keep making it so easy to fall for you.* Before she could stop herself, she asked, "Shawn, are you saying—?"

"Since the first time I saw you." The phone rang. They both groaned, then laughed, simultaneously. "If that's Karla, she's dead meat."

Jaymi snatched up the phone. "Hey, Sara. What's up?...No way! That's awesome! She must be ecstatic...Yeah, Saturday works, there are no gigs this weekend...Yeah, no problem, talk to you tomorrow... 'Bye." She hung up and sprang into a dance around the kitchen.

"So, you want to let me in on the celebration or what?" asked Shawn, as she watched Jaymi's happy dance.

"They're publishing Devin's book! She got the call today."

"Wow, that's great."

"We're throwing her a surprise party here on Saturday."

Shawn's smile suddenly disappeared. "Saturday, huh?"

"Yeah. What's wrong?"

Shawn shook her head and shrugged. "Nothing."

Jaymi playfully grabbed her sleeve and led her into the living room and onto the sofa. "Now, don't give me that. Tell me."

"I was thinking of taking you out to a movie or something, depending on how things went tonight."

"Oh, really? Tell you what, then, I'll be your date for the party, and we'll catch a movie on another night." Jaymi went serious again. "Shawn, were you just trying to tell me that you've been attracted to me since we met three years ago?"

Shawn sighed heavily. "Guilty. Now do you understand why I didn't ask if I could stay with you when I lost my apartment in LA? I knew you had a girlfriend. It would've been torture to sleep on your couch, knowing you were in the bedroom with another woman. I just couldn't do it."

"I had no idea you felt that way. I guess I can understand why it would have been difficult. Still, I wish I had known you were homeless. I feel awful that you were out on the streets when I could have given you a place to stay."

"But your girlfriend—how would she have felt about it?"

Jaymi let out a disgusted sigh and rolled her eyes. "I doubt she would have noticed you were there. She wasn't home much. And she trusted me, so there's no way she would have worried about me fooling around on her."

Shawn smiled and slid in closer to Jaymi. She lightly traced her fingers through Jaymi's hair and rested her palm on her cheek. "If I *had* stayed with you, I would have given her a reason to worry."

Jaymi covered Shawn's hand with her own, squeezed her fingers, and removed them from her face. "I don't cheat."

Shawn smiled mischievously. "Ah, come on, you telling me you wouldn't have even been tempted?"

"*I don't cheat.*" Jaymi stood up, letting go of Shawn's hand. "It's late, and we both have to work in the morning."

Jaymi headed down the hall and slipped into the bathroom to ready herself for bed. She glared at the mirror. *You're overreacting. Shawn's just flirting with you. You're stressed and she hit a nerve. Do you want to be like Peach and sabotage what you have with her because you're scared?*

That was it. *You're scared.* She flinched as if the truth had slapped her in the face. *You're falling for Shawn and you're scared out of your wits. Did you really expect to go through the rest of your life without letting yourself love again?*

She splashed water on her face, took a deep breath, and let the air out slowly. She repeated this until she felt her pulse slow, and then she stepped into the hall. Shawn had retreated to her room and closed the door. Jaymi knocked lightly.

Shawn opened the door silently. The wounded look in her eyes was heartbreaking.

Jaymi gingerly ran her fingers through Shawn's thick hair. "Hey," she said softly.

"I'm sorry," Shawn said. "I didn't mean to remind you of what she did to you—or imply that you're capable of cheating. You're better than that and I know it."

"No, I'm sorry." Jaymi caressed Shawn's cheek. "I'm taking out my insecurity on you, and that's not fair."

"Guess I have to work on that flirtatious side of me. It tends to get me into trouble."

Jaymi smiled. "It's a part of who you are, so don't change it on my account. I don't want you feeling like you have to walk on eggshells around me and watch everything you say. I'm the one that has the problem letting go. I feel bad that I spoiled our first date."

Shawn took a step toward Jaymi and took her into her arms. "The only thing that can spoil our first date is if you tell me there won't be a second," she whispered.

Jaymi shivered at the sensation of Shawn's hot breath in her ear. She nuzzled Shawn's neck and said, "That depends on whether or not I get a good-night kiss."

"We'd better not. I might not be able to stop at just a kiss."

"Then I guess it's a good thing that I never jump into bed on a first date."

"Oh, you are such a tease…"

"Take it or leave it."

❖

Jaymi lay in bed alone, trying desperately to fall asleep.

What-ifs started running through her head again. What if Mom had never become ill? What if she had stayed in California? What if things had improved with Peach once she'd finished school and they had time to focus on their relationship? Would they still be together? Would Passion Play be closer to accomplishing their dream of a recording contract?

What if Shawn had asked Jaymi for help in California? Would she have hit rock bottom as she did? Would Shawn's crush have eventually gone away? Would she have developed feelings for Shawn in return?

She flipped over and punched her pillow in frustration, longing for the questions to cease and for sleep to find her. She prayed for a clear mind and consciously focused on her breathing, slowing it down, forcing her body to relax. Finally, after some effort, it began to take effect. She began to drift into sleep.

Then the screaming started.

Jaymi burst into Shawn's room and grabbed her flailing hands, calling her name repeatedly until she came to. She pulled Shawn's body into her own and rocked her gently. "I've got you, Shawn, I've got you. Shh. You're safe. I've got you. Easy."

Once the tears finally subsided, Jaymi placed an arm around

Shawn's waist and helped her up. She led her into her own bedroom and settled her into bed. She shut off the light and crawled in beside her. Shawn curled into the fetal position but let Jaymi wrap her arms around her. She fell asleep in Jaymi's arms as Jaymi caressed her face and peppered her head with gentle kisses.

The temptation was getting too difficult for Jaymi to resist. Shawn was in her bed, wrapped warmly in her embrace, and Jaymi couldn't deny the willpower she needed to keep from confessing her feelings, throwing all caution to the wind, and making love to her right there and then.

No. Shawn was in her bed because of Brinkman's attempted rape and the fact that it had left her with deep scars. There was no way in hell she wanted that image in Shawn's mind when they made love for the first time. The magnitude of the trauma Shawn was dealing with only increased Jaymi's growing desire to be there for her. It wasn't that she wanted to rescue her. She simply wanted to prove to Shawn that for once in her life there was someone who wasn't going to abandon her in a time of need. Jaymi wanted to be that someone.

If she was having reservations about moving forward now, maybe it was more about giving Shawn the time she needed to deal with the attack. Jaymi couldn't imagine the horror and fear Shawn must have felt as it was happening. Every time Shawn had one of these nightmares, it became clear how badly the experience had affected her.

Jaymi had been so worried about being the one that wasn't ready, that she hadn't considered the extent to which Shawn might not be ready, either. They had talked about taking things slowly. Were they taking things slowly enough? It hadn't been easy, but they had refrained from sex, despite the temptation. That alone indicated a solid foundation for a mature relationship.

Jaymi knew she couldn't fix Shawn—she needed professional help. Jaymi wondered if Shawn would be willing to meet with LaKeisha for counseling at Sara's youth center. She decided to ask her about it in the morning. For now, she was just glad Shawn was able to sleep.

She thought about the events of the last five weeks. She couldn't deny the positives that had developed since Shawn moved in. Her creative juices had awakened with a vengeance. Each workday while she was on the road, her mind flooded with lyrical ideas. Numerous times throughout her shift, she had to pull over or take a few minutes in the car between deliveries to scribble lines in her notebook. She had picked up Shawn's practice of carrying a pocket recorder with her to hum or sing melodies that rushed into her head at the most unexpected times. And more and more, she came home from work and headed directly to her studio to put the songs together while Shawn cooked dinner.

*She's like the perfect little housewife,* Jaymi mused. *And she's spoiling me rotten. Perhaps if I simply bask in this warm feeling and focus on the present, savoring this moment, I'll sleep.*

Instead, she found herself comparing Shawn to Peach. Peach was so strong. She exuded confidence, nearly to the brink of arrogance. She studied her brains out to be the best—determined to outdo everyone. But much of her strength had been anchored in her fierce competitiveness. Peach hated to lose. Yet she had an amazing ability to discern when defeat was imminent. And she could accept her losses with dignity and bow out respectfully.

*So she sabotaged her relationship with me. She knew it was a losing battle. I was coming home to be with my mother no matter what—with or without her.*

Jaymi knew it wasn't that simple, though. Love for a parent could be as strong as love for a partner. Jaymi's gut and heart both told her an unconditional lover would know she wasn't choosing one over the other. It wasn't a competition. Or, at least, it shouldn't be.

*Peach would probably think Shawn is weak,* thought Jaymi. *Shawn isn't weak. She's one of the strongest people I know, and not because she prides herself in it. She isn't even aware of her own inner strength.* There was something familiar about it. A quiet strength that Jaymi had seen in the two people she admired most: her parents. *No wonder I feel such a connection with her.*

Shawn was a survivor. *She knows who she is and what she wants.* She drove cross-country and moved to California on her own. Without the support of her family. Without a lover or friend by her side. Totally alone, and that took guts. She was intimidated by Nikki, yet she stood up to her anyway and earned her respect. *She didn't let Karla get away with harassing me. She went to bat for me, and is still protecting my privacy.* She dealt with the deaths of her mother and her aunt. By herself.

An unexpected rush of emotion surged through Jaymi's heart. *I didn't want this in my life now. I'm not ready. Or am I? How would I know if I am ready?* Shawn was real. Her presence attracted attention in subtle ways. People were drawn to her because there was something genuine about her. No pretense. *She steps on a stage and bares her soul through her guitar strings. Through her voice. She shows her wounds through her music.*

Jaymi knew it wasn't easy for Shawn to trust. *But Shawn trusts me. She came to me with an instinct that I wouldn't turn her away. And that's why I can't make the first move to make love with her. It has to be when she feels safe. When she knows I won't abandon her. When she trusts my feelings for her.*

*Whatever those feelings are.*

# CHAPTER EIGHTEEN

Shawn exited LaKeisha's office feeling more empowered than she could ever remember feeling. It would take time to recover from the post-traumatic stress she was suffering from Brinkman's attack, but she felt confident that she would do so. She was incredibly glad Jaymi had talked her into going to counseling after her last episode of nightmares. As reluctant as she'd been to relive the nightmares of her past, being able to open up about them suddenly took a hell of a lot of the sting out of them.

There was a small waiting area a few steps down the hall. Four cushioned chairs were lined up against the wall with a small square table in between. While waiting to make her next appointment, Shawn tried to avoid eye contact with a young woman seated in one of the chairs, but couldn't shake the feeling the woman looked familiar. She was dressed in well-worn jeans, work boots, and a heavy, slightly oversized leather biker jacket. Her dark, unkempt hair fell across her face. She looked up when she sensed Shawn's scrutiny and recognized her immediately.

"No fucking way! Shawnie, is that you?"

"Mel! What are you doing here?"

"I could ask you the same thing. Shit, I haven't seen you since high school. You, like, disappeared off the face of the earth."

"I've been in California. Just got back about a month ago."

"No shit. Man, I can't believe it. I thought I'd never see you again."

"I didn't plan on coming back."

Mel looked Shawn up and down and smiled widely. "You fucking look good, girl. You lost weight, but, shit, you fucking look good. Can I take you to dinner? Fatten you up a bit and give us a chance to catch up? I'll only be fifteen minutes or so—just gotta give sexy Ms. LaKeisha in there the good news that I'm still sober. Three weeks today without a drink."

"Good for you. But tonight's no good, I'm beat. And my…" *My girlfriend? My roommate?* "My ride's waiting for me."

"Oh. Well, maybe some other time, huh?" They stood in an awkward silence for a moment, both shuffling their feet, eyes fleeting. "Good to see you, Shawn. Damn, I've missed you." She raised her pale brown eyes slowly to meet Shawn's. It was a familiar look, one that had weakened Shawn numerous times in the past. It still worked.

"Tell you what. Let me give you the phone number and address where I'm staying." Shawn grabbed a notepad and pencil off the waiting room table. "There's a party Saturday night—nothing big or wild or anything. Why don't you stop by?"

Mel beamed as she accepted the invitation. "Cool."

"I hope it doesn't make you uncomfortable if LaKeisha's there."

"Shit, no. She can help keep me in line if I'm tempted to drink. LaKeisha's the best."

❖

Shawn hurried outside to join Jaymi, who was waiting in the truck. During the ride home, Jaymi offered to spend nights with her while she overcame her nightmares, but Shawn politely declined, explaining that she would be more empowered by finding her own strength to deal with them. Shawn knew Jaymi had no ulterior motive, but the temptation to touch her was too strong. The last thing she wanted was sympathy sex.

Shawn told Jaymi about her encounter with Mel and talked about their past. They had come out together in their junior year of high school. Their insecurities and fears had sent them into a period of wild partying and, eventually, sleeping together. Together they'd explored their newfound sexual identities, wrapped up in the joy of their sexual encounters. After four months, they realized they were incompatible as a couple and that sex wasn't enough, and they broke up just before the end of the school year. But during senior year, they'd learned that they were better off as friends, and they'd remained close until graduation.

Shawn hadn't thought about Mel much since then. Now she

wondered if there was any chance of reviving their friendship. Or if she even cared to. She stared out the window of Jaymi's truck and shifted uneasily. Perhaps inviting her to the party wasn't such a good idea after all.

❖

Devin's party began without a hitch. Sara had brought her to the apartment on the pretense that they were joining Jaymi and Shawn for a simple dinner. Instead, a roomful of friends greeted her and she was completely surprised.

Shawn took great joy in meeting the amazing, warmhearted people Jaymi welcomed into her home. Devin's best friend, Jen, who had been her college roommate, was the first to arrive. Jen bubbled with so much excitement, one would have thought it was *her* book they were celebrating. LaKeisha arrived with two large bouquets of flowers, one of which came with an apologetic message from another college friend who lived in Michigan and couldn't be there.

After enjoying salads and brick-oven pizzas delivered from a local pizzeria, Nikki arrived with Randi. Soon after, Mel was introduced to the gang and a toast was made to Devin with sparkling grape juice, the stereo was turned up, and everyone set about mingling.

"Holy fucking shit!" Mel exclaimed to Shawn, who was leading her down the hall to show Mel her room. "I can't believe you're living with Jaymi Del Harmon! And you know Nikki Razer, too?"

"Geez, Mel, don't you know musicians are people, too? I just played a gig with them last weekend."

"You're really making it, huh? I always knew you would. I always told you you're fucking awesome." Mel dropped herself onto the futon. "I like your room. Nikki's even hotter in person. Do you think—oh, never mind, I wouldn't have a chance."

"No, you wouldn't. Randi you might have a shot at, though. She's a wicked flirt."

"No shit. What about Jaymi? She's cute. Think she'd go for me?"

"Actually, Jaymi's taken." Shawn walked to her desk and closed a notebook, hiding the lyrics she had been working on earlier that day. *Maybe I shouldn't have invited her here,* she thought as she stared out the window.

"Really? I didn't notice her with anyone."

"You know, Mel, I didn't invite you here so you could hit on all my friends." Shawn spun back around and glared at her. "Especially Jaymi."

"Easy, girl. Do I sense some jealousy here? You telling me that you and Jaymi—"

"Yes, me and Jaymi. But please, don't say anything to anyone. We haven't really gone public with it—"

"Wow. You lucky dog." She smiled and patted the seat. "So I take it you don't sleep on this futon."

Shawn retreated to the bathroom; she needed to figure out a tactful way to get Mel to leave. *She hasn't changed.* Shawn looked at the mirror and, for the first time, acknowledged strides in her own growth as a person, knowing in that instant that she and Mel wouldn't be renewing their friendship. She didn't belong in Jaymi's house, and she needed to think of a reason to get her to leave.

She returned to her room to discover Mel lounging on the futon with a lit joint pinched between her thumb and index finger.

"What the hell are you doing?" Shawn fumed.

"Hey, it's a party, ain't it? Wanna share with your friends?" From her coat pocket, Mel revealed a small plastic bag full of rolled joints.

"It's not that kind of party. And Randi's a cop."

Mel laughed. "Then you better help me finish this before we get caught."

"Put that thing out before someone smells it. I thought you were trying to get sober."

"Hey, I'm not addicted to pot, just beer." Mel stood and held the joint in front of Shawn's face. "Come on, Shawnie, take a hit. You seem a little tense."

"Damn it, Mel, put it out." Mel continued to wave the joint back and forth in Shawn's face. In a defensive reflex, Shawn batted it away, accidently knocking it from Mel's grip and onto the floor. "Shit!" Shawn fell to her knees and picked it up, hoping it hadn't burned the carpet.

At that moment Jaymi stepped in. "Hey, you guys want to—" Her eyes flew open at the sight of Shawn kneeling on the floor, holding the smoldering joint. "What the…?"

Shawn swiftly extinguished the joint on the side of her shoe and stood. "Jaymi, it's not what you think."

Mel looked from Shawn to Jaymi and back to Shawn again. "I think it's time for me to split." She brushed by Jaymi but stopped just long enough to lean into her and say, "Shawnie's a good fuck, isn't she?"

❖

Shawn had never seen Jaymi so angry. Jaymi put on a brave face for the sake of upholding her hosting responsibilities to Devin and her friends, but she was obviously avoiding her. Shawn kept to herself, trying not show her inner turmoil.

A few minutes after Mel left, Randi came back inside and came over to Shawn with an extra bottle in hand. "Hiya, cutie. Brought you a refill."

"Thanks." Shawn traded bottles with her but didn't take a drink.

Randi shifted closer. "You okay?"

Shawn looked across the room. Jaymi was standing at the breakfast bar chatting with Devin and Sara. Jaymi smiled, laughed at one of Sara's jokes, and gave her shoulder a playful push before making a comment to Devin, who rolled her eyes. Devin shrugged and leaned over to kiss Sara's cheek.

Randi watched the exchange then turned her attention back to Shawn. "Cute couple, Sara and Devin, don't you think?"

"Yeah."

Randi crossed her legs and rested her arm on the couch behind Shawn. "Lots of beautiful women here tonight. I feel like a kid in a candy store."

Shawn leaned forward and rested her elbows on her knees, holding her beer in both hands. She didn't feel like drinking, and after a moment she set the untouched bottle on the coffee table.

"Funny what you can learn just from sitting back and observing people," continued Randi. "All these wonderful, gorgeous women in one place, all of them single except for one couple, and no one's hitting on anybody. But I see at least three broken hearts in this room."

That caught Shawn's attention. "Really?"

"Definitely. For example, that butch chick over there who's built like she could bench-press a truck—what's her name again?"

"Brandy. She's a hockey player."

"Well, that explains the legs of steel. She's barely taken her eyes off Devin all night. She's got it bad for her. But look at Devin. Totally into Sara. And it's making Brandy crazy. I mean, see the hunger in her eyes? But then she'll catch herself and look away, all guilty and hurt. And she's spent most of the night talking to Jen—who's straight and happens to be Devin's best friend."

Shawn was listening politely, but her focus hadn't shifted from Jaymi.

"Obviously Sara's happy as a clam with Devin and vice versa. Jen's straight, so she's not looking to hook up with anyone here. But Jaymi. Jaymi, Jaymi, Jaymi." Randi released a big sigh. "That sweet girl seems to always be carrying around a heartache. Oh, she tries hard to hide it. One hell of a great attitude about life. And shit, dealing with Nikki all the time, she's gotta have the patience of a saint. But I wonder just how long she can manage to keep up that protective wall."

"She's a hell of a lot stronger than everybody thinks."

Randi brought her arm down across Shawn's shoulders. She tilted her head toward Shawn's and spoke softly. "Which brings us to heartache number three, right here. Am I right?"

Shawn squeezed her eyes closed and shuddered. She had to admit the attention from Randi felt good. So did the proximity of her body. A year ago, she would have been all over Randi. She knew her type. No strings. Just sex. Charming and ungodly beautiful with a body to die for—and preying on a vulnerable victim. Shawn felt her face flush with shame as she opened her eyes and was relieved to see that Jaymi wasn't looking in their direction.

"You're wrong," Shawn said defensively, hoping to discourage her predator. Randi smiled.

"Am I?" Randi stood and faced her, placing a hand on Shawn's shoulder. "If you change your mind, I'd love to take you out sometime."

As she watched Randi make her way around the room to bid farewell, Shawn caught Jaymi's look, her expression questioning the exchange she must have just witnessed. As if on cue, the other guests began hugging each other before gathering their coats and saying their good-byes. Shawn joined Jaymi in politely thanking everyone as they left.

They cleaned up the apartment in silence. Just when Shawn couldn't bear it anymore, Jaymi started talking.

"I'm still upset with you."

"I know."

"And what was going on between you and Randi?" Shawn sensed a hint of insecurity in Jaymi's voice. Was she jealous?

"Just talking."

"Was she hitting on you?" Jaymi smiled a crooked little smile. "It's okay, you know. Randi hits on everybody—including just about everyone here tonight."

"What?"

"Oh yeah. Brandy. LaKeisha. Even Jen, and Jen's straight."

"Not you?"

Jaymi laughed. "She knows better. Nikki would kick her ass."

"Jaymi, I'm sorry. I shouldn't have invited Mel. I thought she'd changed. I mean, she's going to the center for help—"

"Shawn, do you realize the position she put us all in tonight?" Jaymi's demeanor grew dark again. "What if Randi had known she was smoking pot? What if it got into the papers there was a drug bust here— the band's reputation would have been at stake. Do you realize that?"

"I had no idea she'd bring a bag of weed. And the truth is, I had already decided to ask her to leave. I went back to my room and she was sitting there smoking. She was waving it at me, trying to get me to take a toke, and I knocked it out of her hand onto the floor. That's when you walked in. I don't do drugs. You should know that by now."

Jaymi inhaled deeply and looked into Shawn's eyes. "Can I tell you something?"

"Yeah. Anything."

"When you first got here, I suspected you might have gotten into the drug scene in LA."

"Why would you think that?"

"Well, you were in pretty bad shape, and I don't mean just physically. Musicians are notorious for doing drugs and partying—"

"I haven't touched drugs since my wild high-school days. I stay away from those kind of people. I screwed up tonight with Mel. I'm sorry. I thought she would've grown up by now." Shawn was so angry with herself. She had earned Jaymi's trust and respect. She hated to think that Jaymi might be second-guessing her trust over something that wasn't even true.

She looked seriously into Jaymi's eyes, placed a hand on her shoulder, and said, "I have no interest in ever seeing Mel again or ever doing drugs. Please, Jaymi. I need you to believe me."

Jaymi's eyes softened. "Okay. I believe you. It just surprised me, and it made me nervous, you know, with Randi here. Maybe I overreacted. I'm sorry." Jaymi smiled slightly. "And why does she think we're having sex?"

"Uh…I didn't tell her anything—not really. She was going to hit on you, so I hinted that we were together. She said that to you to spite me because I shot her down. I'm so sorry—you didn't deserve that."

"You're right, I didn't."

"Are we okay?"

Jaymi ran a finger through Shawn's bangs and put her other hand on her hip. "Yeah." She kissed her lightly on the lips. "We're okay." She kissed her again and pulled her closer.

Shawn tasted champagne on Jaymi's lips and groaned with pleasure as Jaymi found her tongue with her own. Her head swam with relief and pleasure. She wanted to take her to bed. She wanted so desperately to feel Jaymi's naked body next to hers, to taste every inch of her, to make love to her and express the overload of feelings that were so foreign and wonderful. Then Jaymi pulled away and the separation struck Shawn like a rush of frigid air.

"Shawn. Shit, this is so hard." Jaymi exhaled a huge breath. "If I don't stop now…listen, sweetheart, I need you to understand something."

Shawn tried to catch her breath. *She called me sweetheart. God, that sounded so nice.* The term of endearment took a bit of the sting out of the apprehension of what Jaymi was going to say next. "What?"

"You just started counseling. You're dealing with something very difficult. It's important that you have time to get through that."

"Yeah. I know."

"I don't want anything, or anyone—including me, or whatever this is going on between us—to interfere with that, okay?"

Shawn nodded, understanding and deeply touched by Jaymi's selflessness. "Yeah. Okay."

"Good. It's late. We better get some sleep."

"Which means—"

"Which means we're sleeping in our own rooms."

# CHAPTER NINETEEN

Despite a nearly sleepless night, Shawn rose early the next morning and went to work in the barn. She dove into her chores, releasing her anger and frustration in the strenuous physical labor. When she had finished cleaning the stalls, she wandered into the pasture and gathered up her favorite horse, Scout. Shawn led her into the barn, where she gave her a thorough groom.

She spent as much time as she could with the horses, avoiding Jaymi until she had to leave for rehearsal. She was grooming her third horse when she heard the hard crank of Jaymi's truck. Then there were curses and a door slammed. Shawn peeked out the barn door to see Jaymi stalking toward the main house.

"Jaymi," Shawn said, just loud enough to stop her in her tracks. "Want a jump?"

Jaymi glanced at her watch. "I'm already late. I'm going to ask Alice if they'll let me borrow Pete's truck."

"Why don't you just use my car?" Shawn tossed Jaymi her keys. "It's got plenty of gas. Go ahead, I've got nowhere to go today."

Jaymi managed a slight smile. "Thanks." Shawn helped transfer two guitars into her car and watched her drive away. As soon as she was out of sight, she walked up the front porch and knocked.

"Morning there, Shawn," Alice said, drying her hands on a floral dish towel. "What can I do for you?"

"I need a favor, Alice."

"That so?"

"I wanted to see if you could give me a small advance, and if I could borrow Pete's truck for about an hour. Oh, and if I could use the garage this afternoon."

Alice rubbed her chin and cocked an eyebrow. "That sounds like three favors."

"Uh…"

Alice burst into laughter and slapped her knee. "I'm just razzing you, kiddo. No problem. How much do you need?"

"About fifty dollars, if that's okay. I'll help you out after work to make it up to you, and I can pay you back on Friday, as soon as I get paid, I promise."

"What're you up to, honey?"

"I'm going to fix Jaymi's truck and surprise her. New battery, tune-up, oil change. The works. But I let her take my car, so I need your truck to go get everything."

"You're a good kid. That's awfully kind of you. You should find all the tools you need in the garage."

❖

Passion Play's rehearsal wasn't one of their best. Nikki's moods swung from giddy, to cocky, to bitchy, to secretive. Jaymi had trouble focusing on anything. Kay and Brian stole looks at each other, wondering what was up with their bandleaders, but they dropped it when neither woman opened up when questioned.

Jaymi eventually conceded that she was accomplishing nothing and left early. She drove mindlessly for a while, going no place in particular, losing herself in a favorite Mary Chapin Carpenter CD in an attempt to calm her nerves. She snapped back to reality when she spotted blue lights behind her. Had she been speeding?

She grudgingly pulled over and let out a groan. *Just what I need.* Her stress lessened slightly when she looked into the rearview and saw Randi approaching her side of the vehicle. She rolled down the window.

"License and reg—Jaymi? Didn't expect to find you behind the wheel." She grinned and lowered her sunglasses for a wink. "What a sweet surprise."

"Was I speeding? Sorry, I—"

"No, not at all. Shawn's car, right? It's got a taillight out."

"Oh. Do you have to give me a ticket for that?"

"No, but I will have to ask you to step out so I can frisk you."

"Nice try, Randi." Jaymi chuckled. "Maybe next time."

Randi swept her hand sideways with an *aw shucks* snap of her fingers. "Got to follow protocol, though, which means I do need the registration."

Jaymi checked both the visor and the console before dropping open the glove compartment. Her hand froze when she reached for its contents.

"Can't find it?" asked Randi, peering in. "What the hell is that?"

❖

Shawn bolted upright from her crouch beside the truck's rear quarter panel and dropped her waxing cloth. Her mouth dropped open in shock. Jaymi had just flung open the door of the garage and she stood with her feet braced wide apart, fists at her sides, her jaw clenched. Her body language spoke fury, yet her crystal blue eyes were drenched and confused.

"Jaymi, what's wrong?"

Jaymi's eyes darkened. "You told me that pot was Mel's."

"It was—"

"Then why the hell did I just find it in your glove compartment? Or rather, why did the *cop* that just pulled me over find it in your glove compartment?"

Shawn could feel her stomach twisting. "What?"

"You heard me. The only reason I'm not in jail right now is because it happened to be Randi that stopped me."

Every muscle in Shawn's body tightened. "Mel, you goddamned asshole."

"Excuse me?"

"Mel must've ditched it in my car when she left. That punk."

"So you're *still* telling me it wasn't yours?"

"Jaymi, do you honestly believe I would lend you my car knowing I had a bag of pot in the glove compartment?"

"After last night, I really don't know what to believe."

"Jesus Christ, when have you ever known me to use drugs, huh? Mel was pissed at me when she left. Pissed enough to pull a stunt like

this. I've known her for years and this has her name written all over it."
Jaymi looked at her skeptically. "Jaymi, come on." Shawn took a step
closer. "I wouldn't lie to you."

"Why should I believe you? You've lied before. You admitted
lying to Nikki to get her back in the band."

"That's different—"

"I can only imagine the lies you told those women you seduced so
you'd have a place to sleep."

Shawn's stomach recoiled as the color drained from her face. She
swallowed hard and choked out her words. "You're throwing my past
in my face? You, Jaymi? You know why I did those things. I've been
honest with you about that, and everything else. All those things I did
that I'm so ashamed of—I didn't have to tell you about any of that stuff.
But I did because I trusted you. Because I felt safe. So if I was honest
enough to tell you my most humiliating secrets, why on earth would
I ever lie to you about something like this?" She let the tears fall, not
bothering to wipe them from her cheeks.

"Oh God, Shawn, I'm sorry. I'm just angry, I didn't mean to say
that." Jaymi lowered her eyes and her voice. "I was scared. I could have
been arrested."

"Jaymi…" Shawn lightly touched a palm to Jaymi's cheek and
looked intensely into her eyes. "I would rather die than risk anything
like that happening to you. I would never do anything to hurt you."

Jaymi's shoulders began to heave. "If it had been any other cop…"

Before the first teardrop could run down her cheek, Shawn had
her in her arms. "I am so sorry, Jaymi. I never should have asked her to
come. I am so, *so* sorry."

They held each other for several silent minutes. Then Jaymi
looked up and saw her pickup, its metallic forest-green paint shining
like new. She pulled away slightly. "Did you wash and wax my truck?"

"More than that." Shawn gave Jaymi a peck on the cheek and
released her. She opened the driver's side door, popped the release, and
lifted the hood. She pointed inside. "New battery. New oil and filter.
New plugs. New air filter. Oh, and I also vacuumed it out, polished the
interior, cleaned your windows and upholstery, put air in your tires,
checked all your fluids, gave it a lube job, and filled your windshield
washer."

Jaymi stared at her. "You did all that yourself?"

A slight smile emerged with a nod. "Alice gave me an advance and loaned me her truck so I could get the parts. And while I was there, I picked up a bulb for my taillight. With everything that's been going on, I forgot all about that thing being out."

Jaymi shook her head. "I can't believe you did all this. That's a lot of hard work. Thank you so much."

"No sweat."

Jaymi checked out the interior. "It looks good as new! How much did all that cost? I'll reimburse you—"

"No. No way. I don't want you to pay me."

"I have to give you something. Come on, what do I owe you?" Shawn grinned and Jaymi blushed and playfully slapped Shawn's arm. "You are such a flirt."

Shawn walked to the workbench and picked up a pencil. "Tell you what," she said, as she began writing on a notepad. "I'll bill you." She scribbled a bit more, tore off the page, and handed it to Jaymi.

Jaymi's face lit up as she read it.

*Tune-up: two hugs*
*Oil change: one kiss*
*Battery: one hug and two kisses*
*Wash and wax: one dinner date*

The seductive look in Jaymi's eyes made Shawn's knees buckle. Jaymi said, "I'd like to pay for the oil change right now."

# CHAPTER TWENTY

Shawn closed the door to Karla's office behind her, glad for a moment to breathe. Ever since Karla had realized she was gay, she called Shawn into her office frequently. With no one else to confide in, Shawn seemed to have a new role as Karla's best friend and personal handbook to being a lesbian.

Today, she left Karla's office with an offer of a permanent position with benefits and a raise, and the news that Karla had come out to her husband and was leaving him. There was no mention of Jaymi or a meeting, which Shawn saw as a good sign that with more pressing matters on her mind, perhaps her bizarre infatuation had subsided.

It was the third week of March. Temperatures were starting to rise. The snow was beginning to melt. Daylight lasted longer. Shawn hurried home after work Monday feeling much more secure about her financial situation and went right to work in the barn.

She began in the stall on the farthest end. After only a few minutes, she had worked up a sweat and removed her jacket, and when that wasn't enough, off came her sweatshirt. In only jeans and a gray long-sleeved thermal shirt, she raked out the old hay. With each stroke, her thoughts were on Jaymi. It seemed their relationship was finally taking a step forward, despite the Mel incident that could have ruined everything. Jaymi was no longer angry about it, but Shawn sensed she was holding back. Was it because of her ex? Was she still afraid? *Maybe she's afraid to trust me.* On several occasions it seemed that Jaymi was about to say something but stopped herself. What was it she couldn't bring herself to say? Was she having doubts?

One official date, that's all they'd had. But they had shared Jaymi's bed more than once, though they'd done nothing but sleep. It had been nearly impossible to keep her hands off her. She loved the warmth of Jaymi's body. The gentleness of her touch. The soothing sound of her voice. The instinctual ways she cared for Shawn's needs. The ease with which they cowrote songs. How magically their musical ideas flowed when they jammed. How relaxed they were in each other's company. How smoothly they had fallen into a routine living together. Had Jaymi felt it too? Did Jaymi know how bad she wanted her?

Shawn was burning up. She felt herself throbbing with arousal and tried to force her thoughts elsewhere. She couldn't remember going without sex for this long before.

She hauled a wheelbarrow of discarded hay outside, without bothering with her jacket, in hopes of cooling her desire. After four trips, it was no use. She was even hotter than before. She pictured them kissing again, lying face-to-face on Jaymi's bed. She could feel their bodies pressed together, her palm across Jaymi's flat stomach, moving up to caress her breasts. She groaned out loud and tried to shift the seam of her jeans away from her aching clit. Acknowledging that she was alone in the far end of the barn in the corner stall, she was tempted to shove a hand down her pants and release her need now.

Instead, she shook her head furiously in frustration. One by one, she picked up three bales of hay and heaved them into the stall. She pulled out her pocketknife, sliced the twine on one of them, and began to fork the hay onto the floor.

"Well, look at you go, girl."

Startled, Shawn stopped and looked up. Randi leaned against the doorjamb, her arms folded, dressed in tight jeans, black leather boots, and a waist-length black winter jacket over a bright blue collared shirt. The shirt, Shawn noticed, was only buttoned high enough to barely cover her breasts, her enticing chest exposed.

Shawn shuddered with the penetration of Randi's dark eyes, which shamelessly looked her up and down. *What is she doing here? The pot! She's here to question me about the pot.*

"Good God, honey," Randi said, taking a step toward her, "you look like you've seen a ghost."

"Randi, I swear, that pot was Mel's. She planted it in my car to get back at me—"

"Honey, relax. I'm off duty, and officially, I have no right to question you." Randi took another step closer. One more step and Shawn would be backed up against the wall. "God, you're sexy when you've worked up a sweat. Just like when you sing."

Shawn didn't know how to reply to that, so she said nothing. She should move. She knew that. But she couldn't. Randi knew it, too.

"So, what can I do for you?" Shawn managed to say.

Randi gave a slow, seductive smile. "That's a dangerous thing to ask me. But since you did..." She slipped a hand into her jeans pocket and withdrew a small plastic bag. "I need help destroying this evidence." To Shawn's amazement, Randi pulled a joint out of the bag, placed it between her lips, and lit it. She inhaled deeply, choked down the smoke, and then held it out to Shawn.

"What the...?"

"Something wrong?"

"But you're a cop."

"You've heard the expression *good cop, bad cop,* haven't you? Guess which one I am?" She grinned, took another toke, and again offered it to Shawn, who shook her head.

"No. No, thanks. I gave up that shit way back in high school."

"Suit yourself." She reached over Shawn's shoulder and ground out the joint on the wall. Keeping her arm there, within inches of Shawn's face, she leaned into her. "So, how're things with Jaymi?" she asked in a quiet voice.

"Things are fine, everything's fine," Shawn whispered, increasingly aware of the heat emitting from Randi's body. Or was it her own?

"You sure? You, look a little flustered to me."

"I said I'm fine."

"Don't feel bad. Like I said the other night, she's been burned. Bad. Figure that's why she's been keeping herself off the market—not in any hurry to hook up with anyone anytime soon. She turned me down once, you know. God, is it fucking hot in here, or what?" Randi lowered her arm and, without backing off, removed her coat and let it drop. She inched slightly closer. "Anyway, when a woman says no, it leaves me terribly frustrated." She moved her cheek next to Shawn's and whispered into her ear, "Know what I mean?"

The tips of her breasts touched Shawn's, ever so lightly. Shawn gasped, feeling her body respond. This wasn't good—not after her arousal just moments ago while thinking of Jaymi.

"Want to know what I do about it?" Randi asked, as she pulled her head back and locked eyes with her, their lips within an inch apart. She took the final step into Shawn, pressing her groin into her and placing both hands on the wall.

"What?" Shawn's voice was barely audible.

"I go out and fuck another woman."

Shawn's breath caught as Randi teasingly moved her mouth even closer, without touching hers, but just staying there, obviously knowing full well the torture she was inflicting.

"I feel your pain, Shawn. Let me ease it. Let me do to you what I've wanted to do since the moment I saw you at the club singing your heart out. You looked so fucking beautiful and sexy I wanted to nail you right there on the stage."

"But…"

"Do you find me attractive?"

Shawn couldn't lie. "Yes."

"I find you fucking irresistible." Randi lowered her arms and wrapped them around Shawn's waist. Shawn felt one hand slide under her shirt onto her bare back. Before she knew what was happening, their lips were pressed together in a searing kiss. Shawn found her arms around Randi's tight body. She needed to come so badly that for several moments all she could focus on was her physical need and the surprise of how good Randi's lips felt, and how scintillating her touch was on her skin. Shawn's resistance weakened further when Randi's tongue found her own. An argument ensued in her mind, a devilish pest trying to persuade her to give in to Randi's advances and relieve her craving. The devil lost the argument easily. She spun around with the intention of pushing Randi away, but they lost their balance. Shawn stumbled back a step and wound up sitting on a bale of hay.

"I hate to see a woman in pain." Randi placed her hand on the back of Shawn's head and pulled her face into her breasts. "Feel that? Feel my heart beating for you?"

"Oh God…"

"I want you, Shawn." Randi came down onto Shawn's lap, straddling her on the edge of the bale. "Why pine after someone who plays hard to get when I'm willing and able to give you what you need right now?" She kissed Shawn on the forehead and began rocking her hips, grinding into Shawn's groin.

"God, oh God, Randi, you have to stop."

"You don't want me to stop—"

"No—"

"Good. Let me make you feel good—"

"I meant no as in *stop,* Randi. Please, stop. Get off—"

"Oh, you said it, baby, I'll get off all right." Randi's lips traveled across her ear and down her neck. Shawn's hands pushed against Randi's shoulders, but Randi continued to press with her body. "Oh, Shawn," she whispered into her ear, "come on, you know you want this."

"No, please, stop, get off me. *Get off me!*" In an instant, Shawn was back in the motel room with Brinkman. But this time, she didn't have to forcibly remove her attacker. Randi sensed the terror in Shawn's voice and immediately backed off. Shawn broke out in tears and continued to sob. "Get off me, get off me…"

"Oh shit, oh shit, shit, *shit.*" Randi raked her hands through her hair. "Shawn, my God, you've been raped, haven't you?"

Shawn hugged herself and rocked, her tears falling shamelessly.

"Oh, fuck. Shawn, I am so sorry, honey. What have I done?"

"Please, leave," Shawn finally managed to say.

"I can't just leave…I've hurt you."

"What's going on here?" Jaymi stood just outside the stall. When Jaymi saw Shawn crumpled on the hay bale, she shot Randi a fierce look before kneeling at Shawn's side. She placed a hand on Shawn's knee and brushed the bangs off her face. "Sweetheart, what happened? Are you okay?" She recognized the terrified look in Shawn's eyes and took her into her arms. She looked at Randi again. "What the hell happened?"

"I'm sorry. I'm so sorry. I fucked up. Shit, Jaymi, there's no excuse for what I did. I made a pass at her. I came on strong—you know me. She freaked—I didn't know she'd been raped. Not that it's an excuse—"

"Shut up, Randi," Jaymi said in disgust, steadying Shawn and standing up. "Just shut up. Did Nikki put you up to this?"

Randi's eyes shot open wide. "What?"

"Come on, Randi, don't lie to me. I know how she works. She'll do anything to keep me single and focused on the band."

"Jaymi, look, what matters here is that Shawn's okay." Randi stole a glance at Shawn. "Are you all right?"

"Jaymi," Shawn said in a raspy voice, "it's all right. I'm okay."

"I like Shawn," Randi said to Jaymi. "I thought—you know—maybe she liked me, too. I mean, look at her, she's adorable. Well, I know she's a mess right now, but God, she's sexy as hell. Why wouldn't I like her?" She turned to Shawn again. "I do, you know that. But hey, if you're taken, I'll back off. I may be a horndog, but I have enough sense to not go after someone else's girl."

The three were silent for a long minute until Randi let out a sigh. "Okay, I'll go. Please, Shawn, forgive me." She turned slowly and left.

Jaymi held Shawn's face in her hands, her thumbs gently wiping the moisture from beneath her closed eyes. A streak of afternoon sun streamed through a nearby window and highlighted Shawn's rusty mussed hair. A faint whisper escaped Shawn's lips. "I need to finish the stall."

"It can wait, Shawn. Let's get you upstairs—"

Shawn shook her head. "No. I have to finish and get the horses in before dark."

Jaymi stood and looked around her. "What's left to do? I can help."

"Thank you, Jaymi. But I think I need to be alone right now."

"Are you sure?"

Shawn rose from the hay and shrugged her shirt back into place. She took one step toward Jaymi and swallowed hard. "Yeah. I'll be up soon."

❖

The ground was softening, the mud becoming a more prominent cover than the snow, so Shawn took care in how fast she took Scout around the pasture. The ride was just what she needed: the fresh air, the oneness with the horse, the time to think. Until today, she hadn't fully acknowledged the extent of the trauma she'd suffered at Brinkman's hand. In an ironic twist, her flashback had actually been a blessing. Her weakness with Randi could have ended any chance she had with Jaymi.

And yet, she'd told Randi to stop before the flashback. It was Jaymi she wanted. No one else would do.

Shawn rode Scout to the farthest boundary of the pasture, turned her around, and stopped. The sun had just set in a spectacular palette of colors above the surrounding trees. She could barely make out the light shining in Jaymi's windows in the distance. She wondered what Jaymi was doing. Writing? Sitting at the piano? Making supper? Pacing the living room worrying about her? *Calling Devin or Sara to question why she had become involved with such a nutcase?*

She lightly dug her heels into Scout's sides and brought her to a slow trot around the perimeter of the field. She forced her thoughts to what she had learned with LaKeisha. Shawn had questioned why she was suddenly recalling details of Brinkman's attack and having nightmares. LaKeisha had helped her to understand that she felt safe in Jaymi's presence, which in turn allowed her subconscious to flow freely. This would allow Shawn to face the memories and thus deal with them, ultimately empowering her to overcome her trauma. She would need practice tapping into her inner strength to conquer the fears, so that eventually she wouldn't be crippled by the horrible experience. She needed to remind herself that not only had she fought back, but she had survived. Her focus now had to be on the present and her goals for the future.

Shawn knew she could also apply these ideas to her family. It wasn't her fault her mother had died. It wasn't her fault that in his grief, her father had chosen to blame Shawn for her death. She wasn't perfect and that meant she would still make mistakes. And that was okay. She was okay.

She had also had enough. Enough of wasting time dancing around her insecurities. Enough of letting her past control her present. *I don't want to waste another day without her knowing how I feel.*

❖

Jaymi pried her shoes off by the heels, dropped her keys on the bar, and hung up her coat. She couldn't believe the strength it had taken to leave Shawn alone. But she knew Shawn was right; she had to face her demons and deal with this thing on her own. No one could do it for her.

She wondered what exactly had happened between Shawn and Randi before she had shown up. Whatever it was, Randi would be discouraged from ever coming on to Shawn again. *God, I hope so.*

She changed out of her work clothes and into a T-shirt and jeans. Lacking an appetite, she poured a glass of wine. In the living room, she briefly perused her CD stand and selected a Mozart piano concerto. She turned the volume down to a soothing level and curled up on the end of the couch. She nursed her wine, and by the end of the first movement of the concerto, she realized its usual calming effect was failing her tonight.

Something wasn't right. She should be pissed at Randi, but it was Nikki who was on Jaymi's mind. She knew Nikki was behind Randi coming on to Shawn. Randi's evasiveness to Jaymi's question had all but confirmed it. But why? Despite being a player, everybody knew Randi only made moves on single women. Then again, no one really knew that she and Shawn were together. Well, sort of together. Working on it, anyway.

*Why do I care what Nikki thinks? Why does Nikki distrust Shawn so much?* Jaymi hadn't shared much about Shawn with anyone. But she knew that Nikki would see red flags waving all over the place: Shawn's bad choices in California, her job working for a crazed fan who nearly became a stalker, her decision to bring Mel to Devin's party. The drugs in her car.

How far had Randi's pass gone? *Was Shawn about to cheat on me? Wait a minute. We've never discussed whether or not we're exclusive. Are we even really a couple?*

She got up and looked outside. She was surprised to see someone riding one of the horses. She looked more closely and saw that it was Shawn, heading in from the pasture toward the fence. *God, she's a natural. Just like on guitar. She's so damn cute. I don't know how I'm going to do this. How am I supposed to live with her day after day and not tell her how I feel?* She sensed Shawn's feelings for her were just as strong. Her desire was increasing by the day. Every time they touched. Every time they kissed. Every time they talked and felt close. And after what just happened in the barn, in that instant that their eyes had met, Jaymi knew her eyes had given her away. *Your eyes tell no lies,* her mother had told her when she was a child. Anyone who had ever become close to her confirmed it. And the two people who could always call her on it were Peach and Nikki. Every time.

Twenty minutes passed before she heard Shawn ascending the stairs. Fearing her eyes would betray her once again, Jaymi retreated to her room and closed the door. *She said she needed to be alone,* she told herself, using her respect for Shawn as an excuse. She heard Shawn sigh as she came down the hall. Was that relief? Exhaustion?

Jaymi sat rigidly on the edge of her bed, her chest tight. She heard the bathroom door close and the shower running. She emptied her drink and set it on her nightstand. She was about to get ready for bed when she saw the doorknob turning. When Shawn came in, she recognized the look in her eyes and knew it matched her own.

Shawn's determined gaze was glued to Jaymi's. She stepped deliberately toward her. "She kissed me. It all happened so fast. She just showed up out of nowhere and was talking all this nonsense—flirting with me, and next thing I know, she's got me pinned against the wall and—"

"Shawn, it's okay, you don't have to explain—"

"Yes, I do. I don't want you thinking I cheated on you like Peach did."

"But, Shawn, we've never talked about—"

"Let me finish, please, I need to say this before I lose my nerve." Shawn slowly walked to the window and stared out for a moment before taking a deep breath. As she exhaled, the glass fogged and her voice cracked. "The only reason it got as far as it did was because my hormones were going nuts because all I could think about all day long was how badly I've wanted to make love to you." She dared not move. She raised her eyes and could see Jaymi's reflection, her face backlit from the glare of her bedside lamp, but Shawn could make out the hint of a smile. Jaymi's hands were shoved into the front pockets of her jeans, and her weight was shifting back and forth on her bare feet.

Shawn finally turned around. Jaymi's cheeks were slightly flushed and she remained silent. Suddenly, the butterflies were back. She briefly squeezed her eyes shut and inwardly shook off the insecure thoughts, knowing she couldn't turn back now with the words she had just spoken still hanging in the air. She moved toward Jaymi. "I know you feel it, too. I know you've been holding back because you're afraid—but I don't blame you. You've been burned before, and I understand why you have doubts about being with me." Shawn's eyes began to water.

"Shawn—"

"I don't want to mess up your career plans—I know this is all bad timing, so we don't have to…I mean, I can back off, or move out—"

Jaymi gently rested an index finger against Shawn's lips. Her other hand came around Shawn's hips and pulled their bodies together. "Don't you know by now that my plans include you?" She caressed Shawn's cheek.

Shawn surrendered to Jaymi's arms as their lips came together. They had kissed before, but this time it was different. The physical connection intensified as the exposed feelings flowed between them. Shawn found Jaymi's soft tongue with her own. Instinctively, her hands found their way under Jaymi's shirt and she savored the smoothness of her back. Jaymi took a step back and slowly sat on the bed. Their lips remained locked as Shawn straddled her lap. The kiss lingered a few more minutes until Shawn withdrew and raised her face to the ceiling in an attempt to slow down, when she wanted to do anything but. Jaymi kissed her neck as their breasts pressed together. Shawn slowly pulled Jaymi's shirt over her head and caressed her shoulders as she unhooked Jaymi's bra and slipped it off. She peppered the hollow of Jaymi's throat with light kisses as she worked downward to her supple breasts. Jaymi's chest heaved as Shawn took a nipple into her mouth, massaging it with her tongue and teasing just long enough to make it taut before she did the same with the other.

Shawn raised her arms so Jaymi could remove her shirt. She was braless, her small breasts already flushed as she leaned into Jaymi so she could enjoy them. Together they slipped onto the bed. Shawn unbuttoned Jaymi's jeans and expertly unzipped them, moaning in pleasure as Jaymi continued to attend to her breasts. Soon after, in a blur of motion, the light was shut off and they wrestled with their remaining clothes and the bedding. Their naked bodies came together in a welcomed warmth and softness.

Jaymi ran her fingertips along the length of Shawn's torso so lightly that it brought goose bumps to every surface of her flesh. She felt Jaymi tremble. Their lips met again in a passionate embrace. Shawn slid her hand down Jaymi's stomach. Jaymi's breath caught as it came to rest on the trimmed triangle of hair below her navel.

Their lips parted and Shawn looked into Jaymi's eyes. Even in the dark, she could see the clear crystal blue of her irises, her pupils wide with arousal and anticipation.

"Make love to me, Shawn," Jaymi whispered.

Shawn tenderly brushed her lips against Jaymi's. She could feel the heat rising in their bodies as she deepened their kiss. She knew Jaymi's long period of celibacy might make her climax almost immediately, and she wanted to make sure that didn't happen. She wanted time to show Jaymi how much she was feeling, how much she cared for her, and how much this meant to her.

She lightly pressed her fingertip to Jaymi's clit and began a gentle circular motion. Jaymi's breathing hitched and she made an ever so slight upward movement with her hips. But Shawn refused to take the bait and teasingly whispered, "Not so fast. I'm going to make this worth your wait." Jaymi moaned her approval and reclaimed Shawn's lips, placing her own hands on Shawn's ass. Shawn withdrew her finger and traced a line to Jaymi's breast. She circled the nipple several times, then lightly began a massaging pinch between her thumb and index finger. She did the same to her other breast, and then replaced her fingers with her mouth. As she sucked and licked, she was surprised by the arrival of Jaymi's hand between her legs, and she raised herself to give her better access.

Jaymi, too, was touching her in a maddeningly light manner, and it only excited her more. They kissed again but couldn't hold it long because their breathing was growing more and more rapid.

"God, Shawn, you're so wet and feel so good," Jaymi whispered. "Please, I need you to touch me like I'm touching you." Shawn complied and again found Jaymi's soft wetness. They mimicked each other's strokes, their rhythms as perfectly synchronized as when they played music together. "Oh, Shawn, that's it…Oh, baby, I could make love to you like this all night."

"I will, all night and every night."

"Together," Jaymi moaned. "Oh God, Shawn, take me, come for me. We'll come together."

They cried out in pleasure simultaneously. They wrapped their arms around each other as their bodies convulsed for several minutes and then, finally, relaxed into deep satisfaction.

Shawn pulled the sheet over them and cuddled into Jaymi's body, savoring the soft smoothness of her skin and the pounding of her heartbeat. Shawn whispered hoarsely, "God, that was amazing." She shimmied downward under the covers. "I want you again. This time, I want to taste you." She settled herself between Jaymi's legs and placed a light kiss on each knee. She continued a deliberate series of kisses, alternating between legs, gradually working her way up each thigh. Jaymi quivered in anticipation and gasped at the first touch of Shawn's mouth to her sex. Shawn stroked her gently with her thumbs, opening her, and then released a hot breath into her.

"Oh God, Shawn, you're making me crazy."

"Mmm, crazy…" Shawn briefly touched her with the tip of her tongue.

"Ooh, yeah, baby. Tease me. I want you so bad, but I want it to last." A quick flick. "Mmm…" A short stroke.

"Oh, Jaymi." Another stroke. "God, you are so wet for me." Another smoldering exhalation. A slightly longer stroke. "So sweet, you taste so sweet."

"Kiss me there…"

Shawn's lips pressed softly, and then her tongue began a steady stroke. And as Jaymi's breaths quickened, Shawn's pace followed, and she tasted every inch of her. And then she slipped her tongue inside her, and that was all it took. Jaymi screamed as her hips lifted and her hands grasped Shawn by the hair and pulled her away. Shawn collapsed on top of her, in awe of Jaymi's beauty as she rode out the orgasm.

For several minutes, they lay motionless, listening to each other's heartbeats.

"I have never felt more wanted in all my life." Jaymi's voice broke the silence.

"Maybe nobody's ever wanted you as much as I do. You are so beautiful." Shawn propped up on one elbow and tenderly brushed back a lock of Jaymi's hair.

"I never thought I could feel this way again. Not after what she did to me—"

"No, don't do this. Don't think about her. I know I'm not as smart, and I'm probably not as pretty, but—"

"You're better, Shawn. In every possible way. This is better. What we have. Don't compare yourself to her, because there is no comparison. Not a one. She has nothing on you, and I don't just mean what we just shared. I'm talking about everything we share. The way we connect. The way we balance each other out. The way we can make each other laugh. The way we relate to each other. The way we meet each other's needs. The way we're there for each other, not because we're obligated as lovers. With us, it just happens naturally."

"So maybe I'm not so bad at this relationship stuff after all?"

"You're very good at it. And you know why? Because you follow your heart."

"It's the only way I know."

"With you, I can just be me. All the time. I love that about you."

"Why the hell would I want you to be anything else? The way I see it, that's why you fall for someone—because of who they are. Not because you want them to be someone else. What the hell's the point of that? If you want to change them, then you're obviously with the wrong person, right? My God, Jaymi, to me you're the most perfect creation. Not that I'm saying you're perfect—no one is—and I wouldn't want you to be. Why would I want to change anything?"

Jaymi smiled widely. "I wouldn't change a thing about you, either."

Shawn leaned down and kissed her. "If that's the way you feel now, then I've made progress, because I needed to make some changes. But you make it easy. When I first got here, I was so ashamed of how I'd been living, I thought no way would I ever have a shot with you. Not that I was thinking in those terms." Shawn dipped her head, suddenly bashful. "I mean, I had a crush from before, but I thought you were so out of my league—"

"Oh, come on, it's not like I'm some head-turner like Nikki."

"Jaymi, if you could see yourself the way other people do, you'd know that Nikki is not the only head-turner in the band."

"Yeah, Kay and Brian are pretty gorgeous, too."

"Would you stop it. Anyway, what I was trying to get at is that, with anyone else, I would've been scared shitless to talk about some of the stuff I've done. But with you, I'm not afraid. I can tell you anything. And you've never judged me or made me feel bad about myself."

Jaymi drew her hand to Shawn's cheek. "So I guess you can say we both see beyond what other people see in us."

"Yeah, I guess."

Jaymi rolled over on top of her and placed a lingering kiss on her lips.

Shawn kissed her back, then smiled. "Does this mean I don't have to find my own apartment?"

"Don't you dare."

She cradled Jaymi's face and kissed her firmly, claiming her tongue as she pressed her thigh upward. She broke the kiss and breathlessly challenged, "I dare you to find out what makes me scream."

"Baby, I can't wait to discover *every* way I can make you scream."

Jaymi reclaimed Shawn's tongue for several minutes and then planted kisses on every inch of her neck and throat. Shawn began to squirm, but Jaymi took her time, her lips traveling across her shoulders, down each arm, and then she softly sucked each finger. Shawn's moans grew louder and more desperate with each touch. She then placed light kisses on the flesh of her breasts, maddeningly avoiding her taut nipples. When Shawn's moans turned to begs, she relented and sucked one into her mouth, as her fingers caressed the other. After she had had her fill, her lips and hand traded places.

"Jaymi…Oh God, Jaymi, if you don't lick me soon I'm going to come without you."

"Mmm-mmm, oh, no you don't." Jaymi delicately touched a finger to Shawn's clit and Shawn jerked upward. Jaymi's kisses proceeded down her stomach, and Shawn spread her legs apart, agonized sounds groaning involuntarily from deep within her throat.

"Please, I'm going to explode. I need your mouth on me."

Just when Shawn believed she couldn't wait a second longer, Jaymi took her into her mouth. Her tongue kneaded her gently at first, then slowly stroked in and out, in and out, in and out. Shawn's hips rocked in rhythm. Jaymi flattened her tongue and drew one long taste. Then another. And another. Faster. A little harder. Jaymi exhaled a long, fiery breath and then plunged her lips onto her, sucking and licking hungrily, the vibrations of her own moans tantalizing Shawn into a frenzy. Shawn was so close, and then, without warning, Jaymi slipped a finger into her drenched core and Shawn came. And came again. And came again. When her body finally finished, Jaymi was quieting her screams with a possessive kiss that lasted for half an hour.

# Chapter Twenty-one

Rain pelted the windshield of Shawn's car as she navigated her way to work. She was going to be late. She didn't care. Karla could write her up a thousand times today. She didn't care. They could fire her. She didn't care. *Karla should be grateful I'm even coming in today.* If it hadn't been for Jaymi urging her to be responsible and shoving her out of bed after their amazing night of lovemaking and only three hours of sleep, she would have called in sick.

Shawn's focus wasn't on packing coffee orders. She wanted desperately for the workday to be over so that she could get home to Jaymi and pick up where they had left off this morning—exploring each other's bodies, talking softly between satisfying each other, holding each other close and savoring the absence of clothing. Shawn barely contained her smile all day.

Karla paged her to the office just as she was punching out. *Here comes the write-up for being late,* she thought as she marched her way down the hall, expecting the usual seated pose with crossed arms, downward stare, and scowl.

She sighed heavily and was surprised to find that though Karla's arms were indeed crossed, her face held a wide smile as she entered. On the corner of her desk was a large bouquet of flowers in a glass vase, a large red ribbon tied around it.

Shawn returned the smile. "What's up, Karla?"

Karla leaned forward slightly and nodded toward the flowers.

Shawn winked teasingly. "Looks like you've got yourself a sweetheart, boss."

Karla's smile disappeared. She unfolded her arms and shoved back in her chair. "They're not mine, you nitwit. They just came for you."

Shawn's jaw dropped. No one had ever sent her flowers before. Her insides fluttered. Her heart raced as she heard her inner voice scold her for not beating Jaymi to the punch. *Why didn't I think of this?*

"Well, don't just stand there. Get 'em the hell outta here. I'm jealous enough already. I don't need any more reminders that Jaymi has no interest in me." With that, Karla's smile returned as Shawn scooped up the vase and thanked her on her way out.

Shawn grabbed her jacket and rushed to her car. Her appointment with LaKeisha was in twenty minutes. She carefully balanced the bouquet on the passenger seat and started the car to run the heat. She rubbed her hands together to warm them, and like a kid on Christmas morning, anxiously removed the tiny envelope from its plastic holder and pulled out the card. Her heart sank when she read the message: *Shawn, I am so sorry for yesterday. I hope you can find it in your heart to forgive me. Randi*

❖

"My dear, you've had an eventful week," said LaKeisha. "How are you feeling about everything?"

Shawn shifted in her chair. The room was comfortably dim, lit only by a small lamp on LaKeisha's desk. They sat opposite each other in large, overstuffed upright chairs. Several tea lights flickered in the room—LaKeisha explained she purposely chose scentless to avoid inadvertently triggering any of her clients' memories. Shawn expressed that she was overjoyed about Jaymi but was confused about her feelings toward Randi. Why did she feel so willing to forgive Randi, yet feel nothing but animosity toward Brinkman?

"Because their intentions were completely different. Even though both actions were sexually charged, Randi was after just that: sex. She's obviously genuinely attracted to you—I saw that myself at Devin's party. For Brinkman, though, it was all about having power over you. He tried to bully you into thinking you had no choice. If you wanted what he had to offer you, you'd give him what he wanted. When you had the audacity to say no, you took away his power, which meant his male ego also took a blow, and that's what drove him to force himself on you."

LaKeisha leaned forward with her hands clasped. "Let me ask you this: If Jaymi wasn't in the picture, would you have reciprocated Randi's advances?"

Shawn's heart rate increased and she swallowed hard. As much as she tried to ignore it, she knew in the back of her mind that LaKeisha was a friend of Jaymi's. As if she could read her mind, or perhaps just the look on her face, LaKeisha smiled and said, "It's okay, Shawn. Remember, these sessions are strictly confidential. Nothing leaves this office, okay? I'm not here to judge, only to listen and to guide you through your feelings. You don't even have to answer if you don't want to."

Shawn inhaled deeply and sighed. "Yeah, I know all that. I honestly don't know if I would have let anything happen with Randi. Maybe, maybe not. You know, I think I *have* changed, and maybe I'm just now realizing it. Because if I had met Randi back in California, I would've slept with her in a heartbeat. But when I left there, I made a promise to myself that I was going to make some major changes in my life. First and foremost was to respect myself. And I needed to rediscover my old self. Get my priorities back on track, that sort of thing. Jaymi's just made it that much easier to do it." They quietly smiled at each other. "So if I freaked out over Brinkman and Randi coming on to me, why didn't I freak out with Jaymi?"

"Because with Jaymi, you feel safe. She let you make the decision to move forward and gave you even more reason to feel safe by letting you know the feelings were mutual." LaKeisha smiled. "Our time is up. Which means, off the record, may I just add that as a friend of Jaymi's, I am very happy for the both of you." Her face became suddenly stern. "Now you treat her right, you hear?"

Shawn stiffly jerked a hand to her temple in a mock salute. "Yes, ma'am!"

❖

Shawn stopped abruptly in the hall outside LaKeisha's office. Mel jumped up from her seat and grabbed Shawn by the arms. She led her into an empty room and shut the door.

"Shawnie! Did you find it?"

"What're you talking about?"

Mel nervously looked around her, as if an interruption was imminent. She yanked Shawn toward her by the arm and whispered, "My joints."

Shawn shrugged herself loose from Mel's grip and took a step back. "No, I didn't find them—Jaymi did when she got pulled over by the cops."

"What the hell are you talking about?"

"What were you thinking, pulling a stunt like that? She could've been arrested if it hadn't been Randi that pulled her over."

"Pulled over for what?" She held her hands up defensively. "I don't even know what Jaymi drives. Is it that truck that Nikki was sitting on? Because if it is, I never got inside it."

"You mean you didn't put them in my glove compartment as a prank on me?"

"What? You think I'm going to give up a hundred bucks' worth of weed on a fucking prank? Gimme a break. I can think of better ways to yank your chain than that."

"Wait a minute, Mel, you said you saw Nikki?"

"Yeah. See, I just passed that Randi chick on the stairs, and remembering she was a cop, I was gripping my bag in my coat pocket real tight, to make sure she didn't see it. I was heading to my car, and that's when Nikki called me over—she was sitting on the tailgate of a truck. She asked me about you. Of course I didn't tell her anything. I know we'd just had a little tiff, but I don't dis my friends, you know? She wanted to shake my hand. That's when the bag must've fallen out of my pocket. I was hoping you might've found it."

"And Nikki picked it up when you left. How convenient. Yes, the picture's becoming perfectly clear to me now."

❖

The members of Passion Play spilled out into the lobby of Jenkins & Malden Entertainment Management. They were bubbling with the step they had just taken to increase their chances of success in the music business: Lance Jenkins had agreed to manage the band. The partnership included a booking agent and a marketing/publicity specialist to complete the team. After resisting the pleas of her bandmates to join them for a celebration dinner, Jaymi explained that she was exhausted and had other business to attend to before heading home.

She beamed at Nikki, Kay, and Brian as the elevator door closed with them inside. She yawned and went to the restroom to freshen up before she worked up the nerve to ask the receptionist if Mr. Jenkins could spare a few more minutes of his time.

"Ms. Del Harmon, so lovely to see you again. What's it been, ten minutes?" Mr. Jenkins rose in gentlemanly acknowledgment and shook her hand.

"Please, call me Jaymi."

"Only if you call me Lance. Please do sit down, Jaymi." He held his tie to his torso as he lowered his long, slender frame into his black leather executive chair. "Did we forget something?"

Jaymi handed him a letter-sized manila envelope and took a seat. "Now that we're officially business partners, I hope I'm not being too presumptuous, but I was hoping you would consider listening to this. I've included contact information, a few photos, and a CD. Granted, it's just a home demo and a few live recordings of rehearsal, but I think you'll be impressed with her. She hasn't done many paid gigs, but she's really getting a following at open mikes. Her name's Shawn Davies."

Lance gave a warm smile. "If she's any bit as good as you, then I'd be happy to see what I can do."

"You won't be disappointed. She's got the talent, she just needs some help with the business end of things, you know, to take her to the next level. I'd really appreciate it. Thank you."

❖

Jaymi came in and stifled a joyful greeting when she saw Shawn asleep on the couch. She quietly removed her coat and shoes and tiptoed to the living room. She smiled when she heard the tiny purring snores. She lightly touched her lips to Shawn's and the snores changed to a sexy moan of pleasure. Without opening her eyes, Shawn reached for her and pulled her on top of her. Jaymi plunged her tongue deeper into the kiss as she felt her bra being unfastened and the now-familiar touch of Shawn's hands upon her breasts. She unbuttoned Shawn's jeans and lowered the zipper before sliding her hand inside to find the soft wetness she had been craving all day. Shawn's lips closed around Jaymi's nipple and her tongue followed the rhythm of Jaymi's fingers, slowly at first, and then speeding up with increasing urgency. Jaymi pulled herself away, breathlessly pleading for Shawn to touch her. Shawn swiftly obliged. Shawn's hips raised, taking Jaymi into her farther as they climaxed simultaneously. Jaymi collapsed on top of her.

They dozed off for several minutes before Jaymi awoke with the excitement of her news. She lifted her head and was about to shift onto her side next to Shawn when she spotted the bouquet on the end table next to the couch. She sat up and smiled.

"Those for me? Oh, Shawn, you're so sweet."

Shawn's mind went into a tailspin. *Oh, how perfect would this be if I were to let her think that. Maybe I could. What harm would it do? But it's dishonest, and if she found out...But what are the chances she'd run into Randi anytime soon?*

"They're not for you, Jaymi, I'm sorry. Actually, they're mine." Jaymi's crushed look about broke Shawn's heart in two. "I'm sorry, I wish they were. Read the card, you'll understand." Jaymi plucked the card from the holder and puffed out her lip in a phony pout. "Ah, please," Shawn said. "You're killing me." She ran a finger along Jaymi's cheek. "Come here." She pulled Jaymi into her and held her close. Was Jaymi crying? She couldn't tell. No, she wasn't crying, she was laughing, and then without warning, she was tickling Shawn all over, sending the two of them tumbling to the floor. Shawn escaped and began crawling on all fours away from Jaymi. But Jaymi grabbed a pants leg and tugged as Shawn moved away. Shawn wriggled her way out of her jeans and ran several steps before stopping suddenly.

"What, am I crazy?" she exclaimed, as Jaymi held up her jeans, laughing. She tackled Jaymi and the tickling resumed until Shawn had succeeded in wrestling off Jaymi's pants, as well as half her shirt. They sat giggling for a minute. Jaymi lunged at Shawn and yanked off her shirt and before long, both were completely undressed. They were soon making love again on the plush carpeted living room floor.

"Do you think we can keep our hands off each other long enough for me to share my good news?" Jaymi finally asked afterward, as they were gathering clothes and redressing.

Shawn grinned mischievously. "I hope not."

"You little devil, you." Jaymi shook her head and stood. "In that case, I'd better go in the kitchen and find us something for supper. I'm starved." She scooted past Shawn's outstretched tackle attempt. "Have you eaten? Wait, don't answer that, I'm talking about actual food." She proceeded to throw a frozen pizza in the oven and fill her in on Passion Play's new management team, as well as her pitch for Shawn. Conversation was animated throughout their meal, but Shawn grew quiet as they cleaned up.

Jaymi, noticing the change in her demeanor, hooked her fingers through Shawn's belt loops and pulled her close. "Hey," she said softly. "You all right? I wasn't out of line giving him your CD and stuff, was I?"

"Oh no, Jaymi, uh-uh." Shawn shook her head. "I'm psyched about it. Couldn't be more grateful."

"If it's about those flowers Randi sent you—"

"I haven't even been thinking about that. But I would've been happier if they were from you."

"Next time, they will be." Jaymi kissed her lightly and smiled. "Come on. Tell me what's bugging you."

"I don't want to cause trouble with the band. Especially now. I mean, you guys have a manager and everything—"

"Shawn, don't worry. J&M knows you have your own act and your own agenda. If they decide to take you on, too, it won't interfere with the band. If anything, it will help you get your own career off the ground."

Shawn let out a long breath and walked away. "It has nothing to do with that." She went through the living room to the slider doors and looked out over the pasture. When she turned around, Jaymi was waiting patiently where she had left her but was now leaning forward on the island that separated the kitchen from the living room. Shawn walked back over and sat on a stool on the opposite side. "It's Nikki. She hates me—"

"She doesn't hate you. She's a pain in the ass with everyone I date. Don't let her get to you."

"I don't give a shit about how she treats me, Jaymi. It's the way she disrespects you that I can't stand. And today I found out...Forget I said anything."

Jaymi leaned toward her, her eyes searching. "What, Shawn?"

"If I tell you this—and it's really only a suspicion—you're going to be pissed at Nikki, and what if you guys have another fight and she quits again and she'll blame me and—"

"Shawn, you're rambling. I can handle Nikki. God knows I've been handling her for years. Why don't you just tell me what's going on?"

Shawn deeply exhaled. "Mel didn't put that bag of pot in my car. Nikki did."

Jaymi straightened. "Are you sure?" Shawn recounted her conversation with Mel earlier that day. "And you think Mel's telling the truth?"

Shawn nodded. "Nikki wants me out of the picture, Jaymi. I think she was trying to set me up."

Jaymi shook her head in disgust. Then her eyes widened. "So maybe it wasn't a coincidence that Randi pulled me over. Maybe Nikki tipped her off, then it backfired when she found me driving. But, I don't know, Randi seemed as surprised as I was when I opened the glove box and saw that bag in there. And I can't see Randi going along with something like that."

"And what about the pass at me? You made a comment about Nikki putting her up to that."

"Now that wouldn't surprise me so much. Although it was already obvious that Randi likes you. And we haven't exactly been open about our relationship. It's possible that she really didn't know we've been dating."

"You don't think Nikki might have given her a little push? I mean, look at the flowers she sent me—is that part of some master plan, too?"

"No, I doubt it. Randi may be a womanizer, but she's not an asshole. I think she really feels bad about what happened."

They were silent for a moment. Jaymi finally went to the fridge and poured herself a glass of water. Shawn turned down her offer for a drink, and then followed her into the living room. They sat together on the couch. It was Jaymi who broke the silence.

"I don't know what to do. I don't understand why she always does this."

Shawn ran her hand through Jaymi's hair. "I think I know why."

Jaymi looked at her, bewildered. "You do? Well, then would you please explain it to me, because I think I've hit my limit with her need to control my love life."

"Isn't it obvious?"

"She's always been protective of me. When my mom got sick, it was Nikki who was there for me—especially after Peach and I had that fight about me moving back home. Nikki understood and was supportive. Nikki was there for me every day. And when I came home that night and found Peach had been with another woman…" Jaymi covered her face with her hands and began to sob. Shawn put her arm around her shoulder, but Jaymi pulled away and slid to the other end of the couch, tucking one leg under her as she turned sideways to face Shawn.

"Jaymi, God, I hate it when you cry. Peach didn't deserve you. I hate to see you cry over her."

"But I'm not crying over Peach, don't you understand? I'm crying because I don't understand how my best friend can be so kind to me, yet be so cruel to want to deny my happiness."

"Because she loves you, Jaymi."

"I know she loves me. Sometimes it's more of a love-hate relationship, you know, like Lennon and McCartney. One day we're fighting like siblings, the next day we're the best of friends, writing songs together—"

"No, listen to me." Shawn lowered her voice. "I know she loves you. But did it ever occur to you that the reason she doesn't like you dating is because she's also *in love* with you?"

Jaymi's head shot up and her fingers raked her hair as she rose and let out a frustrated growl. "Not you, too! God, I can't go through this again."

Shawn's heartbeat raced in terror. *Oh shit, I've screwed this up already!* "You did say that Peach thought that, too. But, Jaymi, I know you don't have those kinds of feelings for her."

Jaymi was still pacing. "She used to insinuate all the time that there was something going on between me and Nikki. I've *never* had a romantic interest in Nikki. There was an innocent crush for a month or two—when we first met—but it was more of an infatuation because I envied her confidence onstage. And because I had just come out and I admired her courage to be openly gay. But it was never more than that."

"But that's you." Shawn spoke calmly. "What about Nikki's feelings?"

Jaymi shook her head forcefully. "She's never given me any

indication that she wants more than friendship and a working relationship. If she really wanted to be with me, she would have quit the band—"

"Because of your no-office-romance rule?"

"Exactly."

"That puts her in a pretty tough situation, then, doesn't it? Either sacrifice her feelings for you, or sacrifice her career with the band."

Jaymi slumped back onto the couch. "What am I supposed to do? You think she's pulling all this shit to trigger a fight with me so one of us will quit? That doesn't make any sense. It's not like that's going to make me fall in love with her."

"I don't think she's thinking that way. Maybe she doesn't want to sacrifice *anything*. If the band stays intact, at least she can spend time with you. And as long as you stay single, she still has hope that maybe someday, the rule won't matter once the band has made it. Then she can make her move."

Jaymi sighed heavily and scrubbed her face with her hands. She emptied her glass of water and looked at Shawn thoughtfully.

Shawn wrung her hands nervously, convinced she'd already damaged the fragile bond they'd created.

Jaymi inched her way across the couch and closed the gap between them. She placed her hands over Shawn's. "I meant it when I said that my plans for the future include you. Whatever happens with Nikki or the band is irrelevant."

"But…your career?"

Jaymi squeezed her hands. "I'll have my career, whether it's with Passion Play—with or without Nikki—or solo. It doesn't matter. I will have my career. But I don't want any of it if you're not by my side to share it with me."

# CHAPTER TWENTY-TWO

Jaymi was in no hurry to get to rehearsal. She found herself wishing it was a longer ride. She still hadn't determined how she was going to deal with Nikki. After the speculations she and Shawn had discussed last night, she'd tossed and turned for an hour before Shawn finally lulled her to sleep by softly singing to her. And then the confusing dreams began. Images of herself in various intimate scenes with Peach, Nikki, and Shawn prompted her at one point to wake up and wonder which of the three was actually in bed with her.

She didn't want Shawn to feel guilty about revealing the truth behind the marijuana incident because she knew Shawn was right: Nikki's vindictive prank could have been disastrous for the band. And if her suspicions about Nikki's feelings for her were right, Jaymi had doubts about their friendship and the band's future.

The timing couldn't have been worse. Irreconcilable differences between Jaymi and Nikki could blow the whole J&M deal. By the time Jaymi pulled into Brian's driveway, she had resolved to force the issue aside for the time being and take a more subtle tactic.

"Before we get started, there's something I want to share with all of you," Jaymi announced after they had finished setting up.

"Did Lance get us a recording contract already?" joked Brian.

"I wish. He's working on it, don't worry. No, this is something personal." Nikki abruptly stopped adjusting her microphone stand and tried to act nonchalant by crossing the room to retrieve her bottled water from a table. She unscrewed the cap and took a swig. Jaymi was relieved that Nikki was at least keeping her promise to abstain from alcoholic drinks during rehearsals. "I don't really know how else to say this other than just saying it. Shawn and I are together now—as a couple, I mean, officially."

Brian broke into a huge grin and jumped out from behind his drum set. He engulfed her in a hug and gave her several kisses on the cheek. "I knew it! Pay up, Kay."

Kay smiled. "I ain't paying you nothin'. I'm the one who said I thought they had a thing for each other a month ago." She turned to Jaymi and said, "I'm happy for you, girl. It's about time."

Jaymi looked at Nikki to find her still standing by the coffee table holding her drink. Jaymi searched her eyes, afraid she might see the heartache that had been so obvious to others, yet not to her, and saw nothing new, just her usual black, guarded stare.

"Is this really what you want?" Nikki finally said, taking another swallow.

"Yes. It is."

Nikki slowly walked to Jaymi and leaned into her. "Then I want you to give Shawn a message for me."

"And what would that be?"

"Tell her that if she ever hurts you the way Peach did, I'm gonna kick her cute little ass." She backed away slightly and grinned. She wrapped her arms around Jaymi and held her for what seemed much longer than she had ever hugged her before. When she finally released her, she seemed herself again. "Now let's kick ass on some music, shall we? We've got a contract to earn." She took her place and grabbed the mic.

Jaymi picked up her acoustic guitar and slung it around her shoulder. "You'll also be happy to know that I have finally broken through my writer's block. I have a new song I want to play for you. I wrote it for Shawn. Now that you know about us, I think it's time to add it to our repertoire."

"The drought is over," exclaimed Brian. "Let's hear it."

She heard a similar response from Kay, and before Nikki could say a word, she began to play. It was a simple guitar and vocal tune that needed no other accompaniment. When she was finished, they all agreed to add it to the set list for the gig in Boston on Saturday.

❖

After she'd done her barn chores and showered, Shawn called Randi to thank her for the flowers. It was an awkward but necessary conversation. Randi kept apologizing, saying that she could never make up for what she'd done. The tension dissipated considerably once Shawn shared an abbreviated story of Brinkman's assault. Shawn reassured Randi that she had forgiven her, and by the time they hung up, Shawn was not only relieved but could foresee the possibility of a friendship.

Shawn sat down at the piano. One verse and a chorus of lyrics in front of her, she pecked out what she could remember of the chord sequence Jaymi had been playing a few weeks after her arrival. She repeated the progression, thinking her keyboard skills didn't do it justice. Jaymi's playing had produced a much more beautiful sound. She checked the time and figured Jaymi wouldn't be home from rehearsal for at least an hour. Perhaps she could work quicker with her natural instrument. She retrieved her guitar and began finger-picking the arpeggios effortlessly. Much better.

After running through the verse a few times, she made an attempt at the chorus but found she was stuck in the same place Jaymi was. If only Jaymi could bring herself to sing it, she would find the musical idea to fit. Shawn found herself thinking of her own mother. Their relationship hadn't been as healthy as Jaymi's had been with her mother, but Shawn still loved her and missed her. For the first time in years, Shawn began to shed tears for her mother, and for the closeness lost after she had come out to her.

She put down the guitar and cursed as she made her way to the piano for a tissue. Now she understood why Jaymi always kept the box there. Obviously seeking inspiration from her own experiences on this subject wasn't the way to go. After all, this was Jaymi's song, about Jaymi's mother. She would need more information directly from the source.

She gave the tune three more attempts before moving on to practicing one of her own. She was playing another open mike tomorrow night, this one in Portland, Maine. Each week she chose a new location, hoping to widen her exposure. She was definitely noticing improvement in her performances. *Can't wait to start getting paid for them.*

She was working on the third song of her planned set when she caught sight of her one-person audience in the corner. Jaymi's smile beamed across her face as she leaned in her familiar pose against the door frame.

"God, you're good. I swear, if Jenkins doesn't take you on, I'll have to fire him as our own manager, because if he can't see your potential, I'm going to think he's an incompetent idiot."

Shawn slipped the instrument off and placed it in its stand. Without a word, she walked up to Jaymi and kissed her long and deeply on the lips. When they finally parted, Shawn said, "I missed you today."

"Really? I couldn't tell by that greeting."

Shawn gave a sly grin. "Be careful, or I may skip dinner and go straight for dessert."

"You are insatiable."

"Is it a bad thing that I can't get enough of you?"

"Not so far." Jaymi kissed her again before they went to the kitchen.

Shawn set to work on dinner. A half hour later, she was stirring a pot of rice and checking on steamed vegetables and marinated pork chops in the broiler. Jaymi set the table and left to freshen up and change into pajamas. When she returned, she found the lights dimmed and a slim glass vase containing a single red rose in the center of the table. Shawn was plating their food and turned to find Jaymi eyeing the flower and smiling.

"Is it safe to assume that this one's for me?"

"What if it isn't?"

"You're not only down two strikes, you'll be sleeping on the futon tonight."

"And if it is?"

"Then you're still in the batter's box with a chance to hit a home run."

"Looks like I'm swinging for the fences, then." Shawn placed their food on the table. Jaymi grabbed her around the waist and pulled her in close.

"Ooh, baby, I love when you talk baseball to me."

Shawn whispered seductively into her ear: "Four weeks, three days, and seventeen hours till opening day at Fenway Park." She nipped at her earlobe.

Jaymi let out an exaggerated moan. "Oh God, you're killing me."

Another long, sensuous kiss followed before they finally sat down to eat and Shawn asked Jaymi about her day. Jaymi told her about Nikki's non-reaction to her news of their relationship, and her decision to hold off on confronting Nikki about the marijuana stunt to see how she dealt with the news. In the meantime, Jaymi resolved to be aware of any other obstacles Nikki might use to mess up her relationship with Shawn. Shawn agreed that this approach might be in everyone's best interest, especially where the band was concerned. She, too, would be careful not to give Nikki any reason to feel threatened.

They finished eating and retreated to the living room, and Jaymi asked about Shawn's day. Shawn told her about the phone call to Randi. Ever since she'd met Randi, Shawn had sensed a touch of jealousy on Jaymi's part. She wondered if that had changed. *How could she think I want anyone else? Especially now?* "Anyway, we're cool," Shawn said. "I even think we might be friends. Are you okay with that?"

"Well, yeah," Jaymi answered, though not convincingly. "It's not like you need my permission."

"Permission?"

"Oh, Shawn, I'm sorry. At the risk of sounding like an obsessed, jealous jerk, I am feeling just a tiny bit insecure right now."

Shawn leaned over and rested a hand on her knee. "If there's one thing I can promise you, it's that I will never, ever, *ever* be unfaithful to you."

"I know. I'm sorry. Forgive me."

"Come here," Shawn whispered, drawing Jaymi into her arms. "I know how to get rid of that jealousy real fast." She eased Jaymi onto her back and lowered herself on top of her. Shawn pressed into her groin and responded to Jaymi's hungry look by kissing her hard. Jaymi found her tongue with her own and tugged at Shawn's shirt.

Their lips separated and Jaymi said, "Oh yeah, that's working. But I need more convincing."

Shawn straightened up. "Really?" Swiftly, she unfastened Jaymi's pants, yanked them off, and knelt between Jaymi's legs. Jaymi cried out in surprise. Shawn plunged her tongue inside her. As she licked and caressed and tasted, she felt her own wetness soaking through her clothing.

"Oh God, Shawn. Oh, baby!"

Shawn withdrew just long enough to say, "I can't get enough of you." She claimed her again, and she increased the pressure and speed of each stroke.

"Take me, baby. I'm yours, Shawn, I'm y—"

Shawn sank her tongue as deep as it would go and Jaymi screamed and jerked upward. Shawn kept her lips pressed into her until she felt the waves of her orgasm subside before slowly withdrawing and moving into Jaymi's arms. "Convinced yet?"

"Yeah," Jaymi replied, sounding breathless. "A little."

Shawn recoiled. "Just a little?"

Jaymi smiled mischievously. "Okay. More than a little."

"You sure?"

"Oh yes. I'm sure. Do I need to convince you that I'm convinced?"

Shawn grinned. "Definitely." She got up, undressed, and straddled Jaymi.

Jaymi stretched up and removed her own shirt. "Well, since I'm too spent to move..." Jaymi gently pushed Shawn up and scooted herself down between Shawn's legs. She tapped her own slightly parted lips with her finger. "Why don't you come up here and indulge me a bit more."

Shawn shifted, grabbed hold of the arm of the couch, and lowered herself onto Jaymi's mouth. She let out a long moan as the sensation took her higher. Jaymi was moaning in response and gently guiding Shawn's backside with her hands, rocking her to control the pressure and set the pace.

"Jaymi...oh, don't make me come too fast." Shawn's chest was pounding and she willed her body to wait. Jaymi was kissing her center as if she was kissing her mouth, driving her absolutely crazy. It went on and on and on and Shawn never wanted it to end, and yet she was going to explode if she didn't climax soon. Just when she thought she couldn't take it any longer, she felt Jaymi's tongue flatten against her and begin a steady movement. Faster and faster she licked, and then she smoothly slid two fingers inside her. As she glided her fingers in and out, she steadily flicked Shawn's hardened clit with her tongue. At last. Shawn's orgasm gushed through her.

She pulled away and collapsed on top of Jaymi.

Jaymi wrapped her arms around Shawn and kissed the top of her head. "Now I'm convinced."

# CHAPTER TWENTY-THREE

Lance called Shawn to declare his interest three days after his agreement with Passion Play. He attended Shawn's next open mike and introduced himself immediately after her performance. He went to work scheduling auditions for a backup band for her. Both acts were in the process of recording professional demos, had promotional photos and posters printed, and were playing one or two paid performances each week all over New England. By the middle of May, both Passion Play and Shawn were enjoying success under the guidance of their manager.

With the pasture thick with a lush, fresh growth of grass and the ground finally dry, and the trees in full bloom, Shawn had convinced Jaymi to let her take her horseback riding one Sunday. Jaymi was happy to wrap her arms around Shawn's waist. The long months of backbreaking physical labor had hardened Shawn's body with sensuous muscles. A vibrant glow had replaced the gaunt, undernourished, tragic figure who had shown up, desperate and alone, months ago.

Shawn slowed Scout and halted her in the middle of the field. After they dismounted, they made themselves comfortable on their backs. Scout wandered away a few yards and began to graze. Looking up at the cloudless sky, they were silent for several minutes before closing their eyes to enjoy the clean air bristling across their faces. Jaymi rolled onto her side and propped herself up on her elbow. She brushed Shawn's bangs off her eyes, thinking how cute she was, even when in need of a haircut. Shawn's eyes remained closed as she sighed heavily and smiled in satisfaction.

Jaymi said softly, "I don't think I've ever been so happy in all my life."

Shawn turned to look at Jaymi. "Really?"

"Really."

"'Cause of me?"

"Because of you. Because of how great the band's doing. Because I love it here. Because I'm so glad I moved back home. Because I'm writing again. Because our careers are taking off. Because I'm on the verge of having everything I've ever wanted. There's only one thing that's missing."

Shawn watched the deliriously happy eyes turn sad. "Your mom." Jaymi managed a slight nod before the tears began to fall. Shawn scooted over and took her into her arms. She let her cry as long as she needed to before speaking. "Your mom isn't missing any of this, don't you know that? She's right here." She pointed to Jaymi's heart. "She's *always* right here, with you every step of the way. And I bet she's got the brightest smile in Heaven right now, hearing you talk about your happiness. She has never left your side, Jaymi."

Jaymi hugged her tightly. After a few minutes, she seemed to collect herself, thanked Shawn for her kind words, and sat up. She grinned mischievously.

Shawn looked at her sideways, suspicious of the source of this unexpected expression. "What is it?"

"Ever been to New York City?"

"No. Why?"

"When's your gig next weekend?"

"Friday in Portsmouth. What are you up to?"

"So you'd be free to go to a show with me in New York on Saturday?"

Shawn playfully shook her lover. "Are you shitting me? What is it? A Broadway show? A concert? What?"

"Sorry, nothing that big. Shoot, I hate to disappoint you—"

"Wait a minute. You always have a gig on Saturday nights. How can we go—" Jaymi's grin widened as Shawn jumped to her feet, startling Scout into a short spurt across the pasture. "No way!"

"Yes way."

"Passion Play's got a gig in New York?"

Jaymi stood. "Not only are we playing in New York, but a rep from a major record label is going to be there."

"Holy shit! When did you—"

"Lance called while you were in the shower this morning. Apparently, the rep was in Boston last week and heard about us. He caught our last set, found out we were managed by J&M, and he called Lance. Fortunately he has other business in New York next weekend, and he actually rearranged his schedule so he can see our show."

"My God, Jaymi. Do you know what this means?"

"This could be our big break."

"This is so unbelievable—I'm so happy for you, babe!" They jumped up and down in silly happy dances before embracing and kissing. "We need to celebrate. I'm taking you out to dinner. My treat. Anywhere you want to go."

"I'll take you up on that. And what about dessert?"

Shawn smiled devilishly. "Well, you may have to wait till we get home for that."

"I'm counting on it."

❖

After a six-hour ride on a Greyhound bus, a hotel check-in, a two-hour rehearsal, and a sound check, Passion Play grabbed a much-needed meal at a neighboring restaurant and were then ushered backstage to dress and warm up. It had been an exhausting day following a sleepless night, and soon their lives might be forever changed. Lance had arranged for a driver to transport their instruments by van the day before; the venue had its own sound system, so they only had to worry about bringing their guitars, keyboard, and Brian's drum set, along with Nikki's so-called lucky microphone. Since Shawn wasn't a band member, Jaymi had paid for an additional bus ticket with her own money to avoid making waves with Nikki.

The group seemed uncharacteristically nervous for the first two songs. But it wasn't long before the music took over. Shawn had never seen them more on top of their game. Their harmonies were flawless with an intoxicating energy. Jaymi's guitar solos took on a life of their own, Brian and Kay's rhythm section was so tight it was as if they shared a soul, and Nikki's stage presence and vocal delivery rocked the place into a connection with the crowd that gave Shawn goose bumps.

It made Shawn hungry for her own success. She could feel the craving growing inside her with every song and every response from the audience. And although she enjoyed every aspect of the show, she had a difficult time taking her eyes off Jaymi. *That's my girlfriend up there. I'm living with her. Sleeping with her. She's never looked more beautiful.* At one point, she looked around her, wondering how many women in the predominantly lesbian audience were lusting after her. Jaymi could have any one of them if she wanted. So could Nikki. It scared her. Then she thought, *Someday there may be women feeling the same way when they see me perform.* She thought of Randi's comments about how sexy she was onstage. She chuckled inwardly and warmed to the knowledge that she never had to worry about any of that. She and Jaymi had each other, they were happy, and there was no way in hell Jaymi would ever be unfaithful. Jaymi was always oblivious to that kind of admiration because all she cared about was what they thought of her musically. *I have got to be the luckiest person in this room.*

The two-hour set went by entirely too fast. Shawn hated to see it come to a close. She hated how time had flown by during the performance, and now it dragged as she paced outside the office door where Lance and the band were meeting with Alan Marsden from the record company.

When the door opened at last, Lance came out with the exec and introduced him to Shawn. Shawn's voice cracked and she felt as if she had stepped outside her body as Alan shook her hand. Lance explained that he had given the man her demo and had invited him to attend one of her upcoming performances. As Lance walked him out, Shawn heard Alan say he would be in touch soon, which Shawn took to be good news. Lance returned a minute later with a smile and said, "You're next. Would you like to be the first to celebrate with the band?"

"Celebrate?"

"We're meeting with him on Monday with our lawyer to discuss a recording contract."

❖

Jaymi made arrangements with the hotel's front desk to stay one more night and decided to grab a cup of coffee in the lobby's café while Shawn was in the shower. She sat alone at a small round table and began reliving the events of last night. This was it. Passion Play's big break had finally come. If all went well, they would soon be signing a record deal, making their first album, and then possibly touring as the opening act for a major artist.

She savored each sip and closed her eyes, sending up a prayer of thanks, followed by an imagined conversation with her beloved mother. *See, Mom, I'm on my way. We're gonna make it, you'll see.*

When she opened her eyes, she was startled by an approaching figure, familiar, but far removed from her present life. She suddenly wanted to hide, to make sure the woman didn't notice her, but it was too late. Suri, her ex's best friend, was standing in front of her.

"Jaymi Del Harmon, in the flesh! It's so good to see you! Great show last night. I tried to get backstage to see you but they wouldn't let me in. I work right around the corner and I overheard someone say you were staying here, so I thought I'd take a chance and stop by to say hello."

Jaymi glared, appalled at the audacity of the woman. "I can't believe you can walk up to me and act like nothing ever happened."

Suri shook her head in confusion. "Excuse me...am I missing something here?"

"You don't remember sleeping with my girlfriend?"

"What on earth are you talking about?"

"This is unbelievable. There's no point in you keeping up the charade now, Suri. I know she cheated on me with you."

"Good Lord, is that what she told you? That it was *me* she slept with that night?"

"Yes, she said..." Jaymi thought back to that dreadful night. Did Peach actually tell her it was Suri? Or had Jaymi assumed? She slumped back in her chair. "Oh my God. All this time I thought it was you, and she didn't deny it."

Suri pulled out a chair and sat down. "Trust me, Jaymi, I never had any interest in sleeping with Peach."

Jaymi's mind was spinning. "Well, if it wasn't you, then—"

"She wasn't having an affair, if that's what you're thinking. She showed up at my place that night completely distraught over your decision to leave. I told her to forget about my presentation and that she should go find you and make things right."

"Well, she never did."

"No, because she couldn't find you—she couldn't remember where your gig was. I'm so sorry to tell you all this, but you deserve to know the truth. She was freaking out that Nikki was going back East with you and she wasn't. She was insanely jealous of Nikki. She was convinced there was something going on between you two. I told her she was crazy, but she wouldn't listen—you know how stubborn she is. I guess in her mind it justified what she did. She picked up some singer at one of the bars. What was her name? She thought she was a friend of yours, but she wasn't sure. Started with an *S*. She had one of those unisex names, you know? Sam? Shannon? No, Shawn. That's it."

Jaymi limped onto the elevator in a dazed stupor and pressed the button for the twenty-third floor. She felt the urge to cry but couldn't; she was too angry. *How could Shawn have done this to me? All her chivalrous anger at Peach for cheating on me and hurting me—was it all an act? Was all of this Shawn's master plan to win me over? She admitted to a crush on me from the time we met. Did she take advantage of Peach's vulnerability to make her move with the hopes we would split up and she could have me for herself? Or worse, maybe she's been using me to further her own career. And look how well it's working. Maybe Nikki was right—she can't be trusted. I never did confront Nikki about the pot—was Shawn lying about that, too? Is it Shawn that's trying to turn me against Nikki? Oh God, listen to me—I sound like some paranoid maniac.*

The elevator door opened and Jaymi froze. What now? Every nerve ending was numb. The muscles in her jaw were taut. Her teeth were clenched and her throat hurt as she choked down the hysterical words that were fighting to escape. A cold sweat seeped out of every pore. She stepped into the hall just as the elevator doors were closing. She stood motionless for a moment, forgetting which way to turn for her room. She blinked several times, her vision blurring as she stared at the magnetic key card. She turned left and forced her shaking legs into motion. She swiped the card through the reader and let herself in.

Shawn emerged from the bathroom, fully dressed, her head down and toweling her hair dry. "Hey, babe—did you know this tub's got Jacuzzi jets? Maybe tonight before bed we could—" Shawn looked up and saw Jaymi's face. "Baby, what's wrong?"

The betrayal came crunching through Jaymi's stomach twofold. She forced out her barely audible words, without knowing ahead of time what they would be. "You slept with Peach."

Shawn's eyebrows scrunched up, as if she was not sure what she had just heard. "I what?"

Jaymi glared at her. "You slept with Peach. Peach cheated on me with you."

Shawn tossed the towel aside and combed her fingers through her hair. "What the hell are you talking about? I never even *met* Peach, remember?"

"I don't even know what I remember anymore. All I know is that I just ran into Suri and she said she didn't sleep with her that night. Peach told her she slept with a singer named Shawn—are you saying it's a coincidence?"

"Jaymi, I don't know what the hell you're talking about. Maybe I don't remember the names of all the girls I slept with out there, but I sure as hell wouldn't have slept with someone named Peach, because I would have known she was your girlfriend. It's not exactly a common nickname."

Jaymi was shaking as bits of memories of their final argument bombarded her. *Don't call me that anymore. It was cute as your little pet name for me, but you've got everyone calling me that now, for Christ's sake. I can't possibly be taken seriously as an attorney with a name like Peach.* Her imagination began to piece together scenarios of how the seduction had played out, and now it began to make sense. She closed her eyes. "Alex."

"Who? What?"

Jaymi wandered over to the unmade king-sized bed where she and Shawn had drunk champagne and made love the night before. She swallowed hard and began to feel queasy. Shawn took a few tentative steps toward her and was standing about a yard away.

"She told you her name was Alex, didn't she?" Jaymi turned away and waited in agony for Shawn's reaction, hoping against hope that

Suri was mistaken. "Wavy red hair, tight jeans, collared dress shirt with a blazer. Gorgeous."

Shawn cursed under her breath and Jaymi knew the truth. She felt her heart rip to shreds.

"Oh shit. Oh God, Jaymi." Shawn gently tugged on Jaymi's elbow and turned her around. "I didn't know who she was."

"So you admit you slept with her?"

"Yeah, but I didn't know, Jaymi. She said her name was Alex. And the way she talked, she made it sound like her girlfriend had already left her. I would never sleep with someone else's…Oh, Christ, I'm so sorry."

"I can't believe this. You. Of all people."

"Jaymi, you know me. If I'd known who she was, it never would've happened, you have to believe that. Please, we can't let this come between us—"

"How can it not? I can't even bear to look at you right now." Jaymi began to back away.

"But I didn't know I was sleeping with your girlfriend!"

"It doesn't matter."

"It doesn't matter? It sure as hell matters! You're blaming me for something Peach did to you—she *knew* she was cheating on you. I didn't."

"I don't know, Shawn. I don't know. All I know is this hurts like hell. I need to get away from you. I need to get out of here."

"Don't do this, Jaymi. We need to work this out."

Jaymi headed for the door. She paused and withdrew a fold of bills from her pocket. She counted out six twenties and slapped them on the table. "That's enough for the bus home. I think you should go. Now."

Shawn paled. "You want me to go home? Okay, if that's what you want. We'll talk about this when you get home tomorrow, give you time to cool off—"

Jaymi shook her head. "I want you to move out."

"No, Jaymi, you can't mean that. You're kicking me out? Where am I supposed to go?"

Jaymi jerked open the door. "I'm sure you can find someone to fuck for a place to stay."

She slammed the door behind her.

# CHAPTER TWENTY-FOUR

The next twelve hours were grueling. The day-long bus ride felt like a month. After grabbing a taxi home, it took Shawn only an hour to gather her belongings and cram them into her car. She left Jaymi's money on the table.

She drove for hours, tortured by the idea of another desperate night searching for a place to stay. She couldn't turn to any of Jaymi's friends, that wouldn't work. And how was she going to explain this one to LaKeisha? Karla was out of the question. As was her father. There was only one other person to consider. She had the space. She would sympathize with her situation. The only problem would be her friendship with Nikki, but for some reason, Shawn had the impression that might not matter.

Shawn checked the time—8:45. She hoped to catch her at home before she left for work. She was relieved to see her car in the driveway when she pulled in. This time when the door opened, she was greeted by a police officer in full uniform, minus the cap. The look was impressive. Confident. Strong. Powerful. And seriously beautiful.

Shawn swallowed past the pain. "Hey, there."

"Shawn. What's wrong?"

"You wouldn't have a spare room I could rent for a night or two, would you?"

"Shit. You and Jaymi have a fight? God, look at me, leaving you standing in the doorway. Get in here, will you?" She ushered Shawn in.

"Worse than that, I think it's over." She dropped her pack to the floor and broke down sobbing. "She asked me to move out." Randi hesitated briefly before pulling her into a loose hug.

Randi's body felt strange to Shawn. Her metal badge was cold against her cheek, her uniform was starched and stiff, and the wide leather belt around her waist was hard. Unlike the last time she had been in Randi's arms, there was no temptation to relieve any sexual frustration on this night. She craved the softness of Jaymi's embrace.

She detached herself and asked to use the bathroom, sick to her stomach.

❖

Jaymi went through the motions of listening intently to the negotiations of the band's pending contract before each member took a turn to affix their signatures. If the contract was approved, a series of meetings would follow. Selecting a producer. Recording sessions. Photo shoots. Publicity appearances. Album designs. Music videos. Release dates. Tours.

And Jaymi didn't care. At least, it felt like she didn't care. Yesterday she had returned to an empty room and spent hours soaking hotel pillows in tears. Nikki finally knocked on the door around three o'clock, only to find an emotional wreck of a best friend huddled in a trashed bed covered with tissues. Jaymi hated to tell Nikki what had happened, fearing an I-told-you-so lecture, but ended up blurting out the whole story. But Nikki simply hugged her, listened, and did her best to comfort her. After two hours she had managed to talk her into showering and getting into clean clothes so they could join Kay and Brian for dinner. When they asked where Shawn was, Nikki answered for her, saying that Shawn was unable to get the next day off from work and had to leave, which wasn't a complete lie. They both knew something was up, but sensing that Jaymi didn't wish to discuss it, the subject was dropped.

The worst part was walking into her empty apartment Monday night. The only surviving evidence of Shawn's residence was a solitary rose on the center of the dining table. Jaymi set her bags down and pulled it from its vase, bringing it to her nose to torment herself with a flood of memories of the past four months. How were they going to survive this?

Jaymi knew in her gut that Shawn was telling the truth; she'd had no idea that Peach and Alex were the same person. In all the months

Jaymi had hung out with Shawn at gigs, Peach had never once shown up. There was no way in hell Shawn would know who Jaymi's girlfriend actually was. *Why did Suri have to see me at the hotel?* It wouldn't have mattered who the other woman was, if it had been any other woman but Shawn.

She tried to tell herself that none of this was Shawn's fault. That Shawn hadn't done anything wrong. Not that it was okay for her to go home with strange women for sex and a place to spend the night, but they had been through that a thousand times and it was another life, a desperate time in Shawn's life that she was terribly ashamed of and deeply regretted. And Jaymi had been able to see beyond that and see the real person that she was. *Is.*

But in her heart, all she could feel was betrayal. And not just by Peach. It was Shawn who had been in their bed. It was Shawn who had made love to her girlfriend. It was Shawn who Peach had chosen to bring home. It was Shawn who was willing to take advantage of Peach when she was rebounding.

As the images pounded through her mind's eye, another word emerged that explained how she was feeling: the whole thing felt incestuous. Again and again, she pictured Shawn and Peach in bed together, knowing from her own experiences how each of them made love to a woman. How each of them felt against her bare skin. How each of them kissed. How each of them had touched her. Caressed her. Needed her. How each of them tasted. How each of them found ways to satisfy her. How she had satisfied them. Had they done the same things with each other they had done with her? It was too much to bear.

Jaymi hurried down the hall to the bathroom, flipped up the toilet seat, and promptly lost what little food she had eaten that day.

❖

Shawn jumped when Jaymi entered her own apartment to find Shawn on a bar stool, pen and paper in hand. Neither spoke. Four excruciating days had passed since Suri had inadvertently shattered their lives. They stared at each other for what seemed like an eternity until Shawn knew she needed to explain her presence. "I just came by to pick up my mail and leave you what I owe for this month's bills. I thought I'd be out of here before you got home."

Jaymi set down her guitars and slid her attaché off her shoulder, letting it drop to the floor. She tiredly shrugged. "I've cut back my hours at Blayne's. I need the time for...well, you know. The band's rehearsing three days a week now and—"

"I'm happy for you, Jaymi. You deserve it. You all do." Shawn crumpled up the note and tossed it across the kitchen into the garbage. "That was just to let you know I was here. Guess you don't need it now." She spun around on the stool to face Jaymi. She tried to hold her eyes, but Jaymi seemed to be struggling with maintaining eye contact. "How are you?"

Jaymi slightly shook her head and looked to the ceiling, a distraught laugh escaping her lips. "I don't really know how to answer that right now."

"You look like hell," Shawn said softly, hoping her charm would open a door.

Jaymi wasn't amused and shot her a glare. "So do you."

"Then what the hell are we doing, Jaymi? We're obviously both miserable. Can't we talk about this?"

Jaymi jerked off her jacket and whipped open the coat closet. "I can't. Shawn, I can't even look at you without picturing you in bed with her."

Shawn slid off the stool and took a step toward her. When Jaymi backed away, Shawn's heart deflated. "That night meant nothing to either one of us. Doesn't that mean something?"

Jaymi made a move toward the living room before she spun on her heel to look at Shawn. "I know all that. My head knows it, and I can tell myself over and over it meant nothing to you. But it does to me. I loved her. And you were my friend. I trusted both of you, and you both betrayed me."

"Jaymi, how did I betray you when I didn't even know who she was? We used each other for our own reasons. I was a slimeball, I admit it. But the difference here is that I didn't know she was cheating on her girlfriend, much less know who her girlfriend was. She knew she was cheating on you. I would've never done that to a friend. Especially you, Jaymi. Shit, I idolized you, for Christ's sake. Please, don't give up on me, on us."

Jaymi rubbed her brow. "I just need—"

"You need time. I know," Shawn said softly. "Honestly, babe, I don't blame you for reacting the way you are. I've done nothing but think about how I would feel if I were you."

Jaymi looked up. The dim twilight seeping through the kitchen window revealed tiny puddles forming in her eyes. "I'm sorry."

"Don't be sorry. I'll give you whatever you need. If it's time, you got it. I'll miss you—God, I already miss you so much—and it's making me fucking nuts not to see you, but I'll do whatever it takes. So if that means staying away so you can get over this, I'll do it. But I promise you—shit, I've never promised a girl anything in my whole life—but this I promise you, I am not giving up on us. You're the best thing that's ever happened to me, Jaymi."

Without waiting for a response, she walked over to the door. As she grasped the knob, she turned. "And just so you know, I'll be coming around on the weekends to take care of the horses. I already talked to Alice. I put money down on an amp and a used Gibson SG, since I can't borrow your Strat anymore. Anyway, I won't bother you while I'm here, I'll just do my job and be gone." She pulled open the door and creaked open the storm door, taking one last glance back at Jaymi before charging down the stairs out of sight.

## CHAPTER TWENTY-FIVE

Nikki steadied Jaymi from behind as they staggered up the stairs to the apartment. They reached the landing and Jaymi giggled as she fumbled with the key, failing miserably to slide it into the slot. Grinning helplessly, she turned to Nikki and simply held them out to her.

"I should never let you drink this much," said Nikki, taking the keys and opening the door. "I forgot what a lightweight you are."

Jaymi wandered into the living room. "Thanks for driving me home." Her voice was muffled as she flopped face down on the couch, and she followed it with more giggles. "This is a switch, huh? You hardly drank a thing, and look at me."

Nikki slid an arm beneath Jaymi's shoulders and sat her up. "Yeah, well, I can handle my liquor. Three beers are nothing for me. You, on the other hand…" Nikki knelt beside the couch and took the lapels of Jaymi's blazer in her hands, sliding the jacket back off her shoulders. Jaymi remained seated but wavered, slightly aware of a silly grin on her lips as she studied her friend's eyes. Nikki's face and mannerisms and presence had become so familiar that Jaymi felt like she no longer saw her for the beautiful woman she was. Her large, thickly lashed eyes were a rich chocolate color, her lightly tanned skin flawless, her lips were full, perfectly proportionate to her petite nose.

Nikki obviously became uncomfortably aware of Jaymi staring at her and moved to lay the blazer somewhere else. She began to stand, but Jaymi caught her arm and held it. "How come you're so good to me when I'm screwed up?"

"Because I'm the best friend you got, Jaymz. Haven't you figured that out by now? Haven't I always been here for you? And you're not screwed up—you're screwed over. Again."

Jaymi sighed heavily and slouched back on the couch. "But why? Why am I so stupid when it comes to love?"

Nikki got up. She raked her fingers through her black spiked hair, let out a deep breath, and chuckled. "If we're going to have this conversation for the millionth time, I need another beer." She disappeared into the kitchen. Jaymi heard the refrigerator open and close, and then a fizzy pop sound. Nikki had slugged down half the bottle by the time she returned. Her dark eyes pierced Jaymi's. "I said I wasn't going to say I told you so." Nikki fell into the recliner and shook her head. "So I'm saying nothing."

Jaymi cut eye contact. "I fall too fast. I'm so stupid."

Nikki leaned forward. "You're not stupid, you're a hopeless romantic. Come on—let's find a movie to watch, get your mind off things." She snatched the remote off the coffee table and clicked on the TV, finally settling on an old favorite. During a commercial break, Nikki got up for another beer.

"Hey, how about making us some popcorn?" Jaymi asked, padding by on her way to the bathroom. "And grab me one of those beers, too, will ya? I'm going to get changed."

"Shouldn't I be trying to sober you up?"

"I don't want to be sober right now. I want to get shitfaced and not think about how bad this hurts."

"But—"

"Please, Nikki. I need a break from everything or I'm going to explode. Give me one night like this and let me get it out of my system, okay?"

"Okay, if that's what you need."

Jaymi came back in red Red Sox sleep shorts and a navy pocket T-shirt. She grabbed the drinks and Nikki followed with the bowl. Jaymi curled up on the couch, and Nikki handed her the popcorn and again took her place in the recliner. Jaymi shoved in a handful and looked at Nikki. She patted the couch beside her. "Come sit over here with me. Don't you want some?"

Nikki hesitated, took a drink, and shrugged. "Sure. What the hell."

By the end of the movie, they were both properly drunk, laughing out of control, and reminiscing.

"Know what I miss, Jaymz? I miss the old times, don't you? Just you and me practicing guitar, having a few beers, singing, passing out in your dorm room."

"Laughing our asses off because you couldn't finger a diminished chord to save your life!"

"Yeah, I'd be playing right along, *doot do do wah wah*, then I'd be like, uh, fans, excuse me for half an hour while I fret this chord, then we'll finish the song!"

Jaymi smiled as the scene played itself out in her memory.

"And remember all those shitty drummers we auditioned? What were there, like twenty-five of 'em?"

"We did have a lot of fun. Remember that one guy, Nik, that didn't even know how to play? He just wanted to live out his fantasy of sleeping with two women?"

"Fucking pervert thought he'd get all three of us in bed. Remember how Kay booted him out on his ass before he even knew what hit him."

"Idiot assumed just because we were all lesbians that we were all sleeping together. Funny how it doesn't occur to people that we can be just friends without there being anything sexual going on. Band probably wouldn't have lasted otherwise. Thanks to our no-office-romance rule."

Nikki's smile faded. "Yeah," she said softly, her eyes down. She patted Jaymi's knee and looked up. She cleared her throat and her lips twitched into a listless smile. "Thank God for that, huh?"

"I mean, look at what would've happened if Shawn had joined the band. I never told you this, but when you quit and she filled in for that one show, we—Brian and Kay and I—we talked about it. If you hadn't come back, there's a good chance we would have asked her."

Nikki crawled off the couch and began collecting empty beer bottles. "No wonder she begged me to come back," she muttered. On her way to the kitchen, Jaymi thought she heard her add, "I should've said no."

When she returned, Jaymi asked, "What was that you just said?" She placed her hand on Nikki's arm, interrupting her move to pick up the popcorn bowl.

"I didn't say anything."

Jaymi grasped Nikki's hand and tugged. Nikki plopped next to her on the couch, her head down.

"You mumbled something going into the kitchen. I didn't quite catch it."

"It's nothing, Jaymi."

"Then why the sudden mood change?"

"I said it's nothing."

"I know you better than that, and you know it. Just tell me."

Nikki sucked in a large gulp of oxygen and blew it out. "It's the rule."

"You thinking that with me and Shawn split up, that now it would be okay to ask her to join Passion Play?"

"I'm not talking about Shawn."

"I'm confused. Wait a minute...is there something going on between you and Kay?" Jaymi stifled a laugh, knowing that Kay's taste in women was so far removed from Nikki's looks and personality that any attempt at a relationship between them wouldn't last five minutes.

"Don't be absurd."

"Then, Nikki, just tell me."

"Ah, just forget it." She was up in an instant and yanked her biker jacket off the bar stool. Jaymi followed her and spun her around before she could grab the doorknob.

"Forget what? What are you talking about, Nik?"

Nikki shrugged into her jacket and straightened to her full height. "You really haven't figured it out? Huh? Why I have a problem with Shawn? Why I never liked Peach? Why I never have a steady girlfriend?"

Jaymi knew she shouldn't have pressed. She held Nikki's angry gaze in full acknowledgment of what she was trying to say. "Nikki?"

"Because I'm in love with you, Jaymi." Her voice was just above a whisper. "That's why."

Jaymi's jaw dropped open. She searched for breath. She shook her head slowly, alcohol making her dull. "No, this can't be."

Nikki sandwiched Jaymi's face between her hands and planted their lips together. Caught off guard, Jaymi couldn't immediately protest and became lost in the passion of Nikki's kiss. Nikki had obviously waited a long time for this moment and was taking advantage of the opportunity to express everything she possibly could in this one kiss. By the time Jaymi came to her senses and decided to stop it, Nikki suddenly released her. She escaped full speed, leaving Jaymi alone with her revelation.

❖

Jaymi groaned as the first awareness of consciousness tickled her brain. The first thing she noticed was the incessant throbbing in her temples. She was facedown on top of her fully made bed with her right arm dangling off the side. She shifted onto her side, cringed with pain at the crick in her neck, and cradled her head between her palms. The dull ache consumed her thoughts for several minutes. The notion of being vertical anytime soon seemed impossible.

Curtains wavered with an incoming breeze, causing red and white splatters of sunlight to dance inside her eyelids. She groaned again and rolled over so that her back was to the window. "Shawn?" she whispered. "Baby, you up?"

Instinctively, she reached out to pull herself closer to her lover. Her hand landed with a thud on the empty place beside her. The queasy feeling in her stomach wasn't from the six beers she'd consumed last night. *Shawn's gone.* A grotesque taste of bile crawled up her throat. *And Nikki's in love with me. Or was that just a dream?*

She pressed her fingertips to the inside corners of her eyes. Slowly, she opened them and bravely shook off the cobwebs of the night before. She touched her lips, remembering how Nikki's passionate kiss had shaken her to the core.

*Peach was right. Shawn saw it, too. Why didn't I ever see it? In all the years we've known each other, why didn't Nikki tell me how she felt?* Jaymi knew the answer to that question immediately. It wasn't just the rule. She had never known Nikki to care about rules—except when it came to the band. To Nikki, the band was sacred above all else. The only other thing to which Nikki was as fiercely loyal? Friendship. Crossing the line with Jaymi meant jeopardizing both—something Nikki wasn't willing to do.

Jaymi slid off the bed onto the floor, cursed at the pain piercing through her head, and dragged herself into the shower. She stood without moving for a long time, simply letting the warm water rinse away the remnants of her hangover, in hopes it might also clear her mind. *That was one hell of a kiss.* She wondered how long Nikki had wanted to do that. Jaymi felt what little energy she had draining each time she attempted to process Nikki's confession. There was no way she could deal with Nikki's feelings right now.

She dressed and went to the kitchen to start a pot of coffee. She leaned back against the bar and stared at the dark liquid streaming into the carafe, trying to gauge if her stomach could handle any solid food. A light tap on the door jolted her from her funk.

When she saw who was on the other side, Jaymi smiled for the first time in weeks. She opened the door and stepped back to allow her surprise guest to enter. "Devin."

"Hey." Devin smiled warmly and opened her arms. Jaymi slipped into her friend's familiar embrace, knowing that Devin would hold her for as long as she needed. After several minutes, Jaymi released her and swiped her palms over her wet cheeks. Devin followed her into the kitchen and made herself at home, as she had so many times before over the course of their friendship, and poured them each a cup. She fixed Jaymi's coffee exactly the way she knew she liked it and then fixed her own. They sat at the kitchen table and sipped in silence.

Jaymi had called Devin soon after the breakup with Shawn, but this was the first time they had seen each other since.

"Where's Sara?" asked Jaymi.

"Working. That's what happens when you run a nonprofit organization—you end up doing a lot yourself."

"I can imagine." Jaymi stroked the handle of her cup and held Devin's eyes, which always lit up at the mention of her lover.

"How are you holding up, Jaymi?"

Jaymi shrugged.

"That good, huh?"

"How would you feel in my shoes?"

"Honestly, I can't say." Devin pursed her lips and looked away, as if she were choosing her next words carefully. "I can, however, relate to what Shawn's going through."

Jaymi let out a sigh. "Yeah, I guess maybe you can." She knew she was safe admitting that to Devin, knowing that there would be no forthcoming lecture or clichéd advice.

"If Sara hadn't cut me some slack for the mistakes I made when we first got together, we wouldn't have what we have now." Devin reached across the table and took Jaymi's hand. "At the time, I was so scared of losing her that I didn't always make the right decisions."

Jaymi looked at their joined hands for a moment and then at Devin's face. At no time in their friendship had Jaymi ever been unaware of how beautiful Devin was. There had always been an underlying crush between them, and Jaymi knew in her heart that, had Sara not been in the picture when the two of them had met, she would have pursued more than a friendship with Devin. She opened her mouth to say so, but when she remembered what Nikki had told her last night, she quickly thought better of it. *You're hurt and vulnerable and you'd only be rebounding.* Devin returned the look with love and, as if reading her mind, nervously released Jaymi's hand, further confirming the connection they shared.

"Devin?"

"Yeah?"

"Do you think I'll be able to forgive Shawn, the way Sara forgave you?"

Devin smiled and adorably tilted her head to the side. "I do."

Jaymi sipped the last of her coffee, then took both empty cups to the counter. She stared out the window and braced her hands on the counter in front of the sink. "I'm still so angry," she said, and then spun around to face Devin. "I hate it. I hate that I can feel so much anger and love for her at the same time. I don't know what to do with this *fury*. I want to lash out at her, and at the same time, I want to take her in my arms and make love to her like I never have before. How is it I can feel such opposite emotions simultaneously? What the hell is that?"

Devin chuckled.

"What's so funny?"

"It's no wonder you're such a great songwriter. Such a great performer. You're so in touch with your feelings. I love that about you."

Jaymi smiled, shaking her head. "It's a frigging curse is what it is. Sometimes I'd rather not feel anything. Don't you ever feel that way?"

"Not really. Not anymore. I wouldn't trade one minute of feeling what I feel for Sara, not in a million years. I love her. She loves me."

Jaymi ran her fingers through her hair and felt her stomach rumble. "You're very lucky, you know that?"

Devin shrugged. "I'm Irish." She smirked. "The luck is built in. As for me and Sara, it's more than luck. We have our challenges, but we work at what we have. She's worth it."

"Yes, she is."

"Jaymi?"

"What?"

"I don't think you'd be so angry with Shawn if you didn't think she was worth it."

"It's not that simple, Devin."

"Are you sure?"

"If it was, then why is it so hard to forgive her?"

"I don't know." Devin shrugged. "Maybe because forgiving her means you have to take a leap of faith and trust her again. You couldn't do that with Peach, or any of your other girlfriends, for that matter."

"It's so hard. Did you know she's living with Randi?"

"Yes."

Jaymi grabbed the counter behind her, suddenly woozy. Devin was up and by her side in a heartbeat.

"Hey, you okay? Have you eaten today?"

"No. Just coffee."

"Sit down." Devin settled Jaymi into a chair and opened the refrigerator. It was nearly empty. "Let's go. I'm taking you out for breakfast."

"You don't have to do that."

Devin rested her hands on Jaymi's shoulders, looking intensely into Jaymi's eyes. "You're right, I don't have to," she said softly. "You're my friend, and I'm going to take care of you whether you like it or not."

Jaymi sighed and rested her head in her hands. If only everything was so simple.

❖

"I let her down." Shawn sat in LaKeisha's office. She had just poured out everything that had happened.

"How so? You didn't know who she was."

"That doesn't seem to matter to Jaymi."

LaKeisha looked at her intently and steepled her hands beneath her chin. "So what are you going to do about it?"

"What can I do? I blew it."

"Shawn, you're only human."

"Well, that's comforting," Shawn replied. "I'll just tell her that. I'm sure all will be forgiven."

"Everyone makes mistakes. Hasn't anyone ever let you down before?"

Shawn immediately thought of her father. "That's different."

"Why is it different? Why should you hold yourself to a higher standard? Why should Jaymi hold you to a higher standard? Do you honestly think you can go through life in a relationship and never let your partner down, ever? No one is perfect. And if Jaymi thinks she'll find a lover who will never let her down, she's in for a very lonely life."

"But…"

"But what? If she can't find a way to forgive you, then you have to move on. It's her loss."

"Her loss? *Her* loss? Are you serious? With all the women out there who want her? Trust me, she can do better than me."

"Shawn, you are just as worthy of being loved as she is. Give yourself credit. Think about how far you have come in the last few months. Don't let this one setback negate everything else you have accomplished. You should be very proud of yourself."

Shawn stared at the candle burning on a shelf behind LaKeisha until the flame blurred. The room was too warm, but Shawn felt chilled to the bone. "I hear everything you're saying, but I don't feel very proud of anything right now."

"Give it time. Give Jaymi time, too. In the meantime, I want you to focus on you, and only you. Not on Jaymi. Not on the past. Not on what you may have lost. I want you to focus on what you need right now as an individual."

"You mean, like my career?"

"Exactly. Your day job, your music, your career, and—most importantly—your worth as a human being, with or without Jaymi. You need to stand on your own, whether you're in a relationship or not. Because if you can't, then even if you do get back together, no amount of love for each other can fill the love you each need to feel for yourselves."

Shawn closed her eyes and let the tears fall silently. She knew the advice was solid. But without Jaymi, even her career felt empty. *How do I keep going?*

## CHAPTER TWENTY-SIX

A month passed. June had rolled around with its thick green foliage, plush lawns, clear blue skies, and warming sun. Passion Play was almost finished recording their album, which was scheduled for release in the fall. Lance was aggressively booking them for two to three gigs every week all over New England.

Nikki had insisted that Jaymi forget about her admission, telling her it was her problem and she would deal with it and put it aside for the sake of the band, as a true professional should. When Jaymi tried to get Nikki to talk about it, she was shut down, again and again. It was as though Nikki knew Jaymi didn't love her in return, but couldn't possibly stand to hear it out loud. Rehearsals were often awkward. Fortunately, once the band was onstage, the tension dissipated and they were able to focus on performing. The music, as always, played its role as healer.

Jaymi discreetly kept tabs on Shawn's career through Lance. Shawn had had no news yet from the record company, but Lance was still hopeful and had been booking Shawn for paid gigs in venues all over the region. She was glad for Shawn's growing success, but it tore her apart that she was no longer part of it.

Every Saturday and Sunday morning, Jaymi awoke early, despite her exhaustion from her busy weeks and late-night shows. Trying to go back to sleep proved fruitless. Inevitably, she would fall out of bed, put on a pot of coffee, and sit at the piano. She would sip her coffee and peck out the notes of her unfinished tribute to her mother as the lyrics sat before her, mocking her, begging for completion, awaiting that elusive burst of inspiration that still wouldn't come. She would check the time. Play a little more. Check the time. Sing a little. Check the time. Play a little more. At ten fifteen, she would begrudgingly slide off the bench and scold herself for scuffling to the window hoping for a glimpse of Shawn. She was angry at herself for her weakness, but still she couldn't stop.

And there Shawn was, doing her daily work for Alice just as she said she would. She'd shed her winter garb long ago in favor of jeans and a T-shirt. Her rusty-brown mop flowed in the breeze. Her skin glowed. Her reluctant smile would emerge when she saw Jaymi in the window, before she moved on.

Shawn's sadness might have been well hidden to the unknowing eye, but Jaymi knew better. The sadness had no mercy. She suffered it every minute of the day as well. Why couldn't she get past this pain and welcome Shawn back into her life?

❖

Randi climbed into the passenger side of Shawn's car, grinning. "I thought you'd never get here—those chores took forever. It's a long ride to Boston. Are you sure you want me tagging along?"

"You think I want to play my first gig at the Paradise without a single person I know in the audience for support? This is the biggest place I've ever played. Look at me, I'm a nervous wreck." Shawn held out her hand palm down. It was visibly shaking. Randi took the hand in hers and brought it to her lips. "Hey!" Shawn exclaimed, whisking her hand away. She launched a playful tap on Randi's cheek in a phony slap.

"Sorry. Second nature for me."

"You promised—no flirting."

"I know, I know. But with me that's like telling a wolf he can't howl at a full moon. You know I don't mean anything by it."

"I know. Sorry."

"It's hard enough that you're living under my roof."

Shawn started the car and fastened her seat belt. "Yeah. In the basement."

"Hey, now. It's a *finished* basement. And you've got the whole damn floor to yourself so you can ham on that rocking new guitar of yours as loud as you want."

Shawn burst out laughing. "It's jam, not ham, you knucklehead."

"Well, you are a bit of a ham when you play it, so I think the term still applies."

"You're a jerk."

"I know. We going or what?"

Shawn grinned and shifted into gear. Living with Randi had turned out to be pretty okay, although she ached for the home she'd created with Jaymi.

❖

The audience wasn't as large as Shawn had hoped, but at close to 300 people, it was more than enough to get her blood pumping. Randi had a front-row seat, and Lance stood off to the side of the stage watching his protégé protectively. After a ninety-minute performance, Shawn thanked the roaring crowd and took a final bow. She quickly exited stage left, simultaneously sorry and relieved it was over. She spotted Lance waiting for her wearing a huge smile.

"I have great news."

But before he could continue, the crowd began to chant: *One more song! One more song!*

Shawn's eyes grew wide. "They want an encore! What do I do?"

"You give it to them, silly. Now don't you disappoint your fans. Get back out there and give 'em one more song."

She gave them three. When the lights came up, Shawn's burgeoning fan base finally gave up and began to shuffle its way to the exits. Most of them were taking the handout offered that listed Shawn's upcoming gigs. Randi hustled backstage and greeted Shawn with a big hug.

"Guess what?" Shawn was gushing. "Lance met a guy here that works for Sierra Sparks. Graham Paxton. He wants me—*me*—to be the opening act for her New England shows when she goes on tour this fall. Can you believe it?"

"You're fucking kidding me. She's like the hottest singer out there right now. That's great."

"He said the band that was originally hired broke up last month. This guy's been checking out local talent to find a replacement. He told Lance that Sierra will love me and he's sending her my demo and everything. Can you believe this? I can't freaking believe this. I'm going on tour with Sierra Sparks!" Shawn was jumping up and down like a little kid. "I gotta tell Jaymi."

❖

"I never should have told you," Nikki said. She had shown up unexpectedly that afternoon, but Jaymi didn't really mind. Maybe they'd finally get to talk out the tension. Nikki sat stiffly on a bar stool, fiddling with a pile of junk mail, as Jaymi started a pot of coffee. "I'm sorry."

"I guess a part of me has always known. People tried to tell me, but I refused to see it."

"Really? You knew?"

Jaymi leaned back against the counter and faced her. "You're my best friend, Nikki. I never thought of you as more than that. I'm sorry—I know that hurts, but it's the truth."

Nikki shrugged like she didn't care. "What about the crush you had on me in school?"

"That only lasted a couple months. I had just come out, you know how that is—you tend to fall for the first girl that brings you out of the closet. And really, when I think about it, it was never more than admiration. It still is. I do love you, Nikki. Just not that way." She looked into Nikki's eyes for a long moment until she couldn't stand it anymore. She turned away and fixed their coffee, but remained standing on the opposite side of the bar when she returned. Nikki took a small sip and kept her eyes on the cup as she set it down.

"I think you should give Shawn another chance."

Surprised at the change in the direction of the conversation, Jaymi looked at her incredulously.

"I love you, Jaymi, and if that means letting you go so you can be happy, then so be it. You love her, and I've never seen you happier than when you two were together."

"I don't know if I can—"

"Look. It's not her fault Peach was a lying cheater. I've seen you with Shawn. And as much as I didn't want you two together, I can't deny that she was good for you. I even tried..."

She waited for Nikki to continue, but she remained silent. "What?"

"Shit, Jaymi, I did something really stupid. But it was way back when she first got here and—fuck." Nikki dropped her face into her hand and rubbed her brow. She looked up timidly and released a long breath. "It was me that put that marijuana in Shawn's car. Randi was supposed to arrest her—but then you were in the car and it fucked up everything."

"I'm glad you finally told me."

Nikki's eyes grew wide. "You knew?"

Jaymi explained how she and Shawn had figured out the scheme, and her decision to forgo a confrontation in order to avoid a disruption to the band. As if relieved to have it out in the open, Nikki redirected the talk back to Shawn. "Anyway, in case you were wondering, Shawn and Randi are *not* sleeping together. In fact, they never have."

"Oh? Well, I didn't think so," Jaymi said, though she suspected her tone was less than convincing.

"Randi said she's living in her basement. She hardly comes up for air, just works on her music obsessively." Nikki chuckled. "Randi's frustrated—you know what a horny bitch she can be."

"So, you really think I owe Shawn another chance?"

"Are you still in love with Peach?"

"No." The question seemed so absurd, Jaymi nearly laughed.

"You sure?"

"Of course I'm sure. I haven't had feelings for Peach in a very long time."

"Do you believe Shawn is telling the truth? That she honestly didn't know Peach was your girlfriend when she slept with her?"

Jaymi closed her eyes and concentrated on her intuition. "Yes. I believe her."

Nikki enveloped both of Jaymi's hands in hers and gave a gentle squeeze. Her eyes narrowed. "Then answer me this. Are you in love with Shawn?"

Jaymi immediately felt her eyes well up as she held Nikki's gaze.

Nikki gently caressed her cheek and wiped a thumb under her left eye. "That's what I thought."

Nikki rose, taking Jaymi by the hand and leading her to the couch, where she held her as she cried. When she had run dry, Nikki eased herself from the embrace and retrieved the tissue box from the piano.

"Here's what I think," Nikki said, once Jaymi had blown her nose and composed herself. "You're not pissed about Shawn sleeping with Peach." Nikki arched her eyebrows and pointed her index finger skyward in a give-me-a-minute gesture. "You're pissed because you can't stand the thought of someone else sleeping with *Shawn*."

"Huh?"

"You're not hurting over someone sleeping with Peach—that's old news, you've dealt with that already. You're hurt because you're jealous of Peach sleeping with your girlfriend. Your current girlfriend. Because it's Shawn that you love, honey. Am I making any sense here?"

"Oh my God." Jaymi stood and paced the room. "You're right. Nikki, you're right. Every time I've imagined them in bed together, I'm heartbroken, not because I'm wishing Peach was making love to me—that's what I used to do when I pictured Peach with Suri—but because Shawn's supposed to be making love with me, not her. Oh shit, what if I've blown it? I'm such an idiot. I miss her so much it's eating me alive."

"Then call her, damn it. Because you're making us all miserable, and you're going to spoil all the fun we'll have when our first single comes out."

## CHAPTER TWENTY-SEVEN

Despite celebrating with Randi into the wee hours, Shawn forced herself out of bed early Sunday morning. She wanted to finish with the horses in time to catch Jaymi before she headed out for rehearsal. She hoped she wouldn't mind if she stopped by for just a minute to share her good news.

She completed her tasks ahead of schedule and stared at the stairway leading to Jaymi's place. Slowly, she began to climb, cringing each time one of the steps creaked beneath her weight. *What if she won't see me? What if she doesn't even open the door? She asked for time and I've given her a month. God, I miss her so much I want to crawl into a hole and die.*

She knocked gently and waited. And waited. She took three steps down, stopped, and went back up, rapping her knuckles on the door a little harder this time. Nothing. She headed back down again, only to reverse direction. She raised her fist to knock once more, didn't, and turned and took one step down. After several deep breaths, she finally trudged down the thirteen steps and left.

❖

Shawn leaned against the door, latching it shut with an unintentional slam, and tossed her keys and cell phone onto the kitchen table. After allowing her heavy bag to slip onto a chair, she picked up Randi's note. It informed her that she was on second shift tonight, but she could help herself to leftover Chinese in the fridge. Maybe later. She had no appetite right now. She stared at her cell phone and ached to call Jaymi.

And tell her what? That Graham Paxton had canceled on her at the last minute? That maybe her career wasn't going as well as she thought it was? She'd been on such a high after that show, only to have this door slammed in her face. Although Lance had tried to reassure her that this was only a postponement and the meeting would be rescheduled, that didn't make her feel any better. There was only one person who could comfort her tonight.

She slumped into the easy chair. And so what if this did turn into her big break? Who was there to share it with her? She'd blown it with Jaymi. Blown it before it had even started.

But how could she have known? Peach had lied to her. Well, no, not actually. Alex was her name, after all. But why suddenly ditch her nickname? Her skin crawled as she thought about that fateful night.

*Did Peach know who I was when she picked me up that night? And if she did, was it because she suspected Jaymi had feelings for me back then? Even subconsciously? Was Peach that perceptive?* If that was the case, Peach was one vindictive bitch, Shawn concluded. *Not that any of it matters now.* She fidgeted in the chair; her pocket recorder was jabbing her inner thigh. She was about to stand up to remove it when the doorbell rang.

Before she could open the door properly, it was slammed open, forcing her backward. When she saw who was in the doorway, every ounce of fear lodged in her throat.

"I believe we have some unfinished business to tend to." Warren Brinkman swiftly shoved her away from the door. He sharply grabbed Shawn by the left elbow and twisted. "Don't we, Ms. Davies?"

Shawn's immediate fear was that he would break her arm with his crushing grip, jeopardizing her career, and for that reason alone, she refrained from resisting. Brinkman shoved the door shut with his foot. He pulled her closer, his eyes large as his evil grin spread.

"Such a shame that Mr. Paxton had to cancel your appointment today, isn't it?" Shawn's jaw tightened as she pieced it together. She slipped her free hand into the pocket of her khakis. Her nimble fingers slid over the smooth plastic case of the recorder and pressed *record*.

"You set me up?" Her voice shook slightly as she hoped it would distract him for that split second she needed to withdraw her hand from the pocket. It worked. He tilted his head back and laughed. When he did, his grip loosened on her arm just enough for her to pull away, but as she did so, he lunged toward her, grabbing her shoulders with both hands and shaking her.

"You left me with one hell of a headache, you dumb bitch."

"You deserved it, you fucking bastard—you were trying to rape me."

The back of his hand came across the side of her face with such force it knocked her backward and crashing over a kitchen chair. She swiftly got up on her elbows and pushed with her feet, sliding away from him on the hardwood floor like a crab. Ignoring the throbbing in her cheekbone, she spun herself over onto all fours, got to her feet, and scrambled toward the living room.

As she reached for the phone on the end table, he crashed into her and pushed her back down. "Oh no, you don't." Her forehead smashed into the coffee table and she collapsed facedown onto the floor. Fighting loss of consciousness, she forced herself to blink rapidly. Her brain buzzed as the pain shot through her skull and she struggled for strength to get up.

She turned just in time to see Brinkman lowering his body over her with a lamp cocked over his shoulder. His knees hit the floor, straddling her hips and pinning her down.

"Poetic justice, wouldn't you say?" He laughed.

"No!" Shawn screamed, twisting her body and shielding her face in the crook of her arm as the lamp slammed down. It shattered on the coffee table, sending shards of glass and porcelain in every direction. He laughed again.

"You're right. This would be no fun at all if you were unconscious while I collected on our little agreement, don't you think?"

"And what agreement would that be, Mr. Brinkman?" Shawn said snidely. "I never saw the recording contract you promised me, either. You know, the one you promised me in exchange for sex."

Brinkman squeezed his knees into her ribs and, with a cocky smile on his lips, leaned back slightly and removed his tweed suit jacket. Shawn punched at his chest and tried in vain to squirm away, but he quickly dropped the garment, grabbed her wrists, and shoved them down onto the floor above her head. "If you cooperate with me now, and give me what I asked for six months ago, then perhaps I'll put that offer back on the table."

"Fuck you, Brinkman. I'd rather flip burgers the rest of my life than sell my soul for what you've got to offer." She swiftly spat into his face, and when he reflexively pulled back, she gathered her strength and pushed her body upward enough to tip his balance. She stretched her neck and bit down hard on his forearm. He hollered and immediately let go of her to grab his arm. In an instant, she shoved him off her, with an agonizing grunt as pain shot through her left arm. She took off down the hall toward Randi's bedroom. One thought pounded through her mind: Randi kept a gun in her nightstand.

Shawn ran to the nightstand, but Brinkman grabbed her by the shoulders and yanked her backward before shoving her face down onto the bed. He jumped on top of her and took a fistful of her hair and jerked her head back. He breathed hard onto the back of her neck.

"You're nothing but a useless whore."

"You'll be sorry. I live with a cop."

"Nice try, freak."

*Oh God. This can't be happening. Not again.* "Get off me!"

"Not till I get what I came for, bitch."

"Eat shit and die."

Brinkman laughed. "You are a feisty one, I'll give you that."

With all her might, Shawn whipped her head back and crashed it into his face. As he grabbed for his bloodied nose, she heaved her body upward and sent him tumbling onto the floor. He crawled to his knees and looked up to find himself staring into the barrel of a 9 mm semiautomatic.

Shawn growled through clenched teeth, "I said, *get off me.*"

And then she heard the sweet sound of an unexpected voice. "Party's over, scumbag."

"It's about time you got home, Officer Hartwell." Shawn sighed with relief as Randi entered with her gun drawn. The room went blessedly dark as she passed out.

❖

After a quick, staccato phone call from Randi, Jaymi and Nikki arrived to what looked like a scene out of a movie: three police cars with their blues flashing, two officers escorting a handcuffed man out the front door, and an ambulance parked in the driveway. As Jaymi took in the scene and scanned for someone who might be able to update them, Randi stepped out the door and held it open as the techs emerged, carrying a loaded stretcher.

"Shawn," exclaimed Jaymi, scurrying alongside as they wheeled the gurney toward the ambulance. "Shawn, are you all right?" Shawn's head was bandaged and her cheek was already turning purple and swelling. "What the hell happened?"

Shawn's face lit up at the sight of Jaymi. She cocked one side of her lip upward and said, "Never been better. But it's a long story."

"She may have a concussion, so we've got to take her in," said one of the EMTs.

"Can I ride with her?" asked Jaymi.

"You may ride along, but really, it's up to the patient," said the EMT. He took note of Shawn's nod, but they were delayed one more time when Randi gently shoved her way in and leaned over Shawn.

"We've got him."

"Is it enough?" replied Shawn.

"I think so, but we'll let the lawyers sort that out. Either way, he's going away for a long time. He's wanted on a whole shitload of stuff—fraud, assaults, bad checks, you name it."

Jaymi looked at Randi, puzzled. "What're you guys talking about? Who?"

"Shawn got the whole thing on tape with that recorder she carries in her pocket." She turned back to Shawn and smiled. "Maybe if this music biz thing doesn't pan out for you, you should think about joining our undercover squad, huh?" She placed a quick kiss on Shawn's cheek. "You did great."

"Hartwell! Let's go!" shouted one of the police officers.

"Damn it. Listen, I have to go to the station and fill out my reports. I'll call the hospital to check on you, all right? Don't worry, you're in good hands."

Once they all settled into the ambulance, the events of the evening seemed to catch up with Shawn. She blinked repeatedly at Jaymi, fading in and out of consciousness and struggling to speak. Jaymi leaned over to hear her whispers.

"She said her name was Alex...not Peach. Sorry...so sorry..."

Tears spilled from the corners of Shawn's eyes until she finally lost consciousness altogether.

❖

Shawn was admitted to the hospital and kept under observation overnight for a mild concussion. She awoke at some point during the night to see Jaymi asleep in a chair next to her. She had no recollection of arriving at the hospital or anything that happened once they got there. She vaguely recalled Jaymi in the ambulance with her. She tried to speak, but her voice was barely a whisper.

"Jaymi." Jaymi stirred slightly. "Jaymi."

Jaymi bolted upright, "Shawn. Are you okay? You need me to get the nurse?"

"No." She shifted her weight, tried to roll onto her side, then winced and stopped. "My shoulder…"

Jaymi was now standing by the bed. "It's sprained," she whispered. "Don't get up, just try to relax. You need anything? Drink of water? Bathroom?"

"No, I just need…" A lump caught in her throat.

"What, sweetheart?"

Shawn smiled and closed her eyes. "That was it."

"What was it?"

Shawn's eyelids parted ever so slightly. "You called me sweetheart. That's what I need. I need you."

Jaymi gently brushed Shawn's bangs off her face. "You need to sleep, sweetheart. Okay?"

Shawn nodded and drifted off again.

❖

Shawn awoke the next morning to the sounds of unfamiliar voices asking Jaymi to leave the room. Her temperature was taken. Her blood pressure was checked. Her eyes were checked. Her reflexes were tested. She was asked a series of questions—her name, her date of birth, did she know where she was and why she was there. She figured she must have passed the tests when they told her she'd be going home in about an hour. Jaymi, she was told, was waiting outside at the nurses' station with Randi.

The entourage filed out and it was then that she noticed there were cards, bouquets of flowers, and balloons all over the room. Nikki, Kay, Brian, and Lance came in moments later. LaKeisha was right behind them, carrying a giant Mylar balloon with a teddy bear on it with a bandaged head and a *Get Well Soon* message.

"Where'd all these flowers come from?" Shawn asked, after letting everyone know she was feeling better.

Nikki answered, "Who do you think? Your fans."

Shawn scoffed. "Yeah, right. Fans. Seriously, did you guys do all this?"

Kay pointed to one of the vases. "Just that one, from the band, and there's one from Lance, of course." She flipped over the cards of a few others. "And this one's from your boss, Karla, and your coworkers. Jaymi called her last night. She said you've got sick pay to cover you the rest of the week."

LaKeisha tied her balloon to the bedrail. "This is from me, Sara, and Devin. They both send hugs and wishes to get well."

Nikki grinned. "You made the news last night, kid. Seriously, the rest are from fans. Guess you're more famous than you thought."

Shawn was quietly absorbing this unfamiliar territory and was unexpectedly saddened by one thought. LaKeisha placed her hand on Shawn's arm. "What is it, sweet baby?"

"I don't suppose there's anything here from my father?"

They all looked at each other silently for a minute and, without a word, began checking the tags and cards. When they finished, LaKeisha pursed her lips and slowly shook her head. "I'm sorry, sweetie," she said softly, taking Shawn's hand in hers and giving it a squeeze. Shawn pinched her eyes shut and swallowed hard.

"We're gonna go so you can get some rest, all right?" said LaKeisha. Each visitor took a turn giving Shawn a kiss on her good cheek and a few words of encouragement before heading out.

❖

A doctor walked up to the group of women and looked at them questioningly. "Which of you is taking Shawn Davies home?"

Jaymi and Randi answered simultaneously, "I am."

"What?" Jaymi said. "Under the circumstances, don't you think she'd feel safer with me at my place than at your house where she's likely to be reminded of what just happened?"

"How do you know she wants to go home with you? Do you know how bad you hurt her?"

"Guys, cool it, will you?" said Nikki.

The doctor loudly cleared his throat, interrupting the argument. When he had their undivided attention, he said, "Shawn is ready to be discharged, but she will need a few days' rest and she needs to follow up with her doctor. The nurse will have written discharge instructions to send home with her. I trust you'll figure out which home that is by then?" Jaymi nodded, and a split second later Randi did, too. The doctor left them, apparently satisfied.

"Look, I know I hurt her, but—" started Jaymi.

"Damn right. Who the hell saved her last night, huh? No one can keep her safer than I can. Besides, all her stuff's at my house."

"Are you forgetting that you once hit on her, too? Do you know what that did to her? She's not just another one of your conquests, Randi."

Nikki swiftly wedged herself between them. "God damn it, you guys, would you listen to yourselves? Fuck it, *I'll* take her home if it'll shut you two up. Problem with that is she doesn't give two shits for me, so she probably wouldn't be too happy with that arrangement. Don't you think the logical solution here is to ask Shawn what she wants?"

"She's coming home with me," Jaymi stated. "She told me last night she needs me, and I don't intend to let her down, especially now." She made a move toward Shawn's room, but Nikki intercepted her.

"I'll go. Can I trust you guys not to kill each other while I'm in there? Huh? Just cool your jets a minute." She rolled her eyes, shaking her head at the ceiling, and walked away, muttering, "Jesus."

Nikki knocked lightly and Shawn said to come in. She was dressed and sitting in a wheelchair. Nikki managed a smile and asked, "How're you doing, kiddo? They should have a better set of wheels for rock stars than that old thing."

"As long as it gets me the hell outta here, I don't care. The nurse said they'll be back to get me in a few minutes. Where's Jaymi?"

"She and Randi are out there fighting over who gets to take you home."

A slow smile broke out on Shawn's face. "Really? And who's winning?"

"At the moment, I am." Shawn raised her eyebrows and they shared a nervous laugh. "It's up to you, Shawn. You tell me where you want to go, and I will gladly deliver you there safely."

Shawn was thoughtful for a moment and let out a deep breath. "Jaymi really wants me to come home?"

Nikki pulled a chair up next to her and sat. "You still think of Jaymi's place as home, don't you?"

"Yeah. I do. But we still have things to work through, and I don't want her doing this just because of what happened last night."

"Shawn, she loves you. She would've asked you yesterday, but you were already gone when she got to the door."

Shawn's eyes grew wide. "She knew I was there yesterday?"

"Yeah. You caught her in the shower. By the time she realized someone was at the door, it was too late. Plus…well, she won't admit it, but she's afraid you've got something going with Randi—which I know you don't, and I've told her so—but she's a bit jealous anyway."

"So she still thinks I'm a player."

"No, she's blaming herself for the whole mess—you guys breaking up, you being attacked last night, everything. Bottom line is, she loves you and she's about to start a brawl out there for the right to take you home with her. Which means you better make up your mind fast, and I better get back out there to make sure security isn't hauling them off and tossing them out on their keisters."

Shawn thought for a moment and then said, "Please call Randi in here. And give us a few minutes alone."

"Your wish is my command."

A minute later, the door opened and Randi entered. "Hey, you wanted to see me?"

"Yeah. Randi, I don't know how I'll ever thank you for what you did—and don't just shrug it off that you were just doing your job. You saved my life."

"I don't know about that."

"Well, I do. He might not have killed me, but if you hadn't come in when you did, I might've killed him."

"It would've been self-defense, you know, if you did. Bastard would've deserved it, too."

Shawn dropped her face into her hands and shook her head. Her teeth clenched as she seethed out her words. "I wanted to. I wanted to so bad. I've never felt so much hatred—all the fear I've had to live with, and the nightmares, the way that asshole has tormented me all these months. I wanted to blow him away, and it scares the living shit out of me that I felt that way." She shuddered. Randi knelt in front of her and cradled her hands.

"I know. Trust me, I know what that feels like. It's okay. You're okay now."

"I'm not a violent person, but at that moment, when I pointed that gun at him..." Shawn's voice faltered. "I just wanted him to stop." A tear escaped and ran slowly down her cheek.

"I know. And you did stop him. We stopped him together, and now he's going away for a long time. He can't hurt you ever again."

Shawn nodded, wiping her nose with the back of her hand. Randi stood and searched the room, finding a tissue to hand her. She blew her nose and sat up a little straighter, composing herself. "You've been a good friend to me, Randi." Randi shrugged, her arms folded. "But you do know that's all we'll ever be, right? Friends?"

"Hey, yeah, no sweat," Randi said gruffly, pacing a semicircle. "You know I'm not really a settling-down kind of girl. And you've never led me on to think you wanted more, so don't sweat it, all right?"

"I hope you know how much I appreciate everything you've done for me over the last month or so."

"But you're going home with Jaymi. Fine. That's fine. I understand."

"Randi, it's not that I don't like living with you, but if Jaymi's giving me a chance to work things out I have to take it. I love her. I want to go home."

# CHAPTER TWENTY-EIGHT

Shawn waited on the couch while Jaymi made them tea. Obviously housekeeping hadn't been a priority lately. The place needed dusting and vacuuming. Junk mail was piled up on the breakfast bar. Lead sheets and pages of lyrics and miscellaneous papers cluttered the coffee table. An acoustic guitar was in the recliner. Shawn picked up one of the papers and immediately recognized it as another attempt at Jaymi's song for her mother. No progress since she had seen it a month ago.

Jaymi settled onto the couch next to Shawn with their cups of tea. "I want you to come home. To stay."

Shawn let Jaymi's words hang in the air for a moment. Her gut was reacting much differently than she had expected it to. The underlying tension of this impending discussion had been conveniently kept at bay while they stopped at Randi's to gather a few days' worth of necessities, and then driven the thirty-five minutes to Jaymi's place. After helping her change into sleep clothes, Jaymi had settled her into her own bed. Shawn had slept for much of the day. When she awoke, she took a bath and dressed in a pair of loose jeans and an old T-shirt.

"Jaymi, I know finding out about me and Peach was an awful thing. But you've hurt me, too."

"I know. And I'm sorry."

Here was the moment Shawn had been waiting for. Jaymi was admitting that she wanted her back. But for the first time in her life, she was feeling a love for herself that outweighed the importance of anything else she had ever experienced. As foreign as this feeling was, it felt good. There was no one, not even Jaymi Del Harmon, who mattered to her more now than herself. And, as she had learned from her sessions with LaKeisha, that wasn't a bad thing. Self-caring wasn't the same thing as selfishness. Self-worth was a new discovery that she wasn't about to relinquish. Not now. Not ever.

"Jaymi, you—more than anybody—know how hard I've busted my ass to turn my life around. You made me want to be a better person. And something else happened, too. I felt something I had never felt before. I fell for you. Shit, I wanted you so much. But you had a girlfriend. It killed me. Every day. Every time I saw you. It killed me.

"So I tried to convince myself that it was okay. At least we were friends. It was better than nothing. And then, you were gone." Shawn lifted her head and swallowed hard. Her eyes were filling up fast. "You never even said good-bye. You were just…gone. I had to hear through the grapevine you had gone back home because your mother was ill. I understood why you left. But when you didn't even say good-bye, it was like I didn't matter to you, just like I didn't matter to anyone else."

"Oh, Shawn, you're wrong about that. You *did* matter, I was just such a wreck at that time—I withdrew from everybody, not just you."

"But I didn't know that. To me, things were just the way I had always suspected, that you meant more to me than I did to you. That maybe the friendship wasn't as strong as I thought it was. That's the way I thought back then."

"I'm sorry I made you feel that way. It was never my intention to hurt you the way I did."

"So how do you think it makes me feel when you throw my past in my face? The last thing you said to me in New York was that I could find a woman to seduce for a place to sleep. Do you know what that did to me? I'm not that person anymore, Jaymi. I will *never* be that person again. I need you to believe that. I need you to know that the human being I am is the one you've been with for the past six months. That's who I am. You brought out the best in me, and I am not about to let you or anyone else take that away from me ever again."

Jaymi wanted to hug her. More than anything, she wanted to cradle Shawn in her arms and never let her go. But after her gut-wrenching words, she wasn't so sure that was what Shawn wanted. Had she been wrong to assume that Shawn would automatically take her back? Had she been that arrogant? She remained still and let Shawn cry, fighting off the temptation to touch her by getting up to bring her the tissue box. When she appeared to regain most of her composure, Jaymi finally spoke.

"I was jealous."

"What?"

"When I found out from Suri that Peach had slept with you, I was so unbelievably jealous."

"Well, of course you were, she was your girlfriend."

Jaymi took Shawn's hand in hers and looked her in the eye. "You don't understand. At the time that it happened, yes, that's how I felt. But when I found out a month ago, that it was you she was with, I was devastated. Not because it brought up feelings for Peach again, but because I couldn't bear the thought of you making love to someone else. That's why I freaked out—because it felt like you had cheated on me."

"What're you saying?"

"I don't give a damn about Peach, Shawn. If it hadn't been you she slept with, it would've been someone else. That relationship would have ended no matter what. I'm glad it did." She touched a hand to Shawn's cheek and looked directly into her eyes. "I love you, Shawn."

"You love me?"

"Yes. I do. And I want to say I forgive you, but there is nothing to forgive you for. You didn't do anything wrong. I'm the one who needs to beg for your forgiveness." She squeezed Shawn's hand. "Please." Jaymi's eyes watered. "You've been nothing but good to me. I don't deserve you. Please forgive me and move back home. I don't want to be without you another minute."

Shawn took a deep breath and Jaymi thought she was going to say something, but she didn't. Her hesitation prompted Jaymi to continue. "I promise you, I will never put you down for your past mistakes ever again. I promise. I was angry and confused—that's no excuse, I know, but I've regretted those words since they left my mouth, and I am so sorry. You don't know how proud I am of you for all you've accomplished. How proud I was to be with you. You are a beautiful, loving, giving person, Shawn—I hope you know that. And your talent, oh God, your amazing talent as a performer, musician, songwriter. Whenever I've watched you onstage, I've seen the women in the crowd lusting after you, and I just gloat inside because it's me you came home with and made love to every night."

A slow smile was growing on Shawn's face. "Please, go on. Flattery will get you everywhere."

Jaymi's lips twitched upward. "I love your eyes and your wild, untamed hair."

"And?"

"And when you play your guitar I fantasize about being the strings under your fingers."

"Oh, really? I thought I was the only one who did that."

"And I miss your delicious home-cooked meals."

"Aha! The truth comes out."

"Baby, I've been a wreck since we've been apart. Look at this place—I haven't been able to write. I can barely get myself out of bed and get down to the studio. I should be on cloud nine with the band's contract and all the gigs we've been getting, and I can't feel any love for it at all. I'm just going through the motions for what should be the best thing that's ever happened to me. And last night, when we were on our way to save you from that despicable creep, it was so clear to me that I might possibly have thrown away the best thing that's really happened to me. You. You talk about bringing out the best in someone, well, you do the same for me, sweetheart. Shawn, I love you so much. And I will do whatever it takes to win your heart."

Shawn leaned into Jaymi and rested a hand on her cheek. "Baby, you won my heart the day we met. I love you, too. I love you so much."

Shawn slipped her hand behind Jaymi's neck and pulled her toward her. "I forgive you." Their lips met in a searing kiss. Shawn eased Jaymi onto her back on the couch. One hand found its way under Jaymi's shirt, and she reveled in Shawn's caress. Jaymi wrapped her legs around Shawn. They sat up and Jaymi gingerly removed Shawn's shirt, mindful of her sprained shoulder, and then ripped off her own shirt before lying back down, their naked breasts pressed together.

Jaymi's breath caught as Shawn kissed her throat and neck. Her hand gently circled Jaymi's left breast.

"We need more room. I'm afraid I'll hurt your shoulder." Jaymi held out her hand for Shawn and they left a trail of clothing in the hall in between kisses. Jaymi yanked back the covers and carefully lowered Shawn onto the bed. Their naked bodies came together.

"Oh God," whispered Jaymi, "I've missed you so much."

"I know, me, too. These last few weeks almost killed me." Shawn nuzzled Jaymi's neck. "You're beautiful. So incredibly beautiful. I love you so much."

"I love you, too. More than I ever thought possible." She gently caressed Shawn's bruised cheek and brushed her bangs back. "All I want to do right now is be here with you, in your arms, where I belong." Jaymi wrapped herself around Shawn and held her tenderly.

"It's good to be home," whispered Shawn, sinking into Jaymi's embrace and gentle kisses on her cheek and temple.

❖

The applause quieted as Nikki addressed the crowd. "You all like surprises?" The audience roared affirmatively. "Good. What about you, Jaymi?"

Jaymi cocked her head in confusion. "What are you up to, Nikki?" she answered into her mic. Out of the shadows from the back corner of the stage, a figure approached with an acoustic guitar. The crowd erupted. Jaymi beamed. A month had passed since Brinkman's attack. Passion Play's bookings were back on schedule after a two-week hiatus taken while Jaymi waited on Shawn hand and foot, nursing her back to health and refusing to leave her alone. Shawn had made a complete recovery, other than some residual stiffness in her shoulder that Jaymi was more than willing to massage for her.

"Ladies and gentlemen," said Nikki, "performing a brand-new song for the first time for you right now, please welcome our friend, the amazingly talented Shawn Davies!"

Nikki retreated to the piano as Shawn took her place at the microphone and began plucking the strings of her guitar. Four bars into the tune, Nikki began to play along and Shawn spoke into the mic as she turned to Jaymi. "This is for you and your mom, Jaymi."

Jaymi immediately recognized the melody. Resisting the urge to sing along, she stayed still and absorbed the emotional voice singing her lyrics in a beautiful melody. The effect of the simple guitar and piano accompaniment was genius, and when Shawn launched into the powerful chorus that had eluded Jaymi for years, their eyes locked and her own filled with tears. Jaymi joined in on the second verse and harmonized organically into the final chorus. The song ended and they

spontaneously swung their guitars behind their backs and embraced—
to the delight of the crowd screaming at the top of their lungs.

"Thank you, Shawn. So beautiful. I love you, oh God, do I love
you."

Shawn's voice caught on emotion so overwhelming she could do
nothing but relish the moment—the crowd noise, the joy in Jaymi's
eyes, the loving energy that filled the room. She held Jaymi's eyes and
could say only one thing. "Kiss me."

Jaymi's eyes flew open wide. "Here? Now?"

"Right here. Right now."

Jaymi took Shawn into her arms and they came together in a
passionate kiss. The crowd noise became deafening.

❖

Shawn and the band joyously stepped offstage as the demands for
an encore echoed throughout the concert hall.

"Damn, I love playing in Boston," said Nikki.

Lance joined them and looked like he was about to burst with
pride. "Great show, guys! I hope you all aren't too attached to your day
jobs."

"What do you think, Lance? What's up?" asked Brian.

"Graham Paxton is here."

Shawn groaned. "Oh shit, it's like a recurring nightmare."

"Not this time, darling. The real Graham Paxton. As in the real
Graham Paxton who works for the real Sierra Sparks."

"But why?" Jaymi asked.

"It turns out that Sierra really does need an opening act this fall
for the New England leg of her tour. When Graham told her about what
Brinkman did, she had him check into Shawn for herself. That led him
to check out Passion Play, too."

They looked at him expectantly and he smiled. "They loved it.
All of it." He turned to Shawn. "But their favorite part was when you
performed with the band."

"Wait a minute, who's *they*? Holy shit, are you saying that Sierra
Sparks is here, too?" blurted Shawn.

"No, she couldn't make it. He sent her a video feed from his smartphone. But there's a catch. She wants both acts, but she can only book one to take on the road with her."

Everyone got quiet. Jaymi turned to face Shawn. "It should be you, Shawn. You're the one he came out here to see. It's because of you that they saw us perform."

"But I don't even have my own band yet. You guys are way more ready to tour than I am. This crowd paid to see you guys, not me."

Lance loudly cleared his throat. "She wants all of you. Together. You're going to have to join Passion Play, Shawn, at least temporarily. Don't worry, you'll get to play all your songs, too." The encore chants were growing louder. Lance gestured in that direction. "If you won't listen to me, listen to them. Ask them. Go out there and give them the encore they want, and ask them if they want you to join the band. You'll see that I'm right." He turned to head down the corridor that led to the back rooms. "And by the way, if this stint in New England goes well, you may be joining her in Europe, too."

The group exchanged looks and began to grin and cheer. Except for Jaymi, who looked at Nikki with concern. "What about the rule, Nik?"

Nikki's smile grew wider. "To hell with the rule, Jaymi. Let's go for it. Face it, nothing's going to keep you two apart anyway. We're a better band with her, and you'd only be distracted if she wasn't with us."

The rest of the band ran out onstage to warm up the crowd for the encore, but Jaymi held Shawn back for a second.

"What do you think, babe?"

"I think we better start collaborating on some more songs."

"I think you're right. After all, we do make beautiful music together."

Shawn grinned. "No more red flags?"

Jaymi laughed and shook her head. "Not a one, babe. Not a one."

# About the Author

Holly Stratimore has spent a lifetime expressing herself creatively. She has played guitar and composed songs since the age of ten and performed at open mikes and benefit shows, and she volunteers as the musician every summer at a day camp for special needs students. She discovered a joy for writing fiction during high school when she wrote seven humorous stories that featured herself and her friends as the characters. In 2007, Holly began devoting her creative energies to writing lesbian romance novels.

A native New Englander, Holly enjoys cheering for the Boston Red Sox, attending concerts, walks on the beach, backyard barbecues, and making people laugh—and groan—with her puns and quick wit. She and her wife live in New Hampshire.

# Books Available From Bold Strokes Books

**One Last Thing** by Kim Baldwin & Xenia Alexiou. Blood is thicker than pride. The final book in the Elite Operative Series brings together foes, family, and friends to start a new order. (978-1-62639-230-4)

**Songs Unfinished** by Holly Stratimore. Two aspiring rock stars learn that falling in love while pursuing their dreams can be harmonious—if they can only keep their pasts from throwing them out of tune. (978-1-62639-231-1)

**Beyond the Ridge** by L.T. Marie. Will a contractor and a horse rancher overcome their family differences and find common ground to build a life together? (978-1-62639-232-8)

**Swordfish** by Andrea Bramhall. Four women battle the demons from their pasts. Will they learn to let go, or will happiness be forever beyond their grasp? (978-1-62639-233-5)

**The Fiend Queen** by Barbara Ann Wright. Princess Katya and her consort Starbride must turn evil against evil in order to banish Fiendish power from their kingdom, and only love will pull them back from the brink. (978-1-62639-234-2)

**Up the Ante** by PJ Trebelhorn. When Jordan Stryker and Ashley Noble meet again fifteen years after a short-lived affair, is either of them prepared to gamble on a chance at love? (978-1-62639-237-3)

**Speakeasy** by MJ Williamz. When mob leader Helen Byrne sets her sights on the girlfriend of Al Capone's right-hand man, passion and tempers flare on the streets of Chicago. (978-1-62639-238-0)

**Myth and Magic: Queer Fairy Tales**, edited by Radclyffe and Stacia Seaman. Myth, magic, and monsters—the stuff of childhood dreams (or nightmares) and adult fantasies. (978-1-62639-225-0)

**The Muse** by Meghan O'Brien. Erotica author Kate McMannis struggles with writer's block until a gorgeous muse entices her into a world of fantasy sex and inadvertent romance. (978-1-62639-223-6)

**Venus in Love** by Tina Michele. Morgan Blake can't afford any distractions and Ainsley Dencourt can't afford to lose control—but the beauty of life and art usually lies in the unpredictable strokes of the artist's brush. (978-1-62639-220-5)

**Rules of Revenge** by AJ Quinn. When a lethal operative on a collision course with her past agrees to help a CIA analyst on a critical assignment, the encounter proves explosive in ways neither woman anticipated. (978-1-62639-221-2)

**The Romance Vote** by Ali Vali. Chili Alexander is a sought-after campaign consultant who isn't prepared when her boss's daughter, Samantha Pellegrin, comes to work at the firm and shakes up Chili's life from the first day. (978-1-62639-222-9)

**Advance** by Gun Brooke. Admiral Dael Caydoc's mission to find a new homeworld for the Oconodian people is hazardous, but working with the infuriating Commander Aniwyn "Spinner" Seclan endangers her heart and soul. (978-1-62639-224-3)

**UnCatholic Conduct** by Stevie Mikayne. Jil Kidd goes undercover to investigate fraud at St. Marguerite's Catholic School, but life gets complicated when her student is killed—and she begins to fall for her prime target. (978-1-62639-304-2)

**Season's Meetings** by Amy Dunne. Catherine Birch reluctantly ventures on the festive road trip from hell with beautiful stranger Holly Daniels only to discover the road to true love has its own obstacles to maneuver. (978-1-62639-227-4)

**Courtship** by Carsen Taite. Love and Justice—a lethal mix or a perfect match? (978-1-62639-210-6)

**Against Doctor's Orders** by Radclyffe. Corporate financier Presley Worth wants to shut down Argyle Community Hospital, but Dr. Harper Rivers will fight her every step of the way, if she can also fight their growing attraction. (978-1-62639-211-3)

**A Spark of Heavenly Fire** by Kathleen Knowles. Kerry and Beth are building their life together, but unexpected circumstances could destroy their happiness. (978-1-62639-212-0)

**Never Too Late** by Julie Blair. When Dr. Jamie Hammond is forced to hire a new office manager, she's shocked to come face-to-face with Carla Grant and memories from her past. (978-1-62639-213-7)

**Widow** by Martha Miller. Judge Bertha Brannon must solve the murder of her lover, a policewoman she thought she'd grow old with. As more bodies pile up, the murdered start coming for her. (978-1-62639-214-4)

**Twisted Echoes** by Sheri Lewis Wohl. What's a woman to do when she realizes the voices in her head are real? (978-1-62639-215-1)

**Criminal Gold** by Ann Aptaker. Through a dangerous night in New York in 1949, Cantor Gold, dapper dyke-about-town, smuggler of fine art, is forced by a crime lord to be his instrument of vengeance. (978-1-62639-216-8)

**Because of You** by Julie Cannon. What would you do for the woman you were forced to leave behind? (978-1-62639-199-4)

**The Job** by Jove Belle. Sera always dreamed that she would one day reunite with Tor. She just didn't think it would involve terrorists, firearms, and hostages. (978-1-62639-200-7)

**Making Time** by C.J. Harte. Two women going in different directions meet after fifteen years and struggle to reconnect in spite of the past that separated them. (978-1-62639-201-4)

**Once The Clouds Have Gone** by KE Payne. Overwhelmed by the dark clouds of her past, Tag Grainger is lost until the intriguing and spirited Freddie Metcalfe unexpectedly forces her to reevaluate her life. (978-1-62639-202-1)

**The Acquittal** by Anne Laughlin. Chicago private investigator Josie Harper searches for the real killer of a woman whose lover has been acquitted of the crime. (978-1-62639-203-8)

**An American Queer: The Amazon Trail** by Lee Lynch. Lee Lynch's heartening and heart-rending history of gay life from the turbulence of the late 1900s to the triumphs of the early 2000s are recorded in this selection of her columns. (978-1-62639-204-5)

**Stick McLaughlin** by CF Frizzell. Corruption in 1918 cost Stick her lover, her freedom, and her identity, but a very special flapper and the family bond of her own gang could help win them back—even if it means outwitting the Boston Mob. (978-1-62639-205-2)

**Rest Home Runaways** by Clifford Henderson. Baby boomer Morgan Ronzio's troubled marriage is the least of her worries when she gets the call that her addled, eighty-six-year-old, half-blind dad has escaped the rest home. (978-1-62639-169-7)

**Charm City** by Mason Dixon. Raq Overstreet's loyalty to her drug kingpin boss is put to the test when she begins to fall for Bathsheba Morris, the undercover cop assigned to bring him down. (978-1-62639-198-7)

**Edge of Awareness** by C.A. Popovich. When Maria, a woman in the middle of her third divorce, meets Dana, an out lesbian, awareness of her feelings brings up reservations about the teachings of her church. (978-1-62639-188-8)

**Taken by Storm** by Kim Baldwin. Lives depend on two women when a train derails high in the remote Alps, but an unforgiving mountain, avalanches, crevasses, and other perils stand between them and safety. (978-1-62639-189-5)

**The Common Thread** by Jaime Maddox. Dr. Nicole Coussart's life is falling apart, but fortunately, DEA Attorney Rae Rhodes is there to pick up the pieces and help Nic put them back together. (978-1-62639-190-1)

**Searching For Forever** by Emily Smith. Dr. Natalie Jenner's life has always been about saving others, until young paramedic Charlie Thompson comes along and shows her maybe she's the one who needs saving. (978-1-62639-186-4)